IVY

KINGDOM OF FAIRYTALES
SEASON NINE

You all know the story of your favorite fairytale, but did you ever wonder what happened after the fairytale ending? Well we know. Not all afters end up happily, sometimes the real adventure starts much later...

Following famous fairytale characters, eighteen years after their happily ever after, the Kingdom of Fairytales offers an edge of the seat thrill ride in an all new and sensational way to read.

Lighting-fast reads you won't be able to put down

Fantasy has never been so epic!

QUEEN
OF CLOCKWORK

12 AUGUST

The pocket watch lay heavy in my hand as I brushed my fingertips over its polished metal. The watch cover was closed, so I couldn't see the clock face, but that didn't matter. The regular *ticking* reverberated through me. Standing in the middle of the shop, I *felt* it.

High wooden ceilings and tall plate-glass windows displayed the finished, half-finished, and just-started inventions that stocked the *Emporium of Mechanical Gadgetry and Invention*. The Emporium boasted clean benches and neatly arranged gadgets. Everything shone. It impressed glancing customers with the owners' mechanical prowess. Only I knew what worked and what didn't.

Inside the pocket watch, tiny gears, springs, wheels,

and mechanisms worked together to make the hands move in time. It worked perfectly.

"Are you sure the lass is up to this?" Mr. Pillar blew a ring of smoke from the cigar he held between two fingers. I wrinkled my nose as the pungent smell wafted through the small shop. "She's not even looking at it."

I glanced at my oldest friend, Chesh, Mr. Chet Cheshire, the son of the elder Mr. Cheshire, who owned the Emporium. He grinned and patted Mr. Pillar on the shoulder.

Mr. Pillar had the look of someone softening around the edges with age. He had coiffed his gray hair into fashionable curls around his face, and he wore a three-piece suit of green pin-stripes, carried a cane, and wore a single eyeglass, which made one of his gray eyes appear twice the size of the other. Both his haughty air, his outlandishly fashionable style, and the embroidered family crest on the lapel of his suit marked him as a member of an old family of the Forge.

"If Miss. Rowntree can't fix your watch, nobody can," Chesh assured Mr. Pillar.

I flipped open the lid to look at Mr. Pillar's ancient pocket watch—a family heirloom, apparently—noticing the beautiful face inlaid with rubies. The scarlet jewels were a sign that the late Queen of Hearts favored Mr. Pillar's ancestor.

People rarely displayed their allegiances so readily to strangers.

"It is a beautiful watch, sir," I murmured. "You said it needed fixing?"

Mr. Pillar snorted, raising himself up to his toes, then rolling back on his heels as he huffed another lungful of cigar smoke. "Look at it!"

I frowned. "It appears to be keeping time."

Mr. Pillar jabbed his cigar at me, narrowly missing burning my hand. "Exactly—not one second off." He turned to Chesh. "You might be right about her."

Chesh beamed at me. "I'm always right, sir."

Mr. Pillar chuckled. "Now that we understand each other, Miss Rowntree, send word to me when it's fixed. Mind you, don't delay—I'm eager to have it back where it belongs." Mr. Pillar patted the empty pocket of his waistcoat where he usually kept his pocket watch.

"You mentioned that earlier." I closed my eyes briefly as I rubbed at my forehead, considering the puzzle. As Mr. Pillar turned to exit the shop, I forced myself to ask the obvious question: "If your watch is keeping time, what needs fixing?"

Mr. Pillar's eyes bulged. He glanced behind his shoulder, then stepped closer to both of us. "I've told you," he whispered, jabbing his cigar so that the ash floated in the air. "It's an antique watch. It hasn't worked for 18 years. Not since..." His eyes widened so suddenly that his eyeglass popped out and dropped to the floor. Mr. Pillar looked over his shoulder again at the empty shop, the whites of his eyes showing. "Not since the Queen... fell." His voice was so low that the last words were barely audible.

I stared at him. "Died, you mean."

Mr. Pillar gasped. Like many of the older residents of the Forge, he was afraid to talk about the late Queen. I caught myself before I rolled my eyes, and glanced at Chesh, expecting him to share my bemusement. My friend was still smiling, but a crease between his eyes showed he was as puzzled as I was. I glanced at the pocket watch that lay heavy in my hand.

"Are you saying...?" I started.

Mr. Pillar interrupted. "Suddenly—this morning—

that watch started working again. With no warning at all!"

I brushed my thumb over the clock face, the problem suddenly taking a different shape. A bell tinkled as Mr. Pillar wrenched open the door.

"Make it stop, Miss. Rowntree. That's all I ask." Mr. Pillar's eyes darted from me to Chesh, then back again. He tipped his top hat, turned his back, and hurried away.

"Quite mad." Chesh said, grinning as he hooked his thumbs into the pocket of his gray waistcoat. Never underdressed, he wore a black frock coat over gray trousers, and a necktie around his high-collar shirt, while his top hat rested on the counter. He'd combed his mane of curly blonde hair to the side, and his green eyes twinkled. "I can't imagine you'll have trouble with that request."

"I'm not breaking a perfectly good watch."

Chesh chuckled. "Just let it wind down."

I turned my back and reached for the small clutch bag that I'd set down on the bench.

"Let me," Chesh said, darting out to reach around me for my bag, in a manner that had him lean over my right shoulder.

I started at the gesture as it brought to mind a memory of a dream.

Dark eyes stared into mine, two pools of fathomless darkness. A mouth opened, and white, gleaming fangs sank into the soft flesh at the base of my neck.

I spun around, dropping the pocket watch as my hands clutched at my throat. For a moment, I was there, in the grips of a vampire, his teeth sunk deep into my skin.

"Ivy?" Chesh stepped back, his head cocked to the

4

side. "Are you all right?"

I blinked several times before the strange, pale face was replaced by Chesh's familiar one.

"You startled me."

"Sorry." Chesh bent down to pick up Mr. Pillar's watch. "You might break it if you treat it like this."

I examined the watch again, hoping it wasn't damaged. Satisfied, I slipped it into my clutch.

Chesh straightened his frock coat, settled his top hat on his head, then crooked his elbow at me. "That's enough seriousness. I have a desperate need for a new waistcoat. Perhaps shoes, as well. I shall insist upon your company, and your opinion on the subject."

I placed one hand at his elbow, using the other to smooth my waistcoat and skirts, as I let Chesh open the door for me and lead me out of his shop.

～

I ran my finger along the inner seam of a vest, examining the stitching. A fine piece of tailoring, as I expected from one of the finest tailors in the Forge.

"I trust nothing is amiss?"

I smiled at the impeccably dressed tailor, Mr. Gerrod, knowing he recognized me as an aesthetic inspector—one of many employed by the President to examine public places, including businesses, to enforce the rigorous aesthetic standards required by law.

"Not at all, sir," I replied. "I'm not working today. I'm admiring your wares."

Mr. Gerrod dipped his head in recognition of my compliment. "In that case, may I suggest this deep indigo would complement your unusual eyes? I could make you a dress worthy of your beauty."

"Of that, I have no doubt," I answered about to refuse his offer. Pearl, my non-identical twin, always made sure my wardrobe was bursting with clothes, but I took another look at the rich color of the fabric and hesitated.

"That color suits you," Chesh came to stand behind me. "I must insist you take Mr. Gerrod up on his generous offer."

Mr. Gerrod bowed. "We have your measurements on file, Miss. Rowntree," he said and hurried away before I changed my mind. I turned an exasperated look at Chesh.

"I can't have you wearing the same dress two times in a week," he said, shrugging. "Pearl would have a fit."

"I could hardly wear the same dress twice in a month."

"If you did, it would be splashed all over the front page of The Forge Hart. Imagine the gossip!"

I threw my head back and laughed. Mr. Gerrod raised an eyebrow as he glanced over at us.

"Shush, you're causing a commotion," Chesh scolded. "Now, tell me—does this coat become me?"

Chesh was trying on a new outfit—a frock coat in a deep green, over a yellow-gold vest, and fitted black trousers. He stood in front of me, seeking affirmation. Hovering in the background, the tailor's young assistant stared appreciatively at him. A tall man, Chesh cut a fine figure in a suit, and his cheerful, bubbly persona added to his handsome charm. He turned heads wherever he went. Pearl had, more than once, asked me whether I fancied Chesh. I had answered my twin sister firmly in the negative. He was my closest friend, that was all.

"You know it does," I answered Chesh. "The green brings out your eyes."

6

Chesh straightened his shoulders as he turned to catch his reflection once more in the mirror.

"Very handsome," the assistant blushed deeply as she offered her opinion.

"I shall take it," Chesh smirked at her, as she helped him remove the coat.

While Chesh returned to the changing rooms, I meandered among the displays once more, trailing my fingers lightly over the soft, textured fabrics.

The memory of my dream nagged at me, and I dwelt on the dark eyes that had looked straight into my soul. I wrapped my arms around my waist, feeling suddenly exposed. I dreamed often—silly dreams that flitted from my mind as soon as I awoke—but this one was different.

The perfect curve of the vampire's lips, as red as fresh blood, parted, revealing his sharp fangs. He leaned forward and dipped his mouth to the base of my neck.

I squeezed my eyes shut, my breath becoming short. I scolded myself as I took several deep breaths.

A hand touched my elbow. My eyes flew open to see Chesh staring down at me.

"Ivy?" he whispered, his eyes darting over to the counter where the assistant was carefully wrapping his new clothes. "Are you ill?"

I pushed the images from my dream away. "Nothing a little air won't fix. Are we visiting the cobbler?"

Chesh grinned, flashing straight teeth. "I can't wear shabby, old shoes with a new outfit."

I snorted, making a point of staring at his black shoes, polished to a shine.

The shop bell tinkled as we stepped out onto the neat cobblestones. Sixth Avenue was lined with shops of all kinds. One of the main streets of The Forge, it was framed by tall buildings that sprung up from each side to tower over the pedestrians, blocking all but the midday sun and casting almost perpetual shadows.

Despite the shade, the late summer heat was oppressive. I flicked out my fan with my spare hand as a trickle of perspiration dampened the collar of my shirt.

"Do you mind if I ask you a question, Chesh?" I asked.

Half of his mouth quirked up. "You've never needed permission before," Chesh replied.

"Have you ever met a vampire?"

Chesh laughed out loud. "Of all the things you might ask me—a vampire?" He paused for a moment to consider. "Perhaps once... in a bar." He pulled at the collar of his shirt, and I noticed a flush in his cheeks, which I put down to humid heat.

"I haven't," I murmured, those dark eyes coming once more to mind.

"I should hope not." He raised an eyebrow. "The city would be alight with gossip if you were to keep company with vampires. Anyway, they keep to their own." Chesh stopped in front of *Broderick's Boots*. "Here we are!"

He insisted on a new pair of boots for me to match my new indigo dress. Mr. Broderick took the measurements, then I settled down in a chair in the shop's front, gazing out of the window, while Chesh tried on a pair of shoes he'd ordered a week before.

The new soles clicked on the floorboards as he paced. His voice wafted through the store and, though I couldn't hear his exact words, I imagined him discussing the fit and the spots where the shoes rubbed his toes.

I'd shopped with Chesh often enough to know how he fussed about shoes. I'd be dragged back to the cobbler at least once more before Chesh agreed to take delivery of his order.

I let my gaze wander over the street outside. The buildings were stone and timber, with brightly painted shutters and doors. Once all red, according to the late Queen's taste, now they boasted bright yellows, pinks, greens, blues, and purples. In the late afternoon, the residents of Melfall, capital of The Forge, were settling in at the teahouses and cafes that spilled out onto the footpaths.

I let my eyes wander, smiling at the sight of a woman in a frilly, pink jacket and skirt, wearing a wide-brimmed hat, and walking a flamingo on a leash. In the middle of the avenue, a man in a bright yellow suit rode a black-and-white striped zebra. Behind him, a man stepped up to a nearby doorway. He was tall, his features obscured by his hat, but something about him snagged my attention—even more than the man on the zebra or the woman with the flamingo. I sat straighter, peering at him. He seemed familiar—the pallor of his skin and the darkness of his hair reminded me of the vampire that haunted my dreams.

It can't be him, I told myself. *It's too early for a vampire.*

I glanced up. The late afternoon sun had dropped below the line of the buildings, casting the street into complete shade. Would a vampire risk the fading daylight? I didn't know.

My heart hammered, and I raised a hand to my neck to trail my fingers over my skin.

Then, the man turned, exposing his profile: a hooknose and a long forehead.

9

Seeing imaginary vampires? I sighed, shaking my head at my foolishness. *What is wrong with me today?*

I glanced at the teahouse across the road and decided to insist that Chesh accompany me for refreshment. After all, I'd waited for him in shops for the entire afternoon. I fiddled with the lace on my clutch, then pulled out Mr. Pillar's watch, and turned my mind to its puzzle to pass the time.

I closed my eyes, concentrating on the watch. I imagined the mainspring, the gear wheels, the escarpment mechanism, and the balance wheel—their minute components working together to power the hands on the face of the watch. Without even opening the cover, I felt each of the tiny components moving to make it tick. I knew there were fifteen small jewels inside, carefully placed to minimize the wear and tear of the moving parts. It was a quality watch.

It worked perfectly.

I let my chin fall to my chest. I couldn't break this beautiful antique watch. Surely, someone in Mr. Pillar's household—a servant, perhaps?—had wound the watch when they should not have. When the mainspring lost its compression, the parts would go still again. When that happened, I decided, I would return the watch to Mr. Pillar without charge.

I slipped the watch back into my clutch and opened my eyes.

A large playing card stood on the other side of the cobbler's window. A rectangular body with metallic arms and legs and blinking red lights peering out of a metal orb for a head. On its chest was a single red heart.

My mouth fell open.

A Heart. A legend of the old stories—a soldier of the

late Queen's ruthless army.

I clamped a hand over my mouth as I sucked in a breath and stood so abruptly that I knocked over the chair.

"Ivy?" Chesh called out from the back of the store.

The lights in the Heart's eyes blinked, then its whole body turned, and it marched along the street.

I yanked open the shop door and burst out onto the street.

The Ace of Hearts had disappeared.

I blinked, staring at the cobbled street where it should have been. People meandered along, in twos and threes, talking amicably as they looked in shop windows. Others settled into the restaurants and cafes for an early evening meal. A few delivery boys scurried along the street carrying packages to their new owners.

No one else had seen the Heart in the middle of the street.

"Ivy?" Chesh rushed out of *Broderick's Boots*, uncharacteristically disheveled. "Are you alright?"

He took my hands, as though I might collapse. The heat of the late afternoon pressed against me, and I scrambled for my fan, flicking it open to stir some breeze around my face.

"I saw..." I looked along the street. "I thought..."

"It's unbearably hot. Let's take some refreshment." Chesh looked around, and his eyes lit up. "Tea?"

I was still searching for the Ace of Hearts when someone shrieked in the distance. Chesh frowned, his usual smile absent. "The city is going mad in this heat. Perhaps I should take you home?"

A few people hurried along the street, pulling their hats over their brows, and avoiding eye contact. One was weeping. Above street level, brightly painted shutters slammed shut. Mr. Broderick peered out of his window, then flipped the sign on his door to "Closed."

"The Pinnacle!" a man called out, hurrying away from the circular marketplace in the center of Melfall. In the very center of the market, a clock tower, called the Pinnacle, rose to overlook the city.

I knew, from childhood lessons with my tutor, that the Pinnacle's clock hadn't sounded since the defeat of the late Queen, a little over eighteen years ago.

"What was that man talking about?" I asked Chesh, who had a firm hand on my elbow. Faintly, as though the very heart of the city was beating, I felt the ticking of a clock.

"I don't think—"

"I'm perfectly fine," I said, shaking off Chesh's grip. I straightened my shoulders and strode towards the marketplace.

∽

I stepped quickly along the cobblestones of Sixth Avenue, dodging people hurrying in the opposite direction, determined that Chesh wouldn't prevent me from seeing the Pinnacle for myself. My heart thudded in my throat, and a sense of urgency came over me.

Those fleeing the scene were older—several were weeping, and one had collapsed and was being carried away. But I wasn't the only one drawn to the commotion in the city center. Other young people saw the fuss and spilled into the streets.

The buildings towering over the avenue, suddenly took on the glow of the pink clouds of the early evening sky where the avenue flowed into the open marketplace.

Clusters of people stood, staring upward at the

interlocking struts of the tower of wrought iron that rose like a needle from the middle of the cobbled market. At the top, the great clock stared dispassionately over the city.

The Pinnacle was an impressive structure, standing taller than any other in the Forge. If one climbed to the top, one could see across Melfall's perimeter walls, all the way to the distant boundaries of the kingdom where The Forge met Urbis to the north-east, Oz in the north-west, and the bright blue waters of the Great Ocean to the south.

I had never climbed the Pinnacle. No one did—not since the late Queen's demise when citizens of The Forge had toppled the enormous wrought iron heart that had once crowned the clock tower. Once the symbol of the late Queen's power had smashed into the courtyard below and the clock had stopped ticking, the citizens had pretended the Pinnacle didn't exist.

The ticking was louder now, and I covered my eyes from the late afternoon glare as I stared up at the tower. The hands of the clock moved, unmistakably keeping time.

For eighteen years, the clock had been stopped at 4:17pm. Now, the clock was ticking again. It read 6:54pm.

I pulled Mr. Pillar's pocket watch out of my clutch bag and flicked open the lid.

6:54pm.

I help up the watch so I could see the face of the pocket watch, next to the enormous face of the clock in the tower. I gasped. The hands were ticking in unison.

13 AUGUST

Ibrushed a curl from my face as I leaned over a yellowed newspaper spread across the large bench in the reading area of Alice's Library. The bench was beautifully carved, with small animals—mice, birds, rabbits, and even a caterpillar were engraved around the edges of the dark wood.

Around the long bench were rows of books about The Forge's history. More than that, it held every copy ever printed of The Forge Hart, the daily newspaper, since it started printing over thirty years ago. Alice had set up the library for the citizens of Melfall, but people rarely used it. Not that I minded—the solitude made it one of the few places I came to think.

The fragile newspaper rustled as I turned the

wrinkled pages. I had started my research at the time of the late Queen's demise, about eighteen years ago, and was working backward, searching for any mention of the Pinnacle, how it's clock worked, or who had been responsible for building and maintaining it.

I skimmed the tiny text for stories about the stoppage of the clock, though the logical explanation was whoever had maintained it during the late Queen's reign had stopped once the Queen was dead. Someone had wound the Pinnacle's clock again. Why else would it tick?

I flipped over another page and huffed. There was no information in any of these newspapers about the clock's operation or maintenance.

Instead, I found a sketch of the late Queen, standing on the balcony of the Pinnacle with her army of Hearts lining the circular marketplace, surrounding the gathered citizens. Ignoring the other details of the picture, I peered at the Pinnacle. A raw, but beautiful structure, it looked much like it did now—a metal skeleton with no skin to cover its bones.

I scanned the text. An announcement about the war effort—the Queen had constantly waged war against the other eleven kingdoms—and a triple beheading. A small article wrote that Mr. Finley Knave, Duchess Ada Thornton, and Mr. Gordon Taylor were all beheaded for the crime of displeasing the Queen.

In every edition, an article announced the day's executions. I shook my head. The late Queen had been fond of beheading her subjects.

I turned the page again and sighed.

The door flew open, sending a gust of breeze into the room. I slammed my hands on the papers to stop them from flying away.

"I knew I'd find you here amongst the dust." Pearl's voice was loud against the silence of the library. She gasped. "You're not even dressed!"

I glanced down at myself and drew my dressing gown around me. "I was reading."

Pearl shook her head as she walked over to the reading bench, her nose wrinkled in distaste as she stared at the old newspapers spread over the surface.

"Decades-old newspapers? Honestly, if anyone saw you like this, it would be a scandal. Nobody has seen you, right?"

"In here?" I smirked. "Not a chance."

My beautiful twin sister pursed her lips. Her long, blonde hair fell over her shoulders in ringlet curls, and an ornate fascinator perched on the side of her head. She wore a pink vest over a white shirt with lace frills and a skirt over full petticoats. Perfectly put together— as always.

"Put away those musty things and get dressed," she said. "You must accompany me to the bank."

"Again?" I raised an eyebrow.

"I haven't withdrawn my stipend this week. I have an aesthetic regimen to uphold, you know. This," Pearl waved a perfectly manicured hand towards her face and hair. "Doesn't just happen, you know."

Pearl spent four to five hours, at least, every day on her daily bathing, dressing, facial, manicure, pedicure, massage, and other hair and skin treatments. She wasn't alone. Most citizens held to strict beauty regimens and wouldn't leave their houses if even a hair was out of place. The Forge Hart was always full of articles about maintaining youth and beauty, and advertisements for potions promising wonders with every application.

I sighed. "Can't your maid accompany you?"

Pearl glared at me. "You cannot waste your life in this dreary place."

"I like it," I replied.

"You should claim your own stipend."

I raised an eyebrow. We'd had this conversation many times before. "I don't need it. I work for Mother, and I sell my watches."

"Such a waste of time," Pearl said. "You are so beautiful—you should live on the stipend. You're taking a job from someone who needs it."

I rubbed at my forehead. There was no point in arguing with Pearl or any other citizen who lived on the aesthetic stipend. Why should the beautiful work when they performed such an important public duty— improving the lives of others by making the city more aesthetically pleasing?

"I hear the roads of Oz are paved in gold," I said, raising an old topic to distract her. "Maybe we should go there instead."

Pearl didn't take the bait. "Traveling in this heat would make my hair frizz," she replied. Then she folded her arms across her chest. "Besides, if you want to travel, you must claim—and save—your stipend."

I sighed, knowing that was true enough. "Fine, I'll come," I said, then held up a finger. "To sell a watch and collect my wages."

～

White, stone steps led to the arched entrance to the First Forge Bank. Unlike the wooden buildings that leaned up against each other along the narrow streets of The Forge, the bank was an imposing stone building, its grand entrance marked with carved stone knights standing to attention. As Pearl and I stepped inside, the entrance hall danced with the colors reflected by the sunlight shining through the stained glass dome overhead.

Once the Royal Bank of Hearts, the bank had contained the late Queen's Treasury. Early in her reign, the late Queen—who loved all things beautiful— had endowed a lifelong stipend on the most beautiful among her subjects. She'd also punished those who did not adhere to her standards of beauty, usually with execution. The stipend became entrenched and, by the time she was deposed, the aesthetic stipend was the main income for the most influential people in The Forge.

The new president—my mother—Alice Rowntree— hadn't abolished the stipend with the formation of the new republic, mainly because she was afraid the citizens wouldn't survive another revolution if Melfall's beautiful citizens rioted against the threat to their livelihood.

On our eighteenth birthday, earlier in the year, Pearl and I had come of age, with the benefit of collecting the stipend. On that day, we'd both come to this building, intending to claim our payment, but I'd decided against it at the last minute.

I'd insisted that the payment was unfair since everyone got paid a different amount depending on how beautiful they were. In truth, when Pearl had received the maximum stipend, marking her as one of the most beautiful women in the Forge, I had felt a sudden stab of fear.

Pearl was blonde, with creamy skin, full lips, and a figure with curves in all the right places. She instinctively knew how to do her hair and makeup to bring out her best features. I was the plain sister. The sister that people noticed only if they tore their eyes away from Pearl. In that moment, I hadn't wanted my plainness quantified by a stranger.

So, from that day, I'd stubbornly resisted the stipend while Pearl withdrew it weekly. Also, I doubted there was single Dinah left over at the end of the week.

"Miss. Pearl Rowntree," a banker by the name of Mr. Elliott came over to greet us, smiling warmly at my sister as he gave her a small bow. Then he turned to me. "Miss. Ivy Rowntree. As always, it is my pleasure to welcome you to our establishment. Are you both making a withdrawal today?" His gaze lingered on me.

"Of course," Pearl answered.

Mr. Elliott bowed, without waiting for my response, and motioned for us to follow him.

Our footsteps echoed as we walked between marble columns streaked with the colors from the ceiling dome, as though rainbows danced. Mr. Elliot ushered us into a cozy office, with plush carpets and two high-backed leather armchairs. Pearl was the first to sit, glaring at me until I lowered myself into the second seat.

"May I offer you a refreshment? Tea?" Mr. Elliott asked.

"That would be lovely," Pearl answered. I pressed my lips into a smile to prevent myself from refusing his offer. My instinct was to get this over with as quickly as possible, while Pearl drew it out.

Tea was served in delicate porcelain cups painted with dragonflies. Steam curled up from the liquid, and I inhaled the pleasant, strong aroma.

"Shall we get down to business?" Mr. Elliott asked.

"Wonderful." Pearl flashed the banker a smile. I took a mouthful of tea, scalded the roof of my mouth, then set the cup down with a clatter.

"Do you wish to start?" Mr. Elliott looked at Pearl. She glanced at me. I inclined my head.

Pearl rose from her seat, smoothed her dress, and went to stand on a small spot marked on the floor in the middle of the room. She batted her eyelids at Mr. Elliott as he slowly looked her over, starting with her face and following her figure down to her feet. His expression was impassive and studious, critically assessing her attributes, calculating a monetary figure based on the strengths and weaknesses of her presentation. When his eyes drifted back up to her face, he nodded. "Overall presentation is very nice—well put together. Your beauty is pleasing to the eye, and your presentation amplifies your natural attributes. I see no defects in style or substance. I am pleased to, once again, offer you the highest rate of stipend."

Pearl flashed him a smile, bobbed a curtsy, then took her seat again.

"Thank you, Mr. Elliott." She paused. "Have you raised the rate since I was last here?"

Mr. Elliott blinked. "No, Miss. Rowntree. The rate remains 500 Dinah. We will not raise it until we conduct a full review at the end of the year."

Pearl pursed her lips. "Pity, it's barely enough to cover expenses, you know. Beauty businesses continue to raise their rates. I think they're trying to impoverish us."

Mr. Elliott smiled politely. "I wish I could offer a larger amount. Truly, your beauty and composure deserve it. I may, on this occasion, be able to provide a one hundred Dinah bonus to your usual amount, since you have never presented in less than perfect condition."

Pearl clapped her hands together. "Mr. Elliott, that

is so kind. I'm pleased you appreciate my efforts."

"The pleasure is all mine, I assure you," Mr. Elliott replied. Then he turned to me and

motioned toward the spot on the floor that Pearl had vacated.

I swallowed a lump in my throat, staying resolutely in my seat. Two spots burned on my cheeks.

"I would like to withdraw my wages today, Mr. Elliott," I replied.

Next to me, Pearl sighed audibly. "Really, Ivy," she started. I silenced her with a glare.

Mr. Elliott went to a cabinet and withdrew a file. He opened it, then perched a pair of reading glasses on his nose. "You work as an inspector and advisor to the President. An important job." He barely glanced in my direction as he ran his eyes over my file. "250 Dinah."

I bit my tongue to exclaim at the unfairness that a full-time job paid half the rate of the stipend paid to those who lead a beautiful existence—and mine was one of the better-paid jobs in the city. I opened my clutch and drew out a pocket watch that I'd recently finished making. It was a lovely example—not my best—but as good as any of the examples being sold by Melfall's horologists. "I also have an item for sale. Will you appraise it?"

I handed Mr. Elliott the watch. He didn't have the expertise to gauge its craftsmanship, but an aesthetic rating would increase the sale price.

"A lovely piece." he examined the lid and chain carefully, before flicking open the case and examining the watch's face. "Is it Guild-made?"

I bristled at the mention of the Unified Guild, an umbrella organization that united the Guilds into one voice, with more power than they'd had separately. I did not belong to, but kept my mouth shut as I shook my head.

"Pity. That lowers the price. Still, I rate it at a ninety-five on the aesthetic scale." He returned the watch before closing the file. "Will that be all?"

I nodded.

"In that case, I shall escort you both to the teller to process your withdrawals."

~

I stepped out of the First Forge Bank, my clutch weighed down with Dinah and breathed a sigh of relief.

"I hate that place."

Pearl rolled her eyes. "You're so stubborn. You work yourself to the bone for paltry wages when you could have Mr. Elliott examine your aesthetic worth and receive twice as much."

Or not, I thought. "Maybe next time."

Pearl opened her lace parasol to shelter her fair skin from the midday sunshine while I lifted my face to the sun for a moment, then adjusted my top hat. I glanced across the street, and something caught my eye.

Painted onto the wall of a shop next to an alley, was what appeared to be a small rabbit. A white rabbit.

"Do you see that?" I asked Pearl, then pointed. "Over there. A painted rabbit."

Pearl glanced over. "Hmmm," she murmured, but the contents of the shop window absorbed her attention. "What a ghastly dress! I hope you visit that shop. Their standards are too low for First Avenue." Pearl put a hand on my arm. "I'm going to visit Mrs. Bancroft's Parlor. She has such beautiful things. Will you come?"

Mrs. Bancroft's was an invitation-only establishment

where unusual and distinctive—and expensive—items were available for purchase. The two hundred, fifty Dinah weighed heavy in my clutch, but not heavy enough. I shook my head. I couldn't afford such luxuries anyway, and I preferred to spend my time with the newspapers in the library.

Pearl gave me a look that suggested she guessed at what I planned to do with my afternoon. "Sometimes, I wonder if we're really related. I really do." She kissed me lightly on both cheeks, then set off toward Mrs. Bancroft's Parlor.

~

Fewer people milled in the city center, compared to yesterday. Those that were out walked across the marketplace with their heads bowed, or resolutely looked in the opposite direction from the Pinnacle—as though determined not to see the working clock.

The faint ticking was like music, calling to me.

Once more, awed by the sheer size of the Pinnacle, I stared up, admiring the exposed workings of the clock. Despite seeming unfinished—the symmetrical form of the metal struts holding the enormous clock aloft were naked and unadorned—the clock tower had functional beauty. Even from this distance, I could see the large gears and joins as they rotated.

Today, several workmen dressed in bright yellow vests were standing on the balcony from which the late Queen had once addressed her subjects. They pointed at the clock and waved their arms as though engaged in animated discussion.

I raised a hand to my forehead to shield my eyes from the sun as I stared up. *If they can get to the balcony to see the inner workings of the clock, I can too.* I marched straight up to another yellow-vested man standing at the base of the ladder.

I acknowledged him with a nod and, with no hesitation, stepped around him to put a foot on the ladder.

"What are you doing, miss?" the man said, putting a hand out to stop me from climbing farther.

"The clock is working," I replied. "I should like to see it."

The man's eyebrows drew together. "Why would a lovely young lady want to do that?"

"I like clocks."

"This is no ordinary clock."

"So I gathered," I replied. "It hasn't worked in some time."

"Not since the fall of..." The man looked over his shoulder.

"Yes, I know," I replied. "Since the Queen died."

The workman started. "Lower your voice, miss. You never know who's listening."

"Thank you for the advice. Now, if you'll excuse me." I grabbed the next rung and pulled myself higher.

The workman reached out to stop me again, avoiding—but only just—physical restraint.

"I can't let you, miss. It's a long way up."

"I have no fear of heights."

"It's just boring, dirty gears."

I pursed my lips. "I want to see. I'm curious."

"Curiosity killed the cat," the workman replied. "A young lady like you has got no cause to be curious."

I gripped the rung of the ladder tighter. "I don't see that it's any of your concern what—"

"This area is closed," the workman insisted. "we

allow only authorized people up there."

"Authorized by whom?"

"By the President."

I smiled. "I see." I took my foot from the ladder.

The workman's expression softened with relief. "Wise choice, miss."

"I'll get authorization from the President if that's what's required."

The man blinked. "You'll do what?"

"You heard me." I gathered my skirts and strode away from the man, leaving him open-mouthed in my wake.

Alice sat in her office behind a desk, obscured by piles of papers. Over several a fat, ginger cat, Young Dinah, purred while Alice scratched her ears. In the center of the room, a petitioner, dressed in formal coattails and clutching a hat in his hands, trembled as he spoke to the President.

"So Your Majesty—"

"Please, call me Madam President," Alice interrupted him.

The petitioner went white. "S-s-sorry, Madam President. Force of h-h-habit."

Alice inclined her head, though the slight sag of her shoulders was a sign of the weariness that Mother felt at the constant burden of leadership. Even eighteen years after the death of their previous monarch, the citizens of The Forge still feared the retribution of the Queen of Hearts.

"Please, continue," Mother said. "You have concerns about vampires?"

"That's right, Your... M-m-madam President. I work across from the Blood Bank on Fourth Street, you see—in a patisserie. I'm a baker. I bake the finest danish in The Forge." The petitioner paled. "I should have brought some for Your Maj... Madam President to sample. I'm s-s-sorry."

"I'm sure the danish are excellent. What about the Blood Bank on Fourth Street?"

The petitioner fidgeted with his bowler hat. "Vampires go into the blood bank at night, when I'm just coming onto shift. I start work at 2am so that the pastries are ready for breakfast when people wake up, see? I often see vampires going into the blood bank. When they go in, they look angry—hungry, you know? When they come out, they look refreshed. Still pale, but glowing." The petitioner shook his head. "Abnormal creatures."

"That's not unusual," Alice replied, ignoring the petitioner's last utterance. "The vampires go to the blood bank to feed, they come out well-fed. That's why we set up the blood banks—so vampires can feed without endangering other citizens."

"Yes, Your M... Madam President. But lately, the vampires have come out as angry as when they arrived. They look at me as though I was... food."

Alice frowned. "Go on."

He shuffled his feet. "They should investigate it," he said. "I don't want to be out at night with hungry vampires."

Alice touched a finger to her temple, then noticed my presence at the back of the room. She waved a hand at me.

"Ivy, there might be an issue with low supply at the Blood Banks. Please investigate and bring me a report."

The petitioner shuffled his feet again and gripped his

hat so tightly that his knuckles went white. He glanced over his shoulder, then leaned forward and lowered his voice. "There's something else. Rumors..."

Alice raised an eyebrow and waited. The petitioner cleared his throat.

"Rumors that... *she*... has returned. The white rabbit is gathering her supporters."

I stared at the man, my mouth dropping open. *The white rabbit?*

Alice pressed her lips into a straight line. "Does this have anything to do with the Pinnacle clock?"

The petitioner nodded, eyes widening. "It's another sign."

"The Queen is dead," Alice said in a firm voice. "She has not returned. The white rabbit is not gathering her supporters."

"But—"

Alice raised a hand to stop the man from speaking further. "If the white rabbit were here, I would know."

"Yes, Your Majesty." The petitioner bowed deeply. Alice sighed, waving a hand at her assistant, Jack Chambers, who quickly escorted the man out of her office.

"Shall I bring in the next petitioner?" Jack asked once he'd closed the door behind the man.

Alice shook her head. "I need a moment."

Jack nodded, quietly excusing himself from the room.

"You look tired, Mother," I said. Alice leaned back in her chair, closing her eyes. Wisps of gray streaked her blonde hair, now tied back in a bun, and fine lines marked the edges of her eyes. Her normally rosy cheeks were pale.

Alice reached out to take my hand, giving me a brief

half-smile. "I'm sure it's nothing. People need something to complain about."

"Of course, Mother," I replied. "Shall I also look into the rumor about the white rabbit?"

Alice waved a hand dismissively, though her mouth turned down at the edges. "The Queen is dead. The white rabbit left The Forge long ago." I remembered the painting I'd seen on the wall and was about to tell her about it when she patted my hand.

"You're a comfort to me, Ivy," Alice said. "I'm so thankful to have a daughter who helps me shoulder this burden."

"I'm happy to do it, Mother," I murmured. "Actually, there's something else I wanted to speak to you about."

Alice shifted in her chair, suddenly tense, and took her hand from mine. "I don't really have time just now. There's a queue of petitioners outside. I don't see how I shall see them all today."

I didn't protest and was about to excuse myself when Alice reached out to grab my arm. "You will follow up on stocks at the Blood Banks, won't you?"

My dream of being bitten by a vampire came vividly to mind. I bit my lip.

"Please—I don't need a problem with the vampires right now. A report will assure the baker that there is nothing to fear, and his complaint about vampires will go away. I wouldn't ask if it wasn't important."

My heart beat a little faster, but I discreetly wiped the palms of my hands on the fabric of my skirts. "You can rely on me."

Alice patted my cheek. "Thank you, dear."

At that moment, the door swung open, and Jack strode in, holding a red rose between two fingers.

"For you, Madam President," he said, but he didn't

give the rose to Alice. He stared at it with a horrified look.

"An admirer?" I raised an eyebrow, a half-smile touching my lips. Alice had never had a special man in her life, but she was still beautiful.

"The Queen sent a red rose to those she planned to execute," Jack whispered. "Do you think..."

The smile fell from my lips as I turned to Alice. She fixed her blue eyes on the rose and was white as a sheet.

"Shall I burn it?" Jack asked.

"Mother?"

Alice shuddered, then straightened her shoulders and took a deep breath. "The Queen is dead," Alice said, firmly, and forced a smile. "Put the rose in a vase. As Ivy said, perhaps, I have a secret admirer." Alice gave me a wink, and the tension in her posture fell away. "It's about time."

14 AUGUST

I paused outside the shop window to *Bertha's Bag Emporium* on Fourth Avenue, which boasted over a hundred different handbags in all colors, shapes, and sizes. Displayed in the window were three examples of the handiwork contained inside. I ran my hands over my clothes and glanced at my reflection.

A person could not claim to be an aesthetic inspector without being properly turned out. I tucked a stray curl under my hat, pinned my official badge to the lapel of my coat, and slid on white gloves. Then I pulled out my *List of Aesthetic Indicators*, the official checklist.

I didn't really need it—the list was just for show. Since my eighteenth birthday, when I started working as an inspector, I had memorized the checklist. I wiped a finger over the store window and held it up.

A light brown smudge colored the tip of my glove. An acceptable level of dust after a hot summer, I decided. I made a note on the list. I stepped back and ran my eyes over the window display. Pleasing, though unimaginative. The colors of the bags did not clash, but the placement was not symmetrical and gave a sensation of lopsidedness.

I made another note on my checklist.

I tucked the list under my arm and pushed on the shop door.

The woman standing behind the counter stared at me, then quickly ducked out the back. A moment later, a small, shapeless woman, dressed in black, hurried out. A set of glasses were perched on her nose, and her white hair was tied back in a severe bun.

"Welcome, Inspector," she said as she hurried towards me. "I am Miss Bertha, the owner. May I ask...," Bertha hesitated briefly. "Has there been a complaint?"

"Inspector Rowntree," I said, pulling at the fingers of the glove on my right hand to take it off as I reached out to greet her properly. "Just a routine inspection."

Bertha was visibly relieved, though her eyes darted around, checking that everything was in place. "May I offer you tea, Inspector Rowntree?"

I shook my head. Although offers of refreshments, samples, and gifts were frequent, I rarely accepted. It was too difficult to judge an establishment according to code after accepting such niceties. "I won't be long, Miss. Bertha."

The skin around Bertha's eyes tightened, but she nodded. "Let me know if you need help."

I ran my eyes over the displays, first considering the layout and look of the shop as a whole. It was orderly, without mess, but there was a fussy, cluttered atmosphere—too many items on display.

I turned my attention to the smaller details, ambling over to the nearest shelf, and noting the positions of the display cases and their contents. Another dusty smudge dirtied my gloves. I frowned, making another mark on my checklist.

I picked up one of the handbags, studying it carefully. The stitching was fine, and the leather was of good quality. The inner lining was well sewn and fit. There were no scuffs on the item, and the color was rich and consistent.

"Is everything all right, Inspector?" Bertha hovered at my shoulder.

I put the handbag down. "A high-quality item," I replied, as I wrote the fact down on the list. "I won't be much longer."

"Miss. Bertha?"

The woman hovered at the door leading into the back room. As she called out, I glimpsed her.

She had a defect of the left eye—it didn't follow the right one, but gazed off in a different direction, making it appear she was looking past me.

Miss. Bertha shooed the assistant away but caught my expression. "The poor girl just works in the back. Customers don't see her. It's charity, really. I keep her on because her parents can't work just now."

"She was in the front when I came in," I said.

"She rarely works in the front." Miss. Bertha wrung her hands, frowning. She looked over her shoulder, then leaned toward me. "Don't shut me down. Not for a bit of mercy. Please, Inspector."

I looked at my checklist. A mixed report. "There is some dust on your display cases, and the general layout of your shop is too fussy. However, the quality of your goods is high, so I'm willing to overlook those things." I paused, my eyes drawn to the place where the assistant stood a moment ago.

"Inspector Rowntree, I'd be thrilled to make you a gift. I'll wrap it up nicely." Bertha moved to take the handbag I'd inspected out of the display case.

I held up a hand to stop her. "That won't be necessary. I warn you—keep your assistant out of sight. I'll return in one month to ensure that you have rectified the cleanliness and improved the display. If these things are attended to, I'll give you a passing report."

Miss. Bertha clasped her hands to her chest and dipped a quick curtsy. "Thank you, Inspector. I am most grateful."

I scribbled the note on my checklist, omitting the assistant. As I handed Miss. Bertha a copy of her receipt, I noticed a small business card on the floor, as though someone had dropped it.

There was no writing—only the image of a white rabbit on a black background.

Just like the one painted outside the First Forge Bank.

Miss. Bertha cleared her throat. "Is there something else? Are you sure you wouldn't like that handbag? I am happy to wrap it—"

The shop owner's words drew my attention back to my immediate work. "No, thank you. Remember, I'll return in one month. I shall expect improvement."

～

The door of the Fourth Avenue Blood Bank swung closed behind me, and I blinked as my eyes adjusted to the relative darkness. I had never entered one of the city's blood banks before—I'd never wanted to donate blood, nor experienced any dire need for additional income—so the number of people in the waiting room surprised me.

A chill ran down the length of my spine as I remembered my dream—the sharp fangs sinking into my throat. I froze in the doorway, overcome by a sudden fear of coming face-to-face with thirsty vampires. As I stood there, someone tried to come in, and the door hit me in the back. I stumbled forward, and my throat bobbed as I turned, frightened of who might be behind me.

The man who entered was no vampire. He was ruddy-faced and short of breath, with pock scars on his face.

"Why are you standing in the doorway?" he grumbled, barely glancing at me as he pushed past and approached the reception desk that I hadn't yet seen. He grabbed a number and went to sit on one of the few empty chairs.

I straightened my vest and hat, pulling myself together, before approaching the desk. I glanced around the waiting room, searching for vampires but saw none. The people seated in the waiting room weren't the usual crowd that frequented the establishments of Melfall. Their clothes were unfashionable, too worn, and they were all too short, too dumpy, or too odd-looking to be considered beautiful. Some of them were too unusual even to be considered plain.

"Are you waiting for an invitation?" the receptionist crossed her arms and raised one eyebrow as she watched me. A blush rose to my cheeks before I squared my shoulders and marched over, putting my clipboard down on the desk with more force than was necessary.

"I'm here to inspect your premises," I said, noticing her name badge read Audrey. I flashed my badge at her.

Audrey's demeanor changed instantly. Her eyes widened, and her arms fell away from her chest. She fiddled with the papers on her desk with one hand, while the other smoothed the stray hairs from her face.

"I'm sorry, Inspector. I didn't see you properly."

I turned toward the waiting area. "I must see each of your public spaces. Would someone show me around?"

Audrey tapped her fingers on the desk. "I have to stay here."

"Anyone else?"

"Err..." she looked across the waiting room. A door swung open, and a woman in a white coat stepped out, spattered with droplets of blood.

"Number 24?" The woman called out, casting a bored gaze around the waiting room.

A man jumped up, waving a ticket.

Audrey hurried over, "Miss. Crispin," she called.

"I'm next," the man insisted, pushing his ticket in Miss. Crispin's face.

"Sit down," Audrey snapped at the man. "This is—"

"I'm next," he insisted. "I've been waiting. She just got here." He jabbed a finger at me.

"You can't jump ahead," Miss. Crispin insisted, barely glancing at me. "Take a ticket and wait."

The man smiled. "Exactly. I'm next."

"Now, hold on," Audrey said. "This is *Inspector* Rowntree."

"Who cares?" the man said, but Miss. Crispin's eyes widened as she shot a look at Audrey.

"An inspector? Here?" Miss. Crispin asked.

"As you see," Audrey replied, a smug note to her

voice

"I've come to inspect the premises. Will you give me a tour?" I asked.

Miss. Crispin paused, then pushed the door open with one hand. Before I stepped through it, another woman came out with a bandage around her elbow.

She saw Audrey. "I want my Dinah," she said, without a word of greeting.

Audrey huffed. "Come with me," she strode back to the desk and dropped several coins into the woman's outstretched hand.

"Inspector Rowntree? Please?" Miss. Crispin led the way through the doorway into a long hallway.

I took out my checklist as I followed Miss. Crispin. "Is there another entrance?" I asked. "For vampires?"

Miss. Crispin frowned. "I beg your pardon?"

I motioned a hand toward the now closed door. "There aren't any vampires in the waiting room. Do you segregate those people giving blood from those... err, receiving it?"

Miss. Crispin arched an eyebrow. "You must ask Miss Dixon."

I pursed my lips, then pointed to the spatters of blood on her front. "Don't you have spare coats, in case of spills?"

Miss. Crispin looked down, then crossed her arms over her chest, attempting—unsuccessfully—to cover up the stains. I made a mark on my list. Her eyes darted across the page as though to read it, but I quickly covered it up with one hand.

"This a public hallway?" I raised my eyebrows as I used one gloved finger to slide across the length of a side table. My fingertip came away brown with dust. I looked around the hallway critically, taking my time, while Miss. Crispin fidgeted. "Please, show me your deposit rooms."

Miss. Crispin opened a door leading off from the hallway. The small room was empty, except for a lamp that cast a dim light over a table and a single chair. The table was dented and scratched. A dribble of blood was visible on the table leg.

"This is a working blood bank, Inspector Rowntree—an operational room, not a sitting room," Miss. Crispin said. I glanced at her, surprised by the sharpness of her tone. "I hope you'll take that into consideration in your report."

"I take all factors into consideration," I replied, meeting her stare with one of my own.

Miss. Crispin crossed her arms over her chest again, hesitating a moment before she spoke. "While it's not my place to tell you about the operation of the blood bank, I know that there is only one entrance. It's too early for vampires to be out. The sunlight," she added.

Of course.

"I appreciate your cooperation." I smiled and stepped closer to her, as though sharing a secret. "Tell me—and this is *not* for my report—have you had a sufficient supply recently? Is there enough blood to match demand?"

"You saw the crowd in the waiting room," Miss Crispin replied. "It's always like that. Selling blood is easy Dinah. For these people, it's their main source of revenue. We have a lot of regulars."

"Do you ever turn business away?"

"We value blood donations, Inspector."

I smiled. "Of course. I meant, do you run out of stock? Do you turn away the, err, buyers?"

Miss. Crispin shook her head. "Of course not. We

have stockpiles—shall I show you?"

She led me down a set of stairs into a large, cool basement, where wooden crates were stacked to the ceiling. I removed the lid of the nearest one—it was full of packets of blood, preserved on ice.

"These are all the same?" I motioned to the rest of the crates. Miss. Crispin nodded.

"You never run out of blood?" I asked. Miss. Crispin shook her head. "Have you had much business recently? From buyers?"

Miss. Crispin's eyes darted back up the stairs. "About usual."

"Any dissatisfaction about the product? From the vampires?"

This time, Miss. Crispin frowned. "Dissatisfaction? I shouldn't think so. Blood is blood. I've never heard... No," she replied firmly. Then she caught my eye. "Have you heard different?"

"I cannot disclose such things," I said, but I gave my head a little shake for her benefit. She appeared relieved. Still, her answers gave me pause. The baker had sworn to seeing hungry vampires coming out of this blood bank, but there were plenty of people here donating blood. Perhaps he'd been mistaken? Nothing here appeared unusual.

"Would you like to see the other rooms?"

I shook my head, then remembered the other rumors the baker had mentioned. "Have you heard anything about a white rabbit?"

Miss Crispin raised both eyebrows in astonishment. She didn't need to answer my question—I knew the look on her face was genuine. I took my checklist, and for her benefit, I screwed it into a ball. "Thank you, Miss. Crispin. Would you mind showing me out?"

When I entered the Emporium, Chesh was showing one of his favorite items to a young lady and her fiancée. I paused in the doorway, watching Chesh☐s eyes light up as he draped the necklace around the young lady☐s neck, then pressed a button.

The necklace lit up, and the jewels reflected the interior light so that it bounced all over the store. The young lady gasped. Her fiancée gave an exclamation of surprise, then leaned closer to examine it.

"I must have it," the lady said, batting her eyelids demurely. "I'll be the talk of the city if I turn up to our engagement party wearing this necklace."

"There is just one *tiny* issue," Chesh admitted. "The necklace needs an electrical current to run the light, I'm afraid. It's not very portable."

"Does that mean I won't be able to dance?" the young lady asked.

"If I'm excused from a dozen dances, it'd be worth the price," her fiancée joked.

The young woman shot him a glare. Then her mouth formed an *O*, and she fanned herself, hopping up and down on one foot. "Get it off, get it off!"

Chesh banged a fist on the button, and the light immediately disappeared. "It gets hot, too..." he admitted as he ripped the necklace from her.

The couple strode out of the shop without a backward glance, as the young lady rubbed at her décolletage.

Chesh sighed as he set the necklace back in its cabinet. He shrugged when he saw me. "I'll find the right buyer one day."

"Hopefully, one who is impervious to burns," I

replied, "until you stop it overheating."

Chesh wagged a finger at me. "It'll work. Then every woman will line up to buy one." He reached for my hand and pressed a kiss to my knuckles, then winked. "Don't rush off, I've other things to show you."

"An automatic hairbrush?" I remembered the device he'd demonstrated a week before—it had started well, but one brush slipped out of alignment, leaving the mannequin's hair in a dreadful tangle. "Or perhaps a mechanized nose clipper? Or the machine for tying bootlaces?" I struggled to keep the smile from my face as I thought about other demonstrations of Chesh's inventions that hadn't worked.

"Laugh all you like—one day, my inventions will be famous. Everyone will want one. They'll admit me to the Guild, for sure."

I laughed, nodding my head. Even though I mocked my friend, I knew he was talented, creative, and determined. I really believed he would invent something that people would line up outside his shop to buy. He just hadn't managed it yet.

Chesh put a hand on my elbow and led me toward the back of the shop. "I've been working on something new. Something amazing."

"I've heard that before," I said, flashing him a smile.

Chesh smiled back, unfazed. "This time," he winked. He crouched next to a strange-looking machine. It stood almost as tall as me, with a metal plate on the floor, big enough for a person to stand on, with a pole sticking up from it, and handlebars at about my shoulder height. He put on a pair of goggles. "Allow me to demonstrate," he said and flicked a switch.

The machine whirred into life, rattling, shaking, and hissing. It rocked as a gust of air shot out of the bottom of the plate. The hissing and humming were so loud, it blocked out all other sound. I had to stop myself from putting my hands over my ears.

Chesh grinned up at me from where he crouched next to the machine, his eyes large beneath the goggles that obscured half his face.

"See? It lifts off the ground—it's flying!" he yelled above the noise. I crouched down to see underneath. Sure enough, the machine was hovering about half a handspan in the air. Now launched, it seemed slightly more stable, with less rocking and rattling.

"What's it for?" I asked.

Chesh wiggled his eyebrows as he stood, taking the handle of the machine with both hands. "Watch."

He put one foot on the metal plate, pressing down and testing his weight.

"Be careful," I warned.

Chesh rolled his eyes. He pushed off the ground and put all his weight onto the metal plate.

I held my breath. A moment passed, and Chesh's smile widened. "I'm flying!" He punched one fist into the air.

The *hum* of the engine became a whine, then a loud *bang* ricocheted through the shop, and a cloud of black smoke billowed from under the footplate. I put a hand over my mouth and nose as the machine lurched sideways to throw Chesh to the floor. He landed, hard, while the machine skittered across the room to crash into his tool bench.

Chesh groaned, ripping off his goggles as he sat up and stared reproachfully at the machine.

"Maybe the next one will be a winner," I said, offering him a hand to help him to his feet.

Chesh ran a hand through his hair. "All it needs are

a few minor adjustments."

I looked doubtfully at the parts bent by the impact. "Want me to have a look?"

Though my specialty, and my interest, ran to clockwork, I had a knack for anything with moving parts. They *made sense* to me. I seemed to be able to look at a machine and know what was wrong with it, or what small adjustment would make it work properly. I could never describe exactly how I understood machines, but I did.

Chesh gave me a glare. "And have you and your magical talents claiming all the credit? No, thank you."

"It's nothing to do with magic," I retorted. "It's just—"

"A *knack*," Chesh finished my sentence for me. "I know. You and machines just understand each other. Honestly, Ivy, if you devoted as much attention to the people in your life as you do to your clocks, you might understand them a little more. You might even have some friends."

I blushed and turned away from Chesh so he wouldn't see the red in my cheeks. He was right, though. Machines were logical. They made sense. People did not. Not to me, anyway. "I have friends," I protested. "You. Pearl."

Chesh chuckled and grabbed his coat and hat. "I think it's about time for a visit to *The Tea Party*, don't you?" he asked, as he slid his coat over his shoulders. "I hear it's got something fun happening tonight. Plus, it has the best cocktails in town."

I picked up my top hat. "How can I say no to that?"

~

Chesh stopped underneath a sign that read: *The*

Tea Party. As the door swung open, I heard muffled conversations, laughter, the clinking of glasses, a shuffling of feet, and the scrape of chairs on the wooden floor. A bell rang.

"New partners!"

A deep voice rang out over the noise. As I stepped through the doorway, everyone in the room stood up and moved one place to their left before taking a seat again. As a result, they all sat with a new partner. Glasses clinked again as the new partners greeted each other.

Waiters in white waistcoats rushed around with teapots, pouring liquid into teacups that ran low.

Chesh leaned over to me. "*The Tea Party* hosts the greatest tea parties. There's no telling when it will start or stop—the last one went for fifteen hours straight—but everyone's invited!"

I watched a waiter pouring a pink liquid into a teacup. "What sort of tea is that?"

"Not tea at all," Chesh replied. "What would be the fun in that?" Chesh lifted a hand to get the attention of the barman. The barman nodded, clicked his fingers once, and a waiter hurried over to place two chairs at the end of the long table.

"Dirty flamingo," Chesh said, ordering my favorite cocktail as he held up two fingers. He pulled out the nearest chair for me to sit down.

The pink liquid had barely hit my cup when the bell sounded again.

"New partners!"

The person next to me hauled me to my feet and moved into my chair.

Chesh moved in the other direction. "See you next time!" he winked, then found himself seated in front of

44

a blonde beauty. He leaned over to kiss her hand, then raised his glass in a toast—no doubt, to her beauty—as he gave her his full attention. Chesh had an eye for beautiful ladies, and they for him. He would probably break a few hearts tonight. Chesh understood people. He knew what to say. He charmed everyone. I could never understand how he made instant friends with almost everyone he met.

I was tense in my seat, gripping my teacup of dirty flamingo. An older gentleman with a red nose sat in front of me. He raised his cup to me, then tipped it back and drained it, holding up a hand until the waiter hurried over to refill it. I searched around for something to say, but my mind remained blank. I took a gulp of my drink.

"How long have you been here, then?" he said, slurring his words slightly.

"I've just arrived," I replied, relishing the first mouthful of the fiery liquid as it tore down my throat.

"A newcomer!" His eyes lit up in delight, and he held out his hand to shake mine. "I'm Mr. Bellacott. I've been here for...," he fumbled with his pocket watch, squinting at it. "Eight hours and thirteen minutes. Splendid. I'm determined to break the record. So many fall over, you know, but I won't be one of them." He pointed at the side of the room, where I saw several people passed out on benches.

"Are they all right?"

Mr. Bellacott waved a hand in dismissal. "They will be once they've had a nap. They won't claim the title, though. This tea party goes on only as long as one initial member remains. It's between me and that fellow over there." Mr. Bellacott pointed to a tall man with a long face. "Once both of us fall over, or leave,

45

the party's finished. The last one standing has naming rights for the event—and the honor of it, if the party breaks a record. *Bellacott's Biggest Tea Party* has a nice ring to it, don't you think? Only...—Mr. Bellacott consulted his watch again—"err, five..., no six hours and forty... forty-seven minutes to go!" He snapped his pocket watch closed and tucked it into the pocket of his vest, just as the barman rang the bell again.

I found myself hoisted to my feet by the person to my right. I turned to glare at him as I sat down opposite a young woman with black, curly hair. I lifted my glass.

"Got your eye on anyone?" she asked, leaning forward as she looked along the table.

I shook my head. "I've only just arrived," I replied, as I glanced over to see Chesh seated opposite a busty brunette who was laughing at one of his jokes.

"I have," she stared longingly at the other end of the table, "but he's gone past. It'll be ages until I sit with him again." She sighed.

I sipped my dirty flamingo as I searched around for another topic of conversation. A thought popped into my head and I blurted it out without thinking: "Have you ever met any vampires?"

Her eyebrows shot up as she spat out a mouthful of liquid. "Certainly not. Why would you ask such a thing?"

"Just curious," I said, taking another sip "No vampires here tonight, then?"

She looked around, suddenly alarmed. "I haven't seen any. Do vampires often frequent this bar?"

I shrugged. "Not in particular, but they're creatures of the night."

The woman pursed her lips, shooting a worried glance over her shoulder, as though a vampire might be looming there.

The bell rang before I had to make any further conversation.

As the tea party progressed, I sat across from three more gentlemen and a lady, before finding the place opposite me empty.

Instead, a tall glass of dirty flamingo—exactly the way I like to drink it—sat in front of me. A small card was tucked underneath. In elegant handwriting, the card said: *We choose our future.*

On the back of the card, there was a motif of a white rabbit. The same motif that I'd seen before. My mouth went dry. I waved a hand at the closest waiter.

"Who left this?" I asked, pointing at the glass.

The waiter blinked. "I'm sorry, Miss.?"

I repeated my question, but the waiter shook his head, pleading ignorance. "You might lose your place on the table," he warned me, as I stood up.

I shrugged, picking up my glass, and moved towards the barman with his hand on the bell.

"Excuse me?" I raised my voice to be heard over the din.

The barman raising one eyebrow at me. "A problem with your drink?"

I shook my head. "Someone left it for me, but I didn't see who. There was just an empty chair and a card underneath it."

The barman glanced at me briefly before ringing the bell. Everyone stood and moved along one place, before chinking glasses and starting new conversations.

"Did you see who left it?" I asked the barman.

"I might have," he replied. A waiter appeared at my elbow, putting an empty teapot on the bar. The barman handed a full one to the waiter who hurried away again.

"I don't suppose it matters if I tell you—he didn't swear me to secrecy."

"Who didn't?"

"Raven."

I blinked. "Raven?"

"You heard me."

"Is Raven associated with the white rabbit?"

The bartender started rubbing at a glass with a towel. He shrugged. "I don't know about any white rabbits."

I paused, staring at the card. "Raven is an unusual name," I ventured.

"It's no human name, that's for sure. If you don't know who Raven is, then I can't help you."

I stared down at the card. The bartender was right— Raven wasn't a human name. That meant only one thing: Raven was a vampire.

Not only that, but Raven knew who I was. The knowledge sent a shiver down my spine.

15 AUGUST

Candlelight flickered from hundreds of candles set into elaborate candelabras all around the dark room. The shadows danced, illuminating hats on every surface. So many hats—tall, small, round, square, decorated with ribbons, bows, feathers, bones, gears and cogs—sitting on every available surface.

Despite the rainbow of color they provided, I barely looked at the hats. Instead, I stared at the figure standing in front of me. An impossibly beautiful face—smooth, pale skin like porcelain, black hair that fell to his strong jaw, with piercing green eyes that sparkled like gemstones, watching me.

I couldn't take my eyes from his face, as though an invisible cord snapped tight between us, drawing us *together. A regular thudding pulsed in my ears. My heartbeat drowning out every other sound.*

I felt hot—too hot—and I fluttered my fan with one hand, as I reached out to touch his face with the other. My fingers ran over the skin of his cheek, and a shiver ran through me at the cool touch of his skin.

He caught my hand and pressed a kiss into my palm. Then lowered his face to smell my wrist. I held my breath. He continued up my arm to my elbow, then up my inner arm with a feathery touch so light that it tickled.

His wide, red lips stretched into a smile as he looked up at me through long black lashes. He continued to inhale my scent, moving along my collarbone.

He closed his eyes, as he stopped at the soft skin at the base of my neck. When his eyes flickered open, the pupils were so dilated that his eyes looked black.

"May I?" he asked, and his voice was a low hum, like music. I wanted to hear more. I froze, my eyes locked on his face, my body attuned to his movement, mesmerized by the entrancing sound of his voice.

I nodded once.

Then he opened his mouth wide, and I saw the glint of candlelight on his fangs.

My pulse thudded in my ears like thunder, but I couldn't move.

The vampire bent his head to the base of my neck and his razor-sharp teeth sank into my skin.

I opened my mouth to scream.

~

I sat straight upright, as my heart pounded. I drew my knees to my chest as I clutched at the spot where I thought I'd been bitten. I stared around frantically for the vampire to catch him in the act of escape.

A sliver of light crept in through a crack in the heavy curtains of my bedroom windows. It lit the room enough to banish the shadows. There wasn't anyone else here.

No vampire.

No one.

I looked at my hand, turning it over. No blood, no cuts. No blemishes of any kind.

I exhaled deeply and let my forehead fall to my knees.

A nightmare—the same one I'd been having for days.

I'm thinking too much about vampires because of the investigation into the blood banks.

But no—the dreams about vampires started before my investigation. Besides, I wasn't dreaming about vampires. I was dreaming about one vampire. One impossibly handsome vampire with intoxicating eyes.

I threw back the remaining covers, reaching for my pocket watch. My fingers brushed the metal case, and I saw the elegant script written on the card left for me at The Tea Party: *We choose our future.*

What did it mean? Another puzzle.

I pushed those thoughts aside, flicked open the watch, and gasped. I swung my legs over the side of the four-poster bed, slid into some slippers and shuffled over to my wardrobe to dress.

A maid had left a tray of breakfast on the side table. I nibbled on a slice of bread as I read a note, then groaned. Mother had called for me, and I was already late.

~

"You wanted to see me, Mother?"

Alice was at her desk, reading a stack of papers. The

smudges underneath her eyes suggested she had slept little.

Alice's face lightened as she saw me. "Ivy..." She paused as she studied me. "You look as though you've barely slept."

I cleared my throat. "I was out late with Chesh, then I had nightmares."

Alice pressed her lips together, in an attempt at disapproval, but I could see in the way her lips curled up at the edges, that she wasn't angry. "How is Mr. Cheshire? I haven't seen him lately." Alice raised one eyebrow.

"He's been busy at the Emporium. He's inventing a flying machine."

Alice laughed, and the sound lifted my mood. She didn't laugh much anymore—always too busy for fun. "If he's going to keep you out at all hours, he should do the proper thing and ask my permission for your hand."

"Mother!" My eyes widened as I shook my head. "Chesh is a friend. Nothing more."

"So you say," Alice remarked dryly. "I've not heard Mr. Cheshire's side of the story."

"There is only one side of this story, Mother," I replied, then cast around to change the subject. "Have you had any breakfast? Shall I ring for tea?"

The smile faded as Alice looked down at the stack of papers. "I don't have time. Actually, there was a reason... I wrote it down... somewhere..."

"While you're looking, I wanted to ask you—" I started.

Alice placed both hands flat on the desk. "Did you find out anything about the blood banks?" she interrupted.

I nodded. "I visited the blood bank yesterday. There was a crowd waiting to donate blood. They have plenty of stock."

"No substance to the petitioner's fears? Good," Alice replied. "I don't need a vampire problem. That clock is making everyone crazy. People are terrified the Queen of Hearts is returning. They're refusing to leave their houses."

"Why do you think it started ticking again?" I asked.

Alice looked up again from her papers. "You're not worried, too? You're too sensible for that."

I shook my head. "It makes me wonder, though... Why does a clock start to tick after all this time?"

"I'm less concerned about the clock than about people refusing to leave their houses. We have several staff who didn't turn up to work today. I heard reports of people packing their possessions into a cart and leaving the city—they're willing to take their chances in a strange place because a clock is ticking. Honestly, sometimes I do not understand people at all."

Me, neither, I thought.

I slipped the card out of my pocket and turned it over so that the white rabbit motif faced upwards.

I cleared my throat. "There *was* something else—"

"That reminds me," Alice jabbed her finger in the air, her eyes lighting up. "Will you work an extra shift today? In the Spades Quarter? One inspector didn't show up for work."

I nodded. "I've never been there, but I know where it is." The oldest part of the city, the Spades Quarter was otherwise known as the vampire quarter, because of the large concentration of vampire residences.

Alice nodded. "Be careful and don't linger after dark, do you hear?"

She called out to Jack and requested the specifics of the inspection schedule. As he hurried out of the room to oblige, Alice waved a hand at me. "See you at dinner."

Ignoring her dismissal, I asked, "Mother, what do you know about the white rabbit?"

Alice froze. "What?"

"The white rabbit," I repeated. "The baker mentioned him the other day."

Alice fussed with the papers on her desk, not meeting my eyes. "I remember." She cleared her throat. "He served the late Queen. He was always late. Or, he was always worried about being late. The Queen of Hearts brought out everyone's neuroses."

"What happened to him?"

Two red dots appeared on Alice's cheeks, a sign that she was embarrassed. She looked out of the window. There was a long pause. "He left The Forge," she said, finally. "I have no idea where he went."

"Do you recognize this?" I held out the card with the white rabbit motif. Alice looked at it, but there was no flicker of recognition. She passed back the card.

"Was the white rabbit a vampire?"

"No!" Alice looked astonished. "Why all these questions?"

I turned the card around in my hand, unable to put my thoughts into words. The petitioner had mentioned rumors about the white rabbit gathering the late Queen's supporters, and I'd seen the painting of the white rabbit in several places across the city. Whether it had anything to do with the white rabbit that Alice used to know, I had no idea. But I was sure it was connected to Raven, the vampire.

I hated a puzzle I couldn't solve.

"No reason, Mother," I murmured. "I'll get to work and let you get back to yours."

"You'll ruin me!"

Mr. Thackery clasped his hands in front of him as he dropped to his knees. He was balding, and his remaining gray hair floated around his head, somewhere between short and long. His coat was worn, his collar yellow with wear. His own appearance broke the aesthetic code, let alone the condition of his shop. *Thackery's Fine Antiques* looked as though it hadn't been cleaned since its goods were first made.

"My records show this is the third time an inspector has assessed code violations," I said, taking another step backward to put space between myself and Mr. Thackery. "You cannot continue to operate in violation of the code."

"If I can't open my shop, I can't run my business, I can't feed my children," Mr. Thackery said, reaching out to grab my skirts and holding me in place.

I pulled at my dress to whip my skirts from his grasp. "If you remedy the violations and pay the fine, we will return your license. It's detailed in this list." I held out a piece of paper to Mr. Thackery. "Please, get up."

He slowly got to his feet, then snatched the paper from my hand. He ran his eyes ran over the list of violations, and his shoulders slumped.

"I can't pay for this—I can't even afford the repairs, let alone the fine to get my license back. You're putting me out of business."

"I'm sorry, Mr. Thackery. I can't do any more for you. I detail everything in that list. I wish you the best of luck." I cleared my throat. "Good day."

Without waiting for Mr. Thackery's response, I

pushed through the door and stepped onto the street, taking a deep breath to rid myself of the musty odor that permeated the antique shop. As I stepped away, I made the mistake of looking back and saw Mr. Thackery, sobbing into his handkerchief. My throat seized up. I spun around to look in the other direction.

He'd had his chances, I told myself. *The previous inspector warned him. He broke the rules.*

I didn't feel any better.

I kept my eyes forward as I walked away. When I'd put a block between myself and the antique shop, I looked down at the last item on my list.

Ace of Spades Apothecary. I marched towards it, determined to get the inspection over with. After the day I'd had, I wasn't surprised the regular inspector had stayed home—almost every business I'd visited, had required a warning for a code violation, and I'd had to issue two shut down notices. I'd already decided to tell Alice that she would need to find someone else to take on the regular rounds.

The apothecary was dark. The sign in the window read: *Closed.*

Below, a handwritten note read: *Open 8pm until 8am.*

I flicked open the case of my pocket watch. Almost two hours until the shop would open. Alice had insisted that I not remain in this quarter after dark, but the summer evenings were still long. I should have time to inspect the shop and get home before dark, but I would cut it close.

I turned in a circle and saw the *Reading Leaves Tearooms,* where I could pass the time. I settled myself at the window and raised my hand to draw the attention of a server.

I was waiting out in front of the apothecary when the sign flipped to *Open*. A young man fiddled with the lock, then pulled open door. His eyes widened when he saw me, but he stood aside to let me enter.

I felt no inclination towards small talk. "Inspector Rowntree. Just a routine inspection."

The young man returned to his place behind the desk where he busied himself with what appeared to be accounts. I wandered between rows and rows of vials of colored liquids with fancy descriptions I had never heard of. Though, with labels like *Clorisazole: For use around the eyes to eliminate crow's feet* or *Nobaldogene Perminisec: One spoonful to be taken at bedtime to ward off baldness,* I expected his custom was good among those who could pay for remedies to increase their aesthetic credit.

Running my gloved fingers over the shelves and vials, I found only hints of dust. The apothecary was clean, well ordered, though perhaps more cluttered than was seemly. I was halfway through my checklist when the bell tinkled as the shop door opened.

The timber floorboards creaked to announce the first customer. I didn't look up, but I continued to work my way down the checklist, moving through the shop, while a conversation with the customer continued in the background.

It wasn't until the bell tinkled again that the salutation pierced my concentration.

"Good evening, Raven. Until next time."

My head jerked up, and I dropped the clipboard I was holding. *Raven?*

The door closed with a *thud*. I spun to face it, but there was no sign of the customer who had been in the shop only moments ago.

Had I heard right? Could it be *my* Raven? How many could there be in Melfall? It had to be the same man who had left me his card at *The Tea Party*.

Leaving the clipboard on the floor, and my hat on the counter, I ran to the door and jerked it open. Dimly, the shop assistant called out in surprise, but I ignored him as I stepped onto the street. Looking left and right, I berated myself for not getting a better look at the customer when he'd entered the apothecary.

The streets were dark and empty. I cursed my luck as I looked at the sky. It had become a deep indigo as the last glimmer of light disappeared. I'd promised Alice that I wouldn't linger after nightfall, but the inspection had taken longer than I'd intended.

I took a few steps toward one corner and peered around to look down the next street. It was empty.

"Spades!" I muttered, then stormed back into the apothecary.

"Inspector?" the young man crouched in the place where I'd dropped my clipboard. He held it out to me. "Are you well?"

"Yes," I said, snatching back my paperwork from his outstretched hand. Then I clamped my mouth shut for a moment while I steadied myself. "I'm sorry, I was just…"

I shook my head, collecting my thoughts. "Actually, I need to ask you some questions."

The assistant sauntered back to put the counter between us. He watched me through wary eyes. "If I can be of service."

"The customer who was just here. Who is he?"

The assistant frowned. "I'm not acquainted with him. He came in off the street."

I arched one eyebrow. "You didn't know him?"

A muscle in the man's jaw tensed, as though he was clenching his teeth. "Anyone may enter a store, Inspector."

I stepped up to the other side of the counter, looking him in the eye. I rapped my fingertips on the polished wood of the countertop. "You called him by his name. I surmised that you know him."

"His name?"

"You called him Raven."

"You must have been mistaken. I know no-one of that name," he replied, though I thought I saw his eye twitch.

I paused, watching him. He met my gaze, but I was sure he was lying. "Have you heard of the white rabbit?" I asked.

He paled slightly. I drew out the card that Raven had left for me in *The Tea Party*. "Do you recognize this motif?"

The young man shook his head. "I'm afraid I can't help you. If you have finished your inspection..." He looked pointedly at the clipboard clutched to my chest.

I bit the inside of my cheek. "For now," I said. "Unfortunately, there are some anomalies. I'll have to return soon."

The assistant crossed his arms across his chest, staring at me with an expression of disapproval. I gathered my things, put on my hat, and prepared to leave.

As I turned, I spotted a small vial of dark red liquid identified by a black label. There were no markings, except for a white line in the shape of rabbit ears. I turned back and grabbed it before the assistant could stop me.

"That's not—"

"The white rabbit?" I said. The vial was marked with the same motif as on Raven's card and on the walls around the city. "What is this?"

The man stood still; his thin lips pressed into a line. He didn't answer.

"Did Raven leave this?"

The man's throat bobbed as he swallowed. "I don't know Raven."

I looked at the vial again, swirling the liquid around. "This is blood." My eyes widened as I understood. "Black market blood."

He clutched the edge of the counter and shook his head. "I don't know—"

"You're lying," I pointed a finger at his chest and tucked the vial into my bag. "I'm taking this with me. When I return, I hope you'll have enough sense to answer my questions."

"You're making a mistake," he said as I put my hand on the door. I spun around to face him again. "Go back to your beauty parlors, dresses, and parties."

I gritted my teeth, flushing at his insinuation. "Or what?"

"Or, you might find out what's happening in this city."

"Is that a threat?" I asked.

"Trust me," he said. He walked around the counter to come toward me. I stood frozen in position, holding my breath as he approached. He stood too close, then reached out, as though to grab hold of me. I jumped out of his way.

He took hold of the door handle and opened it,

motioning for me to leave. "You don't want to know."

16 AUGUST

I flicked open the case of Mr. Pillar's pocket watch as I waited. It kept perfect time, despite not being wound in the five days since Mr. Pillar had tasked me with "fixing" it. I flicked the lid closed again, then open, then closed as my thoughts turned like clockwork.

So many puzzles I'd barely slept last night thinking about them. I hated a puzzle that I couldn't solve. Now I had two.

First, this pocket watch that should not be working at all kept time with no winding.

Second, and more worryingly, the mysterious Raven, a vampire who was connected with black market blood, was also linked to the white rabbit. According to the man who'd petitioned Alice, the white rabbit associated with the Queen of Hearts, and was gathering her supporters.

In Alice's office, the claim had seemed ludicrous. The Queen was dead. Now, I wasn't so sure—it made little sense, yet I was sure these things were all somehow tied together.

"Number 13," a feminine voice called out.

I looked at my ticket. 17. I sighed.

The vial of black market blood weighed heavy in my pocket. I'd made another visit to a blood bank—this time, the one on Seventh Street—to see if I could persuade anyone there to talk. I pretended to be a seller rather than announce myself as an inspector. In the last few days, people seemed more wary of inspectors than usual.

The scruffy woman who answered to number 13 shuffled through the sliding door, and I went back to flicking the lid of Mr. Pillar's watch. There was nothing wrong with it, and despite Chesh's suggestion that I break it and collect Mr. Pillar's generous fee, the act of breaking a beautiful and antique pocket watch seemed wrong. No, after the blood bank, I planned to visit Mr. Pillar and return his watch, explaining that I could not take his commission.

Let someone else take a hammer to the watch if they had to, but it wouldn't be me.

The man next to me glared at me, so I slipped the watch back into my clutch and picked up the day's edition of The Forge Hart left on number 13's seat.

The front page blared: *Hearts Return!* An article followed that listed various sightings of robotic Hearts.

I frowned. At face value, sightings were increasing, but how many of these were eyewitness accounts, and how many were people who wanted their names in the newspaper? Still, after having seen one of the Hearts myself, I couldn't discount the story completely.

Another puzzle.

"Terrible, isn't it?"

A man leaned over my shoulder and jabbed a finger at the picture on the front of the paper. I murmured agreement as I noticed dirt underneath his fingernails.

"I didn't even want to come out of my house today, in case I came face-to-face with one. My neighbor was killed by one of them in the old days. You're too young to know what I'm talking about, but things were terrible back then. A Heart would kill you as soon as look at you if you got in their way. Terrible—if the stories are true... Where did it say they've been seen now? I'm making a list of places to stay away from. Mind if I look?"

I shook my head and handed over the newspaper, eager to extricate myself from the conversation. I smoothed my skirts and wondered how much longer I would have to wait.

≈

"Number 17?"

I sprang out of my chair, waving my ticket.

I smiled at the older woman with a nametag that read Mrs. Sprick. "Eager, are you?" she said, mistaking my relief for enthusiasm. "Have you visited us before?"

"No, first time."

Mrs. Sprick raised her eyebrows. "We'll see how eager you are next time, dear. Some people don't like the needles much."

I swallowed. I hadn't planned to go through with the blood donation. I'd only wanted time to ask some questions. The idea of the needle made me break out into a cold sweat. "What exactly are you going to do?" I asked, stalling for time as Mrs. Sprick led me down a hallway into a small room. She gestured for me to sit down.

"Roll up your sleeve, please," she said.

My mind went blank. I stared at the needle she pulled out of a box—she would jab it into me. The questions I'd prepared vanished from my mind.

"What happens to the blood?" I asked, crossing my arms over my chest. "After you... err, take it?"

Mrs. Sprick frowned at me. "Having second thoughts, are you? If you won't let me prick you, then I'd rather you tell me now. I don't want to waste my time when there are so many other people waiting."

"No, no," I stammered, stalling. "I'm just... interested"—I cleared my throat— "in the process."

"You're too pretty to be thinking about a career in the blood bank," she said.

"Do you have any problems with black market blood?" I blurted out, leaning back subtlety as Mrs. Sprick came towards me with the needle.

"What on earth are you talking about? Why would there be a black market when the vampires can get safe, regulated blood from the banks at a reasonable price? Roll up your sleeve," she said. "Above the elbow."

I fumbled with the button on the cuff of my blouse. My fingers weren't working properly. Mrs. Sprick took another step forward, holding the needle up in the air to test it.

"Is there a lot of demand, at the moment, for... err, the product?"

"You *are* squeamish. Can't even say the word. Blood. Is there a demand for blood? There's always a demand for blood. Those vampires are a thirsty lot. Back in the day, a single vampire could hunt down dozens of people in one night. So, it takes multiple donations to quench their thirst. Will you please roll up your sleeve, miss? I can't do this through your blouse."

Mrs. Sprick huffed, then reached down to the cuff of my blouse to unbutton it herself. I shot to my feet, knocking over my chair, causing it to clatter to the timber floor.

"Actually, I've changed my mind. I'll be leaving."

I was still breathing heavily when I entered the oldest quarter in Melfall. After leaving the blood bank at a run, I'd made my way to Mr. Pillar's residence. As a member of one of the oldest families of the city, he lived in a grand house in the Hearts Quarter, once reserved for those supporters of the late Queen. Most of her supporters had renounced the Queen of Hearts after she'd died, but few had moved out of their stately homes.

I hurried towards the address that Mr. Pillar had provided when he'd left the watch with me. As I turned a corner, about two blocks away from Mr. Pillar's residence, I found myself facing the late Queen's palace. An ornate wrought-iron fence twisted into heart-shapes along the top, and beyond the fence, rows of red roses were in full bloom. I stopped in the middle of a driveway of white gravel running toward a fountain opposite the large doorway to her residence, the Palace of Hearts.

The gates were open. The fountain was running. Several groundsmen were tending to the roses. The gardens were neatly groomed, and the palace seemed full of activity.

Far too much activity for an abandoned palace.

I blinked. Nobody had lived here since the late Queen. If that was true, who was maintaining this place and paying the staff? Who was living here?

Another puzzle.

I forgot about my mission to return the pocket watch to Mr. Pillar as I took one step down the driveway. Then another.

Before I knew it, I was looking up at the fountain. It was a statue of the Queen of Hearts, water flowing from her outstretched hand, as though she was giving a gift.

"May I help you, miss?" A butler appeared next to me. "Are the Tweedles expecting you?"

The Tweedles, I thought. *Of course.*

"I imagine not," I replied, peering around the doors. "I thought this place was abandoned."

"Oh no, the Tweedles took up residence some years ago. They thought it was a shame to let such a historic building go to ruin."

I pursed my lips. Tweedle Dee and Tweedle Dum were twin brothers and ardent supporters of the late Queen. They had given Alice lots of trouble, objecting to everything she'd tried to change within The Forge over the years and had become unofficial spokespersons for all opposition to Alice's presidency.

"I would be very pleased to see what they've done with the place. Are they in?"

The butler bowed. "I shall announce you."

The gravel crunched under my feet as we trudged around the fountain and up the steps to the entrance. The butler held the door open as I stepped inside.

"Wait here, please," the butler said, turning on his heel to disappear into the house, leaving me in a hallway of black-and-white tiles laid out like a large chessboard. I tapped my foot, looking around at the large paintings on the walls—all of the late Queen in various poses.

She had the look of a queen—straight-backed with her head held high. Her crown rested on her black hair, pulled back from her face, and in every picture, she was dressed in red gowns, with stiff lace collars that stood straight up from her shoulders to frame her face. Her eyes were cold, and I had the impression that she was looking at me, watching me, where I stood. I shuddered, turning away.

A foolish notion, I thought. *She's dead.*

Still, being in the palace, which was operating as though its owner had never left, was... disconcerting.

"Miss. Rowntree!" A chorus of two voices rang out as the Tweedles appeared at the top of the stairs. They were portly gentlemen, wearing bottle-green coat tails paired with gold waistcoats and black trousers. Their once platinum blonde hair was fading to white. The only difference between the two was that Tweedle Dee parted his hair on the left, while Tweedle Dum parted his on the right. At least, I thought that was it—or it might have been the other way around.

"Welcome to our humble abode," Dee said.

"A pleasant surprise," Dum continued.

"We weren't expecting you," Dee finished.

"I'm sorry I didn't send word ahead, but I wasn't expecting to come myself," I said.

"How did you get here—" Dee said.

"If you weren't planning to come?" Dum finished.

"I was running an errand in the area, and I noticed the old palace was bustling with activity," I replied. "Isn't it odd—the old Pinnacle clock starts working again, and now the palace is in use?"

"A mighty coincidence," Dum said, with a smirk. He exchanged a look with his twin.

"A coincidence indeed." Dee agreed.

"Anyone would think the two events are connected," I said.

"They would?" Dee asked.

"Would they?" Dum asked, at exactly the same time as his brother.

I sighed. "Do you know anything about the clock?" I asked.

The Tweedles looked at each other, raising their eyebrows, grinning. When they turned back to me, they gave me innocent, wide-eyed looks.

"It's tall," Dee said.

"It's round," Dum continued.

"It's got twelve numbers on its face and—"

"Two hands," Dum finished.

"I mean, why has the clock started working again? Did you have something to do with it?"

"Us?" The Tweedles asked in unison.

I crossed my arms over my chest, staring at each of the brothers in turn. "Yes, you!"

"Not I," Dum said.

"Nor I," Dee added.

I hesitated, wondering whether there was any use in pressing them further.

"What about the Hearts? What do you know about them?" I persisted.

"Hearts are red," Dee answered.

"And usually found inside your chest," Dum finished. He turned to his brother and poked a finger at the middle of his chest. "And yours."

Dee grinned, poking him back. "And yours."

I took a deep breath and clenched my fists, fighting the urge to shake both of them. "You know what I mean. People have seen the Hearts in the streets of Melfall."

"Have they?" Dum asked.

"They have?" Dee asked at exactly the same time.

"Surely, you've heard," I replied. "Why are they here? I don't believe you know nothing about it."

"Neither do I," Dee said, turning to Dum.

"Nor do I," Dum agreed, facing Dee.

"It's settled then," the Tweedles said in unison, grinning back at each other.

"Shall we have a song?" Dee asked.

"No," I replied, putting up both hands.

"Oh, yes, I love a song," Dum replied, ignoring me completely. He turned to his brother. "Will you do the honor?"

"After you," Dee said. They both linked arms and strode to the grand piano standing in the corner of the room.

"Wait!" I said, but it made no difference. The twins sat down in front of the piano and began playing a tune in unison with a flourish.

It had neither melody nor rhythm, but the Tweedles seemed very pleased with themselves.

I sighed, shaking my head. Conversation with the Tweedles was impossible. It was nonsense, or lies, or both. I was turning to leave when I spotted something on top of the piano.

A crown.

I blinked, then looked up at the painting of the late Queen in the hall.

The crown on the piano was exactly the same as the crown that rested on her painted head.

"What are you doing with the late Queen's crown?" I said, pointing at it.

"Who me?" The Tweedles said together, looking at each other without pausing from bashing the keys of the piano. They looked from side to side. "Where?"

"There," I pointed at it. "The crown."

"Is it?" Dee asked.

"It is?" Dum said, at the same time.

"You know it is," I said. "Where did you get it?"

"Must have been—"

"Lying around somewhere."

I hesitated again. They were lying; I was sure of it, but there was no point hurling accusations. I tried one more question: "Are you working with the white rabbit?"

The two men blinked at me, their song pausing mid-note. "White rabbit?"

"You heard me," I replied. "What do you know about the white rabbit?"

The Tweedles looked at each other, their 'song' beginning again.

"The white rabbit," Dum started.

I leaned forward slightly, hanging on his response.

"Is always late!" Dee finished.

I sighed, putting a hand over my eyes. I shook my head again, then turned to leave. "I'll show myself out."

"So long—" Dee said.

"Until we meet again..." Dum finished.

Both of the Tweedles burst out laughing as I turned away.

17 AUGUST

I ran my hands over the metallic curves of one of the two machines that stood in the midst of Chesh's workshop at the rear of the Emporium. With one larger wheel at the front and a smaller, but thicker one at the back, and a leather seat in the middle. The metal handlebars and bodywork gleamed, lovingly polished to a shine.

"Bicycles," Chesh said, beaming. "Mechanical bicycles. What do you think?"

I bent to look at the metal struts that joined the two wheels, then glanced at the engine. The bicycle *felt* right under my hands. I grinned back at my friend, then swung my leg over the bike, settled myself on the smooth leather seat, and gripped the polished metal handlebars.

Earlier in the day, I'd been in the President's Library, immersed in old newspapers trying to find out more about the clock, and the Hearts. Then, I'd started looking in the recent newspapers to see what I could learn about the vampires and the white rabbit.

The puzzles nagged at me. I wasn't sure whether the white rabbit's activity was just a rumor possibly started by an old supporter of the Queen, but I was certain that the vampire, Raven, existed. Something told me that finding Raven would help me fit all the other pieces together.

By the time Mr. Hopewell, Alice's butler, brought me a message, my eyes were tired from staring at the tiny print. I opened the message, which read, "I've a surprise for you. Don't delay, you'll love it, Chesh." Grateful for the interruption to my research and I was excited about Chesh's surprise, I left immediately.

When I'd arrived at the back door to the Emporium shortly afterward, Chesh ushered me into his workshop.

"Steam-powered bicycles," Chesh was explaining. "That's what I'm calling them."

I raised my eyebrows at him. "They're powered by a steam engine? Interesting." I tightened my grip on the handles. "Steam bikes," I murmured. "Can we ride them?"

Chesh pulled a leather cap down over his curly hair, then offered one to me.

He settled himself on the other steam bike, grinning from ear to ear. "I didn't bring you out here to sit on them," Chesh winked.

I pulled the cap on, fastening the strap under my chin. "How did they do in testing?"

"We're testing them now," Chesh replied. "Why, are you afraid that your magical 'knack' won't save you?"

I arched one eyebrow, then placed both of my hands on the metal casing over the engine and felt it thrumming. I could see, in my mind's eye, all the elements of the engine working together—each part in its proper place, serving its proper purpose—to make the machine *purr* like a contented cat. It *felt* right. I felt a surge of excitement for Chesh—the bikes were ready, and he might really be onto something worthy of Guild membership this time.

"I'm not afraid, if you're not," I replied, pulling the goggles over my eyes. I kicked the bike stand out of the way and revved the engine. "Follow me."

"Wait," Chesh called as I was about to start out of the back of his workshop. He tossed me a metal tube, which I caught with one hand. It felt cold.

"What's this?" I asked, raising my voice over the roar of the engines.

"Water," Chesh responded. "In case the bikes run out of steam. I've got some too."

I tucked the canister into the bag on the back of the bike. "Ready?"

"When you are." Chesh pulled his goggles over his eyes and revved his engine loudly.

I kicked off, and the wheels screeched as I sped out of the workshop and onto the street.

"Woo-hoo!" The wind tore at my hair as I motored down a backstreet. Several people jumped out of the way, shaking heads and fists as I rode past, but they were little more than a blur. I fixed my eyes on the street, as I felt the *thrum* of the engine beneath me, and the wind pulled at my clothes like I was flying.

At the end of the street, I slowed to a stop and looked back at Chesh. "Shall we take them around the city? Test them properly?"

Chesh grinned and revved his engine. "Ladies first," he replied.

I needed no more encouragement. Taking a right turn, we tore down the backstreets where there would be fewer people milling about. I swerved sideways to avoid a downpour of wastewater as someone pitched it out of a second-floor window, then skidded to avoid several children playing hopscotch.

Winding our way through the backstreets, we traveled through the Diamonds Quarter, toward the docks.

When the water stretched out in front of me, I stopped again, letting the motor *hum* as I looked out over the water. The docks were one of my favorite places in Melfall. Ships came in and out from all over the Twelve Kingdoms, bringing spices from Badalah, dried fish from Atlantice, fresh flowers from Floris, potions from Arcadia, and countless other goods. I could see the marks on the different crates, denoting where they came from, but I'd seen no more of the Twelve Kingdoms than the marks on those crates. I watched as another sailor loaded boxes of machinery made in Melfall—I'd heard Alice mentioning a self-playing piano, a recent Guild-developed invention, which had quickly become highly sought after in the clubs of Renais, the capital of Arcadia.

Out of the persistent shadows of the buildings that towered over the backstreets, the overhead sun beat down on us. My leather cap and goggles now felt restrictive, and a trickle of perspiration ran down the back of my neck. I wished I'd brought my fan.

"Where to next?" Chesh asked as he came to a stop next to me.

"Let's make a circuit around the inside of the wall?" I

said, as my eyes trailed around to the large fortifications where the city wall joined the edge of the docks.

Chesh shrugged and revved the engine. "What are we waiting for?"

I kicked my bike forward again, and Chesh and I raced along the docks, skidding and swerving to miss the carts loading and unloading goods from the ships berthed in the harbor. Several people jumped out of our way, yelling, but I lost their voices in the din of the engines.

As I approached the end of the docks, I took the wide road that ran alongside the first fortification that began the wall that encircled Melfall. The paved cobblestones made for a rougher ride than the timber docks, but I picked up speed and heard Chesh give an excited yell as he followed me. I looked over my shoulder to smile at him when something caught my attention in the edge of my vision.

A flash of red and white. I slowed, staring into the side lane.

A Heart.

The Heart was marching in the other direction, but it was unmistakable.

My breath caught in my throat, and, without hesitation, I swung the bike around, my tires skidded as I sped up onto the side road to follow it.

"What—?" Chesh yelled. I heard the squeal of the brakes behind me, but I didn't look around. I couldn't take my eyes off the Heart, in case it disappeared.

The Heart kept a good pace, but I was on a mechanical bike—it couldn't outrun me. It didn't look around, only trudged onward, oblivious to the noise the bike made as I followed. Perhaps it was oblivious to its surroundings—it was a machine, not a person, although its mechanical body resembled one.

As I got closer, I saw the arms and legs sticking out of its square body. Like a playing card, it had the heart motif and a number on its front, but on the back, there was a regular, gray geometric design like pressed metal.

If I could get close enough—or, better still, if I could lay my hands on the Heart—I could find out how it worked. If I understood its programming, I might discover why they'd suddenly appeared again. I might even find out who was controlling them. The elusive Raven flitted through my thoughts, though it was as much coincidence as anything else that the Hearts and the vampire were both puzzles that had appeared in my life at the same time. Then again, after my visit with the Tweedles, I wouldn't put it past them to have set the Hearts loose as a prank.

I pushed the bike faster so that the buildings on either side of the narrow streets became a blur. I was gaining on the Heart when a yell surprised me from above, then a chamber pot of wastewater splashed on the street in front of me. I gasped, pulling on the brakes, then swerved to avoid the mess.

In front of my adjusted course, a door opened, and a woman with a baby on her hip stepped out of it.

My instincts kicked in, and I screamed at her, braking hard. My wheels squealed as the bike skidded. The woman stared at me, wide-eyed and open-mouthed, frozen in place. I was still moving too fast, heading directly for her. I pulled back on the brakes, as hard as I could, my eyes locked on the woman and her child.

Everything moved slowly.

The woman pulled the baby to her chest, opening her mouth to let out an ear-piercing shriek. The child screwed up its face and howled.

Directly overhead now, the midday sun cast a stripe down the middle of the street. The sunlight flashed off metal, blinding me for a moment. I held my breath, squeezing my eyes shut, then threw myself sideways to avoid the collision.

I hit the ground hard, groaning as the bike slipped out from underneath me.

~

"Ivy!" A voice echoed through the narrow street.

A moment later, there was a hand on my shoulder, and I was being turned onto my back. The bright sunlight shone straight into my eyes, making me blink, and obscuring the face staring down at me. Then the head moved, blocking the light. Chesh gaped down at me, the sun behind him shining a golden halo around his face.

"Are you all right? Answer me!" Chesh gripped my shoulders, his fingers digging into my flesh as he shook me. His eyes were wide, panicked.

"I'm all right," I struggled to sit, sore down the side of my arm where I'd hit the ground. I looked at my arm—I'd grazed it, but the material of my coat, now torn at the elbow, had taken most of the blow. My eyes opened wide as I remembered the woman and child. "The woman. The baby? Did I...?"

Chesh shook his head, looking over at the doorway where the woman was clutching the baby to her breast. Even from where I lay, I could see she was trembling.

"Can you stand?" Chesh asked.

I nodded, and he helped me to my feet. I moved my fingers, arms, and legs, testing myself for injury. There was a scratch on my goggles, but other than the graze on my arm, I'd emerged unscathed. "Really, I'm fine. Just a little shaken."

"What were you doing? I thought we were doing a circuit of the walls?"

I rubbed my throbbing arm. "I saw a Heart and tried to catch it." I looked around for the place I'd last seen the Heart, but it was gone.

Chesh frowned. "What for?"

I shook my head, disappointment blooming in my chest. "To find out how it works."

Chesh gaped at me, then pulled his cap off and ran a hand through his hair. The gesture made it stick up at an unfashionable angle. He shook his head, then pointed a finger at me. "Didn't your mother tell you curiosity killed the cat? It almost killed you today."

"It didn't. I'm fine," I replied. "Really."

"I'm not," Chesh said, but the edges of his mouth were already turning up into his trademark grin. He put a hand over his heart. "My heart might never be the same. I'm sure it stopped back there."

I snorted, then stepped around Chesh and walked up to the woman, apologizing profusely as I approached her. She shrunk away from me, backing further into the open doorway.

I stopped, raising my voice to call to her instead. "Did you see the Heart?"

The baby started wailing again as it set eyes on me, and the woman shook her head, bouncing the baby on her hip.

"Where did it go?" I asked, but the woman had already shut the door firmly behind her.

I walked back to Chesh, who had stood up my bike and was checking it over.

"No permanent damage," he said, rubbing at several

scratches on the metal.

"Sorry," I replied.

Chesh shrugged. "Perhaps we walk the bikes back?"

I hesitated. "Just give me a minute, would you?"

I walked up to a group of people who had appeared in the narrow street, likely drawn by the unusual noise. They watched us, openly curious.

"Excuse me, have any of you seen a Heart passing this way?" I pointed in the direction it had taken. "Did you see where it went?"

People frowned, suddenly wary at the mention of the Heart, and moved away. I sighed, returning to where Chesh crouched next to the bikes.

"We should go back," he said.

I looked down the street one more time, hoping for another glimpse of the Heart, but it was empty. I looked back at Chesh and shook my head.

"Let's keep going—but slower this time, I promise," I replied, swinging my leg over the bike before Chesh could object.

I kicked the bike into action and took us back towards the wide road that ran along the inside of the city walls. We rode at a more sedate pace, and though I searched the streets for any sign of the Heart, I didn't see it again.

However, as I rounded the corner, moving into the Spades Quarter, I saw something else that made me stop.

Across the road, on the wall of a shop, the white rabbit motif was painted. This time, the rabbit seemed to be looking around a street corner. When Chesh came to a stop next to me, I pointed to the street where the shop with the white rabbit on it was.

"Let's take a trip down there," I said. "I've never been

there before."

"I would hope not—that's the beginning of the vampire quarter." Chesh gave me a strange look. "What's down there?"

I shrugged but didn't take my eyes off the white rabbit. "We won't know until we find out."

"You almost killed yourself back there. Now you want to tempt the vampires?"

"It's the middle of the day. There won't be vampires around. You're not afraid, are you?" I wiggled my eyebrows at him.

Chesh opened his mouth to protest again, but I kicked my bike into action and turned into the vampire quarter.

~

As promised, the streets were empty. I was being more careful , since throwing myself off the bike earlier, but I could have used as much speed as I wanted here. There was no-one around to run into.

The Spades Quarter, or vampire quarter as it was unofficially known, was a very old part of town. Narrow, three-story townhouses stood right next to each other, as though the houses leaned on each other for support. The shutters on the windows were closed, keeping the light from entering the rooms inside. Still, despite the closed windows and absence of people on the streets, I had the eerie feeling of being watched.

At street level, shop windows displayed their goods, though none were open. There were shops selling clothes, shoes, and hats, shops selling furniture, both new and antique, and shops selling watches, machines, inventions, and many other curiosities. There were no food shops, no bars, and no blood banks. I noticed all the shops were on the pricier end of the scale, catering to the renowned wealth of the vampires who gathered to live in this quarter of the city who had owned their property for generations, and who had had centuries to amass their fortunes.

I slowed, getting off my bike to admire a range of hats in a shop window, *Cappello's Finest Hats.*

I thought of Pearl as I saw one particular item in the window. A fascinator decorated with flamingo feathers in different shades of pink so that the feathers spread out like the brim of a hat over her face. I reached out to touch it, but my fingers came up against the cold glass.

The shop wouldn't open until nightfall, according to the sign on the door. I stepped back, knowing the fascinator would look magnificent on my twin and wishing Pearl was with me to see it. I knew she'd never come into the Spades Quarter.

Perhaps I can bring one to her, I thought.

I looked around, trying to spot a street sign so I might make my way back here when the shop was open when I spotted a small, white rabbit painted on the bottom corner of the shop. It was sitting, staring straight out like it was looking at the passers-by walking down the street. As though it was watching me.

I stepped toward it, reaching out to touch it when Chesh's voice made me jump.

"Are we going to get going?" Chesh said. "This place gives me the creeps."

I had a prickly sensation on the back of my neck, though I didn't want to admit it. Though eerie, this part of the city was fascinating. Not only was the architecture older than what I had seen before, but this white rabbit was teasing me. Twice now, I'd seen it painted on the walls.

The petitioner had said the white rabbit was gathering the Queen's supporters. The vampires had been supporters of the Queen during her reign. Was it a coincidence that I saw the painting of the white rabbit in a place where most of the city's vampires lived?

I pressed my lips together, frowning as my mind worked over the puzzle while I got back on my bike. I rode slowly for another few blocks, my eyes roving at street level for any more signs of the white rabbit. Twice more, I spotted more paintings—each white rabbit in a different pose. Sometimes painted as though it was running down the street, or peeking around a corner, or entering a rabbit hole, with only its fluffy tail on view.

I thought again of Raven's card, with its white rabbit motif on the back: *We choose our future.*

I remembered the vial of black market blood. There was some connection between the blood, the white rabbit, and the mysterious vampire. The puzzle, it seemed, wouldn't leave me alone until I solved it.

The sun was dipping lower in the sky when we finally drove out of the vampire quarter and into the more familiar parts of the city. Chesh seemed happier the further away we rode from the Spades Quarter, but I felt my mind returning there—to the white rabbit, and to the mysterious vampire that haunted my dreams.

As we headed for home, we rode through the marketplace where the Pinnacle clock ticked ominously.

Tick, tick, tick.

～

"I want to get a present," I said to Chesh as we walked the darkened streets.

"For whom?"

"Pearl. I saw a fascinator earlier that she will absolutely love." I didn't tell him where I'd seen the hat or the other reasons I wanted to return there. I knew Chesh wouldn't agree to a journey into the vampire quarter to look for more paintings of the white rabbit. Or to find a particular vampire.

Chesh slowed his pace, putting a hand on my arm to make me turn around. "It's too late. The shops are closed."

I held my breath and looked him in the eye. "Not where we're going."

Chesh blinked at me as comprehension dawned on his face. "No," Chesh shook his head. "No, no—it was bad enough during the day. I'm not going back. Let's go to a bar and get a drink instead."

"Sure. Let's do that," I smiled, looping my hand around his elbow. "After we get Pearl's hat."

Chesh opened his mouth to object, but I cut him off.

"Come on—you won't make me go on my own, will you? Please?" I squeezed Chesh's arm, but he wouldn't move. I hesitated a moment, then used a phrase that Chesh had said to me many times: "You're my lucky charm."

Chesh glanced at me, his eyes going wide with surprise. Conflicting emotions played over his face. Finally, Chesh pinched the bridge of his nose and sighed in resignation. "The things I do for you," he said. "Let's get this over with."

We walked into the Spades Quarter, and a smile spread over my face as I took in the almost unrecognizable streets. The quarter was very different from when we'd been there during the day.

Above us, street lamps shaped into bats in flight

were casting their lamplight over streets full of people. It was almost as though it *was* the middle of the day. Shops were open, tearooms, restaurants, and bars were full, and people—vampires, mostly—strolled the streets. Everyone was well-dressed. Everyone glowed with an ethereal beauty.

I tried to look everywhere at once, entranced by the sights of the evening, but also checking every shop wall and street corner for signs of the white rabbit.

Chesh fidgeted beside me, constantly looking over his shoulder. I squeezed his arm. "This way," I said, pointing towards a side street. "Another block over."

I stepped into the side street, while Chesh hung back a moment. Behind me, he sighed, and his footsteps rang out on the cobblestones as he followed.

The side street was almost empty, except for a figure in the shadows who leaned against a wall, smoking a pipe. I didn't pay much attention to him as my eyes fixed on the snippet of a busier street at the end of the lane, which was—I was sure—where I'd seen *Cappello's Finest Hats.*

I didn't look at the figure until I was almost past him. As I walked past, I glanced at him, and my heart raced. Outwardly, I froze.

His eyes were bloodshot and sunk deep into their sockets, with heavy purple smudges beneath them. His pale, almost-translucent skin stretched tight over his bones like a walking skeleton, and he hunched over, as though it took too much effort to stand up straight.

My throat swelled so I could barely breathe. Blood rushed in my ears. A prickling sensation raised along the back of my neck, then spread until the skin all over my body was tingling.

I'd never met a vampire, but it didn't matter.

Instinctively, I sensed danger. This one was thirsty.

The vampire sneered, and his thin lips stretched over sharp teeth.

I forced myself to move, clutching Chesh's arm, as I started walking faster. Without a word passing between us, I knew that he'd seen the vampire too. Chesh matched my step.

Suddenly, the vampire was standing in front of us.

He sniffed the air.

"Fresh blood," the vampire whispered, his eyes drifting to where my blood pulsed in the vein in my neck. I stepped away from him, and he smiled again, wider this time, deliberately showing his fangs. "We get little fresh blood in these streets at night."

"Leave us alone," Chesh said, trying to move around the vampire. "This young lady is the daughter of the President."

The vampire raised an eyebrow but didn't step away. His eyes roved over my face and body, and I saw his nostrils move slightly, as though savoring my smell.

"You? You're the daughter of the woman who is starving my kind?"

I took a step backward as did Chesh in front of me, although I knew it was pointless. From the very little I knew of vampires, they moved faster than the human eye could see.

I pinned my glare on him, determined that I would not blink and find his fangs piercing my throat.

"What are you talking about?" I asked my voice wobbling as I spoke. "President Rowntree is not doing anything to your kind. She was the one who ensured constantly available blood supply through the blood banks."

The vampires gnashed his teeth, showing his fangs.

His blood-shot eyes darted this way and that. "Available? No one can get blood now. They locked down the blood banks."

I shook my head. "I visited a blood bank yesterday. There are enough stocks for anyone wishing to buy."

"Plenty of stocks for your eyes, but when my kind goes there, we get turned away. No more blood, they tell us."

I tilted my head to the side, frowning as I considered the vampire's information. There was no need for him to lie, but I knew it wasn't the truth. Still, that petitioner had seen a vampire come out of the blood bank, claiming that it looked as though the vampire was still thirsty. There was no reason for that petitioner to lie either. Could it be true?

"It's been a long time since I had fresh blood," the vampire continued, and his words brought me back to my immediate danger. "I don't go hunting—not since the Blood Accords—but when such a delicious meal comes to me, how can I refuse?"

"Ivy, run!" Chesh pushed me behind him, giving me a shove. But the vampire was quicker, grabbing the front of Chesh's shirt in his fist and throwing Chesh against the alley wall before I could move.

Suddenly, the vampire was behind me. His breath tickled the soft skin on my neck where my blood was pounding underneath my flesh. Goosebumps raised over my skin.

"I prefer my meat beautiful," the vampire whispered. "And female. The women are always softer, and their blood is so, so sweet."

I closed my eyes and saw the flash of fangs, a memory of the dream I'd had over and over again. I spun around to face the vampire, backing away. He laughed.

"Always fun to play with my meal, too, my dear," The vampire said. "I forgot how much less fun it is to get blood from a blood bank. There's no thrill in sucking blood out of a tube. It doesn't run, or fight, or plead. The blood is missing the tang that comes from the rush of adrenalin coursing through the body at the point of death. So, by all means, run—I'll get you in the end."

My breath came in short gasps, and I wiped my palms against my skirts. He was right—I could never outrun him, nor fight him off. Even malnourished, he was faster and stronger than any human.

My feet were planted on the cobblestones, and, though my thoughts were screaming at me to run, I couldn't move.

"Chesh, you go," I said. "Save yourself."

Chesh was picking himself up from the ground, stumbling sideways a few steps before leaning against the wall, rubbing the back of his head. "I won't leave you."

"Don't be ridiculous," I retorted. "Go. Tell Mother everything."

I didn't look at my friend as I couldn't take my eyes from the vampire standing in front of me. However, I could see his figure out of the corner of my eye. He hesitated, looking from the vampire, to me, then back again.

"I don't think—" he started, but I interrupted him.

"Go!" I yelled.

The vampire only laughed as the sound of Chesh's footsteps echoed in the alleyway. "Too bad, your lover couldn't save you."

"He's not my lover," I replied, squeezing my fists. My mouth went dry as the vampire stepped toward me again.

"Does he know that?" the vampire purred. The pupils of his eyes widened, and he licked his lips. He took another step toward me, and I fought against a sudden urge to run, knowing it would only hasten my death. As soon as I tried to get away, the vampire would pounce.

I swallowed, seeing the hunger in his eyes. I thought of the vial of black market blood and played my only card.

"Why can't you get blood from the white rabbit?" I blurted out.

The vampire hissed and stopped advancing, his eyes narrowing. "What do you know about the white rabbit?"

"I know that Raven is distributing it. The white rabbit's blood," I said, sensing that my statement had rattled the vampire, but my breath caught in my throat as I spoke again, grasping at straws.

The vampire's eyes narrowed further, the corners of his mouth drawing into a frown that covered his teeth.

"How do you know Raven?"

I swallowed, wiping my hands on my skirts. I cast around for an answer. "He bought me a drink," I replied.

The vampire raised an eyebrow. "Did he?" His voice had a dangerous edge.

"Actually, I've been looking for him," I said, lifting my chin and straightening my shoulders, hoping to convince the vampire I wasn't afraid of him at all.

The vampire grinned, then in a flash, he grabbed me by the throat and pushed me up against the wall of the alley. I gasped for breath as his fingers dug into the flesh of my neck.

"You lie," he whispered.

I tried to shake my head, but the vampire held me too tightly. "Please..."

The vampire chuckled. "Your blood will taste so

sweet," he said.

"I'm not lying."

"Raven doesn't buy drinks for the daughter of the President," the vampire hissed, pressing me hard against the wall. The cold of the bricks seeped through my light summer coat.

"He did. At *The Tea Party*," I said. "A bar in—"

The vampire narrowed his eyes again. "I know the one."

I tried to nod, but he squeezed my throat tighter. I couldn't breathe. Dark spots formed at the edge of my vision as the world narrowed to the sight of his face—his dilated pupils, his thin lips, and sharp fangs.

I tore at his grip with one hand, kicking out at him in desperation. It wouldn't be much longer before I passed out. "Please..."

As everything swam in front of my eyes, I remembered the bottle of blood that I'd taken from the counter at the *Ace of Spades Apothecary*. I quickly dug my hand into my clutch, pulling it out and waving it in the air.

"Raven gave me this!" I hissed.

The vampire's head snapped around to look at the vial without loosening his grip on my throat. My eyes bulged, and my chest was on fire as my body demanded air.

Suddenly, with no warning, the vampire let go of me and stepped away. I crumpled to the ground, sinking into the folds of my skirts, gasping and rubbing at my neck.

I didn't even notice that I'd lost hold of the vial until the vampire spoke again. I looked up at him and saw him holding up the vial in front of him. It was empty.

The vampire licked the last trace of blood from his lips and sighed. His skin seemed less gaunt, the shadows under his eyes were less pronounced.

I opened my mouth to protest, then clamped it shut again and crawled away from him in the direction where Chesh had disappeared.

The vampire's face whipped around to see me, then before I could blink, he was next to me, his fingers in my hair, yanking it back to expose my neck.

He took a long breath as he trailed his nose down my neck. "You would have been sweeter, but I won't cross Raven—just in case." He let go of my hair, standing to take a few steps away. "If you were a wise woman, you would leave this quarter, and never come back." Then he chuckled. "I sense you're not wise, so since that blood took the edge off my thirst, I'll tell you what you want to know."

I was breathing hard, cowering against the wall, wishing the vampire would leave. What was it I wanted to know? My mind felt so fuzzy now that I couldn't remember.

"To find Raven, you must follow the white rabbit."

"What?" I blinked, but the vampire was gone. There was no trace that he'd even been there, except for the empty vial lying abandoned on the cobblestones.

I buried my face in my hands, taking a few deep breaths to steady myself. Then I clawed at the wall, forcing myself to stand. I couldn't stay in the vampire quarter a moment longer.

Putting one foot in front of the other, I forced myself to run toward the end of the alley where Chesh had disappeared. I burst out onto the street, stumbling sideways as the darkness fluttered on the edge of my vision again.

"Are you all right, Inspector?" a voice spoke into my ear. I stumbled away, but a hand on my arm steadied me.

I crashed into someone else, who shouted an exclamation, but it sounded very distant to my ears.

Suddenly, a strange face came into my line of vision. A man with a scar down the side of his face. His mouth was moving, but I couldn't make out the words.

"Please..." I said. "I need to get back to the Palace."

Or at least, I think that's what I said because after that, the darkness closed in on me and I slipped into unconsciousness.

18 AUGUST

Alice sat on the edge of my bed; her mouth turned down at the edges as she watched me. A bowl of steaming broth balanced on a tray on my lap. The scent of it made my stomach rumble. I lifted a spoonful to my mouth, and the warmth of the liquid spread through my body as I swallowed.

"I'm all right, Mother," I said.

"What were you doing?" Alice clucked her tongue, glaring at me. "I checked with your supervisor—you weren't working. Why go into the vampire quarter at night?"

I slowly savored another mouthful of broth to give myself time to answer the question. Then I cleared my throat.

"Chesh and I passed through the Spades Quarter

unexpectedly yesterday—during the day—and I saw a hat for Pearl. The shop wasn't open then, so we had to go back during business hours."

Alice's eyes narrowed, and she pressed her lips into a thin line. "You risked your life for a hat? Forgive me, Ivy, but that isn't like you."

"Not just a hat—a present for Pearl."

"Pearl would rather—" Alice started.

"A present?" Pearl interrupted as she stepped into my bedroom. "For me? Where is it?"

I smiled at my twin sister, for once relieved at her sense of timing. "I'm afraid I didn't buy it. I was..."

"The man who brought you back here said it looked like someone had attacked you," Alice said. "Is that true?"

"A petty thief," I lied. "I tried to fight him off, but I took a blow to the head, then he took the contents of my purse."

"Yet, the thief didn't take your clutch?" Alice raised an eyebrow.

My stomach sank as my eyes slid over to see my clutch lying on my bedside table, next to a vase with a single red rose in it. I had opened my mouth to ask about the rose when Pearl laughed.

"Not a clever thief," Pearl said, then leaned over the other side of my bed and adjusted my pillows.

Alice gave Pearl a disbelieving look, then glared at me.

"I promise, Mother. I'm well. There's no need to keep me in bed. I won't collapse again."

"What happened to Chesh?" Alice asked. "Why didn't he bring you back?"

My mouth fell open as I remembered my best friend. "I... He... err... hasn't called?" Sunlight was streaming

96

in the windows. I'd slept in—it was late morning, at least.

"No, he hasn't." Alice's voice was stern. "I told the staff you are not well enough for interruptions."

"Mother, I'm perfectly well," I protested.

"You heard her, she's perfectly well," Pearl said, turning to smile sweetly at Alice. "Well enough to accompany me to my hair appointment this afternoon."

Alice opened her mouth, but Pearl reached out to take her hand. "Don't worry, Mother. I'll take good care of her. I won't let her out of my sight. We're only going to *Lola's Luscious Locks.* It's barely two blocks from the Palace."

I turned to Alice, squeezing Pearl's hand gratefully. "I can't possibly keep to my bed all day, Mother."

"Besides," Pearl added. "It's almost a crime to let Ivy continue to go about with this hair." She made a face as she pulled at a strand of my hair. I put a hand to my hair and felt the mess of tangles. I hadn't been in any state when I'd come to bed the night before to attend to brushing out my hair. "I'll send ahead and make sure they have space for Ivy to get a treatment too." Pearl smiled at Alice, then spun to me.

"It's settled then." She picked up the tray still heavy with a half-full bowl of broth and set it down on a table closer to the door.

"I was eating that," I said, still holding the spoon.

Pearl rolled her eyes as she pulled back my blankets. "Get dressed. We leave within the hour."

～

Lola massaged my scalp, working the shampoo through my hair as I let my eyes drift closed.

"Ivy needs a change," Pearl said, as she lounged on the seat next to me, foils wrapped all over her head as three different shades of blonde dye set into her hair. "She's had this hair for too long."

"No longer than you," I murmured without opening my eyes. "I think we both had hair when we were first born."

"No, that was you," Pearl interrupted. "According to Mother, you were born with a head of black hair, and it took me almost a year to grow any at all."

"I'd roll my eyes if I could be bothered opening them," I said, lulled into a dreamy state by Lola's fingers.

Lola laughed but didn't stop rubbing the tips of her fingers in small circles over my scalp. "It's not going anywhere, darling—don't worry! We'll just add something a little extra, that's all."

"I'm thinking new color and new cut," Pearl said.

"I'm not sure—" I started.

"Absolutely," Lola replied to Pearl, while completely ignoring me. "Something bright. With her skin tone, she could go bright red or even white blonde. Both would look fantastic."

"Blonde," Pearl said. "We should look like twins for once."

"Wait a—"

"And I'm not dying my hair that mousy brown color," Pearl interrupted again, as though I hadn't spoken.

Lola clucked her tongue. "No, darling. You don't have the skin tone for it. Don't worry, Ivy will be fantastic as a blonde."

"Does anyone care what I think?" I said.

"No," Pearl answered. "Keep your eyes shut—we'll tell you when to open them."

My eyes flew open, and I saw myself in the mirror,

foaming soap all over my wet hair. "What?"

Lola laughed. She tilted my head back to pour warm water over my hair, making me feel drowsy. "I won't do anything to you that won't look fantastic. Trust me— my job is to make you look beautiful."

I sighed and obediently closed my eyes, as Lola rinsed the last of the shampoo from my hair.

"As for the cut, I'm thinking short," Pearl said.

"What?" I said, my eyes flying open. Pearl wagged a finger at me until I pursed my lips but closed my eyes again.

"She always wears it pinned back. I think you should cut it to the line of her jaw. I saw another woman with a similar style at Mrs. Bancroft's Parlor—it made *her* face too round, but on Ivy, it would be perfect."

"I know exactly what you mean," Lola said, moving around me and pulling on the hair on either side of my face. "Yes," she replied, slowly, as she pulled on different sections of hair and twisted them around her fingers. She sounded thoughtful. "I think it would work."

"You don't sound very confident," I nodded, keeping my eyes tightly shut.

"Honestly," Pearl said, and I imagined the eye roll that I knew matched her tone of voice. "You go gallivanting around the Vampire Quarter at night, but you won't try a new haircut!"

"I wasn't gallivanting," I replied.

"The Vampire Quarter?!" Lola exclaimed. "You're not being serious, are you? I've had clients telling me terrible things about..." Lola lowered her voice to a whisper. "vampires. There isn't enough blood, and they've gone back to their ways from the time of the old queen," Lola hesitated, and I imagined her looking over her shoulder to check that the late Queen wasn't standing behind her. "Biting people!"

"No," Pearl gasped. "Who?"

"I can't name names," Lola replied.

"Do you know anyone who has been bitten?" I asked.

"My clients know people, who know people," Lola said.

I didn't answer, but I mulled over this information while Lola snipped at my hair. I'd almost been bitten last night and, though I hadn't met many vampires who had wanted to drink my blood, I hadn't met many vampires.

"I have even heard rumors that the Queen is still alive," Lola said, without raising her voice. "That she's coming back."

"Really?" Pearl asked. "But that's not possible. She's dead. Mother always said so. Didn't she, Ivy?"

I murmured agreement.

"What about the Hearts, and the Pinnacle clock, and the vampires? It's all signs that the Queen is returning. Is our President worried about having to face the Queen of Hearts again?"

"The *late* Queen," I replied. "She's dead. And no, Alice isn't worried about her. She's worried about people panicking over a few strange coincidences."

Lola hummed, but I could hear the doubt in her voice. As her scissors clipped at my hair, I turned over the puzzles in my mind.

The clock. The Hearts. The blood banks. Raven. The white rabbit.

Wait...

If Lola hadn't been cutting my hair, I might have shot out of my chair. The vampire had told me something last night about Raven and the white rabbit. Something that linked them together. I squeezed my eyes shut, trying to block out the conversation between Pearl and Lola about the latest fashion in hats.

Something about Raven and the white rabbit, I told myself. *Think!*

"Am I hurting you, darling," Lola tilted up my chin, and I opened my eyes, shaking my head.

"I'm just thinking," I replied.

"Is this your normal thinking face?" Lola seemed concerned. "You're a clever girl, and I know you think a lot, so please take my advice—don't screw up your face like that when you're thinking."

Beside me, Pearl was shaking with contained laughter.

"You'll get wrinkles," Lola continued, with no hint of humor. "Follow my advice—you'll save a fortune fixing your skin in the long term."

I smiled, letting my eyes drift closed again. My mind grasped onto what Lola had just said: *Follow...*

I sucked in a breath and held it. The word sparked a vague memory. Just before the vampire had disappeared, he'd told me how to find Raven: *Follow the white rabbit.*

I let my breath out slowly, considering the vampire's words. I had assumed that the painted motifs were just decoration around the city, but maybe someone had painted the white rabbits for a reason—to lead somewhere.

The first one I'd seen, across from the First Forge Bank, wasn't far from here, and I suddenly wanted to run outside to see if I could find it again.

Lola put her hands on my shoulders. "Are you all right, darling? You're tense. You're fidgeting. Just relax—I'll do a beautiful job on your hair. Don't worry."

"Sorry," I replied, sighing, as I sank back into the chair again. I pressed my hands to my skirts, so they lay flat against my thighs. I took a deep breath through my nose, then exhaled out of my mouth.

"Honestly, Ivy, anyone would think we're torturing you. It's a *hairstyle*," Pearl said. I opened my eyes to glare at her. This time, I didn't have to imagine anything—I saw her roll her eyes at me.

~

I stared at the reflection of myself, my mouth hanging open. I reached forward to touch the mirror, just to make sure it was really me. My fingertips touched the young woman who stared back at me.

At me.

My now blonde hair fell to my jawline, with my bangs cut straight across to sit just above my eyes.

I looked amazing.

Lola walked over to the hatstand where I'd left my hat when I first came in. She turned it over in her hands, before fixing it at an angle on my head. Then she stepped back and put her hands on her hips as she examined me. "Perfect."

"Beautiful," Pearl agreed with a smile. She came to stand next to me and rested her hand in the crook of my elbow. "See, we finally look like sisters."

"Thank you," I turned to Lola, feeling myself blush. "I'm sorry I doubted you."

Lola shrugged. "I'll forgive you—this one time. Next time, you'll trust me."

"I promise."

As we stepped out of *Lola's Luscious Locks*, Pearl leaned closer to me. "Honestly, that cost me almost half of my beauty stipend this week. I don't know how much the Bank thinks we have to pay for service in this city, but they're not paying enough to keep people looking their best." She glared at a passer-by, whose hair was turning gray and whose buttons were strained over his stomach. "That's why there are so many more people around who look rough around the edges. Does nobody care about appearances anymore?"

At the corner, Pearl turned toward home, but I pulled her to a stop. I thought about the white rabbit painting across from the First Forge Bank. I had to follow it if I wanted to find Raven.

"We don't need to go straight home yet, do we?" I asked.

"Don't you need to rest?" Pearl said, "I told Mother..."

"Don't fuss—I'm fine," I replied. I put a hand to my new short blonde locks. "Actually... this new haircut has me feeling brave. I thought maybe..." I searched around for an excuse. "A tattoo might complete the look?"

Pearl's mouth fell open. "You're seriously suggesting that you want a tattoo?"

Inwardly, I felt uncomfortable with the idea. Outwardly, I shrugged one shoulder. Pearl squealed and grabbed my hand. "If I'd known a new haircut would make you see reason about such things, I would have slipped something in your drink and dragged you to Lola's years ago!" A delighted smile spread across her face. "I know just the place."

"Is there a place you usually go to? In the Hearts Quarter?" I said, trying to remember the tattoo parlors she'd pointed out to me in the past.

"Even better, there's a great place near to here. I promised Mother I wouldn't take you far."

I hesitated. I needed to get back to a place where I'd seen a painting of the white rabbit. "You promised

Mother you wouldn't leave my side," I replied. "I'd rather go to the best place, rather than a second-rate place just because it's closer."

Pearl looked shocked. "Do you really think I'd frequent any establishment that was second-rate? Honestly." Pearl flicked her freshly curled hair over her shoulder and pulled on my arm, forcing me to follow her. "Besides, I need a new tattoo, too. We should get ones that match."

I bit back my normal retort, hoping I'd get the chance to change my mind by the time we got to the tattoo parlor. Instead, I smiled. "Do you have anything specific in mind?"

Pearl's eyes lit up, and she outlined all the ideas she had for twin tattoos. I hummed and murmured at all the requisite intervals, but I wasn't listening. Instead, I searched the streets for any sign of the white rabbit.

～

The name of the tattoo parlor was spray-painted on the window—*Colorful Joker Tattoo Art*. Pearl gripped my arm, squealing in excitement as she tugged at me. I pulled back, still searching the street for the white rabbit.

I hadn't seen a single painting while we'd walked from Fifth Avenue to the tattoo parlor on Third Avenue. It was on the edge of the Hearts Quarter, but not far enough into the quarter to be close enough to the First Forge Bank to see the white rabbit painting.

I pulled back against Pearl. "I'm not sure about this."

"You're not having second thoughts. I forbid it," Pearl said, her hands on her hips. "You can't get my hopes up like this."

"We've talked about this. I've told you how I feel about tattoos," I reminded her.

"You might have talked, but you made little sense," Pearl retorted. "I didn't agree with you. I absolutely insist that you get a tattoo. You won't regret it."

"I might."

"I was right about the haircut."

I pursed my lips, trying to stifle the smile that was creeping over my face. "You were right," I admitted. "But I'm not getting a tattoo."

Pearl rolled her eyes. "As you wish. You still have to come with me. Like you said—I promised Mother that I would stay with you. *I'm* going, and I'm not letting you wander around on the streets by yourself."

This time, I pursed my lips out of a faint sense of annoyance. I wanted to keep looking for the white rabbit, and for Raven, but Pearl was the reason Alice allowed me to leave my room. I relented and stepped into the *Colorful Joker* after Pearl.

The tattoo artist greeted Pearl with a kiss on her fingers, as though they were old friends. They started talking animatedly about a tattoo design.

I wandered around the shop, looking at the sketches that the artist had tattooed onto other customers.

"Behind my shoulder," Pearl was saying. "I want it to peep out when I wear an off-the-shoulder gown to parties. Just a suggestion of what's hidden underneath."

The artist started sketching up some designs, as I wandered away from where they were talking, studying the artist's work.

"... thinking about twin tattoos, but she's got cold feet..." I glanced over my shoulder to see Pearl glaring at me and the tattoo artist watching me with raised eyebrows. I bent over to examine some drawings more closely, pointedly ignoring Pearl. I had to admit, some of the art was very good. I spotted an amazing clockwork design and bent closer to study it.

Despite what I told Pearl, I had nothing in particular against tattoos. I just didn't want to be rushed into a decision. If I was going to permanently mark my skin, I wanted to make sure I'd found the right design. Unlike Pearl, I wanted my tattoo to mean something—not be just another way to improve my "look." Still, the clockwork design gave me an idea. Perhaps I could draw a pocket watch design, and the tattoo artist could...

There was a scuffle at the back of the tattoo parlor, and raised voices floated out. The tattoo artist apologized to Pearl and hurried back, opening a door to a darkened back room.

"Look at this!" A male voice was raised loud enough for me to hear now that the door was open. I glanced up to see a figure standing in front of the tattoo artist on the other side of the half-open door.

"There are sometimes complications with the procedure," the tattoo artist explained in a whisper.

"Complications? It looks like I've got a skin disease. I can't go out like this."

There was a pause, and I strained to hear what was being said.

"Give it some time, the rash might settle down."

"Time? It's been like this for days. I have a party coming up. I can't wait any longer. Besides, it's so itchy, I've wanted to rip my arm off."

"It can get itchy. Have you—" the tattoo artist said. He glanced over his shoulder, suddenly noticing that the door was still ajar. I focused on the clockwork design, hoping he wouldn't think I was listening to his conversation.

106

He drew the door almost closed, and the sound of shifting feet on the floorboards drowned out the rest of his question. I shook my head, looking away from the design. Perhaps I'd been right all along—perhaps a tattoo wasn't for me. I vaguely wondered if Pearl knew about these "complications.'"

"I'm not asking for your apologies," The muffled voice raised another notch. "I want you to fix it."

"All right, wait here."

The tattoo artist jerked open the half-closed door and marched into the front of the shop. He stepped up to the front door, opened it, and whistled.

A grubby street urchin appeared from nowhere. My mouth dropped open. I'd never seen a child so dirty and dressed in rags. The tattoo artist slipped a card out of his pocket and gave it to the child.

As it passed from his hand and into the child's dirty fingers, I saw the white rabbit design. I blinked, and when I looked again, the card had disappeared beneath the child's torn shirt.

The tattoo artist came back into the shop, and, without a word to the man waiting in the back of the shop, he put a smile on his face and walked back to Pearl.

"So sorry to keep you waiting. This was the design you wanted?"

"I can't decide between this one, and..."

I shut out the details of Pearl's conversation and stepped up to the shop window, searching the street for the child.

I ground my teeth in frustration, unable to see any sign of him.

If you want to find Raven, you must follow the white rabbit.

"Sit down, Ivy," Pearl said, over her shoulder. "This will take a while."

I sighed, wondering if I'd just missed my opportunity.

$\sim$

I stared out of the window, sunk in an armchair at the front of the shop. I'd turned it around so I could see out, as I searched the passers-by for the street-urchin. The tinkle of a doorbell startled me out of my reverie.

Another customer stepped into the shop. I casually glanced over to see who stepped in.

I froze, and my fingers dug into the arms of the padded chair where I'd been sitting for the last half-hour. My heart raced, and every particle of my body tingled in response to the sight of the man who'd just entered.

Though I only saw the side profile of his face, I knew.

This was the vampire I'd been dreaming about for a week.

I wasn't sure whether I felt anticipation or fear. I put one hand to the soft skin at the base of my throat, as though checking I hadn't been bitten yet. No—still safe.

Part of me wanted to run.

Another part wanted to reach out to him.

It made little sense. I should fear him—especially after my near-attack in the Vampire Quarter—but I watched him and felt a sense of wonder about this man who had visited my dreams.

Does he know me? I wondered. *Did I visit his dreams in the way he visited mine?*

I couldn't draw my eyes away from him. I studied his profile—the straight line of his nose, the square cut of his jaw, the way his black hair fell to brush his jawline, and his skin, like starlight. From my dreams, I knew he was a handsome man, and my vantage point confirmed it.

Involuntarily, my body shuddered, and I gripped the armchair once more as I tried to work out whether my body reacted with fear or desire.

"Raven?" The tattoo artist attending to Pearl's newest tattoo called out to the vampire, now standing in the middle of the shop floor. He jerked his head towards the door in the back wall. "Out back. Don't come through the front door again."

My mouth dropped open as I stared openly at him. *Raven?*

One piece of the puzzle that had worried me for days was standing in front of me.

Here was Raven.

The vampire who had haunted my dreams.

The man who'd bought me a drink at *The Tea Party*.

The one who'd left me a note.

He knows me.

I swallowed, my breath coming in shallow gasps as the pieces of the puzzle came together.

Raven didn't even glance at me as he tipped his hat to the tattoo artist, then disappeared through the back door, closing it behind him.

My mouth was dry as I stared at the door behind which Raven had disappeared.

"Ivy?" Pearl's voice was laced with worry.

I tore my eyes from the door and looked at her. The tattoo artist was bent over the back of her shoulder, inking the exposed skin. Her mouth was pinched, and she frowned.

"You're very pale. Are you all right?" Pearl asked.

I blinked, barely understanding her as I marshaled

my courage.

Raven is here. This is my chance to meet him.

I shouldn't leave. It's too dangerous.

I must.

The armchair scraped against the floorboards as I stood suddenly. "No."

"You look like you will faint."

I started shaking my head, swaying on my feet.

"Please sit down, I won't be much longer," Pearl begged. She frowned over her shoulder at the tattoo artist as he worked on her. "How long?"

The tattoo artist sucked on his teeth as he looked down at his unfinished work. "Half an hour. Maybe more?"

"See?" Pearl said. "Then I'll take you home."

I shook my head more firmly. "No, I have to go now."

"I'm only half-way through. I can't leave yet," Pearl protested. I held up a hand to dismiss her worries.

I took a deep breath to steady myself and forced a smile to my face. "I'm fine. I'll make my own way home."

Pearl looked doubtful, but the tattoo artist had put his magnifying glasses back on as he leaned closer to the back of her shoulder and jabbed her with another needle. Pearl hissed as she drew in a pained breath.

"I promise. I just need to lie down, that's all. I'll go straight home."

I didn't look back as I took my hat from the hat stand, pulled open the door, and stepped out onto the street.

HEIRESS OF DELUSION

19TH AUGUST

The ticking of the Pinnacle clock marked the passage of the night. I rubbed my hands together, pacing back and forth on the footpath while I waited.

Past midnight now, I stubbornly pushed away any regret at having left Pearl at the *Colorful Joker Tattoo Parlor*. I couldn't leave without confronting Raven. Not after I'd followed him from the back alley behind the tattoo parlor, through the narrow streets of the Clubs Quarter, then into the Diamonds Quarter.

Raven had taken the man with the itchy tattoo into a house with darkened windows, then emerged almost immediately without his companion, and continued at a steady pace until he'd stopped at a bar.

I'd hung behind, and now, I found myself again

on the edge of the vampire quarter in the dark—only streets away from where I'd been attacked the previous night.

I cast a glance around. A man walked the street away from me, his hands in his pockets. He took no notice of me as I leaned against a wall. Otherwise, there was no one around.

Tick, tick, tick.

I ground my teeth against the incessant sound of the Pinnacle clock. During the day, the sound faded into the background, but it was always on the threshold of consciousness. At other times, like now, the sound set my teeth on edge. Sometimes, I wanted to cover my ears and scream, if only it would take away the ticking sound.

Instead, I crossed my arms over my chest and waited, wondering if I should take a chance and go into the bar for a drink.

I was weighing the risks of entering a strange, dark bar versus waiting outside in the dark when a passerby glanced sideways at me. A shiver ran up the length of my spine.

I entered the bar.

"Dirty flamingo," I ordered, as I settled myself on a stool, with a good view of the bar. Through the mirror across the back wall, I spotted Raven sitting at a booth, staring into his drink. Curiously, I wondered whether the liquid inside his mug was blood.

"What's a young lady like yourself doing here?" The barman asked, sizing me up as he slid my drink toward me. His words jerked my attention away from Raven.

"Minding my own business," I replied, sliding a few dinah across the counter and taking a sip. I relished the burn of the liquid, aware of the weight of the barman's

114

stare as he leaned against the bar and polished glasses with a rag.

I glanced toward Raven's booth, and my eyes widened.

He'd gone.

I spun around on my stool, leaping to my feet, and running to the door. Behind me, the barman chuckled.

"Spades," I muttered, looking in both directions along the street.

Raven had disappeared.

Again.

Then a hand clamped down on my shoulder.

I screamed. The sound of it echoed around the street.

Then another hand clamped over my mouth.

"Please don't do that, Inspector," a soft, deep voice purred in my ear, raising goosebumps along my skin.

He inhaled, as though breathing in my scent, then he whispered: "Will you promise not to scream if I release you?"

My breath was coming in shallow gasps again, and black shadows fluttered in my vision.

A memory of the vampire that attacked me flashed through my mind.

I should have gone home. I should never have come here.

I closed my eyes.

"Do you promise?" the soft voice asked again.

I nodded. *What else could I do?*

He removed his hands from where they were clamped over my face and shoulder. I spun around, taking a few steps backward, and saw my attacker.

Raven.

Alone in the darkened avenue, every inch of my body was aware of him as he stood before me with a smirk on his face. I fixed my eyes on him, determined not to lose him again, then wondered why I wasn't running for my life. The truth was, I couldn't move—I couldn't even tear my eyes away from his face.

Raven straightened his coat, tapped his fashionable cane on the ground, then tipped his hat and bowed. "I don't believe anyone has introduced us," he said. His expression was neither friendly nor ominous. The faint hint of a frown marred his otherwise flawless face, and he was staring at me with curiosity. As he straightened again and looked expectantly at me, I noticed the tailored line of his three-piece suit, and his crisp, white shirt. Even Chesh, fashionable as he was, would be envious of Raven's dapper turnout.

"I know who you are," I replied. "You're Raven."

Raven's mouth curled up into a half-smile, and a light danced in the dark pools of his brown eyes. He inclined his head in acknowledgment. "You are Inspector Rowntree. We are not complete strangers."

I wiped the moisture from my hands on my skirts, then twined my fingers in the fabric, trying to stop them from shaking.

"How do you know me?" I asked. My voice trembled, and I lifted my chin defiantly, although I'd also rolled onto the balls of my feet as though making ready to run. He was more alluring, and more frightening, than anyone I'd ever met.

On the surface, he was gorgeous, and the sparkle in his eyes mesmerized me. Then a glimpse of the sharp edge of his fangs brought me back to reality—he was a vampire, and I might be his prey.

116

"I could ask you the same question. Or perhaps this one—why were you following me?"

I shook my head. "I wasn't... wait, you didn't answer my question."

"That makes two of us."

"I asked you first."

Raven crooked his eyebrow as amusement danced in his eyes. "I asked you second. Manners dictate that a lady should speak first. I would not wish to interrupt you, Inspector."

"Please don't call me that. I'm off duty."

"Pardon my manners. I've not introduced myself. My name is Mr. Raven Maddox Cappello." He bowed again.

I straightened my shoulders and dipped my head as I bobbed a curtsy. "Miss. Ivy Rowntree." I frowned. "Wait—Cappello? Are you related to the man who owns *Cappello's Finest Hats*?"

Raven made an exclamation of surprise. He removed his hat and turned it over in his hands. "I *am* the man who owns *Cappello's Finest Hats*. The best hat shop in this city. My father was a milliner. He taught me the trade from birth," Raven cocked his head again, considering me. "Tell me, how do you know of my shop? It's in a place well-bred young women rarely frequent."

"I passed it the other day—during the daytime. I saw a hat in the window I thought would suit my sister very well, but your shop was closed. I swallowed, remembering the vampire attack. "I haven't been back for it."

Raven nodded without taking his eyes off me. "It would please me to show you my hats someday. I believe there is a perfect hat for everyone. It's just a matter of finding it. Or, in my case, making it." He flashed a smile at me, and my breath caught.

I smiled back, dropping my guard. He seemed more imposing than frightening—with the self-assurance of someone who wants for nothing and is certain of their value in the world. Tentatively, I reached out towards where he held his hat in his hands. "May I?"

Raven passed me the hat. A black top hat, well balanced, with a narrow brim that curled up at the edges, and splayed out at the top of the crown. The material was soft beneath my fingers, made from the finest silk. A dark blue ribbon finished it. I peered at it, considering its overall esthetic, and the workmanship to make it. "A very fine hat. Fit for a milliner."

He smiled again. I glimpsed the sharp fangs, and my smile slid away—I'd forgotten to fear him. I passed back the hat and fought the urge to run.

"Tell me, Mr. Cappello, why did you buy me a drink at *The Tea Party*?" I whispered. "Why didn't you stay?"

Raven turned and strolled down the street again, pausing to allow me to follow. Without thinking, I fell in beside him. He held his cane in one hand and put the other behind his back and cocked his head to the side as though listening to something. "That sound is irritating, isn't it?"

In the night's silence, the Pinnacle clock chimed the hour.

"Yes," I replied. "When I can't get the ticking out of my head, I understand why people would prefer it stayed broken."

"I don't think it's the sound, so much as the—"

"Memories," I finished. "Yes, I know."

"It *is* loud," Raven continued. "Especially for my kind. It sounds like that damned clock is shouting at me."

I made a face. "How can you sleep?"

Raven chuckled. "I don't sleep. Not much anyway. My kind needs sleep only about once every month."

I raised my eyebrows at that information but didn't turn toward him. Somehow he was less threatening, less maddeningly alluring, if I didn't have direct eye contact with him. Still, I was aware of him next to me. As I walked, my eyes wandered across the dark, empty avenue.

A thought occurred to me. "If your hearing is so superior, why didn't you hear me following you?"

Raven smiled, darting me a sideways glance. "I knew someone was following me. It was your scent that gave you away."

"You could smell me?" I exclaimed, then pursed my lips. "I washed only yesterday."

"You don't smell," Raven said, smirking. "You have a unique *scent*. I could pick you out of a dark room full of people, with a blindfold—just by your scent. Another strength of my kind."

I turned that piece of information over in my mind. "You knew I was in the bar, didn't you?"

Raven nodded.

"And the tattoo parlor?"

Raven nodded again.

"Why didn't you confront me there?" I asked.

Raven shrugged one shoulder. "A test of your courage, your determination."

I raised one eyebrow. "And?"

Raven frowned.

"Did I pass the test?"

He made an amused sound in his throat. "I find neither wanting," he replied, his eyes sparkling again. I looked away before I lost myself in them again.

"You still haven't told me why you bought me that

drink?" I pointed out. "Or why you left me that note."

I pulled the card out of my bag, its corners rounded and scuffed by use, and held it out to him. "You put a puzzle in front of me: *We choose our future*—what did you mean by it?"

Raven didn't read the card. He didn't take his eyes off my face. "Call it a spur-of-the-moment decision."

I blinked. "I don't understand. What does it mean?"

"It's a saying—one that I often repeat to myself: *We cannot change our past, but we choose our future.*"

Raven started walking again, and I fell in beside him. We strolled in silence. The only sound was our footsteps echoing in the darkness and the semi-regular *tap* of Raven's cane on the cobblestones. We turned a corner, then another, and I looked down at the card in my hand, still puzzling over Raven's response. I was about to press the point when Raven spoke again.

"You mentioned others fear the Pinnacle." Raven blurted. "Are *you* afraid of it?"

I gave a little laugh. "No. It's just gears and moving parts. Complex, but just a machine."

"You're too young to remember the Queen of Hearts, or to fear her," Raven observed.

"The *late* Queen," I corrected him. "Yes, she died the year I was born. I'm not afraid of her, but I know other people fear that she will return."

"Nobody ever found her body."

"Mother said... I mean, President Rowntree said the late Queen was dead. She must have had proof."

Raven tapped his cane on the cobblestones, his brow drawn together as he considered my words. "Unless she wanted to reassure the people she was trying to lead. Unless she was soothing their terror of the Queen."

"The late Queen," I corrected again.

Raven looked at me. "There are always two sides to every story," he murmured.

I saw Raven's eyes dart to the shape of my mouth, before returning to my eyes again.

"You have the most unusual eyes—did you know? Golden circles around your iris. In all my long years, I have never seen another person with eyes like that." He leaned forward as he spoke; his voice was like velvet, a sound that reeled me in like a fish caught in his net. Then he straightened, clearing his throat. "Come," he said, his tone sharper. "My place is here. I wish to show you something inside. Something important."

He offered me his arm, as he turned toward a three-story house towering over the street, the carvings around the doorway were menacing in the darkness. A light flickered inside, and someone screamed.

As the scream split the air, his enchantment broke, releasing me from his power. I jerked backward, stumbling on the cobblestones. Raven leaned forward, reaching out to me.

His lips stretched over the sharp curve of his fangs, and I remembered the man from my dreams—an enchanting killer. A bloodthirsty vampire.

"Get away from me," I screamed, clutching at the base of my neck.

Then, finding my feet, I turned and ran as fast as I could in the other direction.

20TH AUGUST

The sun was setting when I stood once more in front of *Cappello's Finest Hats*. On one side ot it, stood a shop named *Masquerading our Love* that purported to sell both masquerade costumes and love potions. On the other was a taxidermist with a window display comprised of several stuffed flamingos and a hedgehog positioned like a croquet set. Distracted, I stared from one to the other, shook my head, and then focused on the task at hand.

Hovering on the doorstep, I debated between running back home or pushing open the door. My heart thumped a rapid beat.

The man was a vampire. A vampire in a city whose blood stocks were running low.

When I had woken that morning, I'd scoured *The*

Forge Hart for articles about vampire attacks. I had found nothing, but that didn't mean there was nothing to find.

When I'd returned home in the early hours of the morning, I'd found Mother and Pearl had waited up for me. They'd been angry and worried. I'd made excuses and hurried to bed before they'd chastised me.

I'd slept until well past breakfast, but when I'd entered the drawing room for morning tea, I'd found Alice waiting for me. On a vase in the center of the table were five red roses.

"Mother? Shouldn't you be in your office?" I'd asked her. It was then that I'd noticed the dark circles under her eyes and her white knuckles where she had clasped her hands in her lap. She looked down her nose at me, pursing her lips.

"I understand you are a woman, Ivy," Alice had said. "You are a smart woman, capable of making your own decisions. However, your behavior over the last couple of days has been rash and poorly thought through."

"I'm sorry—" I'd started, but she'd held up a hand to stop me.

"I'm not finished," she had said. "It would be remiss of me not to caution you as to the consequences of this behavior. Really, Ivy, venturing into the..."—Alice paused, searching for the right word.—"more dangerous parts of the city? Alone? At night? It is not like you to take such risks. I'm worried about you."

"I'm sorry."

Alice had raised an eyebrow. "I think I deserve an explanation for why I stayed up half of the night waiting for you to come home."

"I didn't expect you to wait up."

"Is that all you have to say for yourself?" Alice had

demanded. "Where were you?"

I'd swallowed as my stomach twisted with remorse. "I took a walk. I met Chesh, and we visited a bar," I had lied. "It's what we often do of an evening."

"You shouldn't even have left your bed yesterday. Let alone frequenting bars. You weren't well."

"I told you I was fine."

"You were unconscious when you came home the night before," Alice had said, raising her voice. "I don't call that fine."

I'd smothered a sigh. "I'm sorry for worrying you. As you said, I'm grown. I may go where I please."

Alice had given me a hard stare. "You may be a woman, but you are still my daughter." She stood so abruptly that she startled me, and my teacup had wobbled on its saucer, spilling its hot liquid. "Please keep in mind what I have said."

Now, I thought about our conversation again—and the row I'd had with Pearl when she'd confronted me about lying to her—as I stood in front of Raven's hat shop. I looked at the hat I'd thought would suit Pearl and decided to buy it. Pearl was more likely to forgive my behavior if I brought her a gift. Besides, it would look beautiful on her.

Swallowing down the lump in my throat, I pushed open the door to step into *Cappello's Finest Hats*. The bell tinkled as I entered.

My mouth fell open as I gaped at my surroundings. The inside of the shop was a cavernous room, empty but for a mirror on one end with an armchair next to it. The ceilings were high, which gave the room a sense of space, but along the walls were rows and rows of shelves that stretched all the way to the high ceiling.

Hats lined every surface—in all colors, all shapes,

and all sizes. For women, for men, for children, for workers, for daytime, for evening, for tea, for the races, and for balls. There were toppers, beefeaters, yeoman, derby's boater hats, helmets, caps, bowler hats, navy hats, marines, half-moons, cross hats, bonnets, berets, cloche hats, fedoras, cocktail hats, fascinators, tiaras, and so many others. Hundreds of hats, at least.

"May I help you?" A young woman came over, smiling.

I looked for Raven, unable to loosen the knot of apprehension in my stomach.

"I'd like a hat," I started, when I didn't see Raven. I stared up at the shelves that climbed the walls. Around the edge, was a ladder on rollers to allow the shop assistants to reach the hats on the highest shelves.

"You're in the right place," the shop assistant said with a smile. "We have the finest hats in The Forge." I noted she didn't have any fangs. She didn't appear to be afraid, although, as she turned her head to consider the shelves, I saw there was an unsightly scar running down the left side of her face. Surprised to see someone so unbeautiful working in a customer-contact role, I stared for a moment, then looked away.

I wondered when the inspector assigned to this part of the city had been here last. I couldn't imagine the young woman's appearance would have passed that inspection.

"Are you looking for anything in particular?" the woman asked.

I cleared my throat, but before I could answer, another voice spoke at the rear of the shop.

"Thank you, Miss. Lapin, I'll attend to Miss. Rowntree."

~

Raven delicately placed a hat on my head, then stepped back to appraise it. He was focused—not on me, but on the hat. He tapped a finger on his chin, concentrating, as though the hat presented him with a puzzle.

Without a word, he whipped the hat off my head and replaced it with another. Again, he stepped backward and looked me over.

With a small shake of his head, he swapped it with yet another hat.

"They're all beautiful," I murmured, eyeing the hats piling up on the armchair.

"Miss. Lapin," Raven called out. "Take these away, please. They're not suitable."

"Yes, sir." Miss. Lapin appeared out of nowhere and gathered up the discarded hats. She slid the ladder along the walls, climbing up and down to put away the hats that Raven no longer needed.

"I like that one," I said, as Raven put another hat on my head.

Raven considered me, then shook his head again. "You present an enigma, Miss. Rowntree," he said, his mouth set in a straight line.

"How so?" I asked, a flutter of nervousness going through my stomach.

"Do you remember me telling you, last time we met, that I believe there is the perfect hat out there for everyone? It is my mission to make sure that every customer who leaves my shop does so in possession of their perfect hat."

"These are all lovely hats," I said.

"Lovely, yes," Raven replied, turning to face the shelves and looking up at the highest shelves. "Perfect, no. That is the problem."

I swallowed and looked at my feet. I wasn't as

beautiful as my sister; I knew that. Now, the knowledge that Raven didn't believe I suited any of his beautiful hats hurt me.

I shook my head. The man was a vampire. An alluring but dangerous man. More than that, young women like myself didn't have friendships with vampires—let alone any more intimate relationship.

Still, I couldn't deny the flare of joy in my stomach when he came near, nor my easy smiles when we talked. I knew I should fear him—I *did* fear him—but not enough to keep my distance.

Raven put a finger under my chin, lifting my face to stare at him again. This time, he wasn't holding a hat. "Don't worry, Miss. Rowntree, I have many more hats in my workshop."

I gave him a small smile. "I didn't intend to be such a problem. I only came for a hat for my sister."

"It's no problem at all," Raven tilted his head to the side, considering me. When he next spoke, he lowered his voice so that only I could hear him. "I don't mean you're not deserving of those hats if that is what you're thinking. Rather, those hats are not worthy of you. You are a beautiful woman. Very striking."

Heat rushed to my cheeks. I couldn't tear my gaze from his face. His warm eyes sparkled, and he held my gaze. Then he dropped his hand from my chin and turned towards the back of the store.

"Miss. Lapin?" he called out.

The shop assistant appeared from the back.

"Watch the shop. I'll be upstairs."

Miss. Lapin nodded. I felt a stab of disappointment that he would be leaving. I'd enjoyed his attention.

He's a shop owner, trying to do business, that's all, I told myself. I gathered my bag and the hat I'd selected for Pearl.

Raven turned to me and gestured towards a staircase in the back corner. "Please accompany me upstairs."

I blinked, glancing over at where Miss. Lapin was dusting the shelves.

"Upstairs?" I asked, my voice quavering.

The side of Raven's mouth curled up in a half-smile. "My workshop is above the shop. I might have a hat in my workshop that would suit you better."

"Of course," I said, blushing again.

Raven smiled, though I noticed he took care to avoid showing his teeth, and he put his hand on my elbow as we started up the steps.

～

"Will you take tea with me, Miss. Rowntree?" Raven asked as he held open the door. I stepped into his workshop and looked around.

If there had been a lot of hats downstairs, there were at least as many in Raven's workshop. The hats were in varying stages of completion—some looked almost finished, others were only half-made and missing decoration, or brims, or crowns.

In addition, there was a huge desk pushed against one wall, overflowing with papers, some pinned to a board, and others that had drifted down to pool on the floor.

An identical armchair stood in one corner, though this one held several folds of cloth over it. Everywhere I looked, there were bolts of material, ribbons, buttons, lace, felt, and pins.

On one side, the curtains were open to the night sky. In the corner stood a small bed. Several suit jackets hung on a rail next to it.

"Do you live here?" I asked, remembering the other building Raven had called "his place"" and the scream that had frightened me away.

Raven looked over at the bed in the corner. "Yes. It suits me to stay here above the shop. I keep a separate residence." Raven looked down at his hands, an uncomfortable expression coming over his face. I wondered if he was remembering the screaming too. "But I spend little time there at present. Now, I use that for... well, I have put it to better use. How do you take your tea?"

"White, no sugar," I replied. I was about to ask about the screaming when Raven turned his back and moved over to the corner by his bed. I saw that he had a teapot set above a stove there too. As he made the tea, I wandered around the workshop, looking at the various half-made hats. As I moved closer, I recognized designs drawn on the papers scattered everywhere. Hat designs. I leaned over the desk for a closer inspection. Dozens of detailed drawings of hats were scattered over the table and pinned to the wall. Beautiful designs— some of them, outlandish and with a tendency to defy gravity—and all of them unique. I'd never seen hats like Raven could make.

Raven cleared his throat. When I turned, I saw that he'd cleared away the fabric draped over the armchair and set a tray of tea on a small side table.

"Please," he motioned for me to sit, before drawing a chair up to sit down across from me.

I sipped at my tea, breathing in the scent.

"Thank you," I said. "I didn't mean to trouble you about the hats. I only intended to buy something for my sister."

"It's no trouble, at all," Raven replied. "Finding the right hat for my customers is my job. It's the reason I established a hat shop." Raven smiled, catching my eye. "Finding the right hat for *you* is my pleasure."

I blushed again, dropping my eyes from his gaze. I took another sip of my tea.

"How is your work coming along?" Raven asked.

"It keeps me busy," I replied. "With all this business about the clock, we've had people not show up for work. I've been taking extra shifts to cover for those who won't leave their homes."

Raven watched me. "Why did you become an inspector?" he asked. "It's an unusual occupation for a woman like you."

"Mother suggested it. She said that if I decided to earn my own money, I should serve the city and work for her."

"Is your sister an inspector, too?"

"No," I said, then chuckled at the thought. "My sister can live on her esthetic stipend. She doesn't need to work."

Raven frowned. "You don't? I imagine your stipend would be more than enough for you to live on. Yet, you work as well?"

"I don't collect the stipend," I replied, swallowing as my throat threatened to close over. "I work instead."

"Why do you refuse the stipend?" Raven asked.

I set down the now empty teacup on the side table and clasped my hands in my lap. "I was uncomfortable about being evaluated for the stipend. It's not always easy to have such a beautiful twin. We're not identical, and we're always compared. So, I turned my passion into some income—I make pocket watches," I shrugged. "But I don't earn enough selling watches, so I took a job."

"You are an artisan yourself?" Raven raised his eyebrows in surprise. He pointed to the watch tucked into the pocket of my vest. "Is that your work?"

I pulled the watch out of my pocket and flicked open the lid, then held it out to Raven, who leaned over to examine it.

"Very fine workmanship," he replied. He sat back in his chair, examining me. I squirmed in my seat under the weight of his gaze. "You're a surprising woman. Not at all what I expected."

I tipped my head to the side, frowning. "How so?"

"You are a fine artisan—you shall become a master watchmaker should you follow your talent—and you care for your sister very much. You are intelligent, courageous, and determined—traits rare in your social class." Raven paused, frowning. "You don't enjoy being assessed for your looks for the esthetic stipend, yet you work as an esthetic inspector. In doing so, you hold others to an esthetic standard that you dislike being held to yourself. You seem to be a kind woman, yet you put people out of business, making them destitute. No," Raven said. "I'm not sure what to make of you, Miss. Rowntree."

I stared, wide-eyed, as I absorbed his words. I felt the sharp cut of his criticism, and his observations lay heavy and uncomfortable with me.

"The esthetic laws say that a public place must be esthetically pleasing. Everybody knows the law. I don't put people out of business without fair warning," I protested, feeling the need to defend myself. "Nor do I enjoy it—I don't make the laws, but I have to uphold them."

"Perhaps everyone knows the law, but not everyone

can be beautiful," Raven replied. "Nor can they all remain young and shapely, nor unmarked by accident or disease. The esthetic laws punish those who do not conform to a long-held ideal of beauty."

"Even the unbeautiful can make themselves more pleasing to others. As you know, the right hat, or a well-fitted suit, an appealing hairstyle, or well-applied makeup can improve one's appearance."

"All of which cost dinah," Raven replied. He stood and walked over to the window, looking into the night. "Yet those maimed, scarred, crippled, or elderly, have no way of earning an income. They do not qualify for the esthetic stipend. They cannot find work. These people can't afford food or a roof over their heads, let alone tailored suits or regular hair styling."

I noticed his well-cut coat and trousers, his polished shoes. Raven might not approve of the stipend, but he wasn't averse to making himself presentable.

"Is that why you employ Miss. Lapin in your shop?" I asked.

"Miss. Lapin works here because she is good with customers. She had an accident as a child that marked her face. She can't hide it, so she must live with it. I don't see why she must remain out of sight because of an old scar."

"There can't be many like her, though," I said. Raven turned to me, his eyes wide with surprise. "My work takes me all over the city, to shops and workplaces," I explained. "I've seen very few people whose physical appearance matches your description."

Raven looked like he was about to say something. Then he stopped and turned away. He cast an eye around his workshop. "I don't have the right hat for you here," he said. "I will need to apply myself to the problem of your hat." He waved a hand towards the desk, which was overflowing with designs. Raven straightened his coat, avoiding my gaze. He tapped a finger on his leg. Then, as though he'd decided, he gave me a serious look. "Last time we met, you asked me about the note on the card. Do you still want to know why I left it for you?"

I frowned, surprised at the sudden change in the conversation. I gave him a jerky nod, though his fierce demeanor made me reluctant.

"In that case, there's something I'd like to show you. Before we leave, though, you must promise me you will not breathe a word of this to anyone. Not even your mother, nor your sister. Can you promise me, Miss Rowntree?"

I slipped my hand into my clutch and felt the tip of the card with Raven's handwritten message. Raven offered a solution to the puzzle—how could I refuse?

The alley smelled like piss and vomit. I wrinkled my nose, wondering when the street cleaner was due. Ahead of me, Raven stepped into a spotlight cast by a mushroom-shaped street-lamp. The warm glow of firelight illuminated a circle of gold, like a crown, on his black hair. He turned, looking over his shoulder to meet my eyes. There was a smirk on his face as though he was amused by the fact that he'd caught me admiring him. My face flushed hot, and I looked down at my feet.

When I looked up, Raven had stepped out of the light and was crouching in the shadows. He turned his head to peer up and down the alleyway, then he pulled up a metal disk to reveal a hole in the street.

I moved closer to see what he was doing.

"I'd like you to see something," Raven said as he looked up at me.

I hesitated, then leaned forward to peer into the hole. I couldn't see anything—it was dark, as though it fell into a bottomless pit.

"Is this what you wanted to show me?"

"No." Raven's mouth curled up into a smirk. "This is the way."

I looked at the hole in the ground. "To where?"

Raven wagged a finger at me. "I have to show you."

"You can't expect me to go down there!" I said. "It's just a... hole."

"This is one of many entrances to a network of underground tunnels that run beneath the city."

"Underground tunnels?" I exclaimed. I peered down and saw a ladder disappearing into the dark. "Why did I not know about these before?"

"Vampires have not always been... welcome in Melfall. Our presence here has become tolerated, but it was not always so. We kept our tunnels a secret, in case the prevailing attitude towards my people turns to prejudice once more. The tunnels always provided a way for vampires to move around the city unnoticed, or during the day."

I glanced upwards to see a sliver of the night sky between the roofs of the buildings that towered over the street. There was not even a hint of light on the horizon.

"It's far from dawn," I replied.

Raven quirked one eyebrow. "There's something down there you should see." He held out a gloved hand. "I won't let anything happen to you."

My heart raced at the thought of going down into a dark tunnel with a vampire. I remembered the vampire who had attacked me nearby, but I didn't get the same feeling when I was near Raven. My stomach flipped and my heart thundered, but the terror was absent. Rather, I wanted to be close to him and to know what he had to say. Our conversation at his workshop had rolled around in my mind as we'd walked together, weaving through the backstreets.

I told myself that Raven could have attacked me during our walk together, yet he hadn't. That thought didn't reassure me, but it gave me some comfort.

However, the thought of climbing down a ladder into an unknown darkness, where any manner of vampires could be lurking, gave me pause.

"Will there be other vampires?" I asked.

"You'll be safe with me," he replied. "Though it's not gentlemanly, I'll go first—if it would give you some comfort?"

I watched Raven step down onto the first rung of the ladder, then the next, and the next until he disappeared into the hole.

I crouched down and peered into the darkness. I saw the faint outline of his white shirt.

"Miss Rowntree?" Raven's voice rang out as an echo. "You may follow."

I hesitated a moment longer before my curiosity got the better of me. I knew so much about Melfall, yet there was a whole network of tunnels underneath this city I'd never known about until now. I wondered if Alice knew about them. Chesh did not, or he would have told me about them—if not taken me for a tour.

I inched closer to the hole, then bunched my skirts together and set my foot on the first rung. Carefully, I stepped down to the next rung. As I continued down until my face was level with the street.

"Miss. Rowntree?" Raven called up to me. "Pull the cover of the manhole over the top of you, so no one can follow us."

"Who would follow?" I called back, looking up at the dim light of the night above. The only light that filtered down into the darkness.

"The cover must be closed. It's the code of the tunnels," Raven replied.

I was breathing quickly as I reached up and pulled the cover over my head, plunging myself into darkness. The manhole cover fell into place with a thud that echoed all around. I clung to the ladder as I blinked, over and over, trying to force my eyes to adjust to the dark. My breaths became shallow, and my hands were slick as they gripped onto the metal rung.

"Miss. Rowntree?" Footsteps rang out on the rungs below, coming closer. Suddenly Raven's body was next to mine, where I was clinging to the ladder. His body pressed against my back; he put his arms around mine and covered my hands with both of his. Raven's chin hovered just above my shoulder, and he whispered in my ear.

"I apologize in advance for this inappropriate invasion of your space, but if you will allow me, I will guide you down. You need not be afraid."

"I'm not afraid," I said, but my voice wavered as I spoke.

Raven chuckled silently, and I felt the suppressed laughter shudder through his body as it pressed against mine. A bubble of laughter rose to my throat too, and a giggle escaped my lips, the sound amplified by the echo chamber around us.

Suddenly, we were both laughing aloud, pressed together, clinging to the ladder as our only anchor in the darkness. At the moment, I felt as though there was no one else in the world except for myself and Raven. That thought did not frighten me.

Raven leaned closer to my ear again, and his words tickled my ear. "My eyesight is better than yours. I will guide you down. You'll feel better when your feet touch solid ground."

Raven guided my hands down each rung of the ladder. His body pressed against mine as we descended deeper into the ground. Unable to see anything except Raven's pale hands where they gripped my own, I gave myself over to his guidance.

"Take a deep breath," Raven whispered. "Then, exhale through your nose."

I did as he said, then the impact of his words hit me, and I stopped climbing as I whispered back. "I didn't know vampires can read minds. Do you know everything I'm thinking?"

A shudder of suppressed laughter vibrated from Raven again. "I can't read your mind," he said. "I can smell your fear."

When my foot hit something solid, a wave of relief washed over me. When both of my feet were on the floor of the tunnel, Raven gave my hands a quick squeeze before stepping away to put space between us. I was aware of his physical absence, and part of me wished he would embrace me again.

Raven kept hold of one hand and tugged me forward. I took each cautious step, unable to see the path ahead of me.

"Not much further," Raven said. "Can you hear them already?"

I strained my ears. Nothing. Then I tilted my head to the side.

"Yes," I said. "What is that?"

Muffled sounds grew louder as we moved further through the darkness. Then Raven came to a stop. A door swung open with a shriek of metal grinding on metal.

I blinked, blinded by the bright light within.

A fire blazed from a hearth at the far side of what looked like the living room of an ordinary house. I squinted into the dim light.

Gathered in small groups were far more people than the space should accommodate. Some were sleeping; others huddled together under tattered blankets. Still others shared drinks or food, many sharing plates, cups, and utensils. A few small children ran around the corner of the room, playing a game known only to themselves.

They were dirty, malnourished, and dressed in rags. They noticed us, and it was only a moment before everyone in the room was staring at us. Their eyes bulged from faces with skin pulled tight over their bones.

I gasped.

A man, his shoulders wrapped in a worn blanket, stepped forward. "Mr. Cappello?" he asked. He smiled, his mouth was half-full of rotten, blackened teeth, the others missing. He limped with a lopsided gait, and I noticed one of his legs was bent at an odd angle.

I swallowed, forcing myself to stand my ground as he came toward us. Raven tightened his grasp on my hand.

"Mr. Burke," Raven gave him a bow. "Please allow me to introduce an acquaintance of mine, Miss. Rowntree."

Mr. Burke nodded his head at me, curiosity deepening the lines that creased his forehead. "A pleasure, Miss. Rowntree."

"Mr. Burke," I replied, but my voice cracked and wavered. I searched around for something else to say, but Raven saved me.

"How do you all fare, Mr. Burke?" Raven asked.

Mr. Burke bobbed his head, pulling his blanket tighter around his shoulders. "Well enough." He jerked his head towards the corner. "Got another family in yesterday. Inspector shut the shop. They ran out of money, couldn't pay the rent. Ended up on the streets."

I looked over in the direction where Mr. Burke was pointing to see Mr. Thackery, from *Thackery's Fine Antiques*, which I'd closed for code violations last week. I remembered how he'd kneeled on the floor of his shop and pleaded with me to spare his livelihood, so he could feed his family.

A sudden weight pressed down on me. I shrank back as though trying to hide from sight, but Mr. Thackery saw me, and recognition flickered over his face. He wrinkled his nose, as though he'd smelled something unpleasant, then turned his back, putting an arm around a thin woman, nursing a young child.

"Do you have spare food and blankets?" Raven asked.

Mr. Burke nodded again. "We'll manage," he said. "There's always something to share."

I looked around at the malnourished people, and I understood the lie in his words. These people had nothing, yet they shared what little they had to make sure that the others wouldn't starve.

I noticed a young girl marked down one side of her face with scars, evidence that she'd once suffered the pox—a disease that sometimes ran through the more crowded sections of the city. Sitting next to her, a young boy had a stump in place of a hand. I wondered whether it was punishment for theft.

Everywhere I looked, I saw scars, missing limbs, signs of sickness, or of old age. They were all ragged, dirty, and their shoulders and backs slumped, as though they bore great weights on their shoulders. I couldn't help but stare. I had never seen so many unbeautiful people. How were they all living beneath Melfall?

Raven touched my elbow. I blinked, noticing that Mr. Burke had wandered away. "Are you ready to leave?"

I nodded; my throat so tight that I could not form words to answer him.

Raven pushed open the manhole, and, once he'd climbed out to street level, he bent down to take my hand and pull me out. I took a deep breath of the clear air, pleased to be free of the dark tunnels, and the strange feeling of being enclosed in a small space, as though there wasn't enough air to breathe.

I brushed the dirt from my skirts and petticoats, shaking them out as I avoided Raven's eye.

"Miss. Rowntree?" There was an uncertain quality to Raven's tone. "Are you all right?"

Clasping my hands in front of me, I said, "The new family down there,"— I struggled to keep my voice steady—"I recognized them. Last week, I closed their shop."

I pressed my lips together as my throat closed, and tears prickled at my eyes. "It is my fault," I whispered, then covered my mouth to stop the sobs from escaping.

Raven stepped forward, taking my hands in his. I couldn't meet his eye until he put a finger underneath my chin and turned my face up to his. "I didn't know that. I didn't take you down there to upset you. Only to show you that these people exist, hidden away beneath a city that accepts only the beautiful and perfect. You may not see them on your streets, but they exist."

I nodded, unable to speak as the weight of regret filled me from the inside. I took a gasping breath.

"I'll walk you home," Raven said as he tucked my hand into the crook of his elbow.

I pulled away and turned to face him. "Why did you take me down there if not to show me what I'd done?"

"We cannot change the past," Raven said. "But, we choose our future."

Tears prickled my eyes. "Can we? Can they?"

"They choose to make the best of what they have," Raven replied, then he took a deep breath. "I choose to help them. You can choose to help them, too."

I stood still. "How?"

"You asked me why I left you that card. Those people are the reason."

"I don't understand."

Raven hesitated, studying my face. "I need someone close to the President."

"You said I wasn't to tell anyone. Not even Mother."

Raven tapped a finger on his leg. "I need to know about the President's movements."

My throat went dry. "You want me to betray my mother?"

"I want you to help those people who are powerless because of your mother's laws," Raven replied, his voice quiet.

I opened my mouth to argue with him, but no words

142

came out. After a long silence, Raven reached out to take my hand, tucking it into the crook of his elbow, then guided me through the streets.

We walked most of the way in silence. He placed his hand over mine as I rested my hand on his elbow. The light touch of his fingers gave me some measure of comfort, but they also reminded me of my failures. Part of me wanted to cling to him, another part wanted to turn my face away in shame, and yet another wanted to rage at him for putting me in this terrible position.

As the ring of our footsteps echoed on the cobblestones in the night, I thought of the gaunt faces of the unbeautiful people, living underground with no place in their own city, cast out because of things they could not change. I wondered how many people I had rendered homeless because of my callous application of the law.

My eyes trailed the ground as I walked, unaware of my surroundings, absorbed by my own thoughts, so I didn't even notice where we were. I'd forgotten my fear of Raven the vampire and put my faith in Raven, the man. But was he a friend? Or was he using me to get to Alice?

When Raven coughed, I blinked and looked around, surprised to be standing in front of the Pinnacle. Raven was staring up at it, his mouth set into a line.

"You have some skill at clockwork," Raven said. "What do you make of the clock?"

I blinked at him, surprised by his question. I'd been so distracted I hadn't considered that Raven's might have taken a different path.

"It... is a beautiful example of craftsmanship, from what I can see," I replied. "Though I haven't been able to get a closer look. It's also a puzzle—the way it stopped working, then started again. I don't know how that has happened. Though I think the Tweedles might have something to do with it."

Raven frowned. "Why?"

"They usually have a part in any mischief regarding the late Queen."

Raven tightened his grip on my hand. "I have little acquaintance with the Tweedle brothers, I'll admit, but I don't see how they could have any connection with the strange happenings around this clock."

"Why do you say that?"

Raven looked up at the clock again. "Do you know much about the history of the Pinnacle?"

I nodded. "I've been researching it, and I have found that the late Queen liked to use the Pinnacle clock as a platform for her addresses to her people."

A smile flitted across Raven's face before he became serious again. "Yes, she did," he said. "She commissioned that clock. It was a symbol of her power."

I frowned. "She can't have. That clock is old—it must have been around for a hundred years."

Raven nodded.

I blinked. "You mean, the late Queen's mother built it?"

Raven shook his head. "The Queen of Hearts commissioned the building of this clock, to celebrate the start of her reign over The Forge."

"That isn't possible," I murmured, noticing a tightness in my chest as I looked at him.

"She was also called the Red Queen."

"Red is the color of hearts," I said.

"Red is the color of blood." Raven raised his eyebrows just a little.

Vampires drink blood, I thought.

Raven said nothing, though I wondered again whether he could read minds since he seemed to know what I'd been thinking.

After a pause, Raven spoke again. "One reason vampires were so despised after the Queen's reign is that my kind had always allied with her. We sided with her because she allowed us to hunt—it added to the sense of fear among her subjects, a fear that she exploited for her gain. We also supported her because she was one of us."

I thought about all the photos I'd ever seen of the late Queen. She'd always looked beautiful. And the same, I realized. Beautiful.

Ageless.

"Our President has done a lot for my kind, by setting up the blood banks, by trying to break down the barriers between my kind and yours. My kind hear the clock, and we fear it too."

"Why does your kind fear the Pinnacle clock? You exist outside of time!"

Raven laughed—a surprised bark that seemed louder in the city's silence. "I've never heard it described that way. You're right, we don't age, but we experience the passage of time, all the same."

"You haven't answered my question," I pointed out.

I saw the lump in Raven's throat bob as he swallowed. "That clock was linked to the Queen's power. It stopped when her reign ended. Now it has begun again... Not just that, my kind hears all the city's cogs starting to move once more. All the signs point in the same direction."

"Signs of what?"

"That The Queen of Hearts is returning."

I was shaking my head. "The late Queen is dead."

"She is a vampire. A vampire can die, but not easily.

Trust me, the Queen was defeated, but she is not dead."

My mouth fell open as I gawked at Raven. Then I turned my face towards the Pinnacle again, and the relentless *ticking* filled my mind as I watched it.

"Let me take you home," Raven said, covering my hand on his elbow. "It has been a long night for you, I think."

We'd barely stepped off the square and onto Sixth Avenue, and were approaching the President's Palace when I saw a small painting of the white rabbit on a corner. It was sitting, watching me, as though waiting for me to notice it.

"What about the white rabbit?" I asked.

Raven raised one eyebrow. "You are more astute than I thought," he said.

He took my hand from his elbow and held it to his lips to kiss me farewell.

"This is where I leave you tonight," he said, looking at the guards who were opening the small door in the side gate to let me through. He pressed his lips together, as though debating whether to say anything more.

"Aren't you going to answer my astute question?" I said, gripping his fingers so he could not drop my hand.

"Not tonight," Raven replied.

"I heard the white rabbit is gathering the late Queen's supporters. You say she is back. Is he?"

"I can't tell you about the white rabbit," Raven said.

"Yet you use his symbol on your card? Why should I believe you?"

"I can't say any more," Raven insisted. He held up a hand to put a stop to my protests. "If you come to see me again, I might reconsider."

My eyes narrowed. "Why can't you tell me now?"

Raven tapped his fingers on his leg again, staring off

146

into the distance, thinking. I held my breath, wondering if he was about to relent. He met my eye, but the friendly twinkle was absent. "I'll tell you more about the white rabbit, if you bring me information on our President's movements."

I glared at Raven. He stepped back, tipped his hat to me, then disappeared into the night.

21ST AUGUST

Alice glared at the face of the pocket watch that I'd made for her, while she listened to a petitioner in the great hall of the President's Palace.

"It should never have received a permit," the petitioner grumbled. "His shop is only three doors from mine. It's undercutting my business."

"Rubbish. Our patronage overlaps. You can't handle a little competition," a woman stepped up to stand next to him, glaring at the petitioner, before she turned to Alice.

"My President," she started. "He's trying to shut me down because I make better cakes. I can't help it if customers want to eat my cakes and not his."

Alice rubbed at her forehead as she snapped the lid

of the pocket watch shut. "There are rules around this kind of thing," she said, turning to Jack. "Aren't there?"

Jack hesitated, looking nervous. Alice's expression was thunderous.

"I'll consider your complaint and provide my ruling in due course," Alice said, her tone sharper than usual. She turned to Jack again. "Make a note of that. Find out what the laws say. Next!"

A small man stepped up, wringing his hands.

"You may speak," Alice said.

"My President, I know you are very busy. I wouldn't come to you if I didn't think—"

"Yes, yes," Alice said. "Get on with it."

"Yesterday, I saw a Heart marching in Diamonds Quarter. I was just going about my business—everyone was—when the Heart attacked someone. In broad daylight. I knew him—a young apprentice in the Guild. He fought it off, but..." the small man's mouth turned down at the corners. He clasped his hands in front of his chest, as though in prayer. "Something must be done. They'll kill someone if they're not stopped. My President, where are they coming from?"

Alice shifted in her seat, surprised by the direct question. She tucked her hair behind her ears—the gesture of a small girl—and a mannerism I knew showed her stress. "I'm aware of the Hearts," she raised her voice to address everyone in the hall. "I am taking every measure to get them under control."

"Why are they here? Where did they come from? Is the Queen coming back?" The questions spilled out of the petitioner's mouth, and a ripple of murmurs spread around the hall.

Alice smoothed her hair behind her ears again. She raised her voice over the chatter. "Do not panic. I'm taking every measure to ensure the safety of everyone in this city."

The chatter only increased in volume. Alice turned to Jack; her lips pressed into a thin line.

I stood near the entrance to the great hall, hoping to get a few minutes of Alice's time. I'd promised not to tell her about the people living in the tunnels—and I didn't want to get them into any further trouble—but it troubled me that Raven wanted to know about Alice's movements. For what purpose? I was still sure he had links to the white rabbit who was gathering supporters. If that was true, then his interest in Alice was a threat. What else could it be?

As Alice spoke to Jack, she noticed me across the room and beckoned me with a wave of her hand.

"Dismiss everyone," Alice ordered Jack, who was nodding his head. "Fetch the Head of Security. I want a strategy to deal with these Hearts. They cannot roam the city. Tell him—" Alice looked up as I approached. "Ivy. I hope you're feeling better?"

"Much better," I assured her. "Mother, I was wondering whether I might talk to you about something."

Alice closed her eyes, exhaling. "I am very busy with the menace of these Hearts." Alice's voice contained a note of caution. "I will give any proposal you have due attention. Another time."

"But Mother, I think—"

"I don't have time right now." Alice snapped, glaring at me.

Jack shuffled his feet, then moved away to give us some privacy. Alice rubbed her forehead.

"I'm sorry," she said. "I'm sure whatever you wish to bring to my attention is very important. I *will* consider it. At. Another. Time."

I bit back my protest, then nodded my acquiescence. I was about to leave when Alice reached out to take my hand.

"Be careful. The Hearts used to be dangerous. Until we bring them under control, I'd prefer it if you didn't wander the city at night."

My eyes widened, remembering Raven's promise to reveal the secret of the white rabbit—if I visited him again. Although I had no intention of giving him any information about Alice.

"But—"

"You're a grown woman, but you are still my daughter," Alice said, giving me a stern glare. "Please, be careful."

I signed again before nodding.

Alice turned back to Jack, leaving me feeling both shackled and empty-handed.

～

The midday sunlight beat down on the street, and my clothes clung damply against my body even after walking only the short distance to Chesh's shop.

His face lit up when he saw me, and he skirted around the counter to fold me into an embrace so tight that he lifted me off the ground and spun me in a circle.

"So good to see you!" he said as he put me down, still grinning from ear-to-ear. "When I sought help the other night..., I began.

Chesh looked like he'd swallowed something sour. He grasped my hands, shaking them as his eyes filled with tears. He took a deep, shuddering breath. "Pearl told me you were fine. I can see for myself that you are as beautiful as ever." He leaned forward as though sharing a secret. "I came back for you, but you'd disappeared."

I pulled my hands out of his, uncomfortable as the conversation brought back the memories of the attack. Raven and the people in the tunnels had consumed my thoughts for most of the day.

"I'm fine," I said, even as I touched my throat, where the vampire had almost bitten me.

Chesh's face split into a relieved grin. "Excellent." He tugged my hands. "In that case, come and see what I've been doing since the last time I saw you."

I let him lead me into the workshop at the back. "Though your absence left a hole in my life, I haven't been idle." He winked at me. "In fact, I've made modifications to the steam bikes that will lengthen their range."

"Are you taking me for another ride?"

"No," Chesh replied, but his eyes brightened when he came to stand next to the hover vehicle he'd shown me the last time I'd visited his workshop. "I had a breakthrough!"

He put his goggles on, then stood on the metal plate of the hover, gripping the handles with both hands. "I think I've got it working."

The hover whizzed and hummed as it lifted. His grin grew wider as the vehicle hovered about a foot off the ground.

I held my breath and watched, waiting for something to go wrong.

"Don't give me that look, Ivy. This time, I've done it," he said. "It's all about the weight distribution. Last time, it was hovering before I stepped on. This time—"

The machine vibrated so that Chesh gripped so hard to the handles that his knuckles turned white. Before he could step off, it belched black smoke, then shot another foot up into the air, before crashing back onto the floor, with Chesh tumbling down beside it.

I winced, then held a hand out to my friend. "Are you all right?"

He sighed, then crouched to peer at what now looked like a harmless piece of bent-up metal.

"It was an improvement, right?" he asked, his expression hopeful.

I shrugged one shoulder. "You were in the air for longer this time."

"That's right." Chesh grinned, then ran a finger over the machine as his expression sobered. "I can't work out why it's doing this. After the last time, I pulled it apart, replaced the broken cylinder head—the cause of the explosion. I can't tell why the cylinder head came off..." He ran a hand through his hair, making it stand on end.

I nodded, but as Chesh talked about the machine, I remembered the events of the previous night again.

Every time I thought about the Thackery family, now living in the tunnels underneath the city, I flushed with shame. Raven hadn't blamed me for putting the Thackery's into poverty, but I felt responsible for their current circumstances. How many other people had I condemned to such a life? The guilt gnawed at me. Raven said I could help people by helping him, but how could I betray Alice? What would Raven and the white rabbit do to her if I passed along the information they wanted? Alice spent her life working for the good of our citizens. It wasn't fair to put her in danger for something that wasn't her fault.

I sighed, leaning against the workbench.

"Did you hear me?" Chesh frowned in concentration.

I blinked, trying to remember what we'd been talking about.

154

Chesh stood, putting one hand on the hover as he turned to face me. "Come on, I know you know what's wrong with it. Just tell me."

"You'll regret it," I warned. "You said you wanted to fix it yourself. Give yourself some time to work it out."

"If you don't want to do this, then don't let me keep you," Chesh said. He folded his arms across his chest, and I could tell my inattention annoyed him.

"I was just thinking," I murmured.

Chesh raised an eyebrow. "That much was obvious. I assume you're not consumed by ways of getting this heap of junk to work?" He threw a rag at the hover. "What have you been working on then?"

"Why do you ask that?"

"Whenever you have that expression on your face, you're trying to figure out a puzzle—usually related to a machine, or a clock. Which is it?"

"Neither—though it is a puzzle."

"Are you going to tell me, or do I have to guess?"

"Do you remember the reason we returned to the Spades Quarter?"

Chesh frowned, shaking his head.

"To buy a hat for Pearl—remember?"

Chesh shrugged.

"I went back to the hat shop."

The blood drained from Chesh's face. "By yourself? What were you thinking?"

I held up my hands to placate him. "I'm fine, Chesh. I..." I hesitated, wondering how much to tell him. Then I scolded myself. He was my best friend. We didn't keep things from each other. "Do you remember going to *The Tea Party* last week? Someone left me a card. I saw him again—it turns out he's a milliner who owns that hat shop. So, I visited him—"

"Only a vampire would have a shop in the Spades Quarter," Chesh said. "Please don't tell me this chap is a vampire."

I shrugged one shoulder.

Chesh started shaking his head. "No hat could be so beautiful that you should risk your life for it. Pearl wouldn't want a hat if you bought it with your life, no matter how lovely."

"I wasn't in danger," I replied.

"A thirsty vampire attacked you in the Spades Quarter only days ago," Chesh's eyes flashed. "I'm your friend, and I've roamed this city with you, gone to bars and parties with you, but I'm telling you now that you cannot wander around in the vampire quarter at night. Not by yourself—and I'm not going there again. Not after last time."

"That's not what I was trying to tell you," I said, frustrated that Chesh wasn't listening. "The gentleman—"

"The blood-sucking vampire," Chesh interrupted.

I pursed my lips. "The *gentleman* showed me—"

"You went somewhere with him?" Chesh slammed his hand on the bench. "Honestly, Ivy, you're smarter than this. I've never known you to lose your senses over a man, no matter how handsome he was. Now you're following a vampire around—"

"I'm not following him around. This is not about his looks. You're not listening to me—"

"No, and I refuse to listen to any more of this nonsense. Promise me you won't do anything so stupid ever again."

I glared at Chesh, lifting my chin. "You're my friend. Not my keeper."

Chesh hesitated a moment, his eyes flashing. "If you

don't promise to stay away from the vampire quarter, I'll... I'll tell your mother. Everything."

My mouth went dry as I took in Chesh's words. I reeled back, as though physically struck by his words. Chesh's face fell, and he took a step forward, reaching out for me. I stepped back again, and he stopped, still out of reach. "I only want the best for you. If you can't see how dangerous he is..."

I spun around and marched out of the shop.

~

I stood outside the Emporium, clenching my fists into the fabric of my skirts. I closed my eyes, took a deep breath, then exhaled.

Chesh can't stop me. I'm an adult. I'll go wherever I like whenever I like.

My furious thoughts were crowded out by the memory of Alice's words, ringing in my head like a bell: *"I'd prefer it if you didn't wander the city at night. You're a grown woman, but you are still my daughter."*

I let my chin fall to my chest as the breath went out of my resistance. If I visited Raven again, I'd not only be out at night, against Alice's wishes, but I might also have to give up information about my mother. Then there was the strange pull that I still felt toward Raven. I felt torn in two—I didn't want to betray Alice or cause her to worry, but I couldn't stay away from Raven either.

And then there was the puzzle of the white rabbit. Raven might know the answer, and I needed to solve it.

The door swung open behind me.

"Ivy?" Chesh laid a hand on my shoulder.

I hesitated before turning to stare up into his green eyes, which lacked their usual brightness. One of his dimples sunk deeper as he gave me a rueful expression. He turned the wrench he was still holding over and over in his hands.

"I'm not apologizing," I said when he said nothing.

The rueful smile dropped away, and Chesh's expression was serious again. "Nor I."

"I'm not a child. I'm not *your* child."

"I don't think of you as a child," Chesh said. "You're a woman. You're... my friend. I care about you. I can't ignore it when I see you doing something—"

I held up my hand. "I'm not arguing with you. You've made your point."

Chesh shook his head. I bunched my fists in my skirts again, expecting another argument. I prepared to launch into my defense. This time it was Chesh who held up his hand to stop.

"At least, tell me you've heard my opinion, and you'll think about it."

I pursed my lips, reluctantly nodding. At that, Chesh smiled, producing his dimples again. He winked.

"In that case, let's not talk about this anymore. I don't want to fight with you."

I nodded, then turned to walk home.

"Wait a moment," Chesh ducked back inside the store, and when he came out again, he'd left his wrench inside, and put on a tweed coat over his shirt and vest. He wore a bowler hat on his head.

"Let me walk you home?"

"I don't need—"

Chesh rolled his eyes. "I know you don't, but I like to spend time with you, and it is my pleasure to accompany my lady to her place of residence."

I laughed, rolling my eyes at him, but we fell into step as we walked the well-trodden streets toward the

158

Palace.

We wandered at a dawdle. In the background, the clock's *ticking* was an unrelenting sound. I let my eyes and my thoughts wander.

We were coming around a corner when a metallic scraping noise from above drew my attention upward. I sheltered my eyes from the sunlight that was still peeping over the rooftops as it made its afternoon descent to notice what I'd always thought were nothing more than metal decorations along the rooflines of the buildings.

"What are you looking at?" Chesh asked, touching my hand.

"Do you see that?"

Chesh peered up, squinting as he did so. "What am I looking at?"

"The decorations on the roof there—look! They're moving."

"So they are," Chesh murmured.

"They appear to be cogs," I said, shifting position so that the glare of the sun didn't impede my vision.

"On a rooftop?" Chesh shook his head, looking away. "It's just a trick of the light," he said, taking my arm.

I let him lead me away but looked up at the cogs on the rooftop again. It was no optical illusion—they were moving—but why would anyone put cogs on the tops of the roofs?

I tripped over a loose cobblestone, and Chesh caught my arm to stop me from falling.

"Thank you," I murmured. Chesh patted my hand.

When I regained my balance, I glimpsed a painting of the white rabbit, appearing to peer out from behind a cart selling flowers. I stopped, staring at it, wondering if it was taunting me.

"Are you looking at those flowers?" Chesh asked. I blinked. I was facing the flower cart. I started to shake my head, but Chesh was already moving to engage the flower merchant in conversation.

The cart sold an array of different flowers from all over the Twelve Kingdoms. One was bright, with large petals that looked like someone had thrown purple, orange, and blue paint at them, leaving irregular spots of colors overlapping each other.

"What would you recommend for a beautiful lady?" Chesh asked the florist. She pointed to a bunch of tulips with a sign that said they were the Queen's Tulips from the Kingdom of Floris.

Chesh gave me a sideways glance. The merchant looked over too. "It seems she likes something more unusual," she said. "That is a Speckled Weeper, a rare native to The Forge that grows along the northern border."

"It's unusual and beautiful," I murmured, reaching out a finger to stroke the petals.

"Don't touch!" the woman snapped, her hand darting out to bat my hand away. I blinked in surprise. "The petals are poisonous," she explained. "And it's a flytrap, but it's got sharp teeth along the rim of the petals that will take half your finger off if you touch it."

I stepped away from the plant.

Chesh gave her a look. "I don't believe you," he said.

The woman raised an eyebrow. "Watch this," she said. She touched the middle of the large petals with a stick. The Speckled Weeper snapped shut with alarming speed, and with such force that it snapped the twig in half.

Chesh laughed, his eyes sparkling. "I'll take it. A present for a beautiful lady who might—if provoked—

160

react with a fury that could leave you without a limb!"

I rolled my eyes, assuming he was only joking, but when I returned to the Palace, I was the new owner of a Speckled Weeper.

22ND AUGUST

"**C**an one overfeed it, do you think?"
Pearl broke off a small amount of cheese and lobbed it towards the Speckled Weeper. As the cheese made contact, the plant's petals snapped closed. Pearl shrieked with laughter, as she had the last five or six times she'd done the same thing.

"What are you doing?" Alice walked into the dining room and sat down to breakfast. It was the first time in a week we'd eaten together.

"Chesh gave Ivy a man-eating plant," Pearl said, winking at me. "Isn't that romantic?"

I glared at her. "It wasn't romantic. He doesn't feel that way about me."

"Men only give women flowers when they're in love with them," Pearl replied. "They're always giving me flowers." She tossed her hair and lobbed another piece of cheese at the Speckled Weeper, then giggled.

"Stop playing with your food," Alice glared at her. "Anyone would think you were a child, not a grown woman. You should try being serious now and then. It would do you some good."

Pearl rolled her eyes. "You two are both serious enough for the three of us."

Alice reached for the bread and cheese when Jack entered with an armful of the day's newspapers, and a red rose that he held between two fingers.

"Another rose for you, Madam President," he said, and nodded towards the vase on a side table that now held about a dozen roses. "Shall I put it with the others?"

"Is there a note with it?" I asked.

Jack shook his head, then put the rose into the vase with the others and turned back to Alice.

"I've some urgent matters for your morning briefing, Madam President," he said, hovering a few steps from the table while eyeing the food.

"I haven't even eaten breakfast," Alice complained. "I suppose you can brief me while I eat." She glanced at Pearl and me. "You don't mind, do you, girls?"

"Yes," Pearl answered, but Alice silenced her with a glare, then waved at her advisor to get started.

"Your morning newspaper, Madam President," Jack said, putting the latest edition of The Forge Hart on the dining table.

"Just summarize it for me, would you?" Alice asked Jack. "Reading while eating gives one indigestion."

When Alice didn't take the newspaper, I reached over to slide it towards me. Jack eyed me, then turned his attention to Alice. "The Forge Hart is reporting more attacks this morning."

I glanced over the front page, which led with an article

about the Hearts being sighted again. When I flicked over the page, I noticed an opinion piece speculating about the causes of the return of the Hearts.

"The editor, Elias Doyle, wrote in his column he thinks the Queen's return is imminent," I interrupted, looking up at Alice.

Alice sat back in her chair and brushed her hair behind her ears. "She's dead!"

I remembered what Raven had said about the Queen of Hearts being a vampire. "How do you know, Mother?"

Alice pursed her lips, giving me a glare that told me not to ask any more questions. Jack hurried on. "More people are locking themselves in their houses and stockpiling food. There's also been an increase in people reporting their neighbors for esthetic code violations. Our inspectors are rushed off their feet dealing with minor code infractions."

"Why?" I asked. Jack looked at me, then back to Alice, as though seeking permission to answer.

Alice sighed, pushing her food around on her plate, before settling her knife and fork on the porcelain with a tinkling sound.

"Like this Elias Doyle, people believe the late Queen of Hearts is returning. During her reign, any mark of imperfection was punishable by death. She was very strict about the esthetic code. She chopped off people's heads in the most severe cases or turned them over to her vampires to feed upon if the infraction was only slight. It terrified people. Now, they're worried she might come back, so they're trying to put themselves in a position to deflect attention from themselves. If they accuse someone else of esthetic violations, the Queen's wrath might not turn on them."

"But you don't believe the Queen is coming back?"

I asked.

Alice glared at me again. "The late Queen," she corrected. "The dead rarely come back."

My Speckled Weeper snapped its petals shut with a loud clicking sound, and Alice and I started at the noise.

Pearl shrugged when Alice turned to glare at her. "What? You were both starting to sound boring again."

"There are several petitioners already waiting to see you in the great hall, Madam President," Jack interjected, just as Alice opened her mouth to reply to Pearl. Alice groaned, and the chair scraped over the floorboards as she stood. She was almost out of the door when she looked around. "Oh, Ivy, I wonder whether you might do something for me today?"

I glanced up from my plate. "Yes, Mother."

"I'm supposed to visit the perimeter wall. My regular visit. Unfortunately, I won't get through the list of petitioners in time. Are you feeling well enough to make the visit in my stead?"

I smiled. "Of course, Mother."

"Of course, Mother," Pearl mimicked my words in a high voice, rolling her eyes and tossing her hair. I glared at her before taking my leave from the dining room to change into something more appropriate for a perimeter visit.

The wind tugged at the strands of my hair. Much shorter now, it was impossible to tie back from my face, and though I'd grown to like the style—Pearl was right, it suited me—the wind now whipped the short hair into my eyes. I stood on top of the Twelfth Tower, which looked out to the north, beyond the boundaries of Melfall and out over the lands of The Forge as they stretched out to the horizon.

I'd never been beyond Melfall, The Forge's capital city, though Alice took a tour through the countryside every couple of years. She said there were many little villages scattered throughout the land, though none were visible from my vantage point. In the foreground were rolling hills, and in the far distance, I could see hazy mountains, barely tipped with white in the heat of summer. Though I couldn't see it now, I knew that if I visited the Seventh and Eighth Towers, I would see to the coast to the south and the glittering sea beyond.

I'd walked along the perimeter wall before; the first time was when I was a child and had argued with Alice about the size of the sky. I'd said the sky was small—I'd told her it was the width of my hand. She'd given me a curious look, and I'd held up my hand above me, to show her that it blocked out the sky over the width of the buildings that lined Sixth Avenue. Alice had tried to explain that the sky was much larger and that in the city we couldn't see it so well because the buildings got in the way. I didn't understand her, and so she'd taken me for a visit to the perimeter wall.

I remembered stepping out onto the wall-walk and trailed my fingers along the ramparts, as I craned my neck to see above me. With my other hand, I'd held it up to the sky, amazed that my hand covered only the slightest section of the sky. I had gazed around at the azure ceiling that spread out in every direction to meet a hazy horizon in the far distance.

Many times, I'd returned to the perimeter wall, and climbed the stone steps to one of the towers—there were twelve towers in all, each marking the end of twelve straight avenues that ran from the marketplace around the clock tower like the spokes of a wheel. I'd now walked every section of the wall that encircled the city, at least once, but I'd never tired of this view.

This time, though, I wasn't here to enjoy the view or to walk the wall-walk. I was here to get a report from the Captain of the President's Guard, or city guard as people knew them, whose job was to patrol the perimeter and guard against any threat to the city.

Alice formed the Guard at the start of her presidency, to replace the robotic Hearts who had formed the late Queen's army.

Remembering Raven's story, an unwelcome thought crept into my head. *She might still be alive. No, it's not possible.* I shuddered.

"Miss. Rowntree?" The Captain stood to attention next to me, touching his forefinger to his forehead in salute.

"Captain Walsh," I gave a curtsy, and he relaxed his stance somewhat, though he still stood straight under his plate armor, with his helmet tucked under his arm as he greeted me. His hair was damp, and beads of sweat had formed on his upper lip.

"You must be hot in all that," I said. "Doesn't the President's Guard have a cooler uniform for the summer?"

"No, miss," Captain Walsh said. "It's too dangerous to wear anything but full armor when on patrol."

I glanced down at the cotton vest I wore over my corset and shirt.

"No need to worry yourself, Miss Rowntree," Captain Walsh added. "You are under my protection. I would shield you with my life if it came to it."

"Thank you, Captain," I replied. "Do you expect an

imminent attack? I understand we have accords of peace with each of the other eleven kingdoms. Where are we expecting this attack to come from?"

"Expect the unexpected," Captain Walsh said, turning to stare at the horizon. "We must never neglect our duty to our President nor to Melfall." His words boomed.

Several guards saluted as they marched past, also in full plate armor. When they had gone, Captain Walsh leaned toward me to whisper. "Between us, Miss. Rowntree, you're right. The Forge has no enemies and nothing to fear. There has not been an attack on Melfall, or The Forge, these last eighteen years, since the Queen's defeat."

At the mention of the Queen, the breath left my lungs. Still, I forced a smile. "That's reassuring, Captain."

"However, we must be diligent. I drill that mantra into all the guards under my command. We are ever mindful of our duty."

"I will include that in my report to our President."

Captain Walsh smiled, looking pleased with himself. "I'm at your service. What would you like to see?"

"What does Madam President do when she visits the perimeter?"

"Madam President takes a tour of the wall-walk, greeting the soldiers. It's encouraging for the troops to have a moment with one's superiors, you know."

"I'll do that then," I said.

Captain Walsh led me along the wall-walk, and I spoke to several pairs of guards standing watch at regular sections of the parapets. I made small talk, learned that most of them had served on the President's Guard for only a few years, and complimented them on the gleam of their armor. We strolled in the full glare of

169

the sunshine. By the time we came to the First Tower, my shirt was damp, and my hair was clinging to the sheen of perspiration on my skin.

"No need to continue," Captain Walsh said. "Word will spread about your visit. You need not chat with every man on the wall, no matter how much they'd like to bend the ear of a beautiful, young woman."

I blushed, thanking him for the compliment.

"Shall we take the covered walk back to Twelfth Tower? I think you might prefer to be out of the sun?"

I hesitated, turning my face towards the sky to appreciate the limitless azure above. As if in answer, the wind whipped my hair again, and I turned my back on the view to cover my face.

We were about to take the stairs, when I glanced in the other direction, over the city rooftops.

I noticed the cogs that lined the apex of the rooftops and halted. I covered my eyes with one hand to shield them from the glare, squinting at the sight. From this vantage point, I knew the cogs were moving.

"Captain Walsh?"

He turned to me.

"Do you know what they are?" I pointed at the cogs on the rooftops.

"I'm not sure what you mean, miss?"

"There is machinery on those rooftops. See there? There are similar moving cogs on most of the roofs."

Captain Walsh peered out. "I see them."

"I'm sure they're moving," I said, leaning out over the inner ramparts, wishing I could get a closer look. "But what are they for? What do they do?"

Another puzzle.

Captain Walsh was less interested. He straightened and turned away. "Mere decoration, I'm sure. Every citizen of Melfall devotes themselves to the esthetic glory of our city. Beauty is the goal."

I pressed my lips together. "It's moving—like a machine. Nobody builds machines for beauty. They're built for a purpose."

"I'm merely a captain. You're a much better judge of esthetics. In any case, the eyes of the President's Guard should always focus on what is beyond the perimeter. I spend little time scrutinizing our own citizens. Shall we?"

He gestured towards the steps that descended the first tower. I reluctantly turned from the rooftop cogs and took the steps back to street level.

A trumpet bellowed. Captain Walsh saluted, followed by the guards who stood in a line behind him.

"You have honored us with your visit, Miss. Rowntree," Captain Walsh said. "Please give our respects to Madam President."

"I will, Captain." I smiled at the guards standing as still as statues. Then I noticed something unusual.

Behind them, at the place where Twelfth Avenue met the Twelfth Tower, the gates in the perimeter wall—one of only two entrances to Melfall—stood open.

I hesitated, frowning at the sight.

"Do we get much overland trade?" I asked Captain Walsh.

"I beg your pardon?"

I pointed to the open gates. "I would have thought it is harder to bring goods by the northern roads. Doesn't most of our trade come by ship?"

Captain Melfall didn't even glance at the gates.

"Those gates are not open to admit a caravan of traders."

"Oh?" I tilted my head. "Why would the farmers travel so far when it isn't a market day?"

"It's not to admit the farmers either."

He shifted his weight, and I saw the hair sticking to the moisture on his forehead.

"Then why are the gates open?"

"The gates to our city are always open."

I frowned. "They are?"

"These gates have not closed for eighteen years."

"You leave them open all the time?"

"That's correct."

I stared around, trying to understand. "You just told me that the President's Guard was always vigilant against an attack. Yet our gates remain open? Always?"

Captain Walsh shrugged his shoulders, though faint pink blotching rose up his neck. "The Forge has no enemies, Miss. Rowntree. There is no need to close the gates. That's what Madam President said."

I stared at the gates that had stood open for eighteen years. I was still shaking my head when I turned away.

"Thank you," I murmured. Then, abruptly, I remembered something and turned back.

"Captain Walsh?"

He stood straight. "Yes, Miss. Rowntree?"

"Have you ever heard of the white rabbit?"

The captain frowned. "The white rabbit? Of course, I have."

I blinked. "You have?"

"You're probably too young to remember the white rabbit. A supporter of the Queen, and a member of her inner circle."

"Have you heard rumors that he has returned?"

Captain Walsh shook his head. "Nobody has seen the

white rabbit since the Queen... well, since your mother became Madam President—long may she reign."

~

Moving parts on every rooftop. That's what I saw as I retraced my steps along Twelfth Avenue towards the President's Palace. I kept my eyes focused on the line of the roofs. Had those parts always been moving? If so, why was I only noticing them now?

I cursed myself for my previous inattention. How much happened in this city I was unaware of? I'd grown up in Melfall. I'd been nowhere else. I thought I knew the city well, but the last couple of weeks had shown me parts of the city that I never knew existed.

First, I'd discovered people living underneath Melfall. Now, there were machines atop every rooftop, and I couldn't be sure it hadn't always been so. Surely, I would have noticed?

I bumped into someone on the street and stumbled. My top hat fell from my head and rolled into the middle of oncoming traffic.

"Watch where you're going!" an older woman's voice scolded me.

I waved an apology as I dodged a steam-powered carriage motoring along the road. It's horn blared, and the driver slammed on the brakes, before brandishing a fist at me as he rolled by.

I waved another apology, setting my hat back on my head. Out of the corner of my eye, I saw a flash of red. It drew my eyes into the alley leading off the busy avenue.

A Heart.

Without taking my eyes off the robotic card, with the mark of the late Queen's patronage on its chest,

I stepped off the curb again to dash towards it. More shouts and blaring horns followed, but I ignored them all.

I stepped into the deserted alley, my footsteps clattering over the irregular cobblestones to echo off the walls of the buildings as they loomed overhead.

The Heart was marching in the opposite direction, keeping a regular pace, holding a spear in one hand.

"Stop!" I yelled out as I dashed after it.

The Heart didn't stop or turn. It kept up its steady pace along the alley. It came to a corner, jerked to turn around it, then continued without pause.

I gathered up my skirts, hoisting them above my knees, as I dashed forward. Breathing heavily, and wishing I hadn't laced my corset so tight this morning, I rounded the corner after the Heart.

"Wait!" I heard my voice echo off the walls. "I need to talk to you!"

The Heart didn't pause, and I wondered whether it could hear me. All the stories I'd heard about the Hearts told they were programmed to respond to verbal commands, to answer simple questions, and undertake complex actions. This one, however, wasn't reacting as I'd expected.

I forced myself to run faster. The Heart marched at a regular pace, so I caught up before the Heart reached the next corner.

I yelled out again, before putting a hand on the Heart's spear arm and coming around to stand in front of it.

"I'm talking to you," I said and struggled to catch my breath. I looked into its robotic face, getting a good look at it. The body of the Heart was like a playing card, flat and rectangular, decorated in the Nine of Hearts motif.

174

Its arms and legs were modeled to appear human, and when I stared up into its face, a shiver ran down my spine.

The Heart had a face, smooth and devoid of expression, but its eyes were cameras that rolled around so it could "see." I heard a faint hum as the camera swiveled to focus on me.

I swallowed down my uneasiness and raised my voice. "Nine of Hearts," I addressed it, "What are you—?" I said, but the Heart reached forward and grabbed the front of my shirt. It hauled me upwards, without effort, so that my feet were kicking in the air.

"Hey, what are you—?" I repeated, louder this time, as I tugged at the Heart's fist where it bunched my shirt in its fist. I searched for a panel on its chest or a latch that I might open to see how the robot worked. Perhaps I'd even be able to disable it and take it back to the President's Palace for further study. The Heart's grip didn't loosen in the slightest as I struggled, and I used my most commanding voice. "Let me go!"

At first, I thought the Heart hadn't heard me, but then I hurtled through the air before slamming against the brick wall of the building across the street.

A stab of pain tore through my head. I blinked, as black shadows flickered at the edge of my vision. I crouched on the footpath, leaning against the wall and holding my head in my hands.

When I'd gathered my wits to look around again, the Heart had disappeared.

23RD AUGUST

The 'closed' sign hung on the door of *Thackery's Fine Antiques*. I peered into the window, hoping I'd see some evidence of movement inside, some sign that Mr. Thackery was remedying the code violations I'd used to withdraw his license for operation. The shop was quiet, empty.

I closed my eyes.

"*I have children to feed,*" Mr. Thackery had said when I'd taken away his license. I heard the echo of those words now, and I couldn't shake the heaviness that had lodged in my stomach when I'd visited the tunnels and seen how my strict adherence to the esthetic code had cost Mr. Thackery his livelihood, his home, and his family.

I leaned my forehead against the cool glass of the

shop window, wondering what to do next.

I wondered if I could find the tunnel entrance without Raven, or if I should even try—perhaps these people would rather be left alone than to be confronted by the architect of their miserable existences? I touched my stomach as the heaviness persisted. I couldn't do nothing, but how could I help them? How could I undo the damage I'd done?

I saw Raven's face in my mind as I remembered his offer: *You can choose to help them.* I hung my head. I should help them, but I couldn't betray Alice to do it.

I sighed, opening my eyes as I turned to leave. A movement snagged my attention from the corner of my eye. My gaze snapped back to the shop, and this time, I pressed my face against the glass to see past the window's reflection.

Someone *was* inside.

I rapped at the door. The figure lurking in the back froze.

A moment passed.

Then the figure hurried out of sight.

"Spades," I cursed underneath my breath and ran to the corner of the street to get around to the rear of the building to see if I could head the person off before they disappeared.

As I rounded the corner, I saw a mess of gray hair and the dirty suit that Mr. Thackery had been dressed in when I closed his shop.

"Mr. Thackery!" I yelled out and ran toward him.

Mr. Thackery turned, his eyes narrowing as he saw me. "What are you doing here?" he asked.

I came to a standstill a short way away from him, giving him space. "I wish to say—"

"I don't want pity, girl," Mr. Thackery sneered. "Not

from you."

I grasped my hands in front of my chest. "I just wanted to say..."

"What? You're sorry? Is that it?" Mr. Thackery pushed a hand through the mess of his hair. "A little late for that, isn't it? You took away my shop, my business—I spent years building it up, you know. It's tough, in a place that only values shiny, new things, to encourage people to find beauty and value in things that are tarnished and imperfect. There's character in things that have been used and passed from one person to the next. Every scratch and every dent tells a story. Few people in the Forge are interested in stories, though. All they want is the latest thing, as long as it's shiny, beautiful, and perfect. That's all people care about around here. Nothing's changed. Not really. I remember what it was like before, under the Queen. Not that you'd understand—all you know is peace."

I clasped my hands together, searching for the right thing to say. "Is there anything I can do? Anything you need?"

Mr. Thackery stared at me in disbelief, then snorted. "Apart from my life back? My daughter is on the verge of death, sick from the damp darkness of the tunnels. I lost my home because I couldn't pay the rent. My business might not have succeeded, according to your esthetic measures, but I paid my way. Now..." Mr. Thackery turned away, fishing out a handkerchief from his pocket to dab at the moisture that had filled his eyes.

"When the Queen disappeared, I thought things would change." He shook his head. "Things are just as bad now as they ever were. Mark my words—"

"What do you mean?" I asked.

A set of footsteps made Mr. Thackery jerk. He looked around, wide-eyed, and shrank away from me. "It's the Hearts! They're coming."

A jolt of fear tore through me, and I froze, listening for the sound. All I could hear, though, was the sound of footsteps a short way away. It didn't have the steady robotic frequency of the Hearts.

"Mr. Thackery..." I reached out to touch his arm, to slow him down.

"Don't say my name," he hissed. "Don't talk to me. I can't be seen with you."

"What are you talking about?"

"She's back. Or she will be soon." Mr. Thackery turned away, hunching over as though trying to disappear under the worn collar of his coat as he moved along the back alley. I started after him.

"I only want to help you," I called out.

"I can't risk my family again. I won't."

I leaned against the wall, defeated, watching Mr. Thackery's retreating figure as he hurried away.

It was only then that I noticed the painted form of the white rabbit on the wall opposite.

I ran a finger over the motif. A white rabbit with a black bow tie, black waistcoat, and its ears stuck out from under a top hat. It seemed to sniff the air, one paw curled up as though it was mid-stride.

My mind turned over the puzzle again. One of many that I just couldn't stop thinking about.

Follow the white rabbit, the starving vampire had said when faced with his injured customer. Raven had promised to tell me more about the white rabbit if I brought him information about Alice's movements. Perhaps, if I found the white rabbit for myself, I could solve the puzzle *and* keep Alice safe. I flipped open my pocket watch. There was plenty of daylight left. Still, I felt a twinge of regret at the thought of breaking my word to Alice. She'd only worry about my safety.

I studied the white rabbit motif again. *Follow the white rabbit.* The words echoed in my mind, and I wondered if they should be taken literally. I turned in the direction the white rabbit seemed to face and started walking, meandering along the narrow backstreet, searching for any hint of another painted rabbit.

I walked two blocks before seeing the painted tuft of a fluffy tail. I knelt down next to it and saw the body of the rabbit curving around the corner of the building. A smile touched my lips as I brushed my fingers against the painting. They came away tacky, smudged with white paint.

This rabbit was freshly painted.

I kept walking, keeping my eyes to the base of the buildings on each side of the street, determined not to miss the next clue.

I stopped on the corner, waiting for a steam carriage to pass by, before hurrying down the next block. Then, across the street, I saw another rabbit on the bottom of a wall.

I crossed the street to get a closer look, but as I bent over and brushed my fingers over the paint, I noticed that it had been hastily obscured with a few strokes of black. Was someone trying to obscure the clues? Or perhaps correcting the route?

I took my hand away, noticing that it left no residue of paint on my hands. Perhaps this marking was old? I wiped my hands together, looking back in the direction

I'd come from. If I kept going, would I find another clue that way? Or should I turn the corner here?

"Are you all right, dear?"

I jerked, as an older woman put her hand on my arm. I'd been standing on the street corner, staring into space.

"Are you lost?" she asked.

I shook my head. I needed to decide. I was drawing too much attention by loitering in one place, staring around.

"Are you sure? These streets can be quite confusing, I find." The woman frowned, her hand still on my arm.

"No, I'm fine. I was just...looking for..." I clamped my mouth shut, stopping myself from revealing any more, then lifted my chin. I pried my arm away from her. "I was getting my bearings. I know where I'm headed. Thank you for your concern."

Without looking back, I left the obscured rabbit behind and walked back across the street to continue to follow the clues.

The white rabbit crouched next to an otherwise unremarkable door—this was the sign I'd been looking for.

Another white rabbit.

I walked toward the door, then threw a look over my shoulder. No one noticed me. I tapped on the door.

I waited, pleating the folds of my skirts between my fingers, but no one answered.

I turned my head and pressed my ear to the door, listening for any noise from inside. I couldn't hear anything.

I stepped back, looking up at the windows of the first story. The curtains were drawn, but a movement caught my eye as one of them fluttered. I stared at the window, but the movement didn't happen again.

I looked down at the white rabbit painting on the wall, lying down and looking at the doorway. So far, following the paintings of the white rabbit had led me here. Staring at the rabbit, I had the strongest feeling that I should step through the doorway.

I hesitated, wondering what to do. Then I turned the door handle. The door clicked open and

swung inward. I paused, expecting someone to call out or try to stop me.

Nothing happened.

I threw another glance over my shoulder as I stepped inside.

In the entrance hall, a large vase of sunflowers greeted me. I leaned closer to breathe in their scent but was startled by a crackling sound. A voice spoke:

"How did you get here?"

I jumped, spinning around to identify the voice, but I couldn't see anyone. Then I peered at the sunflower, noticing the sunflower's face move as I did.

"Did you say that?" I asked it, a blush rising to my cheeks. Was I talking to a flower?

"How did you find this place?" the voice spoke again. This time, I noticed a shiny surface in the center of the sunflower. A camera?

"I followed the white rabbit," I replied.

"Well, why didn't you say so? Take the stairs down one floor."

Then the sound disappeared, and the sunflower tipped forward, as though bowing its head. Rejecting the urge to inspect the sunflower—to pull it apart to see how it worked—I walked past the side table and lay a hand on the staircase that wound downwards. I took the stairs one at a time, descending into what appeared to be a dark basement.

When I got to the bottom, a small strip of flickering light glowed underneath a doorway. I paused, then pushed. The door swung open without resistance.

In the room, a line of people were standing against the far wall, looking pale. In the center, a man lay on a bench, while another bent over him.

As the door opened, everyone's heads swiveled towards me.

The man bending over the bench straightened up. An older man with gray hair and a mustache and a stethoscope hanging around his neck put an eyeglass back over one eye as he peered at me.

"Emergency?" he asked.

I frowned, my eyes flickering to the person lying on the bench with his shirt laid open to reveal his bare chest. "I'm looking for the white rabbit."

The man stared at me, then waved a hand. "Wait over there." He turned his attention back to the unconscious, bare-chested man.

I hesitated a moment, then shuffled over to stand at the end of the line, leaning against the wall, as I watched. The man with the stethoscope appeared to be a doctor, though this was not the city hospital.

I watched him stitch a deep cut on the man's open chest. Then, as the line shuffled forward, he examined a rash, pulled a tooth, treated an earache, cleaned and dressed an infected wound, and set a splint for a broken leg.

It was over an hour later, and I was the last in line when the doctor turned to me.

"What ails you, young lady," the doctor asked.

"There's nothing wrong with me," I replied. "I'm looking for the white rabbit."

The doctor set his eyeglass into place as he took a step closer and peered at my face. "Why?" he asked.

I opened my mouth, then shut it again, at a loss for words. Why? "Because..."

Because I need to solve the riddle about the white rabbit. Because I want to find out if the rumors about the white rabbit recruiting supporters for the Queen of Hearts are true. Because I have to know if the Red Queen is really returning. Because I can't sacrifice Alice's safety.

And because I must find out more about Raven.

He frowned. "You're not ill?"

"No, I'm fine."

"Why were you told to seek out the white rabbit?"

"Nobody told me. I just followed the signs."

The doctor rubbed his hands down the front of his shirt. "What's your name, young lady?"

I hesitated, wondering whether I should give a false name. Then I decided against it. I wanted information from this man. I would not get him to trust me by lying to him.

"Ivy Rowntree, sir," I replied, bobbing a polite curtsy.

"Rowntree?" The doctor looked me over, interested. "Alice Rowntree's daughter?"

I nodded. "Do you know my mother?"

A blush rose to the doctor's cheeks. He looked away and popped out his eyeglass to clean it with the tail of his shirt, before putting it back in his eye again. "I did, once. A long time ago. How old are you, young lady?"

I frowned. "I turned eighteen this year," I replied. "Why do you ask?"

"Eighteen," the doctor murmured, and his gaze

drifted away to a point in the distance. "You don't look like your mother."

I pursed my lips. "No, my twin sister is more like my mother," I replied. I'd always assumed that I take after my father, though I'd never met him, and Alice had never spoken of him.

The doctor gawked. "Twins?" His voice hitched a little higher. He turned away and busied himself with his instruments, picking things up to clean them before putting them down again.

"So, do you know?" I asked when he said nothing else.

"Know what?"

"I need to find the white rabbit. Do you know where he is?"

"Oh," the doctor turned back to me. "I'm the white rabbit," he said and held out a hand. "Dr. Wit Lapin, at your service."

~

Dr. Lapin clasped my hand, then motioned toward the door.

"Please, come upstairs," he said. "It's not very comfortable down here. I'll make you a cup of tea."

I followed Wit up a flight of stairs to the first-floor landing, then through a door and into a small sitting room. From brief glimpses through other open doorways, I saw several other people who appeared to be living there too. They were all pale, with dark smudges under their eyes, and threadbare, patched clothes.

Wit bade me sit, and I settled myself in one of two armchairs—its material worn down almost to nothing on the armrests as he poured the tea. As I took the

186

saucer, chipped on the edge, a plume of steam curled up from the cup. I sipped at it, the liquid burning my lips, as I tried to quiet the swirl of questions in my mind.

The cup chinked as I set it down on the saucer.

"So you *have* returned," I said.

"You solved the riddle," Wit said, at the same time. We looked at each other, then Wit sank into the armchair across from me. He rubbed his hands together, pursing his lips. "Many people here won't remain, now that you have discovered our location."

"Are they like the people in the tunnels? Homeless?" I asked.

Dr. Lapin frowned, leaning forward. "How do you know about them?"

I felt the warmth of a blush spread across my cheeks. "Mr. Cappello showed me."

Wit's eyes widened. "You know Raven?"

I nodded.

Wit studied me, his expression serious. "I suppose if Raven trusts you..."

There was a sharp knocking at the door, and another figure appeared in the doorway. It was a woman with long, wavy dark hair, wearing gold loop earrings and dressed in an unusual dress with long layers and oversized sleeves that flowed as she moved.

"Dr. Lapin, here you are!" she said, her eyes lighting up. "If you've finished seeing patients, may I speak with you? I need..."

Wit and I both stood, turning toward the woman in the doorway. She trailed off, suddenly noticing me.

"I didn't know you had company."

Wit cleared his throat. "Miss Rowntree, allow me to introduce you to Her Royal Highness, Princess Gaia of the Kingdom of Badalah. Princess, this is Ivy Rowntree, daughter of President Rowntree of The Forge."

My eyes widened as I took in the princess. Her eyes had a gold ring around the iris, just like mine. I'd never seen it in anyone else before. I dropped into a deep curtsy. "Pleased to meet you, Your Royal Highness," I murmured.

Gaia inclined her head. There was something strange about the way she looked at me, as though she knew me. Curiosity came over her features however, she turned to Wit. "I wish to continue our conversation from the other night if you have a moment?"

Wit glanced at me, clearly wondering whether he might escape our conversation. If I excused myself, he might have vacated this building by the time I returned. No, I couldn't let this opportunity pass by.

"Dr. Lapin and I were in the middle of something important," I said, looking the princess in the eye. Her golden-ringed irises had me on edge

Gaia looked surprised at my boldness. Then her cool mask slipped into place. "You're the President's daughter? The one who lives on the esthetic stipend? Or the daughter who enforces it?"

I gritted my teeth as a hot flush of shame washed over me. I couldn't find the words to respond. Gaia turned back to Wit. "I know The Forge has many problems, but I am desperate. I need that potion."

"Potion?" I narrowed my eyes, looking from Gaia to Wit, remembering the work he was doing downstairs. "What are you doing here, Dr. Lapin?" My voice rang out louder than it should have, over Gaia's commanding tone.

Wit's eyes widened, and he put a finger to his lips. As he did so, the sounds of movement and life in the rooms around us fell silent. Wit closed the door and bade me

188

sit down. He found another chair for Gaia, and the man who stood behind her, who I'd barely noticed in the shadow of Gaia's commanding presence—a bodyguard, I guessed.

"I knew your mother, once," Wit started, wiping his eyeglass with his handkerchief, then putting it back into place. "She had a good heart, and I believe she will have brought you up with her capacity for compassion and her duty to the right thing. So I shall trust you, too. I must insist that you do not repeat these words to anyone who does not know the truth of the white rabbit. Or it will put more people than myself in danger. Do you understand?"

First Raven, and now Wit, demanded my silence before they would speak about their secrets. Narrowing my eyes, I hesitated, then nodded. "I'm not here to arrest anyone," I said. "I came here because..." I thought about Alice and my determination that I wouldn't put her in danger to satisfy my curiosity. Then I remembered Mr. Thackery and my attempt to see him this morning. "I'm here to make amends. I didn't understand that my actions in upholding the esthetic laws had affected people in this way."

"What did you think was happening to the people who lost their livelihoods?" Gaia asked, her tone acerbic. Her bodyguard touched her arm in a familiar gesture. Gaia looked at him. "I won't pretend that Baladah is perfect—far from it. We have poverty enough in my kingdom, but at least we don't pretend that the poor don't exist."

I swallowed, focusing on Wit and not looking at Gaia. "You were saying?"

Wit rubbed his hands together and settled back in his chair. "You may not know this, but I once worked for the Queen of Hearts. I was one of her loyal advisors. I had some training in the art of apothecary, and the Queen—the *former* Queen, I should say—engaged me to concoct beauty potions for her. She wanted to be the most beautiful woman in The Forge—every day, she was determined to be more beautiful than the day before. I was charged with making it happen.

"I had no choice, you see. I worked tirelessly for beauty, under the threat of death. The former Queen was prone to chopping off the heads of those who displeased her. So, I searched for the ingredient that would smooth her wrinkles, brighten her skin tone, shine her hair, and slim her figure. No sooner had I found one solution than I was told to find another, better, potion. She imagined imperfections, even when there were none.

"The former Queen always wanted things immediately, and I was always late." Wit paused, looking down at the hands in his lap, the fingers now swollen in the joints, and the backs of his hands marked with age spots. "At first, it was a privileged position. I lived a life of luxury, as long as I stayed in the Queen's good graces. That was hard enough. Then I tired of the work. I desired to help the people—the ill or injured. The Queen shunned these people and forced them into the fringes of society. Or beheaded them.

"When Alice defeated the Queen, and she disappeared, I was free." Wit's eyes lit up at the memory, and his voice became dreamy, as though in that moment, he was a long way away. "I was free to pursue the work I had always wanted to do. I left The Forge for a time," Wit cast a furtive glance in my direction, then continued. "To continue my studies. I dreamed of becoming a doctor; to use my skills as an apothecary to help people. So, I did." Wit smiled.

"Now, you treat the people of Melfall?" I asked.

Wit nodded. "I treat their ills and injuries, where I can." He pulled at a thread on his waistcoat. "I ask for payment only where I know my patient has the means to pay, and only as much as they can afford. It is not a lucrative life, but I find it more fulfilling than living in the luxury afforded me by the Queen."

I looked at Wit, as though seeing him again for the first time. He wore threadbare clothes, with loose threads and patches on the elbows. His gray hair was messy, with unruly curls, too long and not tamed into a ponytail as worn by most of the gentlemen of Melfall. Wrinkles lined his face, and there were dark smudges under his eyes. Still, when he smiled, his eyes sparkled, and the lines of his face smiled too.

"How does Mr. Cappello fit into this?" I asked.

"Mr. Cappello brings patients to me." Wit explained, with a shrug of his shoulders.

I raised my eyebrows in surprise.

Wit rubbed his hands together. "I met Raven several years ago. I had returned to Melfall and was setting up a practice. I had thought it would be easy. I still had many connections from when I was in the Queen's service, and I believed the wealthy of Melfall would pay enough for treatment, so I could treat the poor for free."

Wit glanced at Gaia, who was also listening to the story with interest. "But the wealthy were after the beauty potions I had once brewed for the Queen. They objected to my treating the unbeautiful in the same consulting rooms, and waiting with them in the same waiting rooms—as though lack of beauty was catching. They demanded I charge the same fees to my poorer clients. Several refused to pay at all when they found I treated a poor, dying man without charge. I refused to change, and, one by one, my wealthy clients abandoned me."

Wit shrugged his shoulders. "It doesn't bother me that those people chose to go elsewhere for medical treatment, but they tried to shut me down. They reported me so many times, and without money for upkeep, I fell afoul of the esthetic code. I was arrested several times, and I have to move my rooms to new locations constantly.

"How can I treat patients if people do not know how to find me when they need me? If they cannot contact me, how do I come to them in their time of need? It troubled me, knowing people were languishing without help, but what could I do? If I revealed myself, I was likely to be arrested. Then, I met Mr. Cappello."

I leaned forward. The mention of Raven made my heart beat a little faster.

~

Dr. Lapin paused, getting up from his seat to walk across the room. He picked up the teapot.

"More tea?"

I looked at the cup I'd set down on the table, half-drunk and now cold. I shook my head. Gaia accepted.

"I don't have a maidservant, Your Royal Highness," Wit said as he poured the tea with shaking hands.

Gaia waved away his concern and gave him a smile as she sipped her tea. Her bodyguard also accepted a cup of tea with a nod to the doctor.

"Is there sugar?" The bodyguard asked. "You drink it very bitter in Melfall."

Wit frowned, then looked around the room. "Yes,

somewhere...ah, here it is."

Wit offered a small sugar pot, but when he opened the lid, he frowned again to see it was almost empty. The man hesitated before taking a tiny amount of sugar to add to his tea.

"I seem to be running low," Wit said, looking flustered as he rubbed a hand over the stubble of his beard.

Eager for Wit to continue the story, I pointedly redirected the conversation. "You were saying you met Mr. Cappello?" I asked.

Wit walked over to a window; he drew aside the curtain to peer outside.

"How much do you know about Mr. Cappello?" Wit asked.

"Is that the vampire who brought us here?" Gaia asked, interrupting.

Wit nodded. I glanced at her, surprised she'd met him too.

"A little. He's a milliner and a vampire." I trailed off.

Wit waited, and when I didn't continue, he looked down to his lap as he took out his looking glass and rubbed at the lens with his handkerchief.

"Mr. Cappello knows the city almost better than anyone. When I met him, he offered me a partnership— he would bring me patients if I would treat them."

Wit smiled, giving a little laugh. "It wasn't much of a negotiation. I didn't plan to give up my work with the ill and injured, so I accepted his help in that regard. He helps me to find new accommodations, when I need to move my treatment rooms. Mostly, though, he helps my patients to find me—the white rabbit was his idea, and his team of orphaned and abandoned children do the paintings."

"He also delivers food for the poor when he can."

I frowned, closing my eyes for a moment, trying to sort through all of this information. "What does Raven get out of this arrangement?"

Wit paused a moment, shrugging his shoulder. It appeared he was about to say something, before changing his mind. He continued to polish his eyeglass on his handkerchief.

"Why would a vampire help the city's poor, sick people?" I asked again, certain that Wit knew something he wasn't saying.

Wit shifted in his seat. "His people suffer too, you know. What with the blood shortage and—"

"What has this got to do with a blood shortage?" I interrupted.

"Well, not so much a shortage, but with the banks refusing to sell to vampires, it's difficult..."

My mouth fell open. "The banks won't sell blood to vampires? How do you know this?"

Wit paled. "Perhaps I've said too much. The point is..." Wit trailed off, and I opened my mouth to ask him another question when Wit spoke so quickly the words seemed to pour from his mouth.

"Mr. Cappello wants to change things for everyone— he was planning something to force President Rowntree to listen to the unacknowledged people of this city. She has ignored us for too long."

My head jerked. I stared at Wit. The petitioner to Alice had spoken about the white rabbit rallying the Queen's supporters, but Wit seemed to imply something different. "*He* was planning? Not you?"

Wit frowned, confused. "I believe he sought you out to see if he could find a way to President Rowntree's ear...?"

I sucked in a breath as Wit's words registered. I

stood, turning my back to walk towards the door.

I took a deep breath, then lifted my chin and straightened my shoulders. "I have taken up more than enough of your time, Dr. Lapin. I believe the princess needs your services now. Thank you for seeing me."

Without waiting for a response from either Wit or the princess, I strode out of the door.

24TH AUGUST

"**A**udrey?" I stood at the receptionist's desk at the Fourth Street Blood Bank. "I have some additional questions. I need to speak to someone immediately."

The receptionist blinked at me, then considered the full waiting room. "It's Monday," she said, by way of explanation. "It's always busy on Mondays. People need money," she whispered the last, then looked down at her paperwork.

"I'm not sure you understand, Audrey," I said, not bothering to disguise the hard edge to my voice. "I have questions, and if you don't answer them, I'll shut down your operation. I'm sure these people would rather wait than be turned away."

Audrey's eyes widened as she looked up at me again,

pushing her glasses back on her nose. "Inspector?" she said, peering at my badge "I didn't recognize you at first, Inspector Rowntree. I'm sure somebody...I'll just call—"

Audrey waved at the next person to come through the double doors. I recognized Miss Crispin and started towards her before waiting for Audrey to explain my presence.

"Miss Crispin? I have some urgent questions for you. You'll understand." I nodded towards the doorway to the blood donation rooms at the back.

Miss Crispin barely disguised a flicker of annoyance as she glanced at the packed waiting room.

"Of course, Inspector," she said, her voice curt.

When the door swung closed behind her, she stood in the hallway and crossed her arms across her chest. "What can I help you with, Inspector? We're very busy today, so it would be best..."

"I've heard a very disturbing rumor, Miss Crispin," I said as I turned to face her, "and if I find it is true, I will be forced to report it to the highest authorities in The Forge."

Miss Crispin paled. "I'm sure--"

"*I'm* sure it will be better for you if you cooperate. I would hate for you to get caught up in allegations of impropriety."

"Impropriety?" Miss Crispin's complexion lost even more color. "I don't know—"

"Are you sure?" I said. "You see, every time I have been here, I have seen a waiting room full of people eager to donate their blood for the payment that this bank provides to them—a payment that is dependent on selling that blood donation to those that need it— our vampire population. The business model of this bank, of all the blood banks, is that they sell the blood

198

to vampires for an agreed price and pay the donors who agree to provide blood for this purpose. Is my understanding correct?"

Miss Crispin nodded. She was clasping her hands in front of her chest, her knuckles white.

"And yet, I understand vampires are unable to get any blood from your blood bank."

Miss Crispin swallowed. "The instruction came from our chief executive officer," she said, looking over her shoulder. She reached out to me, pulling me into a doorway as she lowered her voice to a whisper. "We had no choice. We were to continue daytime collection operations as normal, but all nighttime operations ceased."

"Why?"

Miss Crispin was shaking her head.

I glared at her. She looked around again.

"I... I heard a wealthy patron bought up all of the blood."

My eyes narrowed. "Who?"

"I don't know," she whispered.

I glowered at her again, but Miss Crispin insisted. "Please, I really don't. Nobody does."

Somebody knows, I thought.

"What happens to the blood?"

Miss Crispin glanced behind her, then she motioned for me to follow. She hurried down the hallway, through a small door set into the wall, then down a narrow staircase into the basement. I gasped as I entered the basement storeroom.

Inside, stacked three high were barrels marked by blood type.

"Every day, in the late afternoon, a steam carriage comes to pick them up," Miss Crispin explained.

"Every barrel?" I asked.

Miss Crispin nodded.

"Where do they go?"

～

In the alley, off Fourth Street, I leaned against a wall, watching the back entrance to the Blood Bank as I racked my brain. Who would want to prevent vampires from accessing the blood banks, and why?

The lack of blood available to the vampires in Melfall hadn't caused an attack—yet—but it would be only a matter of time before a dreadful situation arose.

I shivered, remembering the dreams that still plagued me every night. The dream had taken on a different flavor since my visit to Raven's workshop, and I'd woken hot, sweaty, and wanting.

I pushed a strand of hair out of my eyes and focused on the problem at hand. I'd been waiting for the steam-powered wagon to arrive for an hour. Even in the shade of the buildings, heat wafted from the streets. As I waited, perspiration made loose strands of hair stick to the sides of my face.

Finally, the shadows lengthened, and a breath of late afternoon breeze provided some relief.

A rumbling sound caught my attention, and I stood upright, suddenly focused. The wagon rounded the corner into the alley, and two men jumped off to rap sharply on the back entrance of the Fourth Street Blood Bank.

I shrank into the shadows, hiding from notice, but the men barely looked up as they came out with the barrels carried on their shoulders, loading them into the wagon one by one.

200

When they were finished, they covered the barrels with cloth, then tied them down with ropes. Then, with a whistle, they jumped aboard the wagon to leave. The back door to the blood bank swung closed.

The wagon continued on its way to the end of the alley before I pulled Chesh's steam bike out of the shadows and kick-started it.

~

I kept the steam-powered wagon in sight as it chugged through Melfall, passing the Clubs Quarter Blood Bank, and the Central Blood Bank, before heading into the district of the old Royal Palace.

At the sight of the old palace, my heart started to race. The late Queen—or perhaps the returned Queen if Raven was right—was a vampire. Perhaps she wanted the blood donations for herself? It made sense.

As I watched, my conclusions were dashed as the steam wagon didn't stop. It continued to wind through the narrow streets, into the back streets, before it came to a stop at a gate that was not marked by any signage or numbering that I could see.

I looked around to try to get my bearings. We'd come to a lane of service entrances for the large estates, mostly owned by the old families of Melfall. I didn't know the area well enough to know which entrance belonged to which house.

A man jumped from the wagon and walked over to open the gate. It was locked, but the man appeared to have a key, and he held the gate open so that the wagon, now full of the day's blood donations, could enter.

Once the wagon had passed through the entrance, and the man started to pull the gate closed, and I got a glimpse of another figure who'd been standing inside the gates.

I didn't get a good look at his face, but I recognized the garish stripes of his suit.

It was Tweedle Dee.

Or, maybe, Tweedle Dum.

~

"Are the Mr. Tweedles expecting you, Miss?" The butler opened the door and stared down at me over his long nose.

"They are not," I replied, lifting my chin. "I would be very grateful if you could announce my visit."

I prepared to step inside the entrance hall, but the butler stood his ground in the doorway.

"The Mr. Tweedles are not presently at home."

I frowned, certain that it had been the Tweedles I'd seen at the back entrance to a nearby estate.

"Are you sure?"

The butler sniffed, pursing his lips. "Quite sure. I am not expecting them back until very late this evening."

"Do you know where they are?" I asked. "I have a few questions for them, and I would like to see them directly."

"I shall tell the Mr. Tweedles that you called."

I stared at him, but the butler didn't appear to be hiding anything. I supposed that the Tweedles didn't confide in their butler as to their whereabouts. I sighed, then nodded.

"I would appreciate it if you would mention Miss Rowntree called on them."

"I shall be sure to pass on that message to the Mr. Tweedles, when they return. Good night, Miss

Rowntree." The butler gave a bow, then closed the door.

I slowly descended the steps and walked back to where I'd left my steam bike in the driveway.

The bike sputtered to a stop and I cursed. I didn't even have to look to know that the engine was out of water. I stopped the engine, knowing that if I pushed it any further, I'd cause damage to its internal workings.

I was almost at the city center, and only a few blocks from home, so I dismounted and started trudging across the cobblestone market place, now empty for the night.

I heard a shout from overhead and looked up. There were figures standing on the scaffolding that wound around the sides of the clock tower.

My mouth fell open, and my heart thudded inside my chest. Without pausing to consider the consequences, I left the bike to stand in the market and grabbed my skirts in my fists, hiking them up enough to run toward the tower.

I'd been waiting for the opportunity to get close to the Pinnacle clock since it started working again. I had to take it.

I put my foot on the rung of the first ladder and started climbing.

I'd reached the ladder leading up to the third level of scaffolding, where I would be able to examine the clock's inner workings up close when I heard a shout.

Without looking around, I gripped the rungs of the ladder and hauled myself up. The wind tugged at the loose strands of my hair, whipping them around my face. It blew up my skirts and petticoats, but I kept climbing.

"What are you doing up there? Stop her!" The voice came from below. I didn't look down. I concentrated on the next rung, then the next, climbing until I was pulling myself onto the third level of scaffolding.

The platform shook as heavy footsteps approached me.

I stood, holding out my hands for balance. I turned towards the clock, and my mouth dropped open.

It was as though someone had taken the face off of a very complex clock, and I was staring straight at the inner workings. I reached out to run my fingers over the parts, moving in regular synchronicity, making time march forward with the precision of an army. It was one of the most complex mechanisms that I'd ever seen.

A man in a worn, dirty shirt, and torn trousers, approached me.

"You cannot be here. This area is restricted."

I kept my eyes fixed on the clock, and gripped the railing of the scaffold, determined that this man would not drag me away. Not before I puzzled out its mysteries.

"What are you doing?" I asked.

"Trying to fix the clock, of course," he answered his tone gruff. He reached out for my elbow. "Really, Miss, I'm going to have to ask—"

"It doesn't need fixing. It's working perfectly well, as you can see." I pointed out, jerking my elbow away from his grip.

The man signed. "That's the problem, Miss. Now, if you'll follow—?"

I leaned forward to get a better look at the mechanisms inside. "Have you worked out what made the clock start working again?"

"Do you know something about clocks, Miss?" the

man asked.

I nodded.

He hesitated, looking over his shoulder. "There are too many moving parts. It's a very complex piece of machinery, and it won't seem to stop ticking—it's driving everyone mad."

"Who asked you to fix it?" I asked, trying to distract the man, as I continued to study the mechanism. I felt for the familiar weight in my pocket and pulled out Mr. Pillar's pocket watch, which. I still had not returned. I flicked it open. It was still working, though I hadn't wound it since receiving it from Mr. Pillar. As I stared at it, I noticed the second hand ticked in exact time with the audible ticking of the Pinnacle clock.

"Our orders came direct from President Rowntree," he replied.

"From the President?" I flicked the lid of the watch shut and shoved it back into my pocket.

"Yes, Madam President doesn't like the ticking any more than anyone else. Now," he repeated firmly, "I'm going to escort you down to the ground, Miss. We restrict this area. Though this clock hasn't killed anyone yet, I wouldn't want you to be the first."

He took my elbow firmly, and this time, I couldn't shake him off. He turned me back toward the ladder.

I glanced out at the city below, and the sight suddenly stopped me in my tracks. I'd been so busy staring at the clockwork I hadn't noticed that I was standing on the top of the tallest landmark in Melfall. From here, the whole city spread out before me.

"I must insist, Miss," the man said, tightening his grip on my elbow. "I'd rather not carry you down that ladder."

25TH AUGUST

"It's your sister."

Chesh spoke as I stepped into the sitting room for breakfast. I was surprised to see him, particularly this early. He pulled out a seat next to him. I stared at him without understanding.

"What about my sister?" I asked.

Chesh's wide smile was absent, as the worry pulled his mouth down at the corners. "She was attacked last night."

I jumped up from my seat. "What happened? Is she all right?"

Chesh put his hand on my arm, pulling me back down next to him. He gripped my hand and held it, looking into my eyes.

"It was a Heart," he said. Moisture welled in his eyes,

and the dark smudges under his eyes stood out in his unusually pale face. "It happened so fast."

"Is she all right?" I repeated.

Chesh nodded. "I distracted it, then got her away. I brought her back here. She's shaken, but not seriously harmed. The doctor assured us that she'll be fine in a day or so."

I stood from the table. "I need to see her," I said, but the sitting room door opened, and Alice came in. Her figure was slumped with weariness, but her lips were pinched together tightly.

"Pearl is sleeping. You can see her later," Alice said, as she sat down at the head of the table.

"Are you alright, Mother? Did you get any sleep at all?"

Alice waved a hand, as though to swat away my words. She looked at Mr. Hopewell, the butler. "Fetch Jack here directly."

He nodded his head and rushed away to do her bidding.

"Those Hearts are a menace, terrorizing this city. I've had enough," Alice snapped, then sipped at the coffee that had been placed in front of her.

Jack strode inside, smiling as he greeted Alice in the same way he did every morning. Alice didn't bother with polite words as she launched into her instructions. "Tell Captain Walsh that every guard is to search for those cursed Hearts. I want them locked up by nightfall—every one. I will not tolerate another Heart attack in Melfall. Do you understand?"

Jack nodded, wide-eyed, then hurried out.

I watched the door close, wondering at the puzzles that nagged at me: the sudden ticking of the Pinnacle clock, the appearance of the Hearts, the rumors of the

Queen's return, the mysterious buying up of the city's blood stores, Raven's plot against Alice. It had to all be connected.

"Mother, I've been thinking..." I started.

Alice closed her eyes and pinched the bridge of her nose. "Unless it's information about the capture of these Hearts, I don't have time for it today."

I pressed my lips together. "No, it's not about that. I... Do you know there are rumors that the Queen is returning?"

"The Queen is dead," Alice snapped. She gripped the side of the table with both hands, her knuckles going white with the force of it. Beside me, Chesh froze. Alice breathed deeply through her nose before she spoke again. "The. Queen. Is. Dead. She has been gone for eighteen years. A few strange occurrences don't change that. I'm trying to govern this city, and the continued repeating of rumors and speculation does not help me hold the city together."

After a pause, her grip on the table loosened. She opened her eyes to stare at me, then caught sight of Chesh, apparently noticing him for the first time. She blinked, and two pink circles appeared at her cheeks. "I apologize for my outburst, Mr. Cheshire. I'm worried about my daughter, and I'm not feeling well-rested this morning. Please excuse my lack of courtesy."

With one final glare in my direction, Alice rose from the table and left the room.

∼

I paced in Pearl's room, waiting for her to wake. After Chesh and I had eaten our breakfast in silence, he'd left to open the shop, and I'd disobeyed Alice's instructions to come to Pearl's room.

I stared at Mr. Pillar's pocket watch, mesmerized by the continued movement of the second hand. It seemed as though it was trying to tell me something, but I couldn't understand it.

As always, I could feel the mechanism working inside it, without looking. There was nothing wrong with it, but I had never once wound the watch—how did it work if the winding mechanism was not required? I'd opened up the watch, studying the inside, but couldn't work out what was supplying the alternative source of energy.

It didn't make any sense. The movement of the second hand moved in exact time with the ticking of the Pinnacle clock, both of them hammering away, as though saying: *think, think, think.*

The answer seemed just out of reach, and my inability to grasp it was maddening.

"Would you stop that? You're making me tired, watching you."

I spun around to stare at Pearl, snapping the watch case closed. Her eyes were open, but she had barely moved. Her long blonde hair was fanned out on her pillow, her pale complexion as soft as the linens she rested against.

"Are you alright?" I asked, coming to her side to perch on the end of the bed as I took her hand. "Are you hurt?"

Pearl nodded. "My head hurts. My back hurts. Everything hurts." She took a trembling breath. "Did they catch it?" Her blue eyes stared deeply into mine. I saw the fear in them.

I shook my head. "Mother has the city guards searching for the Hearts. We'll find them," I said.

"I was going to the salon," Pearl whispered. "Chesh was walking with me. He was looking for you and decided to accompany me. The Heart came out of nowhere. It grabbed me and threw me against the wall."

"Then what happened?"

"I hit my head—everything was fuzzy after that. Chesh was there. He was very brave. He carried me, brought me back here. I don't know what I would have done without him. The Heart might have killed me." Pearl stared out of the window, her expression distant.

My stomach clenched at the thought that something terrible might have happened to Pearl. I gripped her hand tighter, wishing I hadn't been so busy lately, wishing I'd had more time to spend with my twin.

"I'm so glad you're all right," I whispered.

Pearl blinked, as though suddenly remembering my presence. "No permanent damage. I have no idea what I would do if the Heart had done something that devalued my esthetic stipend. It's barely enough as it is."

I bit my lip, reminded of the unbeautiful living in tunnels, and those who sought Wit's help. Scarred, marked, poorly dressed, or simply plain. None of them could draw on the esthetic stipend for their living, either. It tore at my heart that the city ignored them. The fact that my sister had narrowly escaped a similar fate made me feel sick.

Suddenly, I couldn't sit by my sister's bedside any longer. I had to find answers. I looked outside at the long shadows of the afternoon. There was still daylight left. I made up my mind—there was only one person who knew what was happening in this city. I needed to find Raven and demand answers.

I patted Pearl's hand. "I have some things that I need to do now," I murmured. "Do you need anything more before I go?"

Pearl bit her bottom lip, a habit I hadn't seen her do since she was an awkward girl before she'd grown into her beauty. "Pass me my mirror," Pearl said, and pointed to the small hand-held mirror lying on her bedside table.

I did so, then crossed the room to open the door.

"Ivy?" I turned back to see Pearl staring at her reflection in the glass. "Chesh is very handsome, isn't he?"

I frowned, feeling a sudden tightness in my chest. "Yes, I suppose he is."

"You're not interested in him?"

I paused as the tight feeling intensified. Pearl's eyes slid sideways so that she was looking at me from underneath her eyelashes.

"Chesh is my friend," I replied, surprised to hear the plea in my voice.

Pearl smiled, then looked in her mirror again. I stared at her, hesitating, then shut the door behind me.

The sign on the door of *Cappello's Finest Hats* declared the shop open, and the bell tinkled as I stepped inside.

Miss Lapin hurried around the counter and smiled as she recognized me. "Mr. Cappello will be pleased to see you," she said. "May I bring you refreshment before I fetch him. Tea, perhaps?"

I caught a glimpse of myself in the large mirror hanging on the wall. My hair was ruffled, my shirt rumpled, and there were bright spots on my cheeks. I straightened my shirt and ran a hand over my hair, trying to smooth it.

I forced a smile. "Thank you."

Miss Lapin hurried away, leaving me to browse the shop. Not a moment passed before I heard footsteps on the stairs.

"Miss Rowntree," Raven said. I turned to see his sleek, lithe figure descending the stairs with a regal grace. His eyes sparkled, and the side of his lips twitched. "You have returned. I must admit, I thought you might have come sooner."

"Did you miss me?" I said and instantly regretted it.

Raven chuckled. He turned to me, looking me over as though studying me. He was holding a hat in his hands, and he came over to me to place it on my head. I kept still, as his fingers gently brushed my hair.

He stood back, appraising me, lips pursed. "No, not that one, either." He whipped the hat from my head, tossing it onto the counter. "You do intrigue me, Miss Rowntree, but I will find your hat."

I felt warmth rise to my cheeks. "I'm sorry to have disappointed you, Mr. Cappello," I said.

Raven turned, eyes wide. He reached out to put a finger to my chin, raising my face toward him. "I'm not disappointed in you, Miss Rowntree. Rather, I'm disappointed in my own skills as a milliner. Do not be alarmed, I've never shied away from a challenge."

"Here you are, Miss Rowntree," Miss Lapin appeared with a pot of tea.

"We shall take it upstairs, Miss Lapin," Raven said before Miss Lapin had the opportunity to set it down. She nodded, turning towards the stairs.

"I actually came because—" I started, but Raven put a finger to his lips, glancing at Miss Lapin.

He put a hand firmly on the small of my back and guided me towards the staircase. My heart raced as he positioned himself so close to me that we were almost touching.

Upstairs, Miss Lapin set down the tray with a teapot and two teacups on a small table, then excused herself. Raven poured the tea, then offered one cup to me, before settling himself in the chair opposite.

"I've come—" I started, but Raven interrupted me again.

"How did your sister like the hat you chose for her?" Raven asked. He leaned back in his chair, as though completely at ease. I sat upright, rigid, and aware of every muscle in my body. I remembered Pearl.

"Pearl is the reason I came," I said. "Yesterday, she was attacked. By a Heart."

The smile dropped from Raven's face. He leaned forward, reaching across the table to offer me his hand. I wanted to reach out, but I tightened my fingers around the porcelain saucer in my hands.

"Is she...?"

"Oh, yes. She's alive. She's fine—well, she's not hurt, anyway." The teacup clattered as my hand trembled. Raven reached over and took the cup and saucer from me and set it down on the table. Then he knelt next to my chair and took my hands. I startled, instinctively trying to draw my hands away, but Raven tightened his grip. I saw sympathy and kindness in his face.

"Are *you* all right?"

I closed my eyes, as much to stop myself getting lost in his gaze as to remember my mission. I took a breath. "None of this makes sense. The clock, the Hearts, the cogs, the blood bank..." I was rambling. I squeezed Raven's fingers as I opened my eyes and stared directly into his. "Tell me the truth. What's going on in Melfall?"

214

The door shut behind me, and I was suddenly plunged into darkness. Even the darkness outside was softened by the light of the moon. My heart raced as I heard Raven's footsteps behind me. I touched my throat, on the place where I'd dreamed about the vampire bite.

In my dreams, the face had become Raven—or had it always been Raven—I was no longer sure. I knew my blood was pumping through my veins, and Raven could probably smell it from where he was standing.

With his heightened senses, he could probably see the vein pulsing madly. I put my other hand to my stomach, trying to settle the storm brewing inside.

I heard another movement somewhere in the room, but I couldn't see anything. Was it Raven? But he'd been behind me a moment ago. Or was I turned around? My breath caught.

"Mr. Cappello?" I whispered.

There was a scraping sound, and then a flame appeared. It illuminated Raven's face; the tiny fire mirrored in Raven's dark eyes as he stared at me. The light danced, casting shadows across Raven's face, glinting off the pointed fangs as he smiled at me.

I gripped my throat tighter, stepping backwards. Suddenly, I wasn't certain this was a good idea. Something about Raven made my pulse race, and I wasn't sure whether I liked it or not.

Raven tilted his head, as though he wasn't sure what to make of me, then he stepped sideways and reached out with the hand holding the light. Another light caught, and another. In a moment, a chandelier of candles was burning brightly.

The darkness was chased away, revealing a large sitting room. Large leather armchairs faced an unlit fireplace, a circular rug covered the floor, and several paintings decorated the walls, themselves fashioned with wine-red wallpaper. It was a cozy room, comfortable.

I took a breath and made an effort to stop clutching at my throat.

"I apologize. I think I frightened you, Miss Rowntree. I should have warned you that it was dark in here. I tend to forget that you aren't equipped with my eyesight."

I attempted a smile. "Please, call me Ivy," I said, wishing the storm in my stomach would settle.

"I will call you Ivy, as long as you call me Raven," Raven said, and he smiled broadly at me, revealing his fangs again. I sucked in a breath, then tried to act as though it was natural.

"You are still frightened, Ivy," Raven said, frowning. "I thought you were afraid of the dark. Now I wonder whether it's me that you're afraid of?"

I pleated the fabric of my skirts between my fingers and attempted a smile again. "I..." I tried to shake my head. "I'm sorry. It's just that I've never been friends with a vampire before and—"

"And you've been warned about my bloodthirsty ways?" Raven said. His eyes dropped away, and he stared up at a painting on the wall. It was a portrait of a very beautiful woman. She had glossy black hair, piled on her head with curls tumbling down on one side.

"This woman,"—Raven waved towards the painting— "is my mother. She was very beautiful."

"She was," I agreed.

"I told you that my father was a milliner, did I not?"

I nodded.

"My parents were both human. Both born of Melfall,

more than a century ago. They married, they had five children. I was one of them—the eldest and trained as a milliner, to take over my father's business. I had two sisters and two brothers. Even after birthing five children, my mother was very beautiful.

"One day, she caught the Queen's eye. The Queen was a renowned beauty, too. She appreciated the beauty in everything—did you know that? She was the one who set up the esthetic stipend first. She thought beauty should be rewarded. It wasn't long before beauty was the measure of everything. As you know, in this city, it still is."

I swallowed, remembering the poor, unbeautiful people in the tunnels.

"The Queen asked my mother to be among her ladies-in-waiting. My mother couldn't refuse. No one refused anything of the Queen—it could cost one's life to anger her. At first, it was fine. The Queen was demanding, and my mother spent long hours away from us, but we were old enough to fend for ourselves. I was an adult—barely—and working with my father in the shop. My younger siblings were growing up and made themselves useful. They didn't need the constant supervision of our mother.

"One day, when my mother left for work, my father reached out to touch her hair, laughing. He'd found a gray hair among the black, and said that she wouldn't be able to work much longer for the Queen, who wouldn't hold with such imperfection. My mother didn't come back that night. Nor the next." Raven sighed deeply.

"What happened to her?" I asked.

Raven swallowed, unable to take his eyes from the painting, though he seemed a long way away. "I was in the workshop, designing a new hat. Something special

- a surprise for my mother's birthday. I heard a scuffle downstairs. At first, I just thought it was my brothers being foolish. Then there was a scream.

"I ran downstairs to see what had happened. I found my father, and my brothers and sisters lying on the floor. My mother was hunched over them. Blood poured from her chin. When she looked up at me, her eyes were red. All I could see were the long fangs dripping with blood."

I gasped. "She'd been turned into a vampire?"

Raven nodded. "The Queen turned her. She said it was too terrible to think of my mother's beauty fading with age. This way, she would be beautiful forever. When my mother saw me standing in the doorway, she leaped on me with a strength and speed that shocked me. Her fangs were deep into my throat before I knew what was happening."

"But she didn't kill you?"

Raven shook his head. "Maybe because her thirst was already sated on the blood of my father and my siblings. Or maybe because I'd had the foresight to grab a club as I came downstairs. In any case, I survived to become a vampire myself. While the rest of my family perished."

I wasn't sure what to say. I stood, staring at the aloof beauty of the woman and wondered how long it had tortured her, knowing she'd killed her own family.

"Does she live still?" I asked.

Raven shook his head. "It takes a lot to kill a vampire, and it rarely happens, but it is possible." He hesitated. "I killed her. In vengeance for what she did to the rest of my family. It took a long time for me to learn how to do it. During that time, my mother tried to apologize. She tried justifying her actions as driven by bloodlust.

218

She tried to explain that she, herself, was tortured by the lives she'd taken. I wouldn't hear of it. The night I killed her, I swore that I would never again drink from a human. I would neither kill them nor turn them into a vampire. He wrenched his eyes from the painting. "So, you see, Ivy, you don't need to be afraid of me."

He stared at me, his eyes seemed to droop, and they'd lost their sparkle. When he looked at me, it was as though his eyes were pleading with me, vulnerable and exposed. For what? I wasn't sure.

I crossed my arms across my waist, hugging myself, partly to stop myself from reaching out to him to smooth the sadness from his face.

I thought about how close I'd come to losing Pearl, and it tore strips from my heart. Raven had lost his whole family in a moment because he'd been a little too slow to react to their screams. Or perhaps it had already been too late then. How would I cope without Alice? Sure, she was busy with ruling The Forge, but she'd raised us, cared for us, and loved us. I couldn't imagine life without her. I certainly couldn't imagine being so angry with her that I would kill her. Then, the thoughts of Alice reminded me of why I was here.

"You won't harm humans, yet you're planning to attack my mother?" I said.

Raven's mouth dropped open. "What? No—"

"That's why you wanted information about her movements. Dr. Lapin said you needed someone who was close to her, who knew her habits and her whereabouts. That's the real reason you left me that card, isn't it?"

"No," Raven said. He spoke quietly, but that one word was imbibed with so much force that I stepped back. I waited for him to say something more, but as I waited, I felt the truth of it settle in my stomach. Without knowing exactly how, I knew he was telling the truth.

When I didn't reply, Raven let his eyes drop from my face, and his shoulders rounded as he stared at the floor. "This is what you think of me—that I'm a bloodthirsty killer, and a black-mailer, as well?"

My heart tugged, and before I knew it, I reached out for his elbow to stop him from moving away.

"I'm sorry. About your family, and your mother," I whispered. My heart hammered in my chest as I took a step closer to Raven. He lifted his head and stared at me, eyes widening in surprise.

The vulnerability was still written all over his face, but instead of sadness, there was a sense of hope. Standing before me, he didn't seem like a century-old vampire. He seemed like a young man, his confident demeanor stripped away, uncertain about what to do next.

I felt a pull toward him, as though there was a tether at my chest, connecting me to him. The feeling was so strong that I could barely breathe. I took another step to stand in front of him, aware of his body so close to mine.

I looked up, directly into his eyes, tilting my head toward his. My breath caught in my throat, as I realized I'd been in this moment before.

In my dreams.

I almost laughed. I'd been wrong—my dreams hadn't been warning me of a vampire attack but preparing me for this moment.

Without words, I knew Raven had been telling the truth—he wasn't going to hurt me. He wasn't trying to use me to hurt my family.

Raven bent slowly toward me, and his fangs glinted

in the light of the candlelit chandelier. This time, I wasn't afraid of him.

This time, I wanted him to be closer to me.

He hesitated, barely a millimeter away from me. I yearned for the touch of his lips on mine.

I pushed up onto my toes, closing the tiny space, to press my lips against his.

THRONE
OF CARDS

26TH AUGUST

Candlelight flickered from the chandelier that hung above us, casting an orange light over Raven's black hair. We sat on the couch facing each other, the fingers of my hands entwined in his, while I couldn't tear my eyes away from his face.

Around us, the walls were overlaid with dark wood paneling and windows obscured by heavy, embroidered curtains, as though the room was retreating to give us some privacy. Only the glowing embers in the fireplace were a sign of the passing of the night.

He was staring at me with a sense of wonder, and the seriousness was wiped from his expression as he gave me a shy smile.

"When I first sought you out, I assumed you were a rich, spoiled, young lady. When I started to get to know you—when I understood how wrong I'd been—I developed feelings for you, but I never dreamed you might return them." Raven gave my fingers a squeeze as he smiled wide enough to show his fangs. A blush warmed my cheeks, and I leaned forward to lightly brush his lips with a kiss.

"I was afraid of you," I admitted.

Raven chuckled. "I noticed. When did you stop feeling afraid?"

I ran my hand over the smooth leather of the couch as I tried to remember the exact point when my feelings had changed. "I'm not sure," I started. "I feared you, at first, then my feelings became more...complicated. I'm not sure whether I was afraid of you or afraid of my feelings when I was around you."

Raven ran a finger under the line of my chin, turning my face up to look at him.

"Are you afraid of me now?"

With my free hand, I reached forward to brush the strands of hair that fell over his temples. It was so soft, like feathers against my skin. Then, emboldened, I ran my finger across his forehead, down the side of his face, and over his lips. He opened his mouth, showing his fangs, and I touched the tip of one sharp tooth with my fingertip. The point of his fang pressed against my skin, but I didn't push hard enough to draw blood. Raven froze and didn't move until I removed my hand from his mouth and lay it over his cheek.

"If you'd wanted to drink my blood, you could have done it by now," I whispered.

Raven reached an arm around my waist and pulled me closer. "I want you," he said, pressing his forehead against mine and closing his eyes, "but not like that."

My eyes widened at his suggestion, and I sucked in

226

a breath, finding it suddenly more difficult to breathe. Though we'd spent the night together, and into the early hours of the next morning, we'd sat close to each other, touched each other, and whispered in the firelight, but he'd not pushed his advantage over me. He'd been a gentleman.

Raven chuckled. "I can hear your heart racing from here," he whispered, his breath tickling my ear. "Thundering like the hooves of a racehorse."

He shifted away from me, moving only fractionally, but putting space between our bodies. "It is very late. Perhaps it is time for me to take you home. Before day breaks."

"Not yet," I said, and reached out to cup his face with both of my hands. I pulled him back towards me and kissed him. Our lips touched, lightly, then I pressed toward him, taking the kiss deeper. I wrapped my arms around his neck, erasing the distance between us. I teased his lips with my teeth, then ran my tongue over the sharp edge of his fangs. He held himself back for a moment, then his hands were at my waist, pulling me closer so that I was flush against him.

I was breathing hard, my chest heaving against my corsets. I ran my fingers through the softness of his hair. His hands moved from my waist to my arms, trailing his fingertips up them until he reached my shoulders. Then he was touching my hair and running his fingers down the length of my back.

In the next moment, he was pulling away again. Raven stood up and moved away to stand next to the fireplace.

"Ivy," he said, his eyes sliding over to me, pupils dilated with desire. "I should take you home."

I took a deep breath, staring down at my hands as I

smoothed my skirts. Then, teasing, I looked up at him under my eyelashes and bit my lip. The candles had burned down to stumps, and a slither of light peeped out of the edge of the curtains. I frowned.

"Too late," I whispered and felt a stab of disappointment. "The night is already over."

"Spades," Raven whispered, frowning as he looked at the curtains covering the windows. He strode over to flick at the edge of the heavy fabric, making sure to stay in the shadows. "You're right."

Raven held out a hand to help me to my feet. He pressed a kiss to the back of my hand. "My lady," he said, his voice thick with emotion. "I regret that I must let you make your own way home." He squeezed my hand as he looked me in the eye. "Be careful. Remember—the Queen is returning."

My eyes widened as I remembered why I'd come to see him in the first place. "I wanted to ask you about that. About the Hearts, the Pinnacle clock. You said it was connected—"

"It is. The city is awaking and coming alive, like an animal, but, like my own kind, it has no beating heart. I smell the fear in this city, and not only among mortals. Even my kind is afraid, and it takes a great evil to scare a vampire." He ran a finger underneath my chin again. "Be careful," he murmured, then smiled. "But do not be afraid, my love. I won't let anything happen to you."

∽

I bounced into Chesh's workshop on my way home, arriving so early that I arrived before the shop was open. Chesh eyes widened in surprise, then I noticed him quickly run his gaze over me. I was smiling broadly—I'd

228

been grinning since I'd left Raven's house to make my way across the city towards home. When I'd rounded the corner and seen the Emporium, I'd made an impulse decision to stop by and see my friend.

"You wore those clothes yesterday," Chesh remarked. For once, he wasn't smiling. "Are you alright?"

I laughed loudly, smiling so hard that my cheeks started to hurt. "I'm wonderful. This day is wonderful. Everything is wonderful—wouldn't you agree?"

Chesh's frown deepened, and he looked me over again. "Are you drunk?"

I put my hands on my hips and good-naturedly rolled my eyes at him. "Of course, not. I'm just happy. And why shouldn't I be?" I clasped my hands together and looked up at my oldest friend from underneath my eyelashes. "I think I'm in love."

He froze, staring at me with wide eyes. A hopeful expression passed over his face.

"Ivy, I—"

"I know, it's too soon," I went on. "We've only known each other for a week. We've barely spent any time together..."

Chesh's expression darkened. He turned back and slammed one of his tools down on the workbench.

"But he understands me," I continued, barely noticing Chesh's behavior. "He understands how I feel about the aesthetic—"

"Spades!" Chesh spun around. "Ivy, listen to yourself! Your sister is recovering from a dreadful attack, the city is in crisis, and your mother is stressed and upset. Yet, you've been out all night with a man, and now, you think you're in love?"

I blinked, surprised by Chesh's reaction. The smile slipped from my face as his words brought back the events of the previous day. I started to shake my head when he crossed his arms over his chest and glared at me. "You've never spoken of this man before. Are you keeping secrets from me now? I believed I meant more to you than that?"

My mouth fell open. "I have told you about him. Mr. Cappello, the owner of *Cappello's Finest Hats*. I told you—"

"A vampire?" Chesh's mouth fell open. He ran a hand through his hair, making the tight curls stand up on end like the mane of a lion. "You're not serious?" Chesh's expression softened, and he laughed. "You're joking."

I gritted my teeth. "What's so funny?"

"You're not joking." Chesh's face fell again. "What are you thinking? You can't really be considering a relationship with a vampire. To say nothing of the scandal it would cause for your mother and your sister, but the danger you put yourself in..."

"Mr. Cappello is not dangerous," I whispered.

"He's a vampire. He drinks blood—human blood." Chesh turned his back to me again, shaking his head in anger and exasperation. "You told me yesterday that you've discovered a problem with the blood banks withholding blood from the vampire population. Where is he getting his blood from?"

I shook my head, pressing my mouth into a thin line. The fog of a sleepless night started to close in on me, and I couldn't think of how to answer him. Deep inside, I knew I didn't need to be afraid of Raven, but could I deny Chesh's statement? I remembered the reason I'd visited Raven in the first place, but I'd been distracted from finding out. Did Raven have that much power over me?

Chesh picked up a tool from his bench. His head hung low, and his shoulders slumped. I felt deflated at the sight of him, and suddenly I just wanted to be at home. I turned towards the door and pulled it open.

"Wait!" Chesh spun around at the tinkle of the bell over the door. "I shouldn't have yelled at you—I'm sorry. Please, don't go." His footsteps came up behind me and he put a hand on my shoulder to stop me from leaving. I closed my eyes as I felt his hand on the place where Raven's had been, so lovingly, only an hour before. I didn't turn around, but I didn't leave, either. "I've been working on something. Want to see it?"

I took a shaky breath, fatigue folding around me like a blanket, but I didn't want to reject his peace offering. I nodded.

Chesh took my hand and lead me around his workshop, talking ceaselessly about the changes he'd made to his machines. We ended up at the flying machine he'd shown me the last time I'd been in his workshop. He still hadn't been able to get it working, but he started to explain an idea he had about why it couldn't sustain flight for more than a few seconds.

I nodded every time he paused for breath, but barely heard a word of what he was saying.

Chesh's reaction at my good news had wounded me, and the heady excitement I'd felt when I'd left Raven's place had drained away to leave me feeling low, as though I was dragging myself through a fog.

"Ivy?" Chesh asked. He sighed when I looked up. He'd been trying to get my attention for a few moments. "May I take you to breakfast?" he asked. "You look like you're about to faint."

All I wanted to go was to curl up into my bed, but I nodded, then found myself being steered out of Chesh's workshop and towards the nearest teahouse.

~

I pushed at the runny eggs on my plate with my fork, but I was so tired that my appetite had disappeared. Chesh hadn't stopped talking since we'd sat down at the table in the front window. It was a cozy establishment, with lights that hung low from the ceiling, casting spotlights over small tables. A small bunch of flowers in a vase decorated the table between us, and flecks of bright orange pollen dusted the tablecloth, giving off a faint smell of rot.

As he talked, Chesh glanced at me every few moments. The smile was back on his face, but it was forced.

Out of the corner of my eye, I noticed every one of the places in the teahouse was occupied. Each table was laden with food, and people chatted and laughed as they ate. Several tables were being cleared, the food less than half-eaten. Every person was dressed to perfection, with matching hats, coats, gloves, and bags. Once the gloves and hats were removed, I knew they would likely be tossed into the back of the wardrobe— worn, seen, old—never to be used again.

Were any of these people aware of the poverty underneath their city? I imagined the wasted faces of the people in the tunnels, as though they were pressed up against the windows of the teahouse, stomach's grumbling as they saw food go to waste.

A tinkling sound made my head snap back until I was looking at Chesh, who set down his knife and fork on the plate, which was wiped clean.

"You've barely touched yours," Chesh said. He

reached over to touch my hand. I withdrew it from the table and clasped my hands in my lap. A slight frown creased his forehead. "Are you unwell?"

"I'm just tired," I murmured.

Chesh leaned forward. "I would be more than happy to put myself at your disposal and assist you in cleaning your plate." He winked.

I looked down at my hands.

When I looked up at him again, his smile had vanished completely. He sighed.

"I'm sorry for yelling at you," he said. "I'm only worried for your safety."

I shook my head, holding up a hand to stop him. "Mr. Cappello wouldn't hurt me. He's a good man—"

"Vampire," Chesh corrected.

I pursed my lips. "He tries to help people. Did you know there are hundreds of people starving in the tunnels underneath this city?"

Chesh raised an eyebrow, shaking his head. "Even if that's true—which I doubt—"

"I've seen them!"

"He's a vampire," he continued. "He drinks human blood. If you're right about the blood banks, then where is he getting his blood from?"

I started to shake my head again. "You don't know—"

Chesh stood abruptly, skirting the tables around us to walk up to the counter and take a copy of *The Daily Hart*. He sat down at the table again, pushing the plates aside to spread the newspaper on the tabletop. "People are going missing," Chesh said. "Haven't you been following this?"

I shook my head, truthfully. There had been so many other puzzles jostling for my attention that I hadn't kept up with the news as much as I usually did.

"Look—another one today." He jabbed a finger at a small article about a man who had gone missing the day before. The print blurred together as I stared at the words. After a pause, Chesh read it out to me.

"Mr. Gavin Littleburn went missing from his place of work yesterday afternoon. A proprietor of *Littleburn and Co Mechanical Inventions*, the reports of Mr. Littleburn's absence comes after several people were reported missing the day before, and several others last week. There do not appear to be any links between those reported missing—who were taken from districts all across Melfall—and President Rowntree has downplayed the facts, reportedly discouraging reporters at *The Daily Hart* from causing unwarranted fear among the people of The Forge. Investigations continue."

"You don't really think Mr. Cappello had anything to do with this, do you?" I looked up at Chesh. "There's no proof..."

"Vampires are predators. They feed on human blood. If vampires aren't getting blood from the blood banks, they're getting it from somewhere. I'd put my money on the fact that the sudden spate of missing persons reports is linked to the vampires not being able to get blood by legitimate means."

I shook my head again. "He wouldn't..."

"You're an intelligent woman, Ivy," Chesh banged his hand on the table. Several people at neighboring tables turned to stare at us. He jabbed a finger at the picture in the newspaper. "Don't tell me your head has been so turned by this man that you can no longer think for yourself, or even see the evidence in front of your eyes."

I stood, swaying on my feet. I was too tired to think, to argue. "I want to go home," I said, then marched out, leaving Chesh calling after me.

27TH AUGUST

Uninvited, Chesh dumped a stack of copies of *The Daily Hart* on the side table in the sitting room, interrupting my solitude without apology. I looked up from where I was reading, curling up in a large leather armchair, although my eyes had been sliding over the black print without seeing it. Instead, the memory of Raven's face had been interrupting my thoughts all morning.

All morning, I'd burned alternately with desire and, then, with shame as I remembered Chesh's accusation. I couldn't rid myself of the small voice whispering doubts in the back of my mind—that Raven had sought me out, had wanted to know about Alice's whereabouts, had lured me to him, and fooled me with stories. Now I wondered—was he really attracted to me? Or was he the villain that Chesh warned me about? Had he put me under some sort of spell to get closer to Alice? No, I was being silly. Raven might be a vampire, but he wasn't a magician.

Chesh glared at me as he put a finger on the stack of papers.

"The Ivy I know wouldn't have missed this," he said.

"There have been lots of other things going on," I said and crossed my arms across my chest. "The Pinnacle clock, the Hearts—"

"Yes, and for weeks, people have been going missing every day. It started happening just before the Pinnacle clock started working again. Look," Chesh flipped over the first newspaper in the stack. "Mr. Allen Langstaff, master horologist, went missing on 10 August." Chesh passed the article to me, then turned over another. "Miss Gabrielle Larkin, draftswoman, went missing on 11 August."

I found myself staring down at a sketch of a woman's face. The pile of papers rustled, and Chesh continued, tossing the papers into the air as he read through the names and titles of the missing people. The sheets of paper were floating to the floor like snow, covering the plush rug under the armchair where I sat.

"Mr. Mark Maycock, welder, Mr. Joel Wallace, rigger, Mr. Bartholomew Chickering, mechanical engineer, all missing since 13 August, Mrs. Grace Fischer, machinist, Mr. Samuel Cadwell, blacksmith, both missing since 15 August, Mr. Daniel Dorchester, mold maker, missing since 16 August, Miss Emmeline Beard, technical engineer, Mr. James Rexword, mechanic, Miss Emma May Whitten, mathematician, Mr. Byron Day-Forsythe, mechanical inventor, all went missing on 20 August. Mr. Lucius Perch, civil engineer. Miss Peggy Barclay, automotive engineer..."

My eyes widened as I listened to the list of missing persons. I prided myself on being aware of what was happening in the city, and on being able to advise Alice. How had I missed this?

I stood, going to stand at Chesh's shoulder. He flicked over another page, this time *The Daily Hart* edition of the 23 August. "Mrs. Iris Barclay, electrical engineer," I murmured.

"Mr. Clement Hellyar, robotics expert," Chesh said, flicking over the page to the next edition.

"Mr. Tom Griffin, founder," I added.

"Mr. Gavin Littleburn, inventor, missing as of yesterday," Chesh finished.

We both looked at the papers spread out all over the floor. "That's a lot of people," I murmured, frowning as I tried to make sense of it. "Do they suggest a pattern?"

Chesh shook his head.

"Common elements?" I asked, peering at the latest article in front of me.

"No," Chesh replied. "They're from all over the city. They're not friends, nor colleagues, nor acquaintances. Some went missing from their place of work, or on the way to work, or on their way home, or on their way to the shops, or while running errands." He crossed his arms over his chest. "You know the only thing they have in common," he said, giving me a hard stare.

I didn't pick up on the hard edge to his voice as I stared at all of the faces looking up at me. There seemed to be something about the group that linked them, but I couldn't quite see it. "What?" I asked.

"You know," Chesh repeated. "Think about it."

"If you know the answer, there's no need to keep it to yourself," I replied.

"They've all got blood running through their veins."

I froze, closing my eyes. Raven's face appeared in my memory, soft under the firelight, smiling at me. I put my fingers to my lips, remembering the feel of his kiss. I was shaking my head when Chesh's hands were on my shoulders shaking me. "There's nothing else. Nothing else. They're alive. They're people. They're food. That's what they have in common."

"You don't know that," I retorted. "You're guessing."

Chesh groaned. "Even if you think you've stumbled across the one vampire in Melfall who is starving his natural instincts to feed—which I doubt,"

I remembered the look on his face when Raven told the story about his mother feeding on his siblings. "I know he wouldn't do—"

"Even if that's so, you don't think the rest of them are starving themselves, do you?"

"I've been looking into where the blood donated to the blood banks is going," I said. "I think the Tweedles have something to do with it."

"The Tweedles make mischief," Chesh said. "They don't kill people."

"There's no evidence that these people are dead," I said, though my conviction was hollow. "Have the families been blackmailed? Have there been any demands?"

"None, but if they're not dead, where are they hiding?" Chesh said, but he didn't wait for a reply. "Do you know how many people went missing in July?"

I shook my head.

"None," Chesh said. "Do you know how many people went missing in June?"

I stared at him.

"Or May? April?" Chesh raised an eyebrow. "None.

Only two people have gone missing this year. One turned up a few weeks later after mistaking a hallucination-inducing pleasure drug for an anti-aging tonic. He regained his senses somewhere in a small village in the countryside. The other was stabbed in a disagreement over a woman after a number of strong drinks. The murderer hid the body, then confessed to authorities several weeks later."

"What about last year?"

Chesh shrugged a shoulder. "You don't find this suspicious?" He gave me a disbelieving look. "Ivy..."

I held up a hand. "Yes, I think it seems out of the ordinary. I just don't..." *I don't think Raven is involved.*

Chesh rolled his eyes. He gestured towards the missing persons articles with one hand. "Any other ideas?"

I took a deep breath and turned my attention to the scattered papers. They were a mess of sketched faces and text against the background of the shag rug. I bent down to gather them in a pile. "Let's look at this properly," I said and led Chesh across the hall and into the President's Library.

It looked as though nobody else had been in this room since the last time I'd been here, and I cleared away the newspapers about the Red Queen's reign, and spread the articles out methodically in date order of when the people went missing. As I put down each article, I took a good look at the face, read the article over again, and considered the elements—their age, their place of residence, their place of work, trying to find possible links between them.

"There are no children among them," I noted, once I'd spread the papers all over the table. "Nor very old people. These people are all working age."

239

"There's still a wide variation in age," Chesh replied. "Some have barely finished their studies, while others have decades of experience."

I shrugged, not taking my eyes off the articles spread around the table, as though the solution to this puzzle might leap off the pages.

"Did they have any interaction with the Hearts?" I asked.

Chesh frowned. "None of the articles mention the Hearts."

"Yet, the timing is similar." I walked slowly around the large table, looking at the papers from a different angle, as though it might give me more insight into the problem.

I pointed to a face I recognized. Mr. Byron Day-Forsythe. "Do you know him?"

Chesh nodded. "He's a talented inventor—officially one of our competitors, but we studied together, you know." Chesh pointed to another face. "I also know Mr. Littleburn. He's a friend of my father's. He owns a shop selling the gadgets he's invented across the other side of the city. They're both members of the Inventor Guild." Chesh peered at the articles with renewed interest. "In fact, Byron was an apprentice in the Inventor Guild."

I cast him a quick look, then ran my eye over the other professions listed. "Do you think that might be a common factor? Guild membership?"

"Not of one particular guild," Chesh said, but he made a wry face as he conceded. "They might all be members of the United Guilds."

The first hint of a smile touched my lips as a bubble of enthusiasm grew inside of me. "They all belong to professions related to building or inventing things," I said. "Welder, rigger, different kinds of engineers, machinist, mold maker, mechanic, draftsperson...”

There was a moment of silence. I could hear the ticking of the Pinnacle clock in the distance.

“Perhaps we should check the United Guild—they keep all the memberships of the guilds, right?” I suggested. “I’m sure the grandmasters will provide the membership rolls if Mother asks them. We can check these names against them, to see if a pattern emerges.”

Chesh tapped his finger over the sketch of Byron’s face. An expression of indecision passed over his face.

“What?”

Chesh looked up at me. “I’m not discounting the probability that vampires are involved in this...but I have another friend who is apprenticing in the Inventor Guild. Maybe we should pay him a visit? He might be able to tell us something about this that we don’t know.”

∽

“Why are Mr. Day-Forsythe and Mr. Pankhurst members of the Inventor Guild, and you aren’t?” I asked Chesh as we took the steps up to the residence of Mr. Oscar Pankhurst, an apprentice in the Inventors Guild. He lived in a three-story townhouse with large windows decorated with stained glass. The door was set above street level, only accessible by a set of steps bound by an ornate wrought iron railing.

Chesh removed his hat as he lifted a hand to grasp the heavy knocker, shaped in the beaked head of a flamingo pecking at the heavy wooden door. He paused, looking down at his feet.

I frowned. “Your father is a member of the Inventor Guild, and you’re his apprentice. Doesn’t that give you automatic membership?”

Chesh blushed, dropping his eyes away from me, clearing his throat, but he didn't immediately answer. "Yes," he whispered.

"So, why aren't you a member?" I asked. "Don't you want to be part of the Guild?"

"I do," Chesh responded, meeting my eyes again. His eyes were suddenly alight with passion. "I just don't want to get in because of who my father is. I want to be a member because I have a talent for it. I want to prove myself."

"What do you have to do to prove yourself?"

"If your father is not a member of the Inventor Guild, there is a process by which one has to be recommended by a guild member. Then, one has to present an original invention to a panel of the masters. They vote as to whether the invention, as presented, pushes the boundaries of knowledge and technological creation. It's not enough to be able to build things—that might get a person into the Mechanic Guild, or the Metallurgy Guild, but an invention has to be impressively original and useful to obtain admittance to the Inventor Guild."

"You are a good inventor with a flair for new ideas. I'm sure one of the gadgets you've been working on would satisfy their requirements."

Chesh looked down at his feet. "Not good enough. Not yet. I'm not leaving it to chance. I won't take a half-baked invention to the masters. I won't shame my father by presenting something to them that isn't good enough. One only has one chance."

I nodded my head. "Did Byron have family connections within the Guild? Or did he present to the panel?"

Chesh raised an eyebrow. "He didn't say, and I never asked."

242

"Does Oscar?" I asked.

Chesh sighed. "No, Oscar's father isn't in the Inventor Guild. Mr. Pankhurst Sr. is a respected administrator within the First Forge Bank. He heads the division that administers the aesthetic stipend. Oscar was supposed to follow in his father's footsteps and take a career in the bank. Instead, he became an inventor. His father hasn't cut him off, but he's threatened it. I think he's hoping Oscar will come to his senses and return to the family business. Oscar's a genius, though. We studied together. He's a good friend. He's been a good sounding board about...many things...over the years I've known him. I trust him—he'll tell us if there's something going on that we should know about."

Then, without giving me the chance to ask any more questions, he lifted the knocker to bang it against the door.

We didn't wait long before a butler appeared at the door. He wore a smart suit in black and a white bow tie with his hair slicked back—typical of a butler in a wealthy, fashionable family. He looked down over his long nose with eyebrows raised as he waited for us to state our business.

Chesh introduced me, then asked to see Mr. Pankhurst.

The lines of the butler's mouth drooped as he delivered the news. "I'm afraid Mr. Pankhurst Jr. hasn't been seen since yesterday, sir. His parents have just reported his absence to the authorities. They are most anxious for any knowledge of his whereabouts. You don't happen to know where he might be, do you?"

〜

Chesh paced with his fists clenched. His bright golden curls stood on end, and the back of his shirt was untucked, his vest undone, and he'd thrown his jacket over the back of a chair in a most un-Chesh-like manner.

After we politely asked for our condolences to be passed along to Mr. and Mrs. Pankhurst, we had returned to Chesh's home. Like the workshop, Chesh's house was full of inventions. At the door, an automatic butler had seized my hat and coat. A series of pulleys had lit a lamp as we pushed on a door to enter the sitting room. Everywhere I looked, I saw gears, pulleys, and moving cogs.

Chesh hadn't said a word since we'd left the Pankhurst residence, but the energy emanating from him was like heat from an oven.

"It's alright to be worried," I said to him as I watched him stride back and forth across the room. "We'll figure it out."

Chesh spun around. "There's nothing to figure out. You don't want to see the most obvious solution. It's not members of the guilds kidnapping each other—they wouldn't do that. It's the vampires killing for blood. Why can't you see what's right in front of your eyes?"

I stepped back, physically recoiling from the force of Chesh's outburst. "You don't have any proof of that," I said. I tried to keep my voice calm, but even I could hear the hard edge in it.

Chesh threw up his hands. "Is it because of your new boyfriend? What kind of magic does he possess that he's preventing you from seeing what's right in front of your face?"

I reeled back at the sight of bared teeth in Chesh's angry face. It reminded me of Raven's fangs, though he'd never looked so fierce. "He's a monster. They're all monsters. They'd feast on us all if it wasn't for—"

"For who?" I demanded, rounding on him.

"For the fact that they need us to keep producing, to keep their source of fresh blood available."

"Pragmatic monsters, then?" I crossed my arms over my chest and glared at him. Then I saw the tight set of his face and reminded myself that he was mourning a friend. I took a deep breath and dropped my hands to my side. "I'm sorry. I know you're upset about Oscar."

Chesh turned away, shaking his head.

"I just don't understand why you're so fixated on the vampires. What if it's not them?"

"What if it is?" Chesh spun around.

I threw my hands in the air. "What if it isn't?"

Chesh shook his head again, then stepped forward to grasp me by the shoulders. "If I'm wrong, then we will have locked up a few vampires for a few days. If I'm wrong, we'll let them out. If I'm right, more people will die while we investigate far-fetched theories and non-existent patterns. Who else has to die before you'll see the truth in front of your face? Remember the vampire that attacked you in the alley two weeks ago?"

I shivered as the memory of his desperate face flashed into my mind. I pursed my lips but nodded. "That's what they're like when they need blood. That's why they're doing this."

"It doesn't make sense," I started, thinking of how Raven had helped Wit's patients. Then the memory of the vial of black market blood entered my traitorous mind. Where had it come from?

"It makes perfect sense to me," Chesh retorted.

The fight went out of me, like a hiss of steam, and I sank back onto the cushioned armchair in the corner of the room. I thought about Raven—about the glimmer of the candlelight against the darkness of his hair, about the touch of his lips against mine, about the way he smiled at me with the sparkle of hope in his eyes. Then I remembered the secrets he'd held, that he still held, and wondered whether Chesh was right—was I seeing just what I wanted to see?

Two nights ago, I'd felt perfectly safe in Raven's arms. I remembered the dreams I'd had about him biting my neck. The other night, in his arms, I'd thought I'd been dreaming about him kissing me, but maybe I'd been right in the first place. Maybe my dreams were trying to warn me away from his charming demeanor. Perhaps, he liked to play with his prey. Perhaps, he was enjoying some sort of elaborate game, to lure me into a place of trust, before he drank my blood.

I shook my head, pushing away the memories. Raven had, had many opportunities to attack me if that was what he wanted. He might have secrets, but that didn't mean he was a killer.

Chesh knelt down in front of me, a frown lining his face as he gazed up at me. He put a hand on my skirts.

"I'm sorry," he whispered. "I know you think you're in love. I wish I didn't have to tell you, but if you were to go to your mother or sister, they would give you the same advice."

"What advice is that?" My voice cracked as I choked out the words.

"A romantic relationship between a young woman and a vampire man? It's just not...possible. Not in The Forge. Nobody would accept it. It's like a marriage between a beautiful person and an unbeautiful one. It just doesn't happen."

A lump formed in my throat. I looked outside at

246

the bustle of people on the avenue in their bright, fashionable clothes, with their tall hats embellishing perfect hairstyles, and their servants hurrying behind laden with bags full of more purchases of more clothes and hats and other beautiful things.

They didn't seem beautiful to me now. It was grotesque.

It was wrong. All of it.

"Perhaps it's time The Forge changed," I whispered.

28TH AUGUST

I charged into Alice's chambers. "Mother?"

In my hands, I held a piece of paper with the scribbled notes I'd been preparing all through the night, after I'd left a grieving, angry Chesh at his house. I hadn't been able to convince him, but I was determined to convince Alice that the time was right, finally, for The Forge to change.

In my room, I'd sat at my desk, pushing aside the parts of my latest pocket watch as I tried to gather my arguments in writing. Mostly I'd screwed up balls of papers as I tried to marshal my whirling thoughts into a cohesive petition that Alice could consider. Every time I read over my efforts, I discarded them with growing frustration. Eventually, but only after the candles had burned down to stubs, had I reached a draft that I was happy with.

At the doors to her chambers, Jack tried to stop me, but I strode past him and pushed open the doors. I gripped my notes in my fingers, with such force that I was worried I'd tear the paper in half.

I glanced down at the words I'd written, suddenly full of doubts. Would it be enough to change her mind? Or would she dismiss me like Chesh had?

When I looked up into the room again, I came up short. Alice wasn't alone.

She was with Princess Gaia and her bodyguard, both of whom I'd met at Wit's rooms.

Alice's back was to me, but I could tell from the tense set of her shoulders that something was wrong.

"Mother?" I asked.

Alice turned slowly around. In her hands, she held a handkerchief. Her eyes were red, and her cheeks wet from crying.

"Mother? Is something wrong?" A terrible heavy weight dragged on me. "Has Pearl suffered a relapse?"

Alice shook her head. "Pearl is fine." Her eyes filled with tears again as she looked at me.

I nodded towards Gaia and her guard. "Have they upset you?"

Alice sniffed, then covered her face with her hands. Gaia put her hands at her shoulders and urged her to sit down in an armchair.

"Take your hands off my mother," I said, gritting my teeth.

The guard stepped in front of Gaia. He said nothing, but he would not let me come any closer.

"There's no need for this, my love," Gaia said, coming up behind him to put her hands on his arms. I guess he wasn't her guard after all unless it was customary to call guards love in Badalah. By the way he looked at her with adoring eyes, I doubted their relationship had anything to do with custom. She beckoned me forward. "Your mother has something to tell you," she said. Then she reached out a hand and guided me to sit down in an armchair opposite Alice.

"Mother?" I asked.

Alice glanced at Gaia, who nodded. Alice took a shuddering breath, and new tears sprang to her eyes.

"I'm sorry, Ivy, I should have told you this a long time ago."

I pleated my fingers into the fabric of my skirts, waiting. The papers I'd prepared were scrunched in my lap. "What is it?"

"You're not my daughter," Alice whispered.

There was silence for a beat. Then I started laughing. Gaia and her companion exchanged a look. Alice looked stunned.

"What are you talking about? Pearl looks exactly like you. Even if you wanted to disinherit us, nobody would believe we're not blood relations."

Alice folded her hands in her lap. "You don't understand. Pearl is my daughter. You are not."

"But we're..." *Twins. Non-identical twins.*

"I know that's what I told you. I wanted you to feel like you belonged to us. I didn't want you to feel different from your sister. I loved you—both of you. I still love you as though you were my own." Alice reached out a hand to me.

I stared at her, shrinking away. "Pearl isn't my sister? You're not my mother? But..." Words failed me. I didn't know where to start. I stared at Alice, seeing her tear-stained cheeks and downturned mouth, but couldn't comprehend it. I started shaking my head, waiting for

251

them to tell me I'd misheard. I glanced at Gaia, who was watching me carefully.

"This can't be..." I started. Then I closed my eyes and put my hands over my face. The faint ticking of the Pinnacle clock filled my mind and steadied the whirl of disconnected thoughts.

"Ivy?" Alice reached out for me.

I dropped my hands from my face and clasped them in my lap. "Where did I come from?" I asked her, then glanced at Gaia again. "What are you doing here?"

Alice cleared her throat, looking over at Gaia, as though she suddenly remembered that she hadn't made a formal introduction.

"I'm sorry, Ivy. Please allow me to present Princess Gaia and Genie of Badalah."

"Ivy and I are acquainted already, Madam President," Gaia interrupted smoothly. "She is the reason I sought you out. You see, I believe we are somehow related."

"A connection?" I blurted out. "Between you and me?" I turned to Alice. "If Pearl and I are not sisters, what makes you think I'm related to a distant princess?" I stood abruptly. "None of this makes sense. Nothing makes sense!" I looked from Alice to Gaia and back again, then whirled around with the intention of leaving.

"Ivy, sit down," Alice said, "please."

I stopped, looking over my shoulder to see Alice coming over to me. She took me by the shoulders and turned me to face her. Then she took my face in her hands. "Please, listen to me. I will explain everything."

I let Alice draw me over to the chaise. She sat next to me and held both of my hands in hers.

"Pearl is my natural born daughter. As you say, we look very much alike. On the night she was born, an old woman came to my door, holding a baby. You." Alice smiled, and there was a dreamy, faraway look in her eyes, as though she was watching the memories play out in her mind. "She asked me to take you in."

"Was she my mother?" I asked.

Alice frowned, as though trying to remember. "I don't think so. I believe she was the midwife."

I stared at her without really seeing anything. I felt heavy, as though a weight pinned me down so that I was unable to move, but at the same time, it was as though I'd been set adrift. Floorboards creaked as Genie moved closer to Gaia, placing a hand on her shoulder. A bunch of red roses was like a bloodstain on the side table by the wall. The curtains fluttered lightly next to the open window.

"What happened to my mother?" I heard myself speaking, though my voice sounded strange to my own ears.

"She didn't say. She only said you needed a new home, and that it was imperative for the peace of The Forge—for the Twelve Kingdoms—that I take you in." Alice smiled. "In any case, I couldn't have refused. The moment I set eyes on you, I decided you would be the sister that my Pearl would never otherwise have. I decided I would love you and treat you as my own."

"You were a beautiful baby, Ivy. Your eyes had an unusual gold ring around the iris—they still do." Alice blinked and then reached out to stroke my cheek. Then she turned to look at Gaia. "As do Gaia's eyes... It's so rare. I wonder if you two are sisters."

Gaia walked up to me, staring at me. We looked nothing alike. Nothing at all. Where I was fair with green eyes and blonde hair, Gaia had dark skin, brown eyes, and black hair. She was a couple of inches taller than me. Looking at her, I didn't see any resemblance at all. I looked more like Pearl than the princess, but there was no denying the gold ring around her irises. It was identical to mine.

"Did you grow up with our mother?" I asked Gaia.

She shook her head. "I was brought up as the daughter of the King and Queen of Badalah. The midwife brought me to them, as she brought you to Madam President. I loved them, though—I still do. They are still my parents."

I looked at Alice, who had tears streaming down her cheeks once again. She reached a hand hesitantly toward me. "I love you, Ivy. I hope you always know that."

Tears prickled at my own eyes, and a lump formed in my throat. I couldn't answer her. I nodded as the tears spilled over. I reached over to grip her hand, as though it were a rope, a lifeline. Alice pulled me to her, and tears racked my body as I leaned my head against her shoulder and cried, as she stroked my hair and whispered my name, over and over.

"There are others," Gaia said. "Like us."

I frowned. "What do you mean, like us?"

Gaia and Genie looked at each other. "Ivy," Gaia came to sit on the couch next to me, on the opposite side to Alice. I turned my body so that I could look at her directly. "Have you ever noticed anything different about yourself?"

I burst out laughing. "Many things," I replied.

Gaia elegantly raised an eyebrow. "Such as?"

"I don't seem to fit in here—in Melfall. I don't take the aesthetic stipend. I don't spend enough time thinking about beauty and fashion. I spend far too much time making watches, tinkering with machines, and solving puzzles."

"That wasn't exactly what I had in mind," Gaia replied.

"Do you care to be a little more specific?"

Gaia held up her hand, as though she was pointing a finger towards the ceiling. Then, as she watched me, the tip of her finger burst into flame as though her finger was a candle.

"Magic?" I asked.

Gaia flicked her fingers, and the flame went out. "I have an affinity for fire," she shrugged. Then she pointed to her eyes. "Alice has already noticed the similarity between our eyes. I believe our other siblings will have similar eyes."

"Siblings?" I gasped. "I have other brothers and sisters, too?"

Gaia nodded. "There are at least five of us, so far."

"So far?"

"Strange things have been happening across the Twelve Kingdoms. In Badalah, peace came to our kingdom eighteen years ago. My parents married, and they did much for the poor people of the kingdom. Then, recently, things started to change. My father, the king, started to forget who he was. My mother didn't recognize him anymore. *Nobody* remembered who he was anymore. Then he disappeared and started living like a street urchin, as he had been doing before he met my mother. The reason I came to The Forge was to try to find a potion to bring back their memories."

"The Queen of Hearts disappeared eighteen years ago," I whispered.

"She died," Alice said, closing her eyes and going

very still.

Gaia raised an eyebrow, looking at me.

"It's possible, but her body wasn't found," I cleared my throat. "I heard she was—or is—a vampire. If that's true, she would not have been easy to kill."

"Has anything strange happened here recently?"

I looked at Alice, who was rubbing her temples. Outside, the clock chimed, and I noticed the pink and purple hues of sunset splashed across the sky outside. I was suddenly reminded that I'd planned to go to see Raven this evening at sunset.

My breath caught in my throat as I felt myself pulled in two directions. I wanted to get to know Gaia, especially if she might be able to help me understand the puzzles that had been plaguing me for weeks. On the other hand, I remembered Chesh's friend, Oscar. Raven might be able to tell me what had happened to him. I was still trying to decide whether to excuse myself when Alice stood.

"I think I will leave you two to get to know each other better. I would like to check in on Pearl. Please excuse me, Princess."

"Please, call me Gaia," Gaia replied, but Alice was already out of the room.

When the door clicked closed, Gaia turned to me. "I take it that strange things have been happening in The Forge as well?"

I nodded, turning my body towards her again as I made a decision. Starting at the beginning, I laid out the events of the past couple of weeks and detailed the puzzles that had been worrying me: the Pinnacle clock, the Hearts, the problems at the blood banks, the missing people.

"I can't make sense of it," I said as I finished the

story. "Do you know what's been happening here?"

Gaia looked at Genie then, gently, she reached over to take my hand. "I think it's related to what's happened in the Badalah, and other kingdoms. I can't tell you much more than that, though. I have too many unanswered questions myself."

I sighed as the Pinnacle clock struck the hour once more.

29TH AUGUST

Sunlight streamed into the tall windows of the breakfast room. Gaia leaned over the speckled weeper set into a vase in the middle of the dining room. "Everything is so different here."

A red bird was perched on the mantel. It squawked loudly as Gaia reached out to touch the brightly colored petals of the flower.

"Don't get too close," I warned her. "That plant is not only poisonous, but it eats flesh—it will take the finger off your hand if it catches you in its trap."

Gaia straightened, her eyes widening, and she took a big step backward.

I looked at her, noting the way the light material of her robes flowed and her bangles and necklaces jingled as she moved. The silky darkness of her hair fell in braids down her back.

"I've never been out of The Forge," I admitted. "I've never even been outside the walls of Melfall. Is Badalah very different?"

Gaia smiled, and the act lit up her face with joy. "Very different. Our weather is hot, but also very dry. The buildings in our city are not made of grey stone but of red mud-bricks. There are market stalls on every corner, and the air smells like spices."

"Do you miss it?"

The smile didn't leave Gaia's face, but she looked suddenly sad. "I miss my parents. I know they are not my real parents, but they raised me and loved me. I don't like to see my father homeless and forgotten— not after spending so much of the last eighteen years improving the lives of the poor people in our kingdom. Now that he's forgotten, my kingdom seems to have forgotten everything that happened since he took the throne. My people have forgotten their hearts. They don't care about each other anymore. I love them all, but I don't want to see my home like this. That's why I came here—I need to find a way to help my parents and my kingdom get their heart back."

Genie put a hand in the small of her back. She turned to look at him, her eyes full of concern.

"We will find a way," he said.

"Perhaps our homes aren't so different after all," I murmured. "The people of The Forge lost their hearts too—or perhaps that was already happening when the Queen of Hearts ruled—but the poor, sick, and unsightly among our people are banished to starve underground where they cannot be seen by anyone. Where people don't even know they exist."

Gaia watched me with a serious look on her face.

260

"You see them," she said. "It troubles you."

I nodded.

"I came here to find a memory potion for my parents, for my people, but when I met Dr. Lapin, I saw first-hand the plight of the unbeautiful people of The Forge."

The door to the dining room swung open, and Alice and Pearl walked in. Pearl's hair fell in soft ringlets around her face and spilled over her shoulder, but she was leaning on Alice's arm for balance.

A small crease formed on Pearl's forehead as her eyes were drawn to Gaia. She pursed her lips, appraising the princess, then looked at me with tears in her eyes.

"Mother told me," she said. Her lip wobbled. "I can't believe it."

A heavy feeling settled in my stomach. It hadn't occurred to me that Pearl would be affected by this news too.

I went over to her and drew her into a hug. "Nothing has changed. You're still my sister."

Pearl pulled away, glaring at Gaia. "For how long?" she said. Then she shook her head and moved to sink into the nearest chair. Her face was still pale, and the dark smudges under her eyes remained. She was wearing a robe over her underclothes, tied at the waist—she must have felt worse than she let on since it was unheard of for her to receive guests in a less than perfect state of dress.

"Are you alright?" I asked.

Pearl waved the question away, while Nancy, the housekeeper, hurried to pour tea. Alice settled in the seat next to Pearl and motioned for Gaia and Genie to sit down with us.

"How are you finding Melfall, Princess?" Alice asked, after formally introducing Pearl to Gaia and Genie.

"I was just telling Ivy that it is very different from Badalah."

Alice raised her eyebrows. "Is that so? I will admit that I have not visited your kingdom. Matters in The Forge keep me very busy."

"I'm sure. My family is the same. We rarely travel further than the boundaries of our own kingdom. Though I sometimes wonder whether it would be better for our people if we did. Surely, the exchange of ideas and cultures can benefit more than just those of us who can afford to make the journey? I have, during our few days here, seen several things I would like to take back to my kingdom, to show them what is possible."

"What is it that you have found so interesting in The Forge?"

"The hats, of course," Pearl interjected. "We have the finest milliners of all of the Twelve Kingdoms here in The Forge. Why, just the other day, Ivy gave me the most beautiful hat I've ever seen. It is as though it was made for me. There cannot be another one equal to it anywhere in the world."

Gaia gave her a tight-lipped smile. "There are many beautiful things in The Forge, but there are many beautiful things in my kingdom too. Actually, I was talking about some of the inventions I have encountered here. Your subjects are both ingenious and industrious to create things that make people's lives better."

Alice nodded. "Ivy is an example of such creative industry," she said. "She has an affinity for machines— she always seems to be able to make things work when others cannot—"

Gaia raised an eyebrow at me. "Does she?"

"—and she makes the most beautiful pocket watches," Alice finished. She fished out the pocket watch that I'd made for her several years ago. "She made this watch for me. She made one for you too, didn't she, Pearl?"

Pearl nodded. "Mine is the finest pocket watch I've ever seen."

"That is very clever," Gaia said, examining the watch that Alice handed her. "Where did you learn this trade, Ivy?"

A warm, pleasant feeling spread through me at the joy of my sister's compliment. "I don't really remember," I replied. "I just started taking pocket watches apart to see how they worked, then I found I knew how to put them together again. I wanted to understand them. Sometimes, it's as though I can feel their working parts—the way they should be—underneath my touch." I shook my head, blushing. "I'm not explaining myself very well."

Gaia gave me a strange look. "You have an affinity for them? For watches? Or for all machines with working parts?"

"For all machines, I suppose. My friend, Chesh—Mr. Cheshire—always complains that I find what's wrong with them faster than he can. I guess, I just *know*."

"Mr. Cheshire is also very good at inventions, isn't he, Ivy?" Pearl interrupted.

I looked sideways at her, frowning slightly as I wondered at her interruption.

Gaia didn't seem to have even heard Pearl speak. "That's an unusual gift," she said. "What else do you do? Dr. Lapin suggested that you work for the president?"

I swallowed, about to answer, as Pearl rolled her eyes.

"Honesty, I've told Ivy time and time again that she should collect the aesthetic stipend, like every other worthy person in The Forge—but she refuses!"

Warmth rose to my cheeks, and I cleared my throat. Gaia glanced at me, raising her elegant eyebrows.

"It's an old custom here," Alice explained, forcing Gaia to turn her attention to her. "A remnant from when the late Queen reigned. She held the ideal of beauty above all. She rewarded those who were beautiful and punished those who were not. These habits were so entrenched among the people that change was impossible. In those days, I was barely holding the city together. In the absence of the late Queen—who had reigned in The Forge with an iron fist for a long time— the old families vied for power, the vampires killed indiscriminately, and the city was chaos." Alice sighed. "In fact, these days, it seems as though nothing has changed."

"The vampires are not killing indiscriminately," I spoke up, blushing, as I remembered the conversation I'd had with Chesh two days before. "There are problems with blood supply from the blood banks, but I don't think the vampires are responsible for the missing people in this city."

"Missing people? Are they connected with those who have lost their livelihoods because they don't conform to the aesthetic standards of The Forge?" Gaia asked, pointedly.

I shook my head. "I don't think so."

Alice frowned. "What do you mean?"

"I understand there are people there are who cannot collect the aesthetic stipend, and who lose their livelihood because they do not comply with the standards, who can no longer pay their bills. I have heard that these people are forced to hide away in places where ordinary citizens cannot find them."

"Where did you hear about this?" Alice demanded. "I

264

know of no such people."

I cleared my throat. "Actually, Mother, I have seen them for myself. People who are poor, sick, scarred, or disabled. Physically...unbeautiful."

Pearl shuddered. "I'm glad I haven't seen them. They'd give me nightmares."

I glared at her. "They live in tunnels under the city, by the grace of people who try to help them."

Alice's eyes widened. "That can't be possible."

"I have seen them, Mother," I replied. "It's why I've been trying to speak to you about the aesthetic laws—they must be revoked. The aesthetic stipend, too—"

"Don't be ridiculous!" Pearl exclaimed, and her eyes widened with shock at the suggestion. "How would we live without the stipend? It needs to be raised, if anything. The unbeautiful don't have the expenses of keeping up with the latest fashions and styles. They can simply..." Pearl waved a hand in dismissal, wrinkling her nose in disgust. "Anyway, people wouldn't stand for it. They'd rise up in revolt."

Gaia turned a pleasant look to Pearl. "I'm sure a young woman, such as yourself, would find other ways to earn a living. Wouldn't it be more satisfying to earn a wage doing something worthwhile?"

Pearl looked at her with a look of shock on her face. "Earn a wage? I don't have time to work! How would I maintain my image if I had to go to work every day? Mother works herself into the ground. Ivy doesn't spend nearly as much time as she should on her appearance. Sometimes she leaves the house in such a state of disarray that I'm almost ashamed of her."

"Pearl! That's no way to speak of your sister," Alice said. She turned to Gaia. "Are things so different in your kingdom?"

Gaia shrugged. "There are no laws about beauty in Badalah, but we have plenty of poor people. They are not forced into hiding, but they live difficult lives. My parents and I try to help to feed them, to help them, but more should be done. My home is not perfect, either. In fact, I fear things will have become worse while I've been away." She glanced at Genie. "Before my parents ascended the throne, very little help was given to the poor. Petty crime flourished, and ordinary people starved and lived in squalor."

"Do you fear things are going back to the way they used to be?" I asked.

Gaia nodded. "Something is happening there—my parents have forgotten each other, have forgotten how they have reigned for the last eighteen years, and the people have forgotten them."

"That's why you came here, to find a cure for their loss of memory," I said.

Gaia nodded. "I fear there is no cure."

I frowned, glancing at Alice. "Mother, you said The Forge seems to be going back to the way things were before you became President. In Badalah, too, things have taken a backward turn."

Gaia nodded. "I think you're right. There are problems in The Forge, and it sounds like some of these problems were in place long before the fall of the late Queen. As you've said, it's almost as though society is going backward—back to a time when the late Queen reigned..."

"I do try to do the best for my people," Alice said, and I noticed she was sitting stiffly straight-backed on the edge of the chair. Her cat, Young Dinah, was curled in her lap, but Alice wasn't stroking her soft white fur. Instead, her hands were clasped together. "Sometimes, they seem to be children, needing guidance."

"Mother, this isn't your fault," I said. "You work very hard for The Forge. Nobody doubts that."

"Not hard enough, it seems," Alice looked down and pressed her lips together into a line. Her face was pale, and for the first time, I noticed the lines around her eyes.

"You are a good president," I whispered, gathering my skirts to crouch down next to her. I looked up at her, but Alice wouldn't meet my eyes. "You do your best for our people."

"Your daughter is right," Gaia said, her tone softer. "The events of late are not your fault. The problems in The Forge are not rooted here. There are other forces at work. However, now that I have seen the problems here, I don't think they can be ignored."

"You know nothing about life here," Pearl spoke up. She stood, glaring at Gaia. "It's none of your business. You should go back to your kingdom and fix your own problems."

"Pearl," Alice snapped. "That is impolite. Apologize to our guest. Gaia is as good as family here and is welcome to stay as long as she would like." Alice nodded to Gaia. "I mean that—you are Ivy's sister, and you should consider this your home."

"You are very kind." Gaia inclined her head.

Alice turned to glare at Pearl. "Pearl? Do you have something to say to Her Royal Highness?"

I could see by the stubborn set of Pearl's jaw that this was not going to end well. She glared at Gaia.

"Pearl has had a very difficult couple of days," I said to Gaia, trying to diffuse the attention, and the spotlight, from Pearl. "She was attacked by a Heart a few days ago."

Pearl turned her glare on me. I shrugged at her.

"It's true," Alice said. "These Hearts have been terrorizing the city. Between them and the Pinnacle clock ticking again, people are afraid the late Queen is returning. People are barricading themselves in their houses, they're enforcing the aesthetic standards more strictly—just in case the late Queen returns and punishes them. She was a tyrant." Alice sighed. "Perhaps now isn't the time for change. After everything that's happened in Melfall recently, people are too afraid. Pearl is right—they would revolt."

I shook my head. "There's always an excuse not to change," I started.

"There's no need to change," Pearl said, a little too loudly. Everyone looked up to see her glaring at all of us, two bright red spots on her cheeks, and her hands bunched into fists at her sides. "I don't want to change. This is my home, and I like it just the way it is. Her Royal Highness," Pearl sneered Gaia's title, "says that most people in her kingdom are poor. Why should we strive to be like that? Life is perfect in Melfall, and everyone is beautiful and happy and has the time to do what they want. What's wrong with that?" She crossed her arms across her chest, staring at me, then at Alice. She didn't look at Gaia again.

I sighed. "Not everyone is beautiful and happy with the time to do whatever they want," I said as I got to my feet and went over to stand in front of Pearl. I put my hands on her shoulders and looked her in the eye. "You're my sister, and I love you. But things can't go on like this in The Forge."

Pearl jerked away from me, glaring at me with anger sparkling in her eyes. "They could if you would just leave well enough alone." She turned her back and marched out of the room, slamming the door behind her.

I stood, staring at the door for a moment before I turned back to look at Gaia and Alice. Alice stood, and Young Dinah mewled as she jumped from Alice's lap. Alice gave Gaia an apologetic look.

"I'd better go after my daughter. She's having a hard time—after suffering that nasty attack, and now finding out that Ivy isn't her sister after all. It's difficult for her. I'm sure she'll come around." These last words were directed at me. Alice gave my arm a squeeze as she stepped past me and out of the door.

I sighed, then looked back at Gaia. I shrugged my shoulders, trying to find a way to excuse Pearl's behavior, to show my new sister that my old one was a good person, despite her apparent selfishness. Gaia smiled at me, patting the seat next to her.

"You are very different from your sister," Gaia noted. "I was an only child growing up. I always wished for a sister." She reached forward to take my hand. "I think you and I are alike—we see the way the world could be, and we want to help others. You see the problems in The Forge, and you want to make people's lives better. Alice said that you work as her advisor and that you're always suggesting ways to improve people's lives."

I sighed, remembering all of the times I'd tried to take suggestions to Alice, only to have her tell me she's too busy to consider them.

"Perhaps I should have tried harder to make myself heard. My mother is a very busy woman. She doesn't have time to implement change. She barely has time to keep The Forge functioning normally."

"I don't blame your mother. I know from watching my own parents how difficult it is to rule a kingdom. Still, something needs to be done for those poor people living in the tunnels. It's not sustainable for a city to ignore the unbeautiful. People get old; they get sick; they have accidents. Some are simply not born with the good looks that will allow them to live on the aesthetic stipend. They cannot be ignored. This is their home, too—they deserve to live above ground, with dignity, to earn their living as they see fit." Gaia looked at Genie, who had remained quiet during the whole exchange.

"What should be, and what is, are rarely the same," he said in his low, quiet voice.

"Sometimes, our wishes come true," Gaia reminded him.

Genie smiled at her, his eyes lighting up. They smiled at each other with undisguised affection. I wondered how I'd ever seen these two as anything but lovers. "Sometimes."

I cleared my throat. "Fortunately, we're not the only ones," I remembered what Wit had said about Raven, about how he was leading a movement. I hesitated, remembering his inquiries about Alice's whereabouts, and Chesh's suspicions about the vampires kidnapping innocent people for their blood. Then I forced myself to go on. "I know of others who believe The Forge should change—must change—and they've started a movement."

"A peaceful one, I hope," Gaia replied.

I hope so, too, I thought.

30TH AUGUST

"Can you at least confirm these people are Guild members?"

The man standing at the door to the Guild Hall stared down his nose at me. He stood at least a head taller than me and twice as broad, and he was dressed in a frock coat with the emblem of the United Guild embroidered into the lapel. His unimpressed expression had not changed as I'd approached him from the street, with the list of missing persons in my hand.

"Are you a Guild member, miss?"

I shook my head, suppressing a sigh.

The man cleared his throat. "Entry is restricted to Guild members and their invited guests," he said, with as little expression as though he was reading directly from the rulebook. "Are you an invited guest?"

"No," I replied. "As I said, I just want to speak to someone about a list of your members. It's—"

"That information cannot be given out to the public."

I waved the article about the missing persons—the one reporting Oscar Pankhurst's disappearance—under his nose. "I'm simply trying to ascertain whether these missing people are Guild members."

The man looked down at me once more, his expression, no more interested than before. "Are you a member of the city guard?"

"No," I repeated. "But—"

"Then what business is it of yours to investigate Guild matters?"

"It's not a Guild matter," I said, my voice rising with exasperation despite my attempts to stay calm. "These people have gone missing!"

The man pulled at the sleeves of his coat, looking down his nose at me again.

"Then, I would advise you to take your concerns to the city guard and have them investigate."

"But—"

He held up his hand to stop me speaking. "The city guard are the only ones with the jurisdiction to enter the Guild Hall without an invitation. Apart from the President herself, that is."

My shoulders hunched, as a feeling of defeat washed over me. I didn't want to trouble Alice with this until I knew there was something more to it than just a hunch. I sighed and turned away from the man at the doors without another word. As I moved slowly down the steps, the peal of the Pinnacle clock rang in the distance.

I tucked the article into my clutch and hurried down

the steps, remembering my appointment with Gaia—I'd promised to take her out and show her some of the best places in the city. As I stepped back onto the street, I glanced back at the doorman. He stared over my head without acknowledging me at all.

~

"We need to make the people of The Forge aware of the cost of the aesthetic rules to those who cannot comply. We need them to see the unbeautiful in this city," Gaia said, as she and I walked, arm in arm, down the wide Twelfth Avenue towards the wall. I'd taken her to my favorite teahouse, then she'd asked whether it would be possible to see a view of the city from the wall.

Twelfth Avenue was wide and clean. Steam carriages rolled through the streets, and people strolled the footpaths in hats and gloves, carrying parasols to shelter them from the glare of the midday sun.

As we'd walked past the large plate-glass windows that lined the avenue, we'd glanced into shops selling fashionable men's and women's clothes, hats, shoes, handbags, umbrellas, and other accessories. We'd passed several displays of gadgets and inventions— including an automatic kettle-pourer, a robotic butler, a self-ventilating hat with a fan on the front, a machine with footrests, and a chair that promised to exercise legs while seated, a self-lacing corset, boots with springs to cushion the feet and lengthen the stride, a rack that removed hats and coats on entering through a front door. Gaia had exclaimed at them all, asking constant questions as we walked. Then, the conversation had eventually turned to the situation of the hidden citizens of Melfall.

"They're frightened of the reception they'd get," I said, remembering how Mr. Thackery ran from me when I'd approached him. "What if they're arrested?"

"If their numbers are large enough, the officials can't arrest them all," Gaia replied, though she looked sideways at me and an uncomfortable feeling gnawed at my stomach.

"I don't know," I mumbled.

We walked past a beautiful couple, sharing a slice of cake at a small outdoor table on the avenue. They gazed at each other, obviously in love. Raven's face flitted into my mind, the way he'd looked at me when I'd been at his house in his arms. I wished I could introduce him to my new sister. *Cappello's Finest Hats* wasn't far away. I could take Gaia there now and introduce them. But what if... Chesh's suggestions about vampires kidnapping people for their blood sprang to mind again. I took a deep breath—I hadn't seen Raven since that conversation with Chesh, and I felt uneasy. I didn't think Chesh was right, but doubts lurked at the back of my mind.

Besides that, I wondered what Gaia would say if she knew that I was in love with a vampire. She was my sister, but we still barely knew each other. I didn't know how she would react. I continued past the turnoff that would lead me to Raven's shop, and a lump formed in my throat as I silently cursed myself for being so cowardly. I pushed memories of Raven from my mind and concentrated on the problem at hand. "Perhaps we could start a petition for Mother to reverse the aesthetic laws?"

"Would people sign it?" Gaia asked.

"The people in the tunnels would sign it."

"Unless they're afraid of putting their name on paper

and of the reprisals that might come."

"The biggest problem is that no one even knows they're there," I said. "Chesh didn't believe they existed when I told him."

"Would they believe a list of signatures?"

I sighed, and we walked in silence for a moment, before Gaia spoke again. "It's a good idea," Gaia said, "but I think we need some way of making the ordinary citizens of the city see what the aesthetic laws have done to people who can't comply with them. They need to see, with their own eyes." A line formed between Gaia's eyes as she considered the problem. "What about a parade?"

I blinked, surprised at the suggestion. "A parade? Of whom?"

"The people hiding in the tunnels. The unseen, the unbeautiful. We need the people living here to acknowledge they exist—what better way than to march them through the city? We could take the march down this very avenue—then everyone in the shops and restaurants would see them. We could seek support along the way by asking onlookers to sign a petition." Gaia smiled, her eyes dancing with excitement as she turned to me. "We could go all the way to the President's Palace and present the petition to Alice."

I tried to picture the scene of the people in the tunnels coming out of hiding to march through the most populated parts of the city.

"It could work, I suppose," I said, doubtfully, wondering what reaction they'd get from the beautiful citizens who lined the avenues to be seen at their best. What was the worst that could happen? "If we can get them to come. I certainly don't have any better ideas."

～

"We could start the march here," I pointed to a spot on the map. "Then we could march down Twelfth Avenue, through the market place, and along Sixth Avenue to end up at the gates of the President's Palace. We could publicly present a list of demands to Mother about changing the aesthetic laws."

Gaia and I pored over the maps in the President's library. She was nodding. "When shall we do it?"

I shrugged. "As soon as we can, I think. No time like the present."

"Give your mother some warning. No leader likes to be taken by surprise. She certainly won't expect a crowd of unbeautiful at her gates demanding changes to the laws."

I nodded straightening. "I'll speak to her."

"We will also need to—"

"Mother? Ivy? Where are you?"

Pearl's voice wafted through the door to the library. I stepped away from the maps and opened the door to step out into the hallway. Black and white tiles arranged in a checked pattern along the floor, and a large staircase curled up around the walls to a mezzanine landing on the next floor. The banister was carved with cats— sitting, lying down, walking, pouncing, and watching. A grand painting of a younger Alice, when she was first sworn in as President, with her old cat, Dinah, in her arms.

At the far end of the hallway, Pearl was standing with her back to us. In one hand she held a parasol, and there was a light shawl around her shoulders, as though she'd just come in from outside. Her other arm was looped through that of a young man with a familiar figure. My eyes widened.

On the mezzanine level, a door opened upstairs, and

276

Alice appeared on the upstairs landing, wearing a lace-trimmed dress in her favorite color—blue. Her blonde hair was pulled back from her face, and the glasses perched on her nose suggested she'd been working.

"What have I told you about yelling through the house?" she said, a note of irritation in her voice. Her shoes clicked the tiles as she started down the stairs, one hand sliding down the banister as she went. "What is it, Pearl?" she asked. "Are you well?"

Pearl turned around. As she did so, she dropped the arm that was linked to the young man, only to grasp it again when she'd spun around. She was beaming. I found myself smiling in response to the look on her face.

Then her eyes drifted to the young man on her right, and the smile fell from my face.

Pearl beamed up at Chesh, who patted her hand as it rested in the crook of his elbow. He glanced at me, sideways, but didn't meet my eye. I took a step backward, putting up a hand to rest it on the wall.

"We're absolutely wonderful," Pearl replied. "Aren't we, my darling?"

I stared at Chesh. He'd never shown any interest in my twin sister before—had he?

"Of course," Chesh replied. "It's a marvelous day, and I have one of the most beautiful women in The Forge on my arm, what could be better?" His eyes darted toward me again, and I could have sworn I saw a tint of pink color his cheeks.

"Mr. Cheshire?" Alice looked confused, staring at the couple in front of her, before casting a glance at me. She descended the last steps to come to stand in the hallway. I crossed my arms across my chest, then dropped them at my sides, before fiddling with my hair with one hand. I couldn't stand still. I couldn't meet the eyes of anyone in the hall.

"What a pleasant surprise," Alice continued.

"Chet and I have been on the loveliest outing," Pearl said, and as she did so, she flicked her fan open. "He took me to the most enchanting teahouse, and later this evening, he'll be taking me to the theatre to see the latest production of *Behind the Looking-glass*."

"The theatre?" I said, almost choking on the words. I glared at Chesh. "You don't like the theatre."

Chesh turned a deeper shade of pink, but it didn't seem like Pearl had even heard me. Alice wrung her hands, looking at me, then to Pearl, as though she couldn't decide whether to be happy or upset by this turn of events.

"This afternoon, Chet showed me his latest invention. He's so clever! You never told me how clever he is, Ivy," Pearl gushed.

I felt the words like a punch to the stomach. He was going to show Pearl his latest invention? He'd always shown me his inventions before anyone else. This hurt more than all of the disagreements we'd had over the last couple of weeks.

Chesh dropped his eyes to the floor, turning his face away from me. I clenched my fists and straightened my shoulders. Alice gave me a look of pity.

"I hope you have a lovely time," I said, clipping my words as I spoke. "I'm spending the evening with my sister."

This time Pearl did hear me. Her smile wavered, and I saw a sudden look of confusion in her eyes, as though she was lost. Then she fixed her eyes on Chesh again and patted his arm.

"I'll need time to change, of course," Pearl said.

Chesh dipped his head, then lifted her hand to brush a kiss over her knuckles. "I shall also change. I would not wish to shame you by appearing at the theatre in my day clothes. I will call again in a couple of hours. Until then, my love." Chesh bowed.

Pearl beamed at him again. She dipped a curtsy and fluttered her fan as she looked at him from under her long eyelashes. She was the picture of beauty, of a young woman in love.

Chesh turned to acknowledge Alice, then his eyes flickered towards me again. I glared at him. He cleared his throat, put his hat on his head, and turned to leave, his shoes rapping on the polished floor as he walked.

When the butler closed the door behind Chesh, Pearl spun in a little circle and squealed. "Isn't he wonderful?" she said, though she spoke to no one in particular. Without waiting for an answer, she ran up the stairs to her dressing room.

"Ivy?" Alice asked when Pearl's door closed behind her. "Are you alright?" She took a step toward me.

I started to shake my head. Gaia stepped out from behind me, and I saw her figure in the corner of my eye. She put a hand out to rest lightly on my arm. When I turned to her, I saw concern in her eyes, but there was a soft smile on her face too.

"I am very pleased to be spending the evening with you, too, sister."

A lump rose to my throat, and I took her hand and squeezed it.

∽

I undid the buttons on my vest, shrugged it off, and threw it over the window seat, then stepped out of my skirts. Wearing only my underclothes, I flopped down on my bed, staring up at the curtains draped over the four posts of the canopy. The folds of the light material fluttered in the warm evening breeze coming in from the open shutters. I let my eyes blur, focusing on nothing, as my mind turned inward, ruminating on the events of the day.

Gaia and I had talked and planned during the afternoon and into the early evening, but I'd kept my eye on the carved clock on the mantle in the dining room. When I knew the theatre would be coming out, I made my excuses to retreat to my bedroom. I didn't want to be downstairs when Chesh and Pearl returned. I didn't want to hear about their evening together.

There was a sour taste in my mouth as I deliberately pushed aside thoughts of my twin and my best friend. Instead, I considered the proposal that Gaia and I had worked on over dinner. Alice hadn't joined us, as she'd taken dinner in her office, but it had given Gaia and me time to work on the details of the proposal that we would put to Alice when it was ready.

We would need not only Alice's blessing, but the march also relied on Raven's support, or I didn't think we would get the people in the tunnels to show their faces. My mind turned to the dark-haired man who haunted both my dreams and also most of my waking thoughts. I still hadn't returned to see Raven since the night of our kiss. My fingers absent-mindedly brushed over my lips. I took a deep breath and lay my palm over my forehead and the other hand on my stomach.

I'd told Raven that I would come to see him again, but that was days ago. Why hadn't I gone back to see him? I told myself that I'd been busy, and it was true. Since I'd last seen Raven, I'd discovered a sister and a past that I never knew I had. Still, deep down, I knew it wasn't just that. Chesh's accusations about Raven and the vampires being responsible for the people who had gone missing had affected me, nagging at me every time my mind turned to Raven. I couldn't deny that the circumstances fit the explanation.

If I faced Raven, I'd have to confront him with my doubts. Deep down, I didn't want to know the truth, just in case, Chesh was right. Then what would I do? My head said I would have to turn him over to the authorities. My heart refused to believe it.

I closed my eyes, trying to quiet my thoughts, with little success.

A sudden rapping on wood made me sit directly upright in bed. There was a shadow at the window sill against the inky night sky. Raven's pale face shone in the moonlight, staring at me, unsmiling.

"Ivy?" he said, his voice was deep and throaty as he uttered my name. My breath caught in my chest. I hastily grabbed a robe and pulled it around myself.

"Raven," I replied, standing next to the bed, one hand on the nearest post. Drawn to him, I held onto the bedpost like an anchor to stop my feelings from betraying my reason.

Raven smiled but didn't make any attempt to come inside. There was a hesitant smile on his face, as though he wasn't confident of his reception. I took another step forward.

"What are you doing here?"

Raven cleared his throat. "I'd hoped you would come to me," he admitted. "The days were endless without you. When night fell tonight, and still you didn't come, I decided I couldn't wait any longer."

I nodded, then cocked my head to the side. "Why

are you on the window sill? Why didn't you come to the door?"

Raven shrugged. "I saw the light in the window. I sensed you in here from below. I didn't want to wake the household. Honestly, I didn't know whether you'd told your family about me." He raised an eyebrow, and my cheeks warmed.

I waited for him to move into the room, but he remained perched on the sill. "Are you coming in?"

This time it was Raven's turn to blush. He cleared his throat. "You need to invite me first," he replied. "Vampire, remember?"

My eyes widened slightly. "Of course, please..." I gestured for him to enter.

Raven shook his head. "It's not enough. You need to say it."

I cleared my throat. "Please come in, Mr. Cappello." There was a smile on my face as he entered, and my heart skipped as he stepped inside.

He held his hands behind his back, and as he stepped toward me, he brought out a hat. A molded felt bowler hat, with a large ribbon and flower detail tied around the base, flowing into a ribbon and lace train falling down my back.

He touched me, a brief touch under my chin with one finger to lift my face towards his. He studied my profile with a studious expression.

Several moments passed, then he pursed his lips and whipped the hat from my head. "No, not that one, either." Raven sighed. "You continue to elude me, Miss Rowntree."

I smirked at him. "Have you ever had such a complicated customer?"

Raven raised one eyebrow. "Not one so complicated,"

He gently took my hand in his and raised my knuckles to his lips. "Nor so beautiful."

"You tease me, Mr. Cappello," I said, but I squeezed his fingers, enjoying his attention. A smile spread across his face, and he let the hat fall to the floor. He reached for my other hand and held them both in front of his chest, as though pleading with me.

"Tell me," Raven whispered. "Why didn't you come back? I've done nothing but think about you. Did you think about me?"

A lump formed in my throat. "Yes," I whispered.

"So, why didn't you come?"

A flush spread over me, and I pulled my hands away from Raven's grip. He let them go without protest.

"Tell me."

I took a deep breath. "I... heard reports about people who have been going missing in Melfall. I didn't think... but the timing..." I pressed my lips together, then put a hand to my flaming cheeks.

There was a moment of silence. "You think I'm responsible for those missing?"

I swallowed.

"You think I drank their blood? Killed them?" Raven didn't raise his voice. His eyes became sad, and part of him retreated from me, although he didn't move at all.

I waited, hanging on his response, but Raven didn't say anything. He just looked mournful.

"Did you?" I whispered; the words escaped my lips before I could bite them back. "Or...maybe... one of the other vampires?"

"Does it matter?" Raven whispered. "You think I'm a monster."

I started shaking my head. "I don't think you are a monster," I said, then I steeled myself for what I needed to ask, taking a deep breath. "I saw you with a vial of blood. Black market blood. You didn't get it from the blood banks. So..."

Raven looked down at his hands. "You think I got it from those people who went missing?" He turned away from me then and went to stand by the window, looking out over the rooftops of the city and the stars in the night sky. In the distance, I could see the face of the Pinnacle clock standing proud and tall in the center of the city. In the silence, I heard it ticking, like a heartbeat.

"I tell you truly—I don't know what happened to them, though I am as worried as you are. Do you believe me?"

The lump in my throat persisted for another moment, but as I saw the pain on his face, the doubts drained away, and a sense of relief lifted the load off my shoulders. I nodded.

"When did you see me with a vial of blood?"

"At the apothecary. It was before that night I followed you."

Raven nodded. "I can explain that. Why don't we sit?" He motioned with his hand, making a motion for me to sit on the bed. I looked at it, but it felt too intimate to sit on the bed with Raven in my room. I walked over to the small work table instead.

Raven noticed it for the first time. "What is this?"

I looked down at the tiny wheels, springs, and gears spread across the table. "I'm making a pocket watch for my new sister."

Raven frowned. "You have a new sister?"

I laughed. "Yes." I slipped my magnifying goggles onto my face and picked up the work I had done so far. "Look," I laid it out on my hand. When I looked up at

Raven, his eyes seemed really large as they stared at me. "Sorry," I said, and pulled the goggles off again.

Raven shook his head. "No, keep going. In fact, keep working on that watch. I'll tell you why I had a vial of blood, but do you have a sheet of paper?"

I got up from my seat and brought him a slip of paper. "What for?"

"If I tell you, it will ruin the surprise."

"I don't understand," I said, still standing as Raven took the leaf of paper from my hands.

"You will. Sit there," he instructed.

I sat down at the dressing table that functioned as a workbench and picked up the half-made pocket watch again.

"As you know, I help Dr. Lapin find patients so he can heal the ill and injured in Melfall," Raven started talking. He glanced at me, then leaned the paper against the wall and started making markings with some quick strokes. His eyes darted from me to the paper, then back again.

I stared, noticing the look of concentration on his face as he sketched something I could not see. I leaned forward, craning for a view of the picture. When he noticed me looking, he waggled a finger at me, then pointed to my workbench. I suppressed a smile, then pulled my goggles over my eyes again and stared at the parts scattered over my bench, trying not to be distracted by the vampire on my window seat.

"Dr. Lapin is kind enough to charge people only what they can afford to pay," Raven said, still drawing. "Unfortunately, most of the people he treats cannot afford to pay anything for his services. Dr. Lapin doesn't lead a lavish lifestyle, but he would find himself as destitute as those people dwelling in the tunnels if he didn't find a way to earn an income."

I frowned. "He mentioned that his wealthier clients were not willing to be treated by him when he treated the poor alongside them."

Raven nodded, glancing at me again, then turning his attention back to his sketch. "He no longer keeps the rooms where he used to treat his old clients. It became too expensive. I had been working with Dr. Lapin for some time when the blood banks stopped supplying Melfall's vampires with blood to quench their appetites."

"As soon as I knew what was happening, I feared for my kind. If they couldn't quench their thirst legally, I knew it would only be a matter of time before people would start dying. Then, no amount of money would keep us from the citizens' vengeance. There is little enough goodwill between the vampires and humans in this city."

"With the number of people going missing, some people have leaped to that conclusion already," I interrupted, thinking of Chesh.

Raven nodded. "I feared as much." He leaned back, holding his sketch up to the light of the candle.

"Are you going to show me now?" I asked, looking up at him.

Raven shook his head, tucking the piece of paper into an inside pocket of his coat. "I will show you the finished product."

"A hat?" I asked.

"You shall see," Raven replied. He sat on the window seat, leaning back against the windowsill. The pallor of his skin contrasted with the darkness of the night sky outside. "Now, I was telling you about the blood trade. When I found out about our supply problem, I worried about it for a few days, before seeking out Dr. Lapin. I proposed a trade for his clients who could not pay his bills in coin."

I fixed one of the small wheels into place with a set of tweezers. It was such fiddly work. When I was done, I looked up at Raven again, and his face bulged with the effect of the magnification of the goggles.

"And that was?"

"I knew vampires would pay for fresh blood. I also knew Dr. Lapin's clients couldn't pay for the treatment they were provided. I asked Dr. Lapin to set up a trade—their blood as payment for his services. The vampires then paid him for the blood. I deliver the product and provide payment to Dr. Lapin."

"Does that make Dr. Lapin's patients sick?" I asked, feeling as though this situation was slightly unethical.

"Dr. Lapin takes blood from a patient once they've recovered, or from a willing family member," Raven replied.

"Are Dr. Lapin's patients happy for their blood to be used in this way?" I asked, still feeling uneasy.

"Actually, yes," Raven said, though he seemed a little surprised himself. "Apart from the needle used to draw the blood from their bodies, they do not seem to notice the small amount of blood that Dr. Lapin takes from them. In fact, they are pleased to have a way to repay Dr. Lapin for his services. You might be surprised, but most people—even the poor—would prefer to pay their way, rather than take charity from someone else."

"Everybody benefits," I murmured, setting my tools down on the table again. I removed my goggles and set them down too. Then I got up and went over to sit next to Raven on the window seat. I sat close to him—so close that our knees were almost touching, but not quite.

A sudden energy buzzed between us, a sort of magnetism calling our bodies together.

Raven looked sideways at me. "Did you really think I had killed those missing people?"

I shook my head. "No, but when Chesh suggested it, I couldn't get the idea out of my mind."

"Mr. Cheshire Jr.? Your friend?"

I nodded.

"Is that why you've been avoiding me?" Raven frowned.

I hesitated, then looked up at Raven. "Not the only reason, but... yes, I suppose so."

"What was the other reason?"

I brightened, the smile coming unbidden to my face once more. "I discovered I have a new sister."

"The president is pregnant?" Raven asked, his eyes widening in surprise.

"No." I laughed as I shook my head. "As it turns out, Mother is not my mother—not really. Pearl is not my real sister, either. A woman—a princess—arrived here a few days ago. Her name is Gaia, and she's my biological sister. We've spent some time getting to know each other over the last few days."

"And?"

I looked down at my hands, clasped in my lap, and smiled. "We have a lot in common."

Raven smiled, gently taking my hand. "You both make pocket watches?" he guessed.

I shook my head. "No, but we're both troubled by the fate of the people in the tunnels. We want to help them. We've decided to organize a march, to force the people in this city to see the people who are living in hiding in the tunnels, and to petition Mother to change the aesthetic laws."

288

"A march? Through the city?"

I nodded, twisting my body around to face him. "I was going to come to see you about it, actually. I need your help convincing the people to march. Do you think they'll do it?"

The excitement of the idea bubbled inside of me again, but Raven didn't seem to share my enthusiasm.

The smile slipped from my face. "Don't you like the idea?"

Raven put his hands in his pockets. "Do you really think it's necessary? Why can't we just speak to the President? Surely we can petition her for changes without the need for a march?"

"What's wrong with a march?"

"Your mother could change the laws without a march."

"People in the city don't believe the people in the tunnels exist. A march would—"

"These people have been forced out of the public eye. They have been ridiculed enough." Raven was shaking his head. "Making them march...Don't you think it will be like putting them on display as though they're curiosities to be stared at? They'll be jeered at, mocked, maybe even stoned. This city is their home, they should be able to enjoy it like every other citizen. That's why the President must change the laws."

I sighed, closing my eyes. "Mother can't just change the laws on a whim."

"Why not?"

"She's not the queen."

"She's the ruler of The Forge. If you asked her—"

"Mother needs to see the people in the tunnels for herself," I interrupted.

"If we spoke to her, told her about them, then she'd

know. If you don't want to be the one to tell her, then let me. I'm not afraid to tell her the truth about what is really going on in Melfall."

I pulled my goggles off my face and crossed my arms across my chest. I remembered Wit said Raven had been looking for me, even before he'd left that card for me at *The Tea Party*.

"Is that the reason you're here? So that I will introduce you to my mother?" I glared.

Raven froze, a guilty look passing over his face.

My stomach dropped, and my cheeks blushed, red and hot. Raven held up his hands as though in surrender.

"At first—yes, that's why I left my card at your table. I wanted to find a way in to speak to the president, to find a way to plead for the people living underground." Raven gave his head a little shake. "Then I got to know you, and you surprised me. That's why I'm here—to be with you. But the people living in the tunnels still need help. The President could change their lives with a word."

"It's not that I don't want to help, but I know it won't work."

"But—"

"Mother is afraid the people will revolt against her. When she first became president, The Forge was in chaos. Recently, with the people's concerns about the Hearts and the rumors of the return of the Queen, the chaos is again bubbling just below the surface. The aesthetic laws are entrenched, and many people earn their living from the aesthetic stipend. Mother is afraid that if she changes the aesthetic laws, people will move against her. She doesn't want to disrupt the peace in Melfall."

290

"The people hiding in those tunnels are her people too, whether she likes it or not."

I sighed. "I know that, but Mother doesn't. If she *sees* them for herself, she will feel differently; I'm sure."

Raven stared at the other side of the room. By the small wrinkle above the ridge of his nose, between his eyes, I could tell he was thinking. After several moments of silence, he nodded. He stepped over me and took my hands, squeezing.

"Perhaps you're right. The people have been hidden for too long. Out of sight, out of mind—as the saying goes. Still, the idea of a march makes me uneasy."

A familiar laugh wafted through the open window from outside the front entrance below.

Raven raised an eyebrow.

"It's Pearl," I replied. With Raven sitting next to me, I was less troubled about the idea of Pearl and Chesh enjoying each other's company as a couple. "She went out to dinner and the—"

Raven froze, then his eyes widened, and a small smile appeared on his lips.

"Dinner," Raven echoed. His smile broadened as he turned to me, taking my face in his hands and pulling me forward for a quick kiss. "That's it!"

I blinked at him, part of me wondering what he was talking about, while the other part relished the jubilant look on his face. His eyes danced, and he smiled wider than I'd ever seen.

"What is it?" I asked. "What are you talking about?"

"Forget the march," he answered. "I've got a better idea."

31ST AUGUST

I put the pen back into its holder and blotted the paper. I'd finished writing my report on the blood banks that Alice had requested. Still, it felt unfinished. Someone was taking all the donated blood, but I hadn't found out who it was or why they were doing it.

My nerves jingled at the promise of the night ahead. I stood abruptly, unable to sit still, and paced around my bedroom. I couldn't stay here all day, fussing over my hair and clothes and preparing for the night ahead. The wait would drive me crazy.

Perhaps, I had time for one last attempt at finishing my report properly.

I crouched at the base of a nondescript wooden fence near the gate where I'd seen the carriage enter with the day's stock of blood. There was nothing special about it at all, neither the fence nor the gate—the two were held together by old nails and a rusty latch.

The sun beat down overhead, and I repositioned my hat to provide some shade over my face. It would be hours before the carriage came past again, but I would need to be home by then to meet Raven.

There was only one thing for it.

I looked left and right, then, seeing nothing, stepped up to the fence and stood on my tip-toes. The fence was too high, and I couldn't see over it.

I reached up, straining to get my fingertips over the edge of it. I was just a stretch away from getting a grip. I jumped, getting a hand on the top of the fence, but couldn't hold on, coming away with a painful splinter in my forefinger.

I sucked on my finger as I examined the gate. I tried to force it open--the latch was rusty but unfortunately, solid. It held fast.

I heard people moving around inside and took several steps backward to conceal myself behind the fence again.

I squeezed my hands into fists, frustrated at being so close but unable to find out what was happening on the other side. I crouched down, gathering my skirts, and crawled along the bottom of the fence to see if I could pry a board loose. I tested them, pulling at them, one by one.

Finally, about halfway along, I found a rotten board and pulled with all of my strength.

With a creaking and cracking sound, the plank broke away.

I froze, certain that someone must have heard me. Pressing my back against the fence, I didn't dare even to breathe. I waited for the cry of discovery.

It didn't come.

Finally, I couldn't hold my breath any longer. I sucked in several lungfuls of air, then crouched down again and peeped through the gap I'd made in the fence.

A stack of crates towered on the other side of the fence, and I couldn't see past it.

I paused a moment, then unpinned my hat and shrugged off my jacket, leaving both in a pile outside the fence. Without dwelling on the grass and mud stains I would surely get on my shirt and skirts, I lay flat on my stomach and wiggled through the gap.

The jagged wood scraped down my back, but my shirt took most of the damage. On the other side, there was barely any room, but I managed to crawl into a squat to peek into one of the crates.

I frowned. The crates looked exactly the same on the outside as those that had stored the blood in the blood banks. On this inside, though, there was no blood.

A jumble of cogs, gears and other metal parts, all crowded together like scraps.

I looked around. There were crates stacked all over the small area that stretched between the fence, the driveway, and a wooden building. It didn't have enough windows for a residence, but from the look of the smoke billowing from the chimney, it could be a blacksmith's forge.

I scooted around the crates, edging closer. A door opened, and somebody went inside. Through the open door, I glimpsed the white-orange glow of heated metal.

I crept closer, cautiously, keeping my eyes on the inside of the shed, moving from one stack of crates to the next.

The squeal of ungreased metal rang out, and I dropped to the ground, panting. It was the sound of the gate opening.

A steam carriage came through the gates and stopped on the driveway, near the open door. The carriage door swung open, and a figure stepped out, closely followed by another, identical to the first.

I didn't need to go any closer to recognize them. The Tweedles.

Then someone else was bundled out of the carriage. A man stumbled, blindfolded, before being pushed roughly into the shed.

I inched forward to get a better look, but a shout brought the Tweedles directly back out again.

Someone came running up the driveways, holding something.

My hat and jacket.

Instantly, the Tweedles started issuing orders, and several people appeared from inside the building, spreading out to search around the stacked crates.

I gasped, then started crawling away, keeping low to the ground. I retraced my steps to flee back to the hole in the fence and dove underneath.

The sharp edges of the wood scratched my back as I pulled myself back into the lane, then pushed to my feet and started running.

∼

The street lamp ignited with a hiss, casting a glow over the lamplighter's face as I walked past. In this part of the city, the lamps looked like phoenixes who rose every night in the fire, only to be extinguished again at

296

dawn. I stared up at the majestic bird wrought in glass, the flame dancing inside it. The lamplighter stepped down from his ladder, tipped his hat to me, then swung his ladder over his shoulder to move along to the next lamp on the street.

I waited for him to move along, then swung open the wrought iron gate, and took the steps to the door two at a time. The lamplighter didn't look back as he lit the next lamp on the street. I raised the knocker, in the shape of a top hat, and let it land on the door with a sound that pierced the fading light.

Since two raps were customary in the city, the signal was a single knock. Inside there was a pause before the door opened.

Raven answered the door, pulling it open only enough to show his face. He raised an eyebrow with a smirk. The door wasn't opened wide enough to admit me, and I raised my eyebrow back at him playfully, then rolled my eyes.

"You really need me to say the password?"

"Security is of utmost importance. How am I to know whether you are sympathetic to our cause or an agent of the city trying to worm your way into our secret gathering?" The smirk on his face increased. I struggled to keep a straight face.

"A toast to the Mad Hatter, sir," I said.

Raven chuckled as he swung the door wide. "The Mad Hatter?"

"Well, it was you who came up with this mad plan to begin with," I replied, stepping inside the entry. Raven closed the door behind me.

"The princess and her companion have already arrived. They appear to have sourced every map of the city and have laid them all over my dining room table."

I paused in the entry hall and removed my hat and coat. Raven took them both from me and hung them in the hall closet. "How many are we expecting tonight?"

Raven shrugged. "Not many. I invited Dr. Lapin as he'll be able to spread the word to many of his patients very easily. His niece—you remember Miss Lapin?—will be along when she closes up the shop."

"Well, let's hope we have some more with us tomorrow when the real action starts. Otherwise, it might be somewhat of a letdown," I said. As Raven closed the hall closet, I made to move with him through to where Gaia and Genie were in the dining room. Raven took my arm to stop me.

I looked up at him as he pulled me closer. "Before we greet the others," he whispered before brushing his lips against mine. "I want you to myself—just for a moment."

I rested my hands on the front of his pinstriped vest and raised up on my toes to return his kiss. Our kiss deepened, and Raven wrapped an arm around my waist, pulling me closer until we were pressed against each other, breathing hard.

I let my hand slip up to brush over his shoulder and up his neck to curl in the softness of his hair.

"Ivy," Raven pulled away from me just enough to breathe my name. "I have done nothing but think about you—about kissing you—all day." He pulled back a little further to look deeply into my eyes. "I have counted the seconds until you would rejoin me."

"Me too," I whispered, pulling at his neck until he bent down to kiss me again.

"It really is quite inconvenient," he continued. "I ought to have been thinking about a great many other things, and you quite distracted me."

298

"Would you rather I leave?" I said as I drew a breath.

In answer, Raven tugged me closer to him and kissed me on the soft skin under my ear.

The rap at the door echoed through the hallway. We both pulled apart, looking up at each other with wide eyes. We waited for a second knock, but it didn't come.

Raven pulled away, motioning for me to wait. He went over to the door and opened it just enough to see who was standing on the doorstep.

"Yes?" he asked.

"A toast to the white rabbit, sir," chorused a number of deep voices. It was a clever password, as it called out the person who had invited them to come. These men had been sent here by Wit.

Raven looked back at me, both eyebrows raised as he opened the door. I saw a group of about six men, dressed in worn suits and scruffy flat caps. Raven ushered them inside before closing the door behind them. One of the men brandished a baton, bringing it down on his palm with a slapping sound. I noticed the others were all carrying batons with them. I took a big step back.

"We're ready," the man said, and the others nodded enthusiastically.

Raven looked at me. "What did Dr. Lapin tell you, exactly?" he asked.

"That it's time to change the city. That other like-minded people were planning something. We're tired of living like rats, taking whatever scraps we can get. We want to fight."

Raven edged around the group so that he was standing in front of me. He held out his hands. "We have no plan to fight," he said.

The men looked at each other. The leader let his

baton fall to his side. "But Dr. Lapin said..." He frowned as though he was trying to remember Wit's exact words. "He said we had to stand up for ourselves. We're ready."

Raven nodded. "We are going to stand up for ourselves," he said. "Though there will be no violence."

The men looked at each other. The leader gave a grudging nod, and they agreed to leave their batons with their coats and hats at the door.

Raven escorted us all to the dining room where Gaia and Genie were standing, hand in hand, as they pored over the maps. Gaia's phoenix, with its exquisite plumage, was perched on Gaia's shoulder, as though reading the maps too. Next to her, Genie stared at Gaia with an incredulous look on his face, as though he couldn't believe she was standing next to him. As we entered the room, Gaia looked up at him and caught Genie staring at her with a smile on his face. Her serious expression softened, and her eyes lit up as she matched his smile with one of her own.

Then she noticed us, and her attention shifted, her expression back to serious again.

"You're here!" Gaia stepped around the table and came over to take my hands and kiss me on the cheek. "And you have brought...others?"

"Dr. Lapin sent these men to join our cause," Raven replied.

Gaia smiled at them as they shuffled inside the room to come to stand with their backs to the wall, staring around with wide eyes, looking uncomfortable. Gaia turned back to her maps on the dining table, dragging me across the room with her.

"For the most effect," she said without preamble, "we will need to have a presence in every precinct of the city. There are so many. How many do you think will

300

come?"

I eyed the six men standing around the wall. "It's hard to say," I replied.

Another single knock echoed from the hallway, and Raven hurried back to the door.

"How many will we need?" I asked her.

"More than this," Gaia replied, eyeing the six men. She straightened and addressed them. "Do you men have wives or girlfriends? Will they be joining you tomorrow?"

The men exchanged looks. Finally, the man who seemed to be their leader responded. "The vampire said there would be no bloodshed," he replied.

Gaia nodded her head. "On the contrary, I'm hoping it will be fun."

The men stared at her, confused, then exchanged looks again. Before anyone could say anything else, the door opened, and more people shuffled into the room. More than twenty more people entered, both men and women—all thin, some scarred by pox, some missing a hand or a finger, one with an eye-patch, all dressed in little more than rags. I raised myself onto my tiptoes to see Raven, but the people kept coming in.

Finally, Raven appeared, with Wit by his side. The large dining room was half-full of people, who stood silently, looking wide-eyed about as though waiting for something to happen.

Raven and Dr. Lapin pushed their way over to where Gaia, Genie, and I stood at the table.

"This is more than I expected," Raven muttered.

"They are eager to improve their circumstances," Dr. Lapin replied. "They've nothing left to lose."

"We don't plan for violence," I said in a low voice so that only they could hear. "I hope you have explained that."

"Peaceful protest," Dr. Lapin replied. "Even better. I hope that I will not need to patch up too many of them after the night is over." He turned to Raven. "Are the vampires with us?"

Raven gave a small nod. "I can't speak for all of them, but a great many will stand with those who have been kind enough to donate blood in their time of thirst."

"Do you think it will be enough?" I asked Gaia.

She looked down at her maps. "There is an area in each district, at least. We need people in each one..." She was about to say something else when the knocker sounded again.

I looked at Raven. "More?"

He looked at the table spread with platters of sandwiches, scones, and pastries. Many of those who had just arrived were eyeing the food hungrily. Raven shrugged his shoulders. "I believed we'd over-catered. I might have been wrong."

∾

I stood with Raven at the door as everyone filed out of the door, collecting their threadbare coats and hats as they left. Gaia stood with us, clasping the hand of each person who came by and thanking them.

"I look forward to seeing you tomorrow," she said, making eye contact with each one.

I followed her lead, nodding to them as they passed me. "Do you remember your places for tomorrow?" I asked. The people nodded their heads and murmured their thanks. Many had stuffed their pockets with food to take back to hungry families—I couldn't begrudge them. In fact, we'd made sure all the food went home with someone. There should be no leftovers when people were starving. I knew that many of them had eaten more this evening than they would have had for days.

The meeting had become far larger than we'd planned, with more than one hundred people arriving at Raven's house to pledge their support for the plans.

Gaia, Genie, Raven, and I had quickly split up to speak to each of the small groups, in turn, assigning them to a different district of the city and giving them detailed instructions for the next day.

When the last of the guests had left, Genie was helping Gaia with her coat. As they were about to step out of the door together, Gaia turned to me to draw me into a hug.

"I think this is going to work," she said, and there was a twinkle in her eye.

I took a deep breath, an uncomfortable feeling in my stomach.

"You will speak to your mother, won't you?" she asked. "We will need her support if we're going to be successful. Don't surprise her with it."

I nodded. She leaned forward and kissed my cheek again. I squeezed her hands in return.

"I shall see you tomorrow," I said, then Gaia and Genie were out of the door.

Raven took out my coat and hat from the hall closet. "It's late. I shall walk you home," he said, tucking my arm into the crook of his elbow.

I leaned close to him as we walked down his front steps. "Do you think it's going to work?"

"It will all hinge on whether the president will lend us her support," Raven said. "If not..."

"I know. I will speak with her tomorrow," I murmured.

As we stepped onto the street, I noticed the ticking of the Pinnacle Clock.

"Is that clock louder than usual?" I asked him. Raven frowned, tilting his head to the side as though he could hear something I couldn't.

In front of us, I saw Gaia's gown flutter as she and Genie rounded the corner. In the other direction, other smaller groups of people were also hurrying home in the dark. From this distance, I wasn't sure whether they were the same people who had come to our meeting at Raven's house, or if they were just people who were walking home from dinner or other amusements.

The wrought-iron gate squeaked as it swung open, and Raven covered my hand as it rested in the crook of his elbow, with his own.

"We should hurry," he said, looking one direction down the street, then the other.

Someone screamed. Raven and I started running. Around a corner, a figure lay on the ground—one of those who'd been at Raven's house only a quarter-hour earlier. In the distance, the echoed footsteps of a marching Heart disappeared into the darkness.

1ST SEPTEMBER

I paced a track in the carpet of my room next to my four-poster bed. I hadn't drawn the curtains on my window, and outside, above the tiled rooftops, the sky was spread with pinks and purples. A sense of excitement boiled inside of me. Tonight was the night—either we would succeed or we wouldn't.

There was a gentle rap at the door before I heard the deep tones of Mr. Hopewell, Alice's butler, announcing that Mr. Cappello and his companions had arrived.

Companions?

I spun in a half-circle and took one last look in the mirror. I'd curled waves in my platinum blonde hair and dabbed my lips with gloss for the occasion, but now looking at myself in the mirror, I wondered whether it was too much. I smoothed a hand over the lines of my fitted vest and pulled nervously at the cuffs off my billowing shirt.

Then I shook my head. *You look great,* I told my reflection sternly. *Tonight is not about you. It's about the people in the tunnels. Do it for them.*

"Miss Rowntree?" Mr. Hopewell knocked again. "Are you there?"

"Yes, coming," I replied, then took a deep breath. I turned to the door and wrenched it open. Mr. Hopewell drew back, a look of surprise on his face. Then, he fixed his features back into his usual pleasant expression. He motioned for me to follow him, and I heard my skirts swish as I stepped into the hallway to follow him.

Mr. Hopewell's posture was erect and proper, as always, but I didn't miss the slight raising of his eyebrows when I'd opened the door. My heart galloped in my chest as I followed, beating so loud that I was sure Mr. Hopewell could hear it from where he walked in front of me. I only hoped Raven would appreciate my efforts in preparation for this evening, too.

My shoes clicked on the tiles, and I gripped the railing as I took a first step down the curving staircase that led down to the entry hall.

Raven looked up at me as I came down the stairs. He was holding a top hat in his hands and struck a dashing figure in a purple tailcoat trimmed with silver. His eyes widened a fraction, then a look of joy spread across his face. A smile touched one edge of his lips, slowly pulling the rest of his mouth to follow. My heart skipped a beat, and I felt my own expression mirror his until I was grinning so hard my face hurt.

Mr. Hopewell cleared his throat. I was standing halfway down the stairs, gripping the banister. I almost tripped over my feet as I stumbled down the rest of the steps.

As I made my way down, I noticed a number of others in the hall. Gaia and Genie stood, arm in arm, but Wit was also there. I raised an eyebrow as I saw Chesh among those waiting in the hall.

Raven stepped forward, taking my hand as I took the last two steps. His eyes didn't leave my face as he brought my knuckles his lips, brushing the back of my hand with a soft kiss.

"Miss Rowntree, you look..."—Raven shook his head slightly, as though lost for words for a moment.—"so beautiful this evening."

"As do you, Mr. Cappello," I replied, then caught myself. "H-h-handsome, I mean." I felt a red flush creep up my neck and searched around for something else to say. "Do you expect the others will come?" I added in a low voice.

Raven leaned closer. "I hope so. I really hope there will be a good turnout. Did you speak to your mother about the event?"

I nodded. "She promised to speak to the captain of the city guard this morning."

"And she did," Alice said as she came up behind me, putting a hand on my shoulder.

"Mother?" I looked at her, noticing that she was dressed in one of her best dresses—with layers of blue lace and ribbons, fastened with gold buttons. Her hair was tied into a bun, and teardrop pearls hung from her ears. "Are you going out this evening too?" I couldn't disguise the surprise in my voice.

She raised an eyebrow. "I hear someone has organized a *Big Night Out*," she replied. "I didn't want to be left at home. Besides," she added, as Wit walked up to her and turned a deep shade of red. "Dr. Lapin asked me to accompany him to dinner."

"You know Dr. Lapin?" Then I remembered Wit had spoken of my mother, as though he'd met her a long time ago.

Alice looked sideways at Wit, giving him a knowing smile. He turned an even brighter shade of red. "Dr. Lapin and I are old friends."

"Chesh, darling!" Pearl's voice rang out as she came to stand at the top of the stairway. We all looked up at her, dressed in a beautiful peach-colored gown, with her hair tumbling over one shoulder in ringlet curls. She beamed down at Chesh. When I looked across at him, he looked sideways at me before returning his attention to Pearl. He took her arm, giving her a quick peck on the cheek, before guiding her over to where I was standing with Raven and Alice. I turned my face away, tightening my hold on Raven's arm, as I tried to pretend I wasn't upset by the glow on Pearl's face, or the sight of their arms entwined.

"Where will you be dining this evening?" Chesh asked, looking pointedly at me.

"I believe we were assigned to The Menagerie," Raven replied.

Chesh's eyes lit up. "How fortunate," he said. "We will be dining in the same place. Perhaps we should—"

"And you, Mother? Dr. Lapin?" I asked, cutting Chesh off, both hoping to hide my discomfort at the idea of dining in the same restaurant as Chesh and Pearl this evening, as well as any suggestion that the four of us might dine together. The last thing I wanted was to be watched on my first outing in public with Raven.

"We'll be eating at Fire and Brimstone," Dr. Lapin replied. "I believe it is a new establishment on Third

Avenue."

Alice gave him a smile. "How lovely. It's been a long time since I've stepped out in the city just for fun." She turned to me and kissed me on the cheek. "Have a lovely evening. If there is any sign of a disturbance, make sure you alert the city guard—they have been given strict instructions to keep the peace and to ensure that nobody is prevented from entering licensed establishments on the grounds of their appearance."

She and Dr. Lapin left, accompanied by Gaia and Genie, who were dining at another restaurant on Third Avenue.

"Shall we?" Chesh asked.

"We shall be along directly," Raven answered before I had the chance to say anything.

Chesh looked at me for a moment, before Pearl tugged at his arm. "Come on, Chesh, darling," she said. "It is an absolutely magical evening. Let's take a scenic walk to the restaurant. We'll see you there, Ivy."

Finally, the door behind them closed, and I breathed out, letting my head bow for a moment before I turned to Raven.

He was watching me cautiously. "Are you alright?" he asked. "Are you sure you want to go through with this?"

I swallowed. Raven had taken my relief for disappointment—that Chesh was taking Pearl to dinner, not me. I started to shake my head. "No, no, no..." I waved a hand, trying to get my thoughts in order. Then I took a deep breath. "I'm perfectly well," I said, taking his hand firmly. "Yes, I'm looking forward to our date." I lifted my eyebrows. "What exactly are we waiting for?"

"Them to leave," he replied, then winked at me. He fetched a large box from the entry. "I brought this for you," he said and set the box in my hands. There was a hint of nervous anticipation on his face.

The box was light in my hands. "What is it?"

"Open it," he replied.

I did as I was bid and opened the box. Inside was a hat. I lifted it out and held it up to study it. It was a black top hat, but around the brim was a set of goggles, rather than ribbons and bows, along with a series of small wheels and cogs that looked like they might have a place on the inside of a pocket watch. The metal detailing gleamed copper against the black felt of the hat.

"This is beautiful," I said. "I love it."

"Let me help you with it," Raven stepped closer and fixed the hat on my head. He stepped back, studying me. His look was calculating and critical as he stared.

Then he nodded once. His eyes sparkled, and his smile widened into one of complete pleasure. "Yes," he whispered. "I've found it."

"My perfect hat?"

I smiled, touching the brim of the hat. It sat easily on my head—not too heavy, not uncomfortable, not awkward—made for me. Even better, the way Raven's eyes danced as he looked at me gave me a warm feeling inside.

I caught sight of myself in the long mirror in the hall. "You're right." I smiled, putting a finger on the brim. "It's perfect."

He gave me a slight bow then offered me his arm. "Shall we go, my lady?"

～

The city was busier than usual—far busier.

Raven and I walked slowly down the boulevard, making our way towards our assigned restaurant. We were not in a rush, but there were so many people in the streets that it was impossible to move at any speed. People moved in pairs, or groups, and spilled from the footpaths onto the roads. Drivers sitting on top of steam carriages yelled at the people dashing across the roads, but even they had to accept that the crowds wouldn't allow for any speed through the city.

Along the way, we saw evidence that the unbeautiful of the city had heeded the call to show their faces for the Big Night Out.

Raven's fashionable cane tapped on the cobblestones as we walked.

"Why do you carry a cane?" I asked as we walked. "Don't tell me it's just because it's fashionable?"

"I am very old," Raven raised an eyebrow at me, then winked.

I gave him a look. "You don't need a cane."

"They are very fashionable," Raven protested. "I wouldn't want to shame you by presenting at less than my best."

I gave him a sideways look. He'd certainly made sure to dress for the occasion, and I couldn't fault his attention to detail—he was perfectly put together.

"You know I don't care about fashion," I said. Raven smiled and patted my hand.

"I know, but..." A shadow passed over his face. He looked over his shoulder. "I didn't want to give anyone an excuse to judge me poorly tonight. I have a feeling we're going to attract enough attention already."

As he spoke, he tipped his hat to another couple that he appeared to know from the tunnels. As we made our way along the streets, he wordlessly greeted couple after couple—we'd passed vampire couples, couples who were tattered and torn, even in their best clothing, and those who were scarred and disfigured, yet walking with their heads high.

Regular citizens stared at these unfamiliar faces on the streets of the city, but we endeavored to act as though everything was completely normal. They also stared at us—though neither of us, as individuals, were out of place on the streets of Melfall, it was unheard of to see a vampire and a human woman walking about together.

I realized Raven had brought his cane, not for need or for fashion, but so as to blend into the crowd as much as possible. He'd been under no illusions about what we might face tonight.

On the other hand, I found myself blushing under glares from other people. Now, I could really sympathize with those who were physically disfigured. No wonder many of them had chosen to live their lives in hiding, rather than face such obvious stares and disapproval.

The city guards were to be found on every street corner, making their presence known. I witnessed one man walk up to a guard and demand he "do something" about the presence of a man scarred by the pox. The guard cheerfully replied that the city streets were open to everyone.

Raven and I didn't speak much. I spent most of the walk scanning the streets for evidence that the Big Night Out was going as planned. Not only that, but a heavy sense of anticipation was building inside me as we drew closer to *The Menagerie*.

It was one thing to walk down the street with a vampire, but quite another to gain entry to a fashionable restaurant.

As we walked up to *The Menagerie*, Raven leaned down toward me and whispered, "Are you ready?"

I didn't risk answering him in case my voice trembled, but I lifted my chin and nodded, staring at the door to the restaurant with a sense of newfound determination.

If the unbeautiful people of this city could work up the courage to come out of hiding to show the city what the aesthetic laws had done, then I could be brave too.

As we approached, I saw a city guard striding down the street. I recognized him from my visit to the wall—it was Captain Walsh. I smiled and raised my hand in greeting. The captain saw me, and his eyes lit up in recognition. He gave me a salute and stopped beside us as we approached our assigned restaurant.

"Any trouble?" he asked.

"Not yet," I murmured, glancing at the doorman who was looking at Raven and me hesitantly. "Any reports of disturbances elsewhere?"

"A few minor scuffles, but don't worry yourself with that. They've been dealt with in accordance with our orders."

"I'm pleased to hear it," I replied, turning my attention to the doorman as we stood in front of the door.

The large wooden door was set into an ornate doorframe, with flaming torches set into each side. I hadn't noticed as we'd approached, but now I could see that the doorframe was carved with gargoyles, their mouths open to display their fangs. The shadows cast from the torches made the monsters look as though they were screaming at us in warning. The door itself was carved and set with mother of pearl to look like dozens of pairs of eyes staring out of the darkness at us.

"A table for two, please," Raven said in answer to the

doorman's question.

"For two?" the doorman asked, his eyes flickering to Captain Walsh, who was still standing next to us.

"For two," Raven confirmed.

The doorman looked at me, then glanced behind him. "I'll have to check whether we have any available tables."

"I can see several empty tables through the window," Captain Walsh said firmly, giving the doorman a glare. "Any one of them will be quite suitable."

The doorman shuffled his feet, glancing again at the captain before pushing the door open. "As you wish."

He reluctantly held the door open, and we stepped through the darkened doorway and entered *The Menagerie*.

The contrast couldn't have been more acute—outside the door was dark and menacing. Inside, I wanted to look everywhere at once—the room was a riot of light and color. Near the doorway, there were tables that bloomed like red mushrooms with white spots, with seats shaped into caterpillars, hunched and crawling, or carved to look like snails. The walls were held together at each corner with fawns, hooves on the floor while their human-shaped upper bodies held the domed roof on their shoulders. In the center of the restaurant was a pool, and, as though waiting in the water, a walrus sat on a rock, complete with long-pointed tusks, a curled mustache, and a top hat.

As I stared around me, the chatter in the room fell to a hush. All eyes in the restaurant turned to stare at us as though we were more interesting than the interior of the restaurant. I felt a blush rise to my cheeks, even as I squared my shoulders and walked determinedly between the tables. The doorman pointedly led us past several empty tables at the front of the restaurant, to make our way towards the back.

Near the window, Chesh and Pearl were already seated on chairs shaped like fish standing on their tails at a table that was shaped like a starfish arched upon its points. Chesh turned to look at me as I walked past. He raised a hand as though to wave me over. I gave him a small nod, which he returned with a smile, but I continued to follow the doorman to the back. As we passed, I didn't miss the glare he turned on Raven.

We wound through the restaurant before being seated in the back corner at a table that was crammed into a small space between the wall and the doorway to the kitchens.

Raven pulled out my chair for me as I sat down. Our table was shaped like an upturned tulip, with seats made to look like leaves.

"Well, this is cozy," he said, though there was a strained expression on his face.

I glanced at my surroundings as Raven settled himself opposite me. Though it was inside, the restaurant had the feel of a courtyard, and all of the tables were arranged around the central water feature—the walrus that gave the appearance of overlooking proceedings with an air of aloof superiority. In the water around the walrus, dolphins and whales were carved from stone, water spurting from their blowholes. The water sparkled gold, reflecting the light of the hundreds of tiny lamps shaped like fireflies that hung from the ceiling. Above, the domed glass ceiling, the night sky glittered with thousands of tiny stars.

As I looked around at the restaurant, Chesh caught my eye again. I gave him a quick smile then turned back to Raven once more.

Raven seemed to have seen my exchange with Chesh, and he looked uncertain before reaching across the table to take my hand. I tensed, feeling the eyes and the judgment of every other patron in the restaurant.

"Relax," Raven said, squeezing my fingers. "Nothing is going to happen. We'll eat. We'll drink some wine. We'll go home. Just like any other couple."

I nodded. "I know."

"You're not embarrassed?"

"Why?" I asked, pretending not to know the reason he asked.

Raven raised one eyebrow, clearly not fooled by my act. "To be seen in public with a vampire. With me."

I shook my head. "It's not that."

Raven's mouth flattened into a line. "Really?" he asked, his tone soft.

"I just don't like being stared at."

Raven gave me a half-smile. "That surprises me. You are a beautiful woman. I wonder that you don't attract glances more often."

I felt myself blush. "Even if that's true," I said. "Being beautiful in a city full of beautiful people is not notable—especially with a sister like Pearl."

"Meaning?"

"She is stunning. I'm used to the unflattering comparisons between us."

Raven frowned. "She is beautiful too, I don't deny that, but you are strikingly unforgettable."

"That's very kind," I murmured.

"Not kind at all. Simply the truth."

There was a sudden disturbance several tables away. I glanced over to see Chesh and Pearl following a waiter, who hurried to clear and reset a table only two seats from us. It was shaped like a frog, set with six

316

seats around it shaped like tadpoles. Pearl beamed at me and gave me a wave.

"That other table was entirely unsuitable," she said, loudly. "Do you know who they sat next to us? I was staring at a man missing an eye and a scar down one side of his face! Chesh demanded that we be moved to a table with more pleasing surroundings."

"Shhh," I hissed at her, looking around to see if anyone else had heard. Then I put a hand over my eyes, trying to ignore the blush that was burning two spots into my cheeks.

I glanced at Chesh, who was glaring at the spot where Raven and I were holding hands. I fought the instinct to snatch my hand away, and instead, reached over to take his other hand again and tighten my grip on his fingers.

"Now, we're closer to you!" Pearl gushed.

"This table will be more suitable," Chesh said, clipping his words as he sat down.

My heart sank. They were in earshot of our entire dinner conversation. The feeling of being watched increased.

"Perhaps we should order wine?" Raven suggested, turning his attention to the menu. He leaned forward. "The wine comes from the blowfish," he nodded his head at the opposite corner of the room where a bloated fish with pointed spines all over its body squirted a ruby red liquid from its mouth into a large bowl.

"You mean, that's wine? It's drinkable?"

"Look," Raven pointed as one of the waiters dipped a carafe into the sparkling red liquid pouring out of the mouth of the fish, before hurrying over to deliver the carafe to a table and pour it into wine glasses.

I grinned. "I'm game to try it."

Raven raised a hand to get the attention of the nearest waiter.

She ignored him, stopping at Chesh and Pearl's table to take their order instead. My mouth went dry, hoping the waiter had simply failed to see us.

When she walked past our table again, my stomach sank. Raven's smile wavered. He indicated to the woman again. Finally, unable to ignore us any longer, she slammed down two menus onto the table, then strode away without speaking. Raven wasn't smiling now. His mouth was set into a thin line.

Next to us, a family who had just sat down at a table started speaking loudly to the waiter. They were demanding to be reseated, but I could see that there weren't any other tables in the restaurant, which was now full. A moment later, they were gathering their things and left.

I felt myself stiffen in my seat and swallowed down a lump in my throat. Trying to ignore the feeling that everyone's eyes were on me, I reached out to pick up the menu and opened it.

"Do you have any recommendations about what's best to eat?" I asked Raven.

Raven raised one eyebrow. "I always order a bloody steak, so I'm not sure that I'm the best one to advise you."

I froze, staring at him with wide eyes before I burst out laughing. His serious expression broke into a grin.

"Better a rare steak than taking a bit out of you, eh?" he added.

Then both of us were shaking with silent laughter.

Tears of laughter streamed down my cheeks before I noticed a figure standing next to our table.

I dabbed at my eyes with my handkerchief, expecting

318

to see the waiter had returned to take our order.

Instead, Chesh was standing at the table, his fists bunched by his sides, glaring at Raven. His curly hair, which had been groomed into a neat ponytail with gel, now stuck up at an unusual angle, as though he'd dragged his hand through it.

"What are you doing?" I hissed, glancing around at the other tables whose occupants were now openly gawking at us. Even Pearl was looking at him, her blue eyes wide, and her mouth turned down slightly at the edges as she gripped the edge of the table with both hands.

Raven started to stand, as though to address Chesh when Chesh leaned over and grasped him by the cravat tied around his neck in an elaborate knot.

Chesh hauled Raven forward, dragging him across the table towards him, while Raven resisted and grabbed Chesh's arm, as though trying to loosen his grip on his shirtfront.

Chesh bared his teeth, and pulled back his other arm, about to swing a fist at Raven.

"No!" I pushed out my chair so hard that it fell backward as I got to my feet, throwing myself between Chesh and Raven. There was a sickening crunching sound as Chesh's fist connected with Raven's face. I reached out and caught Chesh's arm a fraction too late, but pulled him back anyway, away from Raven.

Raven had his fingers on his nose, his head bowed so that his black hair hung loosely over his face.

"What are you doing?" I glared at Chesh, raising my voice—no longer caring who was looking. Behind him, Pearl stood up and moved hesitantly over so that she was standing just behind Chesh. She tried to reach out for his arm, but he was looking at me and reached out with both hands to lay them on my shoulders.

I was shaking my head, gritting my teeth, and I shrugged off Chesh's hands as soon as he touched me.

"I heard what he said about you," Chesh started. He ignored Pearl's attempts to take his arm. He reached out again, this time to touch my face, but I jerked away. "I'm sorry. I shouldn't have done that, but it made me so angry. He should never speak so to you. To threaten you that way."

"It wasn't a threat—" I said as I shook my head.

"He said he would hurt you, bite you," he continued, his voice hardening.

"You're—"

"No, listen to me. He doesn't deserve you. You shouldn't be here with him—"

"I can—"

"You should be here with me," Chesh said. The words dropped like stones in the pond. I was staring at Chesh, open-mouthed as the words registered slowly in my consciousness. Suddenly I became aware that everyone in the restaurant was listening. Behind Chesh, Pearl covered her mouth with her hand, and her eyes filled with tears. "I love you, Ivy. There's never been anyone for me but you. I should have told you earlier—before he brainwashed you to believe—"

"No!" Pearl's shriek filled the air.

I glanced over at my sister as Pearl covered her face with her hands. With a sob, she turned and ran out of the restaurant, knocking into a table on her way, overturning it so that the wine glasses smashed into a million tiny shards of glass that scattered all over the floor.

～

320

I stared after Pearl, frozen to the spot, as the restaurant seemed to spin into motion again. Exclamations of shock and surprise filled my ears, and waiters rushed around to clean up the mess.

Slowly, I turned my attention back to my table, where both Chesh and Raven were staring at me.

"Go after her," I said, with an edge to my voice.

"Ivy, I—"

I held up my hand to stop him, then was silent for a moment as I struggled to keep my emotions in check. Then I curled my hand into a fist. "Go."

"Come with me," Chesh said, holding out a hand to me. "Please, I don't want to leave you," Chesh's eyes flickered towards where Raven was now standing. "You'll be safer with me."

"I would never hurt Ivy," Raven replied, his voice like steel. Then he glanced at me and inclined his head. "It is your choice."

"I'll stay," I replied.

Chesh reached out for me, but I stepped back. "Leave."

He paused, as though trying to decide what to do, then he sighed and hung his head.

"Good night, Ivy," he said, reluctantly moving away. Every person in the restaurant stared at him as he left, then turned to stare at us.

I swallowed, suddenly flushing at being, yet again, the center of attention. I looked at Raven, who ran a finger down the bridge of his nose, an action I knew meant he was deep in thought.

I knelt to pick up the napkin that had fallen to the floor when I'd leaped out of my chair. As I stood, Raven moved around the table to put a hand on my elbow.

"Perhaps we should leave?" he whispered, his breath

tickling my earlobe.

I felt the lightness of relief and nodded. I tossed the napkin onto the table and tucked my hand into the crook of his elbow.

The waiters fetched our coats and hats before we stepped out of the restaurant door into the warm evening breeze.

Along the street, tables and chairs overflowed from the restaurants and cafes onto the footpaths, as couples and groups enjoyed the balmy night. With the hundreds of extra people who had stepped out for the *Big Night Out*, the streets were full of people, spilling out of the establishments, or just taking a walk along the avenues.

I saw a guard on patrol on the corner, but there was a smile on his face that indicated that he was enjoying the evening just as much as everyone else.

Mr. Thackery was sitting at an outdoor table with his wife and children. He held his wife's hand and smiled as one of his children wolfed down the meal, barely pausing between bites.

"The night has been a success for some, at least," Raven murmured.

I felt tight all over, wound tight like the mechanism in one of my pocket watches. Out of the corner of my eye, I saw a flash of red and spun around, coming to crouch into a fighting pose.

A woman with three bright red feathers curving in a plume over her head walked past, arm in arm with a girlfriend. They were engaged in conversation and didn't notice my behavior.

"Ivy?" Raven said softly before laying a hand gently on my shoulder. "What is it?"

I straightened, feeling foolish. "Nothing," I replied, though I stared both ways down the street, just to be sure. "I think I saw... Never mind, just my eyes playing tricks on me."

"You weren't expecting the level of animosity that we received at the restaurant?" Raven asked. He tucked his hands in his trouser pockets as he stood in front of me, waiting for me to answer him.

I looked up at his expression, seeing the straight set of his mouth and the hint of sadness in his eyes. I shook my head. "But you were," I said.

He nodded. "It wasn't the evening that I'd hoped for—I wanted to show you a night out that we'd both remember. Well, I suppose we'll remember it, but not for the right reasons. Still, you got a taste of what the unbeautiful people of this city—including vampires—experience all the time."

"I'm sorry," I said. "I didn't expect to feel so... vulnerable." I swallowed, remembering the way everyone in the restaurant had looked at me. As though they found me disgusting. "I didn't expect to feel so disliked."

"I'm sorry too." Raven reached out to take my hand.

"Do you think it will ever change?"

Raven tipped his head, the edge of his mouth curling into a smile. "Of course," he replied. "I have to believe that this is the beginning of something new. Look around—" He spread his hand as though surveying the street.

People sat at tables and chairs, the fashionable seated next to those who were not beautiful or fashionable by any measure. Mr. Thackery's family appeared to be enjoying themselves—or at least the food—as they sat at a wrought iron table and chairs on the footpath. As I watched, though, the beautiful woman seated next to Mr. Thackery's family glanced over her shoulder before shifting her chair a little further away. As though she wanted to put some distance between them. As though somehow a lack of beauty might be catching.

I looked farther and noticed the looks being exchanged by the beautiful people and those who were not.

"Do you really think so?" I murmured uncertainly.

"Believe me, Ivy, this is progress." Raven put a finger under my chin and turned my face up towards his as he leaned down so that his nose was almost touching mine. He paused a moment, looking into my eyes, before brushing his lips to mine in a kiss so brief that I wondered if it had even happened. He smiled at me. "The evening is still young. Perhaps we could walk a little and enjoy the beauty of this night?"

He held out an arm. I grinned at him as I looped my arm through his. We stepped away from the people seated on the footpath and walked slowly along the avenue underneath the lamps. In this part of the city, they were shaped like dragons, rearing up on their hind legs, copper scales gleaming while they hissed fire into the night sky.

We left the crowd behind, and with every few steps, we walked in and out of the pools of light created by the street lamps. We fell into silence. I tightened my hold on Raven, moving closer to him, then leaned the side of my cheek against his shoulder.

After a while, Raven cleared his throat, putting his hand over where mine was tucked into the crook of his elbow. "Ivy, did you want to come to dinner with me tonight?"

My mouth went dry, and a lump formed in my throat. "Yes," I whispered.

"You seemed...unsure," he said. "Afraid, even."

I glanced up at him. "When?"

"When I came to pick you up tonight."

I stopped walking, and he took another step forward. With our arms entwined, he half-turned to me as he came to a stop. "Why are you asking me this?"

The lump in Raven's throat bobbed as he swallowed before he spoke. "Your friend, Mr. Cheshire said some things to you tonight—"

"He was speaking out of turn," I interrupted. "It was rude."

"Yes, it was," Raven agreed. "That doesn't mean he was wrong."

"I don't understand."

Raven turned to face me, taking both of my hands in his. He ran the pad of his thumbs lightly over my knuckles, looking down. Refusing to meet my eyes.

"You and Mr. Cheshire are good friends. Perhaps you are more than good friends. If that is so..." He started to pull his hands away from mine.

"Yes, Mr. Cheshire and I are good friends." I tightened my grip on Raven's hands, pulling him towards me. "That's *all* we are."

"Are you sure?" Raven looked up at me, frowning. I saw concern in his eyes. I started to nod my head, but Raven stopped me. "He's right, you know—this relationship, between us, would not be easy. Certainly not for you. Change takes time, especially when trying to change people's minds. Many of your friends wouldn't want to be seen with you any longer if you were linked romantically with me. You saw how it was in the restaurant tonight. That's how it might always be. Can you live with that?"

His words fell like stones in my stomach. I let my gaze drift from his face, falling until I was staring at his shoes.

"What about you?" I asked, my voice so small that I wasn't sure he would hear me. "Can you just walk away so easily?"

A moment elapsed. Then Raven exhaled his answer: "No." He swallowed. "But I will—if you ask me to."

Could I?

The ticking of the Pinnacle clock filled my mind, obscuring my thoughts. I squeezed my eyes shut, thinking about all of the times we'd spent together— in truth, it was hardly any time at all. We'd snatched a few hours together, here and there. He'd occupied more space in my thoughts than he'd spent next to me. Nevertheless, next to me, or away from me, he made my heart race. More than that, since the first conversation we'd had, he'd challenged my views, showed me things I'd never imagined, revealed a side of the world I'd never seen. I'd always had an inkling that our city wasn't quite right, and Raven had shown me the truth. He'd given me a purpose—more purpose than I'd ever had. He'd given me a reason to fight for change.

I thought about Chesh and the love he'd declared for me tonight. On a certain level, I'd always known our friendship was unequal. While I kept him at arm's length, he would have taken more if I'd given him an opportunity. I'd been jealous of Pearl when he'd shown interest in her, but not because Chesh made my heart race. It was because Chesh was mine—my safe harbor. Someone I'd believed would always be there for me if I ever decided I wanted him.

In the dancing lamplight of the dragon's fire, I knew

what I had with Chesh was different to what I had with Raven. It would never be the same.

And I didn't want it to be.

I looked up at Raven and tightened my grip on his hands. "I can't walk away from you so easily, either." I reached up to wrap my arms around his neck, pulling his face down towards mine. "And I don't want to," I whispered.

~

It was the sound of an upbeat tune wafting through the air that brought us back to the moment. Raven pulled away, cocking his head to the side.

"I do believe that's the sound of dancing," he said. He turned and scanned the avenue. He pointed in the direction of the wide paved circle in the city center, but I couldn't see anything but the row of lamplights in the dark.

Raven held out his hand. "Will you grant me the honor of the first dance, my lady?" He smiled, the gleaming white of his teeth flashing against the darkness.

My smile spread so wide that my cheeks hurt. I bobbed a curtsy, then took his hand. "I believe I shall, sir," I replied.

He laughed and started tugging me towards the music. I shrieked as I stumbled forwards, and the sound bounced off the stone buildings lining each side of the avenue. I kept my feet, then somehow, we were both running down the street, skirts and tailcoats flying as we made for the music.

When we arrived at the city center, a crowd of people had gathered under the spire of the Pinnacle. As we moved closer, I saw a band of four or five musicians playing lively tunes and people dancing under the face of the Pinnacle clock, which glowed as though it was the moon. We didn't pause at the edge of the dance to take any notice of the details—instead, we flung ourselves into the swarm of partners. The music was lively, and dance partners smiled, with eyes only for each other, as they swirled around and around. Raven took one hand in mine, and wrapped the other around the small of my back, holding me close to him as he led me into the dance.

His feet moved like the music flowed through them, and I struggled to keep up, but it didn't matter. One song merged into another, becoming louder and louder, as the night wore on and the throng of dancers grew. As though there was some sort of magic in the air, more and more people were drawn to the crowd and joined in the dancing. It was almost as though the impromptu dancing had drawn the revelers—beautiful and unbeautiful alike—out of the restaurants and bars of the city and to the paved cobblestones of the city center.

In the dance, the distinctions between the beautiful and unbeautiful fell away. None of it mattered. As we moved in time to the beat of the music—and to the rhythm of each other—Raven stared down at me like there was nobody else in the world, and I couldn't tear my eyes away from his.

It was as though everything else in the world ceased to exist, except for Raven and I in this moment. This perfect moment.

Then the music drew into a crescendo, and the bells of the Pinnacle clock started to strike twelve.

～

Dong.

The music stopped in an instant.

Raven swirled me around one more time before taking my face in both hands and kissing me. Around me, people crashed into each other as they looked around to see why the music had stopped. Someone laughed.

Dong.

Raven pulled away, then looked away to the side. He frowned. I glanced around, breathing heavily, suddenly clammy in the evening air. I pushed a stray hair away from my face and looked up at the Pinnacle clock.

Dong.

Raven straightened, suddenly tense. He was looking away from the Pinnacle clock, to the outer edge of the city center. Everyone else stared up, mesmerized by the chiming sound and the glowing face of the clock.

Dong.

I tugged on Raven's shirt and stretched up onto my toes to whisper in his ear. "What is it?"

Raven's mouth was pressed into a thin line. "Can you hear that?" he asked.

I listened. Then I heard it, too—the sound I'd mistaken for the ticking of the clock. The sound of hundreds of footsteps marching exactly in time.

Dong.

"That's the same sound we heard last night, wasn't it?" I asked.

Raven nodded. "The Hearts," he said, and at the very moment the words left his mouth, the first Hearts appeared out of the darkness.

Dong.

Someone screamed, and I jumped. The Hearts didn't advance, but with every tick of the clock, more

Hearts appeared, spreading around so that they made a perimeter around the circular edge of the city center.

Dong.

I spun around to run in the opposite direction but froze. "They're surrounding us," I hissed. A frisson of adrenalin surged through me as I understood what they were doing. I took a step forward, lifting my skirts as I got ready to run towards the last remaining gaps in the perimeter. "We've got to get out of here," I said and raised my voice so that the people around me could hear.

Dong.

The dancers started to scatter, as they came to the same conclusion as I had. Everyone was moving in different directions. Raven grabbed my hand, pulling me towards one of the gaps in the circle.

Dong.

A Heart marched into the gap that Raven and I had been heading for. It stopped, turning to face us, with its broad card-body almost touching the cards on each side of it—like a wall. We couldn't fit through the gap. I spun around again, searching frantically for a way out.

Dong.

What had Alice said about the Hearts? They used to kill. I spun around again, looking for another gap. I ran straight into Gaia and Genie.

"We've got to..." I yelled out to them, trying to warn them about the Hearts. Then I saw Alice, hand-in-hand with Wit. She was staring at the Hearts, her face white with fear.

Dong.

There was another scream, but this time I recognized it. Pearl. I spun around, trying to locate her in the frenzy of the crowd. People were running to and fro, but there was nowhere to go. The Hearts had penned us in, like cattle.

"Ivy!" Raven yelled.

At the sound of his voice, I spun around to face outward the circle of Hearts. They'd made a solid wall with their square card-bodies and were holding their spears at the ready. The pointed tips of the spears glinted in the luminescent light of the Pinnacle clock.

Dong.

As the final chime brought in the new day, the Hearts all marched forward as one.

GODDESS
OF HEARTS

2ND SEPTEMBER

The marching Hearts pounded the cobblestones, deafening as they surged forward, the sharp edges of their spears pointing toward the crowd. Screams pierced the night, as people surged backward, crushing each other. Raven pushed me behind him. He grabbed the cane he'd been carrying and brandished its metal tip at the advancing Hearts like a sword.

I patted myself down. Did I have anything to use as a weapon?

"Go to the middle of the crowd. You'll be safer there," Raven ordered. Then he yelled out: "Vampires to the front!" I saw a number of pale-faced, well-dressed men and women appear to make a wall, taking the brunt of the initial attack.

I looked behind me. People were screaming and

pushing each other, trying to get away.

The Hearts surrounded us in a circle. The vampires might hold them back for a short period, but there were too many of them. In the open central marketplace, there was nowhere to hide.

Beside me, several other men were brandishing their canes, too. A woman swung her folded parasol, and another held a high-heeled shoe in front of her so that the spike pointed out. Another lady swung a long necklace, with a large jewel pendant, like a ball and chain. As I watched her, I had an idea. I took out the pocket watch and swung it around in front of me—it was better than nothing.

I looked up at the Pinnacle clock. The scaffolding that the workers had put up was still there, along with the ladders that the workers used to make it to the higher levels.

"The ladder," I pointed, yelling at the people around me. "Quick!"

Instead of using it to escape, a man with a scar down one side of his face pulled the ladder from where it was fixed to the scaffold and broke it across his knee. He broke it in a few more places and passed around wooden stakes as makeshift weapons.

Another scream sounded as the Hearts charged again. Several bodies were lying on the ground, blood seeping from their bellies. I scanned the place where Raven had been, unable to breathe as I saw him striking a Seven of Hearts over and over again with his cane, knocking aside the spear that it was jabbing at him.

A wooden stake, splintered at one end, was pushed into my hand by the man with the scar down his face. "Protect yourself."

I nodded, gripping the stake in one hand and my

pocket watch in the other. I scanned the area again for the others. Across the crowd, flames flew from Gaia's fingertips. Genie fought beside her, and he must have disarmed one of the Hearts because now he used its spear as his own. Close to them, Alice and Wit were both crouched on the ground. I started toward them, then Alice sent something flying. Wit was digging up the cobblestones with his cane, and Alice was pulling up the loose stones and pelting them at the advancing Hearts.

On the other side, I saw the four men who had come first to Raven's house the other night. Although Gaia had told them that we'd hoped to have no violence, they'd come prepared anyway, because all of them were fighting with their batons.

Several beautiful ladies had hitched up their skirts and were using knives they'd concealed in their garters to defend themselves. Others threw shoes or jabbed at their attackers with the pointy end of elaborate headdresses. Their perfect faces were pulled into expressions of terror, anger, and grim determination.

A woman, whose face was badly scarred by the pox, swung a stone, striking a Heart in the back of the head as it tried to attack Pearl.

I put a hand over my mouth as I saw my sister, almost skewered by a Four of Hearts. My throat closed up, as the Heart crumpled, falling to the ground at Pearl's feet.

Pearl stared at the Four of Hearts, then at the woman who had saved her. A look of astonishment passed over her face; she pulled the woman into an embrace, whispering something in her ear.

The woman pushed Pearl away, bending down to pick up the spear that the Four of Hearts had dropped when it fell. She pushed it into Pearl's hands and pointed. Pearl's look of astonishment, became determination. She and the pox-marked woman let out a scream as they charged a Heart together, holding their weapons aloft.

"Watch out!"

The scream alerted me just in time. I swung around to see a Ten of Hearts lunge at me. At the last moment, I stepped aside, and the spear missed me by a fraction. Then Chesh was next to me, his teeth bared. He leaped on the back of the Heart, grabbing it around its neck.

I rushed forward to help Chesh, raising my wooden stake to use it like a baton and brought it down hard on the Heart's chest plate. It made a hollow sound that echoed through the square, but the impact didn't appear to hurt it. I raised my arm again, bringing the stake down on the Heart, again and again.

Chesh was banging the Heart on the metal helmet over its robotic head. Then he reached forward to cover its eyes with his hand. The Heart stumbled, as though disoriented, then it spun, trying to dislodge Chesh from its back.

As it spun, it's arm knocked me to the ground and I went flying backward, hitting the back of my head on the cobblestones.

I blinked, seeing double for a moment. Then I scrambled to my knees, just in time to see the Ten of Hearts jab the point of its spear over its shoulder, skewering Chesh through the shoulder.

"No!" I jumped to my feet, picking up the wooden stake and rushed at the Ten of Hearts as Chesh fell to the ground. The Heart pulled the spear from Chesh's shoulder, making him scream in pain again as he curled up in the fetal position, clutching his shoulder.

336

I rammed into the front of the Heart before it had the chance to whirl its spear around to fight me off. The force of the impact of my body against the Ten knocked it backward, sending it sprawling on the cobblestones. For a moment, it was like a beetle on its back, waving its arms and legs in the air.

I leaped onto it, hitting it with the stake in my hand. It jabbed at me with its spear, but this time, I grabbed the spear in my spare hand and pulled. The Heart lost control of the spear, and I snapped it in half, wedging a splintered end into the visor of its helmet.

Sparks flew, and the Ten of Hearts jerked, then went still.

I paused, panting as I stared down at the Heart. Slowly, I slipped off the square plate of its body and banged it over the head once more with my stake, for good measure. Then I spun around to see Chesh.

He'd disappeared.

I scanned the area, but there was no sign of him. There were lots of little battles, people fighting against Hearts. The Hearts no longer hemmed us in, though, and as I looked around, I saw the battles were uneven—with two or more people fighting each Heart.

Around the edge, where the Hearts had formed a perimeter, now, the city guards had arrived—apparently summoned by the action—and were fighting alongside the vampires. Beautiful and unbeautiful were fighting alongside each other with vampires among them.

I grabbed a spear lying on the ground and gripped my wooden stake in the other. I rushed to join the group battling the remaining Hearts, pushing them away from the center of the city.

Raven was with the group, and the knot in my stomach loosened a little to see he was unhurt. Then,

I noticed Alice among them too, still holding a chipped cobblestone in her hand, and she was yelling orders at the guards.

"Drive them all the way to the gate," she commanded. "Take Twelfth Avenue, drive them out of the city, then close the gates."

I ran past, coming to stand alongside Raven. He glanced at me as he confronted a Heart, jabbing at it with his cane.

"Drive the cane through its visor," I yelled over the noise. "It'll drop like a stone."

Raven glanced at me again, then did as I'd said. The Heart fell backward, slamming to the ground, a shower of sparks coming from its mechanical eye sockets.

Raven grinned at the sight, then glanced at me.

"I thought I told you to get behind me," he said.

I grinned and stood next to him, jabbing at another Heart with my spear. "I've never been very good at doing what I'm told."

Raven and I stood, shoulder-to-shoulder, both brandishing our weapons in front of us, slowly advancing on the Hearts to force them backward along Twelfth Avenue.

The Hearts drew back to attack again, as though they'd been programmed to go only forward.

Suddenly, the remaining Hearts suddenly went completely still.

I blinked, looking sideways at Raven, who shrugged.

The remaining Hearts turned, in unison, and started marching down Twelfth Avenue toward the perimeter wall. They fell into straight rows, and with their footsteps sounding in time, the Heart army left the city as they had arrived.

"Close the gates," Alice ordered. Her voice was commanding, and she stood erect with her head held high, but her hands shook, and the pallor of her skin betrayed her shock and exhaustion.

It took ten of the city guards, lending their body weight to push each gate closed. The metal squealed on its rusted hinges as the gates protested being moved.

I struggled against the urge to put my hands over my ears as the gates groaned, then finally closed with a *thud*. As soon as the gates were firmly shut, Alice strode forward, pulling out a chain hidden under her shirt. She slipped the chain over her head, then held up a large brass key.

A guard rushed forward with a ladder, offering to take the key from her, but Alice resolutely shook her head. Instead, he held the ladder as Alice climbed the rungs.

When she reached the top, she pushed the large key into the keyhole. With a *click*, the gates were locked. Alice sagged against the metal of the gates, then started to make her way back down the ladder. She took each rung much more slowly than she had done on the way up.

When she reached the ground again, her hands were shaking.

"Mother?" I walked towards her, aware of Raven following closely behind me. I reached out to take his hand as I walked, reaching out to Alice with the other. "Are you alright?"

Alice pushed a lock of grey-blonde hair out of her eyes. She didn't answer but turned to Captain Walsh.

"I want guards posted at every watch along the wall. If those Hearts come anywhere near this gate, I want to know."

Captain Walsh bowed to her. "As you command, Madam President."

He hurried off to carry out her orders, and I moved toward her. Alice held up a hand, then closed her eyes, shaking her head. She was on the edge of breaking down.

"Come, Mother. Let's get out of here."

I put an arm around her waist, coaxing her back down the avenue and away from the scrutiny of those who had helped drive the Hearts out of the city, and those who had come to watch as they'd marched out of the gates of their own will.

"Wit was setting up an area to treat the wounded," Alice said, her voice breathless. "I should go to him."

"You should sit down," I murmured. "Take a moment."

"My people need me," Alice said. The steel in her voice returned, and I knew there was no point fighting her.

A slight glow appeared above the buildings in the eastern sky as a new day dawned. My fingers entwined tighter between Raven's, as I put one arm around Alice's waist.

"We'll go together, then."

∽

The sky was lightening as we walked back down Twelfth Avenue. The avenue was quiet—not unusual for this time of day—but there was an eerie quality to the quiet that made my chest tighten with unease. The lamplighters were out to extinguish the street lamps as the morning dawned, though the sun hadn't yet popped into the sky. It wouldn't be long, though. I looked at Raven.

"Don't you need to go home?" I whispered.

Raven looked up at the sky, frowning. "Soon, yes."

Apprehension twisted in my stomach as I looked at the glow above the buildings. "What happens if you get caught out?"

"Then I'll be sorry, I wasn't more careful," he replied, but he gave my hand a squeeze.

Approaching the center of the city, we saw the first stretchers carrying the injured. Raven stopped a man with a false leg, at the head of a stretcher.

"Where are they taking them?" he asked.

The man didn't stop as he replied. "Dr. Lapin's ordered that the worst of the injured be taken to the hospital for treatment. I'm taking this one there—but I don't know if there will be enough beds. Those with less serious injuries are being treated where they lie on the cobblestones."

I thought immediately of Chesh—were his injuries so severe that he'd been taken to hospital, or was he one of those left to languish on the cobblestones? And what of Pearl? Of Gaia and Genie? What had happened to them?

Raven nodded. "Where is Dr. Lapin?"

"Still under the Pinnacle clock," the man replied, turning his back to us as he continued limping on his way.

"Wait!" Raven called out, and the man stopped. "If there aren't enough beds, take the injured to this address." Raven pulled out a calling card and tucked it into the pocket of the man's coat. "There's plenty of room. Dr. Lapin will attend to him there, directly."

I stared at Raven, suddenly appreciating his calm but authoritative demeanor. It was easy to imagine this man taking charge of an underground movement helping the people living in the tunnels, and those vampires starving for lack of blood stocks. A natural leader.

"We need to see Wit," Alice said, straightening. She looked slightly less pale in the rosy morning light, or perhaps she was recovering from the shock of the night.

We continued down Twelfth Avenue and into the city center. As the avenue widened and the circular marketplace came into view, I gasped at the sight. Dozens, perhaps hundreds, of people were laid out on the ground. Others knelt by their sides, cradling heads in their laps or grasping hands as though holding onto them for dear life. The sounds of pain filled the air.

So many injured. And these were the ones deemed not serious enough to be taken to the hospital.

"There he is!" Alice spotted Wit almost immediately, and she let go of my hand as she strode over to see him. Raven and I followed closely behind, stepping between the people lying on the ground.

A smile spread across Wit's face as Alice walked up to him. "You're alright, my dear," he said and reached out to grab her hands, pulling her towards him.

"You are in your element, I see," Alice replied. "We saw some being stretchered to the hospital."

"The doctors there can tend to the worst of the wounds," Wit said, the smile slipping from his face. "The hospital can take no more, though, and these people require attention too."

"I've ordered for the overflow from the hospital to be taken to my house," Raven said. "Take these there too—

as many as need a bed. The superficial wounds can be tended in place," Raven looked around doubtfully. "But these injured look like they need more than just a few kind words."

Wit nodded. "These aren't the worst of them, but I'm afraid their wounds will get infected without proper care, cleaning and bandages. I'll take up your offer, Mr. Cappello. If you can arrange for the transportation of these injured, I'll attend to them there."

Raven nodded. "I'll get started." He looked at me, as though he was about to say something, but I shook my head.

"No need to explain," I said. "I'll be along when I can, but..." I looked up at the sky again, then gave Raven a pointed look. "Don't you need to get inside?"

Raven frowned, glancing towards the horizon. "Yes," he whispered. "But I can't leave without helping. I'll be careful. I'll take the tunnels."

Raven went to leave, taking a look around, then he stopped. "These people look like they've lost a lot of blood."

"Most have. The worst are at the hospital, as I said. The hospital supplies are running low because of the blood bank shortages. There won't be enough blood for everyone that needs it."

Raven glanced at me, then at Alice, before giving Wit a wry smile. "I know a guy. Perhaps he can sort out a solution to the blood problem." He walked away, calling out to a scarred man that I recognized from the tunnels, starting to give instructions.

"What can I do?" Alice asked Wit, bringing me back to their conversation. "Each of these people fought to protect our city. I want to do something to help them."

Wit put an arm around her shoulders, drawing Alice

close to him. "Walk among them. Thank them. Notice them. It will make all the difference.

Alice gave him a small smile before moving away to bend over the first woman she came across. It was the pox-marked woman who had saved Pearl's life. I startled to see Pearl sitting next to her, holding her hand.

"Mother!" Pearl exclaimed. As she looked up at Alice, I saw the tears staining her face. "This brave woman is Mary Ann. She saved my life."

Mother knelt down and took Pearl's face in her hands, examining her for any injuries. Pearl shook her off.

"I'm fine, Mother. It's Mary Ann. She won't stay awake."

"I've got this, Mother," I said. "You need to see to the others too."

Mother nodded, glanced once more at Pearl, and kissed her on the top of the head before walking away to speak with the other injured.

I looked down at Mary Ann, noticing a trail of blood that ran from her eyebrow to her chin. I knelt down next to her, lay one hand on her shoulder, and held a hand out to Pearl.

"Was she hit in the head by one of the Hearts?"

As the words came out of my mouth, I noticed a pool of blood underneath Mary-Ann's leg. I bent over to see better, pulling the threadbare and now blood-stained fabric of her skirts aside for a better look.

Pearl was shaking her head. "I think she's going to die. I don't know what to do."

I put my hand on Pearl's cheek, looking up at her. "There's a place where they can take her so that she'll get the medical attention she needs."

"The hospital?" Pearl asked. "But they don't have

any more beds. I heard someone else say so."

"Not the hospital. Somewhere else. I'll arrange for someone to move her. Make sure you go with her—she'll want to see a familiar face when she wakes up."

Pearl's eyes widened, and for a moment, I thought she might refuse, not wanting to go to a place where there might be sick, unsightly people. Then Pearl looked down at Mary Ann, swallowed, then nodded.

I got up and hurried towards one of the men who had returned with a stretcher, stepping carefully between the people.

"Excuse me," I waved at him. "There's a woman over here. She's lost a lot of blood."

"I'm not taking anyone to the hospital. It's full—"

"I know," I interrupted. "There's a house..." I passed the man Raven's calling card with his address on it. "I need you to take her to that address. Dr. Lapin is seeing patients there, and I believe there is room for as many as can't be accommodated in the hospital."

His eyes lit up. "That's good news, miss. Shall I spread the word?"

"Please do," I said, then pointed out Mary Ann and Pearl. "This is the woman. She needs to be moved there as soon as possible."

I waited a moment until I was sure that Mary Ann was safely on the stretcher, before moving through the bodies, searching their faces. Everywhere I looked, I saw the bloodstains on their bodies, the pain etched into their features, the worry on the faces of the loved ones clutching their hands—the dark legacy of the attack of the Hearts.

So much pain. So much blood. So much destruction. But I couldn't stop to help anyone in particular. I was driven to search the crowd for one face in particular.

Chesh.

My throat tightened. I should have searched for him when he was first injured, but I'd been distracted by the fight to repel the Hearts. I took a ragged breath. What if he hadn't made it?

That thought jolted my mind into gear. How many people hadn't made it? How many had perished defending Melfall from attack? How many had died in the streets because I had encouraged them to come out of their homes in the tunnels? How many would be alive today if we had never thought of the *Big Night Out*?

I put my hand over my mouth as tears sprang to my eyes. We'd wanted to change The Forge, and we'd certainly accomplished that vision, I thought bitterly. Tonight would go down in the history books as a night to be remembered—but not for the reasons we'd hoped.

I backed up, staring at all of the people who were injured because of me. Stepping backward, I almost tripped over another person lying on the cobblestones.

"I'm sorry, I'm so sorry," I said, murmuring the words over and over again. I turned and moved away, but everywhere I looked, I could see evidence of the destruction the Hearts had brought on our city— the injuries, the torn-up cobblestones, the broken scaffolding torn apart to use as weapons, the shocked and sobbing people who couldn't believe it had happened. Tears welled in my eyes, making the world around me a blur.

I walked straight into a woman wearing a red dress, but I couldn't see her features through my tears, even as I glanced at her face.

"I'm sorry, I'm so—"

"Ivy." The woman put her hands on my shoulders and gave me a little shake.

I blinked away the tears that burned my eyes. Gaia was standing there, looking at me with concern. "Are you alright?"

I sniffed, the tears streaming down my cheeks. "Am *I* alright?" I asked, sounding hysterical. I swept an arm around me. "I'm unharmed, but what about them?"

Gaia frowned, then pulled me over to a small space directly underneath the clocktower.

"You're not alright."

I shook my head. "I'm not injured. I'm looking for Chesh. What if he didn't make it? What if—"

"He did make it. He's fine. He's in the hospital."

My eyes opened wide. "He's alive?"

Gaia tilted her head to the side. "He had a serious injury to his shoulder, but, yes, he's alive, and he will heal."

I let out a sigh and let my head fall forward so that my chin rested almost against my chest. Then I noticed Genie wasn't with Gaia.

"What about—?"

"Genie is alright, too." Gaia smiled. "Or he will be with some care and attention. I left my phoenix there— he has magical healing powers, you know. He'll be in his element in the hospital, though I expect I'll find him in a pile of ashes when I return." Gaia squeezed my arm. "Thank you for asking after Genie's welfare. That means a lot to me."

"You're in love with him," I said, more of a statement than a question.

"Of course," Gaia answered. "It's obvious, isn't it?"

I paused, wondering how to phrase the question that had hovered on the edge of my thoughts since I'd known about Gaia and Genie's relationship.

"Do your parents approve?" I asked. "I mean the

King and Queen—the people who raised you."

Gaia put an arm around my shoulders. "Yes, I still think of them as my parents." Then she frowned slightly. "Why do you ask whether they approve?"

I shrugged. "He just doesn't seem quite the type for...forgive me, but you're a princess. He doesn't look like a prince."

Gaia smiled sadly. "My father wasn't a prince when my mother married him. He was an orphaned street urchin and a mischievous one, at that. Still, they fell in love and got married, and he was a good ruler."

"Was?"

"Until he lost his memory and went back to living on the streets like the orphan he'd started out as." Gaia sighed. "They married for love. I don't think they'd stop me from doing the same." She looked sideways at me. "Sometimes, the person who is the perfect match for our hearts isn't the person that our parents—or our kingdoms—would choose for us."

I nodded my head, then leaned my head against Gaia's shoulder, feeling suddenly exhausted. "I don't think anyone would approve of my stepping out with Raven. Last night made that perfectly obvious."

"You were having lots of fun with him, when I saw you," Gaia replied. "You two danced like there was nobody else in the world."

"There wasn't—not then, but..."

"But then those Hearts arrived and ruined it all?"

I ran a hand over my cheek and wiped away the tears. The mention of the Hearts brought back a thought that had been niggling at me since Alice locked the gate shut.

"Why did they do that, do you think? The Hearts, I mean."

"I've been wondering that too. It doesn't make sense, does it?" Gaia replied.

"Unless they're being controlled by someone else," I continued, thinking aloud. "At the end, when they suddenly stopped fighting, they just turned and marched straight out of the gates. As though someone had given them an order and they were just following it."

I frowned, looking at the people laid out over the cobblestones again, as another thought struck me.

"Where are they?" I asked, getting to my feet. "The Hearts that fell? They're gone."

Gaia got to her feet beside me. "The Hearts that could still move joined the others who were retreating. Those that couldn't move were dragged by the uninjured people and thrown over the wall after them. Nobody wanted any remains of them inside the walls."

I nodded, hesitating a moment as a thought nagged at me. Something that had happened during the fight. Then I remembered with a jerk.

"I saw you shooting fire from your fingertips, again," I said, astonished once again. "How do you do it?"

Gaia smiled. "I was wondering when you might ask more about my magic."

"Is it really magic?"

"Fire magic. It's one of the gifts my parents left me—left to all of us siblings, I suppose." Gaia winked. "You, too."

I stared at her, startled. "Magic? Me?"

"Don't you wonder about your affinity for watches and machines?"

I blinked, frozen into place as my mind whirred with this information. Her meaning dawned on me. Gaia arched her eyebrows and nodded her head. Other questions started to form in my mind, but a wave of weariness washed over me. I knew I should visit Chesh, or help with the injured, or do something, but the scene before me suddenly swam before my eyes, and I almost stumbled.

Gaia clung to my arm. "I need some sleep. You do too."

"You're not going to the hospital?"

Gaia shook her head. "Genie will be well looked after there, and my phoenix will watch over him. He'll only scold me for not looking after myself if I go to see him now. Come, let's get some sleep. We'll be needed later, I'm sure of that."

3RD SEPTEMBER

I sank down in the chair next to Chesh, who was tucked into a hospital bed, sleeping. His curly blonde hair was sticking out, laid out on the crisp, white pillow like curly rays of sunshine—or perhaps the mane of a lion. There were fresh bandages on his shoulder, the same crisp white as the sheets on his bed. His face was pale, and there were dark smudges under his eyes. His expression was peaceful in sleep, his mouth slack, and I wished for the smile that he had so often turned on me.

He'd told me he loved me. Twice.

How had I not seen it before?

Ever since I'd told him about meeting Raven, Chesh had been acting differently—strangely. I realized now that it was jealousy and an over-protective nature that had made him react so badly. I sat very still, in a state of conflict. I wanted to make sure he was alright, and I wanted to patch up our friendship, but I didn't want to drive a wedge even further between us.

Right now, in this in-between state, we could still be friends. If I said the wrong thing, we might never be friends again.

I sighed, reaching over to take his hand, stroking his skin with the pad of my thumb.

"Chesh," I whispered. "Get better. Then we'll make sure everything else is alright."

He stirred at my words, slowly rising to consciousness. He blinked, staring around the room before he turned his head slightly to settle on me.

"Ivy," he said, a sense of weary surprise in his voice. He shifted in bed to turn his body toward me and winced with the movement. To avoid the need for him to move any more, I stood to lean over him.

"You're hurt," I said.

"Yes, I've just remembered that," Chesh replied, sinking back on the pillows. "My shoulder."

"How is it?"

"There's a big hole in it," Chesh said with a grin. "It hurts."

I chuckled.

"You were very brave," I said, remembering how he'd leapt on the back of that Heart to protect me. "Thank you."

Chesh smiled briefly, closing his eyes for a moment, as though the effort of speaking was costing him energy.

"Do you want me to go?"

"No." Chesh's eyes flew open again. "You're not hurt?"

I shook my head. "I'm fine. I was lucky to have such

a great friend nearby when I needed him."

Chesh closed his eyes again, a smile on his face. Then he frowned, opening his eyes again. "I'm sorry, Ivy."

"We don't have to talk about it now." I patted his hand.

Chesh stared up at the ceiling. "I spent all day yesterday in pain, in and out of sleep, and all I could think of was the look on your face when I interrupted your dinner and punched your date in the face. I just wanted..."

His eyes flickered over to me, then he went back to staring at the ceiling. "I should have told you before. Years ago. You were never like other girls. I tried making you jealous, but you never took the bait. Then I thought that if I was your friend, in time, you would come to love me, the way I love you."

Chesh swallowed. I sat very still, saying nothing, my hands clasped in my lap. A lump formed in my throat. The words had been said, and they couldn't be taken back. Chesh needed an answer, and I needed to set my friend free.

"You don't love me, do you?" Chesh looked me in the eye.

"You're my best friend," I whispered, and a heavy, uncomfortable feeling settled in my stomach. I closed my eyes and took a deep breath, summoning my courage. "But no, I don't love you. Not the way you want me to."

Chesh sighed, and it seemed as though his body sank back into the mattress. He closed his eyes, and the smile slipped from his face again.

"I'm sorry, Chesh," I said. "I wish—"

"Me, too," Chesh replied. He lifted his hand, reaching out for mine. I reached forward to clasp it. I held him for a moment before he withdrew. "I think it might be best for you to go."

Tears prickled my eyes. This was it—the end of our friendship. I pressed my lips together, trying to hold my emotions in check.

"I just need some time, Ivy," Chesh said. "Seeing you every day—seeing you with *him*—it's too hard. I'm not saying we can't be friends, in time. I just..."

I stood up, nodding my head. "I know. I hope your shoulder heals quickly, and you get out of this hospital bed as quickly as you can. Then, when you're ready, you know where I live. I'd like to see you."

"Goodbye, Ivy."

I nodded and walked out, stopping in the doorway to glance back at Chesh, who was staring at the ceiling with a pained look on his face. I knew it had nothing to do with his shoulder.

⁓

I walked slowly down the hospital hallway, feeling as though I was floating along. The doctors and nurses rushed around me, like water flowing around a rock. People gathered in the doorways to hospital rooms, hovering around their injured family members.

I felt adrift, still seeing Chesh's grieved expression as I left the room and wondering if I would ever find the same easy friendship with him again. Perhaps, before I'd met Raven, I could have made it work with Chesh. Rationally, we had the same interests, the same sense of humor, and we got along well. We should have made a good match.

In my heart, though, I knew it wasn't love. Now that I'd met Raven, I knew that I couldn't pretend to be in love with Chesh when I wasn't.

I rounded a corner, making my way slowly towards the exit.

"Ivy?"

I looked up to see Gaia coming towards me. She had a light shawl wrapped around her shoulders, and she looked tired and drawn.

"Are you alright?" I asked.

Gaia smiled. "I'm not hurt. I've just spent too much time in this place over the last couple of days."

"Is Genie alright?"

Gaia nodded. "He's sent me away. He said he's disturbing my rest, and I should go home to get some sleep. Besides, my phoenix is there. He won't let anything happen to Genie." She yawned. "I can't say he's wrong. I know I should get some rest, but I can't help fussing over him. I'm lucky he's alive, really. Everyone is—it's a miracle that nobody died."

"Nobody died?" I asked. "Are you sure?"

"I've been asking those who brought the patients to the hospital, and I've checked in with the nurse stations. No fatalities."

I thought about the Heart that attacked Chesh. I'd assumed it was trying to kill Chesh, that it was luck that it put a hole in his shoulder instead of his heart. Perhaps, it chose to injure him, instead of going for the kill? But why?

Gaia smiled and put her arm around my shoulder, pulling me toward the exit. "I know that look. Come, tell me what you're puzzling out now—because I'm too tired to work it out on my own, and I've got to go home. Walk with me."

We stepped out into the heat and sunshine of a hot day—the air was clammy and still. I fanned at my face, while Gaia let the shawl drop from her shoulders. We took the couple of steps down from the entrance to the hospital to the street, then turned down Fourth Avenue back in the direction of the President's Palace, where Gaia was now staying, too.

"I was just thinking that it's more than good luck that nobody died."

Gaia blinked. "You think the Hearts didn't mean to kill anyone? I could've sworn when they charged at us with spears that they intended murder."

"Me too," I replied. "Now that I think of it, though, the Heart that injured Chesh had a clear shot at him. He could have put that spear through Chesh's heart and felled him on the spot. Instead, he put the spear through his shoulder and let him live. Maybe that was purposeful."

Gaia was quiet for a moment while she digested that information. "Genie could have been killed too. But he wasn't. I thought it was luck, but maybe you're right."

"If everyone escaped without life-threatening injuries, it has to be more than luck."

"If the Hearts weren't intending to kill anyone, what were they doing?"

I shrugged. "That's what's so hard to understand. Every time I've seen a Heart, it hasn't been wandering aimlessly. It's been marching somewhere—with purpose. They want something, but what?"

"Or maybe they're going somewhere?" Gaia suggested.

"Where?" I asked. "And why?"

"They didn't appear to have a leader," Gaia said. "But they must have—they were too well coordinated to be acting independently. They must be taking orders from someone."

I stared into my sister's golden eyes, knowing they mirrored my own. "You're right. When they suddenly retreated, it was as though somebody had flicked a switch, and they all just stopped fighting and left, marching at the same pace they'd come. Someone else was in control of them."

"Have the Hearts harassed the city before?" Gaia asked.

I nodded. "Eighteen years ago—they did the work of the Queen of Hearts. They killed for her, so they're certainly capable of it."

"Do you think the Queen of Hearts is controlling them again?"

I rubbed my fingers at my temple. "Raven said he thinks the Queen has returned. After what you said about the things that are happening in the other kingdoms, perhaps... Alice doesn't believe it—she's adamant that the Queen is dead, but Raven said she's a vampire and would have been difficult to kill. If that's the truth, then she might be in control of the Hearts again. Or, it could be one of her loyal servants. There are still those who are loyal to her in The Forge." I thought of the Tweedles and wondered whether they could have been responsible for the attack the other night. Without knowing who was behind the attacks, I couldn't be sure that the Hearts wouldn't attack again. The question gnawed at me, and I resolved to make some inquiries.

"At least, the Hearts are locked out of the city," Gaia said. I murmured my agreement as I wondered what they were doing out there. We crossed the street, arm in arm, passing a greengrocer. I blinked as I recognized one of the women from the tunnels the other night, working behind the register—one of the women who

357

had greeted Raven in the street as we'd walked to *The Menagerie.*

The woman smiled as she caught my eye, and raised her hand to greet me, then turned back to serving her customer.

Gaia caught the greeting and leaned toward me. "Apparently, since so many are injured, the unbeautiful citizens have been given opportunities to work that they wouldn't have had before." Gaia squeezed my arm. "See? The Forge can change. Not all at once, but we've made a difference over these last few days."

I stared at the woman for a moment before turning away. "I've been thinking that if we hadn't tried to force change, a lot of people would not be lying in the hospital right now."

Gaia stopped walking abruptly, then turned to me and put a hand on my cheek. "This wasn't your fault. You've helped people to improve their lives. Look at her—she's not starving in the tunnels, or living off charity. She's working for a living. A few days ago, it wouldn't have been possible. And she is only the start—I'm certain of it."

4TH SEPTEMBER

I walked up the steps of the perimeter wall until I reached the walk that ran all the way around the ramparts. On one side, the city of Melfall spread out, a maze of buildings huddled together around straight avenues, between an interconnecting puzzle of streets and narrow alleys. Once again, I spotted the decorations on top of the roofs all over the city, still moving ceaselessly like cogs in a machine.

I squinted at them—was it my imagination, or were the cogs moving in time to the ticking of the clock? In fact, I had to strain to hear the sound of the ticking. It seemed quieter than it had only days ago.

"Miss Rowntree?"

I turned to see Captain Walsh saluting me.

"Captain Walsh," I replied, and he dropped his hand,

though his posture was still straight and tall.

"Have you come to see our new sculpture garden?"

I blinked at him. "I beg your pardon?"

He chuckled. "Just a little joke, Miss Rowntree. Yesterday, one of the guards mentioned that they were so still; it was like they were statues. Like sculptures—though they're no work of art, in my opinion."

"You mean the Hearts are still here?" I exclaimed, then rushed over to the other side of the walk and looked away from the city, towards the rolling hills that stretched out toward the distant horizon. Only, now, the hills were marked by approximately one hundred Hearts standing in rows.

The Captain was right. The Hearts didn't move. They stood erect and completely still.

"They haven't moved since President Rowntree locked the gates. Not a single movement from any of them—and my guards have been watching them around the clock since the attack."

I stared at the Hearts, standing in straight rows in the same formation they'd taken when they marched out of the city.

"What about the broken ones?" I asked, stretching to look directly down to the base of the wall. "I heard they were thrown over?"

"Well, there's the mystery. The remains of the broken Hearts have disappeared."

"Disappeared?" I looked at him. "Your guards didn't see anything?"

Captain Walsh shook his head. "They didn't, but that doesn't mean they weren't looking. The fact is that the wall is long and, even doubled, my guards cannot see everything."

I clenched my teeth, determined to keep my mouth

shut, despite the obvious questions. I looked over the Hearts again, doing a rough count.

"There seem to be more than the number of Hearts who marched out of the gate," I commented.

Captain Walsh looked out, frowning, and I could see him surveying the Hearts, as though doing some quick calculations of his own.

"Do we know how many Hearts there were to begin with?"

"No, miss. I don't believe anyone counted," Captain Walsh responded. His posture straightened and tensed, and he suddenly sounded defensive. "There was quite a lot going on at that time, and most of my guards were patrolling the city streets instead of manning the towers. President's orders, you know."

I sighed. "I'm not blaming you or your guards," I said, trying to sound diplomatic. "I'm just trying to work out where they came from and who sent them."

Captain Walsh shrugged. "Doesn't matter now, does it? The city gates are locked, and the Hearts have run out of energy. If that's what they ran on, to begin with. They don't seem like much of a threat to me, right now."

I pressed my lips together. *Not right now, but I'm not counting them out completely.*

His words about the Hearts running out of energy struck me, though, and I stared down at them.

Captain Walsh cleared his throat. I became aware that he had asked me something.

"I beg your pardon, Miss Rowntree, but since you're here, I wonder whether you might take a tour of the wall and barracks? All of the guards were pulled back from leave to patrol the city on the *Big Night Out*, and since then, they've been pulling double shifts to ensure the wall is properly guarded. I expect our President is very busy just at the minute, but people think of you as her representative. It would be helpful for morale if you walked among them for a short time, and thanked them for their efforts."

I wanted to say no, but couldn't deny that the city guards had been very helpful in patrolling the *Big Night Out*, then during the Heart attack, and since. I inclined my head in agreement and dutifully followed Captain Walsh to greet the guards.

~

"What are you doing?"

Gaia sat on the window seat underneath my bedroom window. She'd come to see me in my room after having woken from an afternoon nap. I sat at my table with little cogs and gears spread all over. I was wearing my goggles to magnify the tiny gears as I worked on the pocket watch I was making for Gaia.

"Keeping my hands busy helps me to think," I replied without meeting her eyes.

"What are you thinking about?" Gaia asked.

"The Hearts."

"About who is controlling them?"

I nodded. "the Hearts are robots. They have been made to look human, with card armor and helmets, but they aren't human. They're programmed."

I fiddled with one of the tiny round gear wheels with teeth that wouldn't quite fit into place. The placement had to be perfect, or it wouldn't connect properly to the other wheels, and the escapement mechanism wouldn't run properly or keep time. I held my breath as I used a small set of tweezers to fit the wheel into place, but it slipped from my grip. I sighed as I set the wheel down

362

on the table, changed my grip on the tweezers and tried again.

"If they're programmed, then somebody is in control of their responses."

"Someone used them to attack the city," Gaia replied. "We talked about this already."

"Yes, but the fact that they're outside the city, still and unresponsive, doesn't mean they're no longer a threat. They're not dead—they're just waiting for a signal to power up again. While we don't know who's controlling them, we don't know when that might happen."

"We shouldn't wait around for an attack to come."

I shut my eyes and focused on *feeling* the gear into place. I could feel the energy pulsating through my fingers where I held the tiny pieces of the watch. The parts of the watch felt like parts of myself, and I concentrated my mind on *thinking* them into the right place. I heard a *click* as the tiny gear fit into place.

My eyes flew open, and I smiled in triumph before setting the still unfinished watch back on the table. I leaned back to stretch my shoulders. "That's exactly what I was thinking. We should be ready for it," I replied, once again, thankful that Gaia and I seemed to be on a similar wavelength when it came to solving problems. It felt so natural to talk through problems with her—as though we'd been doing it for years, rather than less than a week.

The late afternoon light fell over Gaia's shoulder, setting off her profile with a line of gold, as though she was some sort of goddess. The sun would soon dip beneath the horizon, and I felt a thrill of excitement shoot through me at the notion that it was almost time for me to visit Raven. Part of me scolded myself that I shouldn't be so excited when the city and its people faced so many problems, but I couldn't deny the way my heart pounded when I thought about him.

"You are thinking that your new friend might have the answers to this puzzle?" Gaia asked, looking at me from underneath her long eyelashes, with a smirk on her face.

I shrugged one shoulder in mock innocence. "Raven might be able to answer some of my questions. It's worth a try."

"I suppose that's the only reason you're going to see him?" Gaia teased. "I'm sure it has nothing to do with his handsome face and dashing figure."

I blushed but knew it was pointless denying it. A thought struck me. "You think Raven is handsome?"

Gaia rolled her eyes. "It doesn't matter what I think. You think he is handsome. As it happens, I understand the attraction to a man who looks younger than he is. After all, who can argue with the beauty of youth and the wisdom of age?"

"Is Genie much older than you?" I asked. "He's not a vampire, too, is he?"

Gaia shook his head. "Not a vampire, but yes, he is somewhat older than me. He's a genie—but don't go asking him for wishes. He doesn't have that magic anymore." She stood up and walked to the door, giving me a wink as she left. "Don't stay out too late."

It was dark by the time I stepped down the ladder and into the tunnels that ran underneath the city. I'd tried the shop first, but Miss Lapin told me that Raven hadn't been in since the attack. Then, I'd tried his house, but his butler informed me that Raven had not been seen at the residence since turning it into a halfway house. He also mentioned that Raven had not slept since the attack. The butler seemed rushed off his feet, so I hadn't pressed him for more details, but if Raven hadn't slept for days, I knew that meant he'd been out of the reach of the sunlight.

That meant there was only one place he could be— the network of tunnels that ran underneath Melfall.

As the lamplighter lit the street lamps, I'd retraced my steps to the place where Raven had first brought me down to the tunnels. I slid open the manhole cover and lowered myself down the ladder and into the darkness.

Somewhere, I could hear the dripping of water. It was cooler down here, but the moisture made it feel just as humid as the surface.

I followed the torchlights along the tunnel, and it wasn't long before I bumped into the people who had made these tunnels their home. They confirmed my suspicions and led me through the maze of tunnels to find Raven.

I entered a brightly lit room with a map of Melfall pinned to the wall, alongside other papers scribbled with lists of items and names. A number of people were standing around Raven as they looked at something, and they all turned to look at me as I cleared my throat.

Raven's face lit up with a smile. He wiped his hands on his trousers, which looked uncharacteristically rumpled, and stepped around the table.

The others mumbled something about having "things to do" and scuttled out of the room. Raven didn't take his eyes off me as they left, and when the last of them left the room, he reached out to put a hand on my cheek.

"Ivy," he breathed, speaking my name with such longing. He drew me to him, pressed his forehead to mine, and closed his eyes as though in prayer. I curled my fist in his shirt, and we stood like that for a moment, clutching each other, before he bent down to brush a soft kiss to my lips. "I'm sorry, I haven't come to see you. It's not because I didn't want to."

"Your butler thinks you've abandoned your home to make it into a halfway house. He didn't seem particularly pleased about it."

The edge of Raven's mouth curled up in a smile. "The hospital was full. How could I let my house stand empty while the people of this city bled on the streets? The place is too big for me, anyway."

"He also said you haven't slept in days." I raised my eyebrows in mock admonishment.

"I'm a vampire, I don't need nearly as much sleep as a mortal." He stroked my cheek. "I couldn't rest while the people of this city needed help."

I leaned my ear against his chest as I looked around the room. "What have you been doing? This looks like a base of operations."

Raven chuckled. "I've built up networks over the years, especially since I've been working to better the lives of the hidden, and the vampires of this city. It puts me in a unique position to make sure those who suffered blood loss have access to the blood they need for a full recovery."

"You're supplying the hospitals now, as well as the vampires?" I looked up at him.

"Since we've been unable to get access to the blood banks, vampires have been building up their own stores, paying me for blood that I get from Wit's patients. Now, they're donating their stores to the cause."

"Even though the blood banks are still withholding blood?"

Raven nodded. "I've never known my kind to be so charitable, especially toward mortals."

"You're the go-between, making sure the donated blood gets to where it's needed?"

Raven shrugged, though there was a hint of a pleased smile. "Blood, supplies, medicines—I've got a network of people and vampires who can move things around the city. It's useful to have in a time like this. Plus, I've already got a network established to find places to live for people who need one—the hidden are moving out of the tunnels and back to the surface. Now, we're passing along offers of work to those who might be able to step in to cover for those injured in the attacks."

"I saw an unbeautiful woman yesterday, serving in the front of a shop. Last week, she would never have been hired to serve customers. Things are changing."

"We have to capitalize on this momentum while there is some goodwill in the city. I can't rest while we have the opportunity to take advantage of this crisis to forge a place for the hidden to be part of society again. If we don't, we risk Melfall going back to the way it used to be. I won't let that happen."

I smiled up at him, bursting with pride. "Good. Just make sure you look after yourself. I don't want to see you collapsing from exhaustion—it won't do anyone any good."

Raven chuckled again and brushed a lock of hair from my face. "I've missed you," he murmured as he leaned down to press a lingering kiss to my lips. I wrapped my arms around his torso, pressing myself against him, as though trying to forge our bodies into one.

When we pulled away from each other, I found myself breathless and blinking in the flickering light of the torches on the damp walls.

"As lovely as it is to see you, Ivy, I have more to do, and I don't want you wandering around the city at night. After the attack, I worry about you."

"Would your work allow you to walk me home?" I asked, though I didn't want to leave. "We could talk on the way. I did actually come to see you for a reason."

Raven arched an eyebrow. "Aside from the pleasure of my company?"

It was my turn to chuckle. "Your company is equally alluring," I replied as Raven motioned for me to follow him out of the room and back into the darkness of the tunnels. He didn't take a torch from the walls, and though I could barely see through the darkness around me, Raven moved with the confidence of someone who could both see and knew where he was going. He took my hand, and I wove my fingers between his, thankful for the contact as I moved blindly through the dark.

"What did you want to ask me?" Raven's soft voice echoed off the tunnel walls like the sounds of our footsteps.

"I wanted to ask if you have found out anything more about the Hearts and who is controlling them."

I heard Raven take a deep breath. "No more than guesses. The Hearts used to be controlled by the Queen. I told you that I think she's back. I don't have anything to prove it, but that's still my hunch."

"We need to disable those Hearts so that the Queen— or whoever is using them to attack the city—can't use them anymore."

"Can you do it?" Raven asked.

I bit my lip, hesitating as I remembered what Gaia said about my 'knack' before I answered. "I can try."

5TH SEPTEMBER

"This extraordinary city hall meeting will come to order," The town crier's voice boomed from the front of the large city hall. I stood on my tiptoes in the crowd, stretching to see around the tall feathers on the hat of the woman who stood in front of me. On either side, my shoulders pressed against other people. The chairs had been removed so there was standing room only in the cavernous space

I guessed that had caused some grumbles from those who had arrived first, but now it seemed as though everyone in the entire city was trying to squeeze into one of the few large meeting halls the city offered.

There wasn't even room to fan my face, and in the warmth of the day and the crush of the room, a wave of heat swept over me.

At the front of the hall, Alice stood on a raised stage, waiting for the moment to speak. This morning, she'd left me a note that she was calling a town meeting, and that I should attend, but she hadn't told me what it was about.

I could only guess it was about the recent attack on Melfall, but I hadn't had the chance to speak to her.

In one corner, I noticed a group of vampires with Raven among them. They appeared through a back door and, since the meeting was being held in the middle of the day, I guessed there had to be an opening to one of the tunnels somewhere in the back of the building. I could see Raven looking over the crowd—for me—and I tried to catch his eye, but he didn't see me before Alice stepped up to the dais.

As she did so, another man stood on the side of the stage, watching her as though she was the only person in the world. Wit put his hands together, as though he was clapping—or praying—but he didn't make a sound. I remembered seeing them together at the *Big Night Out*, learning that they had been old friends. By the look in Wit's eyes, I knew there was more than friendship between them—on his part, at least.

The muttering of the crowd fell to silence as Alice paused, waiting for their attention before she started to address everyone.

"Welcome, citizens of Melfall, and thank you for attending at such short notice. I think you will agree that the events of the last few days warrant immediate action."

A ripple of a murmur ran through the crowd as people wondered what Alice was going to say. The pre-meeting chatter had converged on the same topic. Some thought she was going to announce special security measures. Others speculated that she knew the origins of the attack. Still others, worried that she was going to announce that she'd made a deal with the Queen of Hearts, to return the throne to the Queen in return for her life and banishment from the kingdom.

Tension knotted my shoulders, and I wished I'd had the chance to speak to Alice before the meeting. While I was confident that she had done no such deal with the Queen of Hearts, it reminded me of Raven's conviction that the Queen would return.

The woman in front of me moved, and the feathers obscured my vision again. I shifted sideways, too, accidentally stepping on the toes of the man next to me.

"Sorry," I whispered. Several people shushed me as Alice started talking again.

"There are to be changes to The Forge and to the city of Melfall," Alice continued, raising her voice over the whispers of the crowd.

The muttering suddenly ceased. Absolute silence fell like a blanket over the crowd.

"A few days ago, a group of people organized an event. I'm sure you have all heard of the *Big Night Out*— an event designed to call attention to the plight of those people who live in this city but have been ignored and forced into hiding because of the way they look."

"The people who attended the *Big Night Out* risked discrimination and arrest for being on the streets and in venues in flagrant disregard of the aesthetic laws of The Forge."

Alice paused and looked around. Many of the people who had been at the *Big Night Out* were also here in the crowd. I recognized many faces, including Mr. Thackery and his wife, who were now looking at Alice with a mixture of fear and hope on their faces. Alice's next words could change their lives or condemn them.

"If those people had not risked arrest to attend the *Big Night Out*, the Hearts would have outnumbered us. Without them, the Hearts would have controlled our streets. Our city would have fallen to those heartless beings. Of that, I am sure. Whoever controls the Hearts would be standing in front of you now."

"Instead, the people of this city—young and old, rich and poor, beautiful and," Alice paused. "*less* beautiful, humans and vampires—*we* stood together and fought together, to defeat the Hearts and to drive them from Melfall."

The crowd burst into chatter and applause. A small smile tugged at my lips.

"Since the attack, I have watched the citizens of this city rally together—to help the injured, to keep business running while the owners cannot work, to find supplies, to source hospital beds for the injured, to find housing for those without it. All of the citizens of Melfall have worked together—no matter their background, appearance, or income—for the recovery of and betterment of our great city."

"I stand before you to thank you all for your contributions to the life of our city at this time."

People broke into applause, looking around to grin at each other. I could see the pleasure on their faces and the pride that they felt at being part of it. I found myself smiling and clapping along with them. Not because of my part in it, so much, but because I was proud of the people. Yes, I had a hand in getting some of them out of the tunnels and into the streets of Melfall, but the way the people had put their differences aside and fought alongside each other—they had saved themselves, and they deserved to revel in their success.

Alice was smiling too, as she looked around at the crowd. Then she glanced over her shoulder at Wit, who nodded his head once in encouragement. Then Alice turned her attention back to the crowd and held up her hands for silence again.

"Our city cannot go back to the way it was before the attack. We cannot go back to the differences that drove division between us. We cannot go back to the laws that rewarded some and punished others—not for their skills or labor or achievements, but for their appearances."

I held my breath, clasping my hands in front of my chest as I strained on tiptoes to see Alice.

When she spoke again, her voice was sure and authoritative. "Henceforth, with immediate effect, the aesthetic laws will be repealed. Nobody will be able to refuse service or employment to anyone because of the way they look, nor will licenses to conduct business be refused or revoked for aesthetic reasons."

A selection of the crowd cheered. Others looked at each other, gobsmacked. A knot formed in my chest as Alice took a deep breath before she continued.

"Furthermore, the aesthetic stipend will be discontinued."

At Alice's words, the crowd erupted. There were a few cheers, but just as many people who were shouting. The faces around me ranged from shocked to angry to afraid. I heard snippets of the conversations around me.

"...how am I supposed to support myself now?..."

"...that's alright for those with another livelihood, but it will force many into poverty..."

"...about time people did more than just stare at mirrors all day..."

"...I'll be ruined..."

"...my business relies on people receiving the stipend..."

The knot in my chest tightened. I thought of Pearl, knowing she would take the news hard. I looked around, but if she was at the meeting, I didn't see her. At the back of the room, I glimpsed Gaia, who was nodding and smiling. There was no way of moving through the crowd to get to her, certainly not while the people were so worked up. For a moment, I wondered whether the crowd would surge toward the front, taking power from Alice by force and crushing me in the process.

Alice was holding up her hands again, trying to calm the crowd, but it was having little effect. She glanced back at Wit with a worried look on her face. Wit was frowning, too.

The town crier stepped forward. He thumped his staff on the ground, though the sound was barely audible over the crowd. "Order, order!" he boomed.

"Please, quiet now. Quiet, please," Alice called out.

"Order! This meeting will come to order!"

"Let the President speak!" It was Raven's voice that carried over the noise of the crowd. He stepped up to the side of the stage, emanating authority as he stared out over the crowd. From the whispers around me, many citizens knew the role he'd played helping people over the last few days. At his statement, the crowd quietened, though discontent still rippled around the hall.

Alice gave Raven an appreciative look before she continued.

"Thank you, fellow citizens, I know this is a big change. It is a bigger change for some of you than for others. I recognize this. It is for this reason that, while the aesthetic stipend will cease, the city will provide assistance to those who were receiving the stipend to learn new skills and to obtain employment."

"There will also be assistance and compensation to those who have lost their businesses due to the application of the aesthetic laws. Further assistance will be provided to those who have been living in the city tunnels to find new homes. As you have all come together to save this city, so this city will come together to make sure there is a place for all of you. Nobody will fall through the cracks. Nobody will be left behind. This, I promise you."

Alice let her words settle. There was silence now—but it was a thoughtful silence, rather than a silence of anticipation or of fear.

The woman in front of me moved, and her hat now completely obscured my view. I looked around me, wondering whether there would be a protest about the loss of an income that was considered to be vital to many of the people present. I'd never anticipated how difficult it would be to take a payment from people who were used to it and believed they deserved it.

Finally, after a long pause, Alice spoke again. "The Forge used to be a kingdom. Now it is a republic. I am not your queen. I am your president. I do not govern by divine right, but because you—the citizens of The Forge—have chosen me to lead you. So, I now declare the meeting open to those who would like to speak—either for or against the change of laws."

Alice stepped away from the podium and smiled at the crowd.

My throat tightened, and I looked around again. The murmurs of discontent quietened, and people looked around at each other. At the side of the stage, Raven had stepped down to the ground and was now looking around at the people in the hall with his arms crossed.

There was a long pause, and I wondered who would be the first person to speak. Alice stood on the stage, looking around.

Nobody stepped forward.

Alice visibly sighed with relief and was about to step up to the podium when I heard a series of footsteps clicking over the floorboards.

I strained on my tiptoes to see who was there, but all I could see were bright pink feathers in front of my face.

When the person spoke, though, I didn't need to see. I could have identified that voice anywhere.

"My name is Pearl Rowntree," Pearl's voice sounded small and unsure—something I'd never known Pearl to be. "Our President is my mother. I'm eighteen. I've never worked. I've always lived on the stipend. The decision of our President will take away my livelihood. Honestly, I don't know what I will do without it."

My mouth went dry, and I saw a pained expression on Alice's face. There was a murmur among the crowd as Pearl took a breath. Then, she continued: "A few days ago, if Mother had proposed the abolition of the aesthetic stipend, I would have spoken out against it. Now, I'm standing here to say, I think the President is right."

The crowd around me gasped, then chatter erupted. Towards the other side of the room, someone called for quiet so that we could continue to hear Pearl speak.

"The other night, I was in the center of the dancing when the Hearts attacked. I thought I was going to die."

My throat constricted as I heard the waver in Pearl's voice. "I would have died if it wasn't for the brave actions of a woman—a stranger—but who I now know was a

376

friend I hadn't met yet. Her name is Mary Ann. She's in the hospital, recovering from injuries that she sustained when she helped me fight off that Heart. Before that night, she lived in the tunnels with so many others who couldn't show their faces on the streets. She might not be beautiful enough to receive the stipend, but she is truly the bravest person I have ever met.

"So, the only thing to do now is what our President— my mother—says is right. She's always right, and now is no exception." Pearl cleared her throat. "That's all."

I blinked tears from my eyes as I heard Pearl's footsteps. I imagined her stepping down from the stage. Alice waited a few more moments, but nobody else spoke.

Finally, Alice stepped back to the podium. "I know these are big changes for each of you and for our city. Please know, even if you have not stepped forward to speak now, my doors are open to you if you wish to petition me in the future. We will stand together—I do not intend to leave anyone behind." Alice inclined her head. "Thank you all."

~

The crowd flowed out of the town hall like a dam that had burst. There was lots of chatter, and most of it was about Alice's proclamation. I heard a few mutterings and musings about how things were going to work, but most people seemed to be curious rather than opposed. Alice's promises not to leave anyone behind seemed to have mollified most of the initial concerns among those people who risked losing their income and livelihood.

As soon as I stepped out onto the cobblestones of the avenue, I looked quickly around for Gaia. Raven, I knew, would have disappeared into the tunnels since the sun was still high in the sky, but Gaia should still be about. The crowd was too thick to find her, and I didn't want to waste time looking when there was no guarantee that I would find her in amongst most of the population of Melfall.

Besides, I'd promised Raven that I was going to find out how the Hearts worked, and disable them, to make sure they could not be used against the city again.

I turned in the direction of the wall and walked briskly along the almost empty streets. Most of the shops and restaurants were closed, as their proprietors had been at the town meeting and hadn't yet reopened. It wasn't long until I was craning my neck to stare up at the stone ramparts of the perimeter wall.

"Miss Rowntree?" Captain Walsh asked as I knocked on the door of the gatehouse.

"I want to see the Hearts," I said, without preamble.

The captain frowned. "Again?"

He hesitated, waiting for me to confirm my request, then sighed and started to lead me up the stone steps set into the wall. I put a hand on his arm to stop him, then I pointed to the gates, now firmly closed.

"I want to go outside," I said. "I need to see the Hearts up close."

Captain Walsh's forehead furrowed as his frown deepened. He started shaking his head emphatically. "No, Miss Rowntree. I'm afraid that's not possible."

"I understand the Hearts are dangerous...," I said, eager to forestall his arguments and change his mind.

"You do not understand, Miss Rowntree," Captain Walsh said. He crossed his arms over his chest. "I cannot comply with your request."

"I understand you want to protect me. You are one

378

of the brave guards of our city," I continued, clasping my hands in front of me as though in prayer.

"It is not possible," he replied with a firm shake of his head.

I held up a finger. "Anything is possible if you're willing to give it a try."

"It is not, miss." Captain Walsh repeated, his voice rising a notch. "You don't understand—"

"No, sir," I interrupted. "It is you who doesn't understand. All I want is to examine the Hearts. I want to see how they work, to disarm them so that they can't threaten us anymore."

Captain Walsh sighed and rubbed at his forehead. "It is not a matter of will, Miss Rowntree. It's not that I am refusing to open the gates. I simply can't do it. The president has the only key. Our city is on lockdown until she orders otherwise."

"Oh," I stared at him for a moment, then looked down at my hands, feeling foolish.

"So, you see, no matter how good your reasons are for needing to leave the city, or examine those dreadful Hearts, I'm afraid I cannot comply with your request."

I sighed, then a thought struck me. "What if the president orders you to open the gates?"

"As long as the president's orders coincide with her giving me the key to open the gates," Captain Walsh gave me a small smile. "Then, I'd be happy to comply. Well... *happy* might be the wrong word, but I would follow my president's orders." He gave me a small bow in what seemed to be a sort of apology. "I'm sorry I can't help you on this occasion, Miss Rowntree. Still, we can all feel a little safer that nobody but the president can open the gates. I have faith that she will do no such thing until we can eliminate the menace of the Hearts forever. Those Hearts will stay out there, and we'll stay in here. Safe."

I nodded, wondering how we would ever know the Hearts were no longer a threat if we couldn't study them. I took my leave of Captain Walsh, and, lifting my skirts, I trudged slowly up the stone steps to the top of the wall. A cool breeze ruffled my hair as I stepped out onto the walk. I touched the rough stone, leaning over the edge to look down on the Hearts.

At first glance, it seemed as though nothing had changed. The Hearts stood completely still. The wind rustled the tips of the long grass that grew around their feet, but the Hearts were unmoved.

I tapped my fingers on the stone of the battlements, staring at them, as my thoughts turning instinctively to the puzzle of these Hearts. There were lots of them standing at attention outside the walls. Hundreds of them.

The puzzle still gnawed at me. I couldn't believe that the Hearts had voluntarily marched out of the city to die.

I sighed again, leaning my elbows on the battlements to prop my chin on my hands. I would find no answers up here. There was nothing for it.

I'd have to speak to Alice.

The shadows were long by the time I made my way home from my visit to the perimeter wall. The fastest way was directly across the circular marketplace of the city center, past the Pinnacle, and under the glare of the ever-watching clock. As I approached the site of the attack, I hesitated, debating taking the longer way around.

The city center was empty—it had been since the night of the attack. It used to be a place where people milled and mingled. Now, most people avoided this place, and anyone who walked through here did so with their eyes focused straight ahead—as though they were afraid of seeing the blood that still stained the cobblestones.

I gritted my teeth, telling myself that there were no ghosts here, only memories. I forced myself to keep walking. To take the quickest way home. If I was lucky, Alice would be able to see me right away, and I'd have the key to the gates in my hand by morning.

I glanced up at the Pinnacle clock as I strode across the center of the city. I hadn't really intended to look at it, but something caught my eye. I looked up at it again, slowing down until I came to a complete stop.

Something was different about the clock tower. I frowned up at it. What had changed?

I slowly circled the Pinnacle, craning my neck to see. The play of late afternoon light and shadows made it difficult to see clearly, but the clock tower seemed...less intricate somehow. As though someone had removed the gears and inner workings of the clock.

It was still ticking, though—I could hear it clearly.

I put a hand over my eyes to shade from the glare of the late afternoon sun and stared up again. Perhaps the workmen had started working on it once more. But no—the ladder and scaffolding from the bottom level of the clock were still damaged from where people had torn them apart to use the wood as weapons against the Hearts. The workers would have had to fix the scaffolding and the ladder before they could climb up to the upper levels to work on the clock.

I stared, taking a few steps back to get a better look. I stepped into a shadow, where the light wasn't shining straight into my eyes. Within moments, the light dimmed quickly as the sun dipped underneath the horizon. The glare suddenly disappeared.

I stared up, just as the lamplighter started to light the street lamps molded into the shape of Hearts with a flame burning in the center.

The lamplighter moved onto the next lamp, tipping his hat to me as he hummed and moved along. The sound of his lonely tune echoed through the almost empty space. I turned back to the clock, starting to walk again, slowly making my way across the cobblestones towards the President's Palace.

I was on the other side of the market when I glanced at the clock again. It was almost like a compulsion—I'd never been able to find out how the clock worked, and it was another unsolved puzzle in my life.

As I glanced up, I saw some of the gears exposed. I stared. There *was* something different about the clock. It wasn't that the gears had been taken out of the clock. They had been covered. Some kind of sheeting now covered the inner workings of the giant clock.

It couldn't have been the workers, though, because the scaffolding hadn't been fixed. Unless, with everything else that had happened on the day of the *Big Night Out*, I hadn't noticed the changes.

Was that it? I sighed, rubbing my forehead. I couldn't be sure, but the thought gnawed at me. Why hadn't I noticed the other night?

A hand clapped me on the shoulder, and I sucked in a breath as I whirled around.

Raven stood there, one hand in his pocket, his mouth curled up in a half-smile, and his eyes sparkling as he tipped his hat at me.

"My love," he whispered. "I've missed you."

Raven was still grinning when we approached the gates of the President's Palace.

"It was a good day," I murmured.

"I didn't see you at the town hall," Raven said.

"I was there."

"I know." Raven winked. "I caught a hint of your scent."

I slapped him playfully on the arm. "I don't smell."

"I didn't say you smell," Raven replied, chuckling. "You do have a particular scent, though. It is very pleasant."

"Thank you," I blushed. "I think."

"Things did go well today," Raven agreed. "This marks the beginning of a new era for The Forge."

"I hope so," I said.

"Our president was great today—very convincing. Nobody spoke against her."

"It won't be smooth sailing," I replied, thinking about the muttered comments I'd heard around me.

"No, but we have made progress, and far quicker than I ever imagined we would. I hope we'll move everyone out of the tunnels by the end of the month."

"So long?"

Raven looked sideways at me. "We have to find housing for everyone—affordable housing."

"Mother said the city would help with that."

Raven nodded. "She did. Still, it takes time."

The guard at the gate recognized me and opened the gate without a word. Raven followed me to the door, then pulled on my hand to stop me.

"This is where I leave you tonight."

"You don't want to come in to see the others?"

Raven smiled. "I would, but I have things to do tonight."

"Don't you ever rest?"

Raven shook his head. "I don't need much rest."

"Is that how you make so many hats?"

He chuckled, brushing his thumb across my cheek as he inspected the hat I was wearing today. "Yes, although I haven't much time for it at present. My shop is looking distinctly under-stocked."

I snorted and rolled my eyes. "Your shop looked cluttered before. Now, it'll be just right."

"Speaking of hats," Raven plucked at the ribbon on the headpiece I was wearing. "This isn't one of mine."

A faint blush spread across my cheeks, and I wondered whether Raven could see the color under the flickering lamplights along the drive. "Pearl bought it for me."

Raven made a non-committal sound. "She surprised me today. I thought she'd be against the change."

I nodded. "You mean to say your superior senses misjudged her character?" I replied mockingly.

Raven dipped his head, sheepishly, acknowledging my dig at him. "It is rare that I misjudge a person's character, but I'll admit,"—Raven met my eye with a sheepish look—"she might not have been the first person I have misjudged recently."

I gave him a mock-stern look. "As long as you don't hold fast to your first impressions—"

"You know I don't."

"then I suppose you might redeem yourself yet." I winked at him, then turned serious. "I'll admit, I was

384

surprised too. I haven't seen Pearl in a couple of days either. Not since the attack. Though now that I think of it, Alice mentioned that Pearl has been helping to nurse the patients who had been taken to your house to be treated."

"If Pearl can see beyond her friend's appearance, then it gives me hope for Melfall," Raven murmured.

"There's often more to a person than appearances would have you believe," I agreed, though I was thinking of the Hearts standing outside the wall. As though they were waiting for something.

"Alice was smart to move on the changes while the attack was still fresh in the people's minds. I'm going to have to make you a new hat."

I blinked. "A new hat?"

"Since we're discussing appearances, I'll not have you walking around wearing another milliner's hat." He grinned, then pressed a kiss on my lips, then on my forehead. As he pulled away, Mr. Hopewell opened the door.

"Miss Rowntree?" he said. "Welcome home. Dinner has been served, but I'll have someone bring a tray to your room."

Raven brought my hand to his lips and pressed a kiss to my knuckles. "Good night, Miss Rowntree. I will see you again soon."

6TH SEPTEMBER

A serving girl, Rose, stood in the hall, holding out a silver tray laden with a single cup and saucer, and a number of sweet pastries. Alice took the cup of coffee, acknowledging Rose with a nod and taking a quick sip as her ladies maid, Nancy, fetched her light coat and hat. Alice winced as the hot liquid scalded her lips.

"Hurry, Nancy, I'm already late."

"You haven't even had time to sit down for a proper breakfast, Madam President," Nancy protested. "Surely, there is time for a pastry?" Nancy had served Alice since she first became President of The Forge. An older woman, her hair almost completely white, Nancy sometimes acted more like a mother than a maid. "Eating while standing gives one terrible indigestion, you know."

"Thank you for your concern, Nancy, but this is all I have time for today," Alice replied, setting the half-empty coffee cup back down on the tray. She nodded to Rose, who bobbed a curtsy, then withdrew into the kitchens. "I'll be out all day, but I hope to be home for dinner."

"You work too hard, Madam President," Nancy scolded. She tucked a stray lock of hair into Alice's hat as she pursed her lips. Then she relented. "I'll be sure to ask cook to have a hearty dinner ready for you when you return."

Alice gave Nancy a grateful smile. She glanced in the hallway mirror to check her appearance, then spun around and marched to the door. Mr. Hopewell, the butler, opened the door on cue so that Alice didn't even have to break stride as she stepped outside.

"Wait, Mother!" I said, rushing down the hallway after her. "I need to speak to you."

"I'm running late, Ivy," Alice replied, half-turning to glance at me, her lips pursed. "I'm speaking with the grandmasters of the United Guilds about taking on additional apprentices and using their skills to rebuild the city. It really is an important meeting and I cannot—"

"Let me walk with you," I said. I didn't even look in the mirror as I stepped outside behind her.

"You're not even matching, dear," Alice said, but she turned and stepped quickly down the steps. "What will the editor of The Forge Hart say if someone sees you? What would Pearl say?"

"If yesterday's speech is anything to go by, Pearl has turned over a new leaf. In any case, I promise I'll return home to dress properly after we've had the chance to speak."

Alice sighed. "What do you need to tell me so urgently?"

"The gates," I replied. "I need your key."

Alice coughed, startled, and put a hand over her mouth to cover her shock as she looked sideways at me. "I know there are lots of changes in Melfall, dear," Alice said. "But I hardly think you'll like country life any better. Besides, the changes are to take effect in all of The Forge—not just Melfall."

My face broke into a grin. "I'm not leaving the city, Mother," I replied. "I want to examine the Hearts. I want to bring one to my workshop to study how it works if it's not too heavy. If I can't move them, then I'll—"

Alice stopped dead in her tracks. There were furrows on her forehead as she turned a stern expression on me.

"Absolutely not," she replied. "I forbid it."

My mouth dropped open. "Why?"

"The people of this city are too frightened of those dreadful things for you to bring one of them inside the city."

"I need to see how it works—"

"You don't."

"You don't understand—"

"I understand you are too curious for your own good."

"But—"

Alice put a hand on my shoulder, giving me a slight shake. "It's too soon, Ivy. The people of Melfall need to feel safe. There are lots of changes afoot, and we need to make our people feel like they are properly protected. If I let you open the gates and bring those Hearts inside, there will be panic."

"But—"

"No," Alice said firmly. "Chasing down rabbit holes might satisfy your need to know how things work, but I have to lead these people, and they are frightened. Your curiosity will get you in trouble one day—but not today. I will not allow it."

Alice straightened her hat, a stubborn expression on her face. "Besides," she continued, as I hurried to keep up with her. "I've had to pull the guards from their double shifts on the wall to help with moving the people in the tunnels to proper accommodations. There's no need for the guards to watch Hearts that aren't doing anything. If the wall isn't being properly manned, I cannot risk the gates being opened. Not yet."

My shoulders sank, and I slowed to a stop. I watched as Alice turned to continue on her way, raising her hand in goodbye as she walked away.

I stood in the middle of the market underneath the broken scaffolding, trying to work out whether there was any way I would be able to get a closer look at the Pinnacle clock. Slowly, I walked around, noticing the paneling that seemed to cover the inner workings of the clock now. Rather than the tower showing its workings on the outside, like an unfinished structure, panels had been slotted into the grooves between the exposed struts. I ran my hand along them, a cool, smooth finish like pressed metal underneath my fingertips.

I looked up. Above, the paneling stopped, but it had an unfinished look, as though there should be more panels covering the skeleton of the tower.

"Ivy?"

I looked over my shoulder to see Gaia coming towards

me, waving a hand.

"What are you doing here?" I asked

"On my way to visit Genie at the hospital." She glanced up as though searching for whatever had caught my attention. Then she looked back at me. "What are you doing?"

I pointed up. "I'm trying to get a closer look at the clock, but I can't get up to that platform. Do you think you could give me a step up? Then I should be able to reach that rung of the scaffold and pull myself up to the first level. I'll get a better look from there."

Gaia laughed. "Half of the people of Melfall are lying in hospital beds, and the other half are trying to work out what they're going to do with their lives now that they won't get paid for looking pretty. And you want to get a closer look at the inner workings of a clock!"

I put my hands on my hips as I glared at the Gaia, who was still smiling. Then I shrugged my shoulders.

"What can I say? It's bothering me," I replied. "The clock, the Hearts, the attack—there's something going on that I can't figure out. Something's not right, and I'm sure it's got something to do with this clock."

Gaia smiled and shook her head. Then she got down on one knee and laced her fingers together so that the palms of her hands formed a stirrup for my foot.

"Thank you," I said as I put my foot into her hands and reached upwards.

As I stretched, Gaia hoisted me a little higher until all of my weight was pressed down on her hands, and my other foot lifted off the ground. My hands wrapped around the lowest rung of the broken ladder, and I screwed up my face with the effort of hauling myself up.

As I got a grip, Gaia struggled to her feet, continuing to push my feet upward so that she took some of my body weight as I pulled myself up.

Finally, I hoisted my upper body onto the first platform of the scaffold, and I lay there panting for a moment.

"Ivy?" Gaia called up from below. "Are you alright?"

I wiggled further onto the platform until my whole body was lying on it. Then I got to my knees and leaned over the edge to wave at Gaia.

She waved back to me, then turned and kept walking in the direction of the hospital.

Catching my breath, I watched my sister until she disappeared down a street leading away from the city center. Then I turned my attention back to the clock tower.

I kneeled on the platform, to get a better view of the panels below that had slotted into the grooves of the upright poles of the tower. On the outside, the metal had a pattern pressed into it. Hearts and swirls—the pattern matched the rest of the clock.

However, from a vantage point directly overhead, I saw the pattern on the outside of the panel was different to that on the inside. On the inside, the panel was a white color with uneven black and red marking in the corners that I couldn't quite see. I lay down on the scaffold, wiggling forward until I was hanging over the edge. My head hung over the side of the platform so that I could see directly down.

I squinted as I tried to see, wishing I had brought a torch to dispel the shadows on the inside of the panels. I inched further forward, sure that I would be able to see the pattern if I could just get a little closer.

I reached down, just able to touch the panel below me, and tried to press it back just enough to get a proper look at the design on the inside of the panel.

392

I gasped, then almost fell over the edge of the platform.

I wiggled back, getting my legs tangled in my skirts as I pulled myself back to lie flat on the wooden platform. I flipped onto my back and closed my eyes.

It wasn't just a panel that someone had put on the clock to hide the inner workings. It was a card. A playing card.

Thoughts swirled around my mind as the pieces of the puzzle started to fall into place.

The Hearts hadn't attacked the city. They were trying to get to the clock. To become part of the Pinnacle clock tower.

But why?

Tick, tick, tick.

I opened my eyes to look up at the giant clock face above me. It wasn't purely aesthetic to cover the clock in the panels made from the back of the Hearts.

Unless...

I rolled over to get to my knees, pushing myself up until I was standing on the platform, looking up. I covered my eyes to shield from the sun that was shining directly down on me.

There were hundreds of more slots. Enough spaces for each of the Hearts standing outside the gates to have a place on the clock. Like a puzzle.

Or a key.

I rubbed my forehead as I thought.

When a puzzle was complete, it revealed the full picture. A key was used to unlock something.

Once all of the Hearts were in place in the Pinnacle clock tower, what would it reveal? Or unlock?

And why?

My heart started racing as I remembered what Alice

had said when she'd left the house this morning. *"I've had to pull the guards from their double shifts on the wall."*

I knelt down and judged the distance from the platform to the ground. Then, without another thought, I jumped, jarring my feet as I felt the impact of hitting the cobblestones. Then I got to my feet and started running.

I revved the engine, and the back wheel squealed as the steam bike leapt into action. The wind pushed against me as I drove through the streets, whipping at the loose strands of hair that were not pinned down by my helmet. Large goggles covered half of my face, but I was grateful they protected my eyes from both the wind and my hair. I gritted my teeth as the bike bounced and lurched across an uneven section of cobblestones in one of the narrower streets.

I gripped the handles tighter as I leaned into a tight turn, taking the quickest route to the Guild Hall, where I knew Alice would be meeting with the grandmasters. Although Alice hadn't had time for my request this morning, now that I had proof that the Hearts were somehow important, I had to make her listen to me.

I leaned into another corner, dodging a man cleaning windows before hitting the accelerator again. An inexplicable sense of urgency coursed through me. Somehow I knew that every moment that passed was important. Every moment wasted was a missed opportunity. I didn't have a moment to lose.

When I rounded the next corner, coming out of a narrow street to enter the wider Seventh Avenue, I spotted the Guild Hall immediately. Though it was no taller than any other building in the city, it dominated its neighbors through the grandeur of its carved entrance and the copper-tipped spires on its tower roofs.

I drove straight up to the entrance, leaning my bike against a street lamp as I waved for the guard at the entrance to the Guild Hall to watch it. Taking the steps two at a time, I wrenched my helmet and goggles from my head and tugged off the bulky riding gloves. Then, tucking those under my arm, I used my other hand to clutch at my skirts as I ran the rest of the way up the steps.

The beautifully carved double-door entrance to the Guild Hall was closed, and a man—a different guard from last time—stood stiffly at the entrance.

"Are you a Guild member, miss?"

My heart sank a little. His demeanor didn't give me much hope that he would be more cooperative than the last guard I'd met on these steps.

"No, I'm not—" I started. I noticed his name tag read "Craftsman Turner."

He frowned at me, and his eyes roved over my clothing. I touched the now-wild mess of my hair, making a quick effort to comb my fingers through it.

"Do you have business here, miss?" Turner asked.

Then I gave up, straightened my shoulders, and looked the craftsman directly in the eyes.

"I need to see the president immediately, Craftsman Turner," I replied, using as authoritative a voice as I could manage. His eyes widened a little in surprise at my use of his title. "It's urgent."

Turner raised one eyebrow, continuing to study me with a narrow and focused expression. His forehead furrowed, and he hesitated. I thought he was about to refuse my entry and started to marshal further arguments as to why he should open the door when he gave me a curt nod and stepped aside.

"As it happens, Madam President *is* here," Turner said. "If you know that, I suppose you might need to see her, after all."

I gave him a grateful smile. "Thank you, Craftsman."

The door swung open, and I strode quickly inside. Turner didn't move from his post, but he raised a hand and snapped his fingers twice. Another man appeared, wearing the same emblem on his coat lapel.

"Show the Lady to the main hall, Dirk. Madam President is meeting the Grand Masters—but don't let her interrupt their meeting," Turner cautioned, pointing his forefinger to emphasize his point. I opened my mouth to protest, but he continued. "Announce her presence, and let the Grand Masters decide whether she should be admitted or not."

Turner turned back to me. "Apprentice Dirk will take you from here," he said with a bow. I gave the man another smile and followed Dirk into the mysterious Guild Hall.

Few people were allowed into the halls of the Guild unless they were members. I'd never seen the inside of this building, and though I didn't have time to appreciate my surrounds, I couldn't help but see the evidence of the different Guild specialties that were on display in the hall: beautifully wrought metal sculptures made by the Metallurgy Guild, an ornate grandfather clock made from the joint efforts of the Wood-turners Guild and the Horology Guild, and several prototypes of inventions from the Inventors Guild that I really wanted to take a closer look at. There were plenty more pieces on display, but my eyes were drawn to the center of the hall where a glass sculpture stood, in the shape of a woman holding a lamp with a flame flickering inside. The plaque noted it was made by the Glass-blowing Guild—the most beautiful lamp I'd ever seen—and I paused to peer at the inscription, which read: *The Guilds hold the lamp that lights the way to the future.*

Dirk's footsteps clipped across the polished floor as we walked. I was so busy staring around me that when he came to an abrupt stop outside another set of double doors, I almost crashed into him. These doors were even grander than those at the entrance and inlaid with tiny shapes of colored metal, marble, glass, and wood in an incredible mosaic of the same emblem—many hands reaching for the light—that was stitched into the Guildsmen's lapels.

"Wait here," he instructed, then pushed on the door, opening it just wide enough to step through. Inside, the conversation abruptly halted as Dirk's crisp footsteps echoed as he moved inside, leaving me outside, holding my breath and hoping Alice would agree to see me.

I twisted my fingers in my skirts, as every moment stretched out. The urgency built inside me as I waited.

The clipped footsteps returned, accompanied by softer footsteps, and as Alice's face appeared in the doorway, I felt a flood of relief. I caught hold of her hand before I saw the tight pinch of her mouth.

"What are you doing here?" Alice snapped. "This is a very important meeting. I can't just—"

Her tone caught me by surprise, but I gripped her hand more tightly. "The Hearts were trying to get to the clock." I spoke quickly, pouring out the words before Alice could leave. "The Pinnacle Clock. Remember, it started working at the same time the Hearts reappeared. It was drawing the Hearts to it. Somehow they're connected—

as though they're the missing parts of a puzzle—but they're not finished yet."

"I don't see how—"

"I feel it, Mother," I tugged on her hand. "You know I have a "knack" for machines." I couldn't use the word magic. Alice would only laugh and dismiss my concerns. "I just *know*." I took a breath. "Please, listen to me. I would never interrupt such an important meeting without good reason. I know that something is going to happen at the wall. You're the only one with a key. I need to—"

Alice took a deep breath and tugged her hand away. She stared at me for a moment, unblinking, pressed her lips together, and, without a word, turned to step back into the hall.

I reached out after her, "Please..." I whispered, but I couldn't follow because Dirk stood in my path.

"You may not enter," he said. I looked up into his expressionless face and knew that no amount of pleading would budge him.

Alice's voice wafted through the still-open door. Then, to my surprise, Alice stepped out again. She fixed me with a stare.

"Lead the way," Alice said. I blinked, as she strode past me without pausing. She turned her head and gave me a hard stare without breaking stride. "This had better be important."

I picked up my skirts and raced to keep pace.

"You can ride with me," I said as we both walked through the entrance and down the stairs.

Alice gave me a confused glance, then her expression became horrified as I stopped in front of the bike.

"You can't possibly—"

"It's the fastest way to get to the wall," I replied,

handing her the only helmet. I slid the goggles over my eyes, then swung a leg over the steam bike. "We don't have a moment to lose."

I could see Alice starting to formulate all the objections as to why she would not be riding on my contraption, but then a determined expression came over her face, and she took a step forward and swung her leg over the bike too. Her arms tightened around my waist.

"Hold on," I called out to her, before revving the engine and kicking the bike into action.

Alice screamed as we took off in the direction of the wall.

~

Marching footsteps drowned out even the sound of the steam engine when we were a block away from the wall. I swerved out of a side-street and into the center of Twelfth Avenue, putting out one foot to help me take the tight corner. Alice wound her arms around my waist so tightly that she almost squeezed the breath from my body.

A heavy feeling expanded in my stomach as the sound of marching grew louder. I accelerated, forcing the bike faster, and faster. Alice let out another scream, and I was sure that she'd squeezed her eyes shut in fear.

The stone structure of the wall loomed up ahead, but something wasn't right.

I squinted, noticing the thick metal gates weren't in place—they were wide open—but I shook my head, unable to believe what I was seeing.

It can't be, I told myself. *Alice has the only key.*

The thought had barely popped into my mind when I realized the movement at the gates was the Hearts, marching three abreast down the center of the avenue.

Their eyes were fixed ahead, and their progress was relentless. They didn't seem to notice the people running out of their way, darting into shops or doorways or slamming the shutters shut. There was a slight

disruption in the movements of the Hearts in the center of the column. There was something in their path—a mound—but instead of avoiding it, they were marching over the top of it.

On the side of the road, people were pointing at the mound, tears streaming down their faces. It wasn't a something, but a some*one*. A someone who hadn't moved out of their way fast enough.

I gritted my teeth as I slowed the bike to a stop, more carefully this time, so that Alice could dismount before I flung my leg over the bike and leaned it up against a lamp post.

Alice struggled to get the helmet off her head, but I yanked my goggles from my eyes and started running toward the open gates. There was nothing I could do for the person dead in the streets, but I had to do something about the gates before the Hearts caused any more damage.

I didn't even pause as I pushed my weight against the door of the watchhouse and barged inside. I swung my head from side to side as I searched for Captain Walsh.

"What are you doing?" I screamed at a guard, sitting on a seat in the watchhouse next to a system of bells and lights that were supposed to sound in an emergency. His uniform marked him as a junior watchman. He looked at me in astonishment, then jumped to his feet.

"Close the gates!"

The watchman blinked, as though he didn't understand what I was saying. "The gates, miss?"

"Close the gates!" I yelled again, pointing outside. He took a few steps around me, toward the door.

Alice appeared in the doorway of the watchhouse, pale and panting. Despite appearances, when she spoke, her voice rang with authority. "Where is your commanding officer, Watchman Vern?"

The astonished watchman shook his head. "Off duty," he replied, belatedly saluting Alice as he recognized his president.

"Who gave the order to open the gates?" Alice demanded.

Vern shrugged, looking around in bewilderment. "Nobody," he replied. "There's no-one else here. We're on a skeleton staff as we were ordered to stand down from the emergency protocols. We thought the attack was over. Most of the guards have either gone on much-needed rest and respite, or they've been ordered to duties within the city. I'm sorry, Madam President," he said, shaking his head. "I thought those orders came directly from you."

Alice was still struggling to catch her breath. "Don't concern yourself, Watchman. I did give those orders. What I'm trying to understand is why these gates are open and why there are hundreds of Hearts entering Melfall."

Vern looked around and saw the Hearts marching in the street. His jaw dropped open.

"I'll sound the alarm, Madam President," Vern saluted her again, then ran back to pull the levers that rang the bells and sounded the alarm at watch stations all along the wall.

I didn't wait for the watchman to finish what he was doing. Instead, I darted out of the watchhouse and took the steps up the stone wall two at a time, towards the wall walk along the ramparts of the perimeter wall.

At the top, the wind was stronger, pulling my hair into knots and making my eyes water. I turned to face the city, putting my back to the wind and watched the Hearts march down Twelfth Avenue.

My mouth went dry. I'd failed.

I should have insisted on taking a look at those Hearts earlier. I should have figured it out. If I hadn't been so distracted—by Raven, by my new sister, by the plight of the people in the tunnels...

Then I shook my head. This was no time to dwell on regrets. The Hearts had to be stopped before they hurt anyone else. Maybe, if the watchman could get the gates closed again, perhaps we would still trap most of the Hearts outside the wall. There might still be time.

As I turned towards the steps, out of the corner of my eye, I saw two figures leaning up against the outer edge of the ramparts. They both wore garish suits—one was orange with a green check, while the other was green with an orange check—and both wore identical grins on their faces.

I froze, and my mouth dropped open at the sight of the Tweedles. The terrible tightness in my chest grew worse.

"You," I stammered, finally. "You did this."

The grins on the Tweedles' faces grew even wider as they looked at each other like two little boys who'd been given the keys to a sweet shop.

"Who us?" they answered in unison. "Did what?"

I gritted my teeth, trying to keep my temper under control. I took a slow step towards them and pointed

402

a finger at the Hearts marching down Twelfth Avenue. "That!"

"That?" Tweedle Dee asked, looking at his twin with mock confusion.

"What's that?" Tweedle Dum looked around with wide eyes, then back to Dee. "I couldn't say."

"Nor I," Tweedle Dee said. They both shrugged their shoulders and looked back at me, grinning.

I bunched my hands into fists and took another deep breath. "You opened the gates. You let the Hearts back into the city."

"Oh, is that what you're talking about?" Tweedle Dee asked.

Tweedle Dum looked at his twin. "Is that what she's talking about?"

I ground my teeth together. "Yes, that's what I'm talking about."

Tweedle Dum scratched his chin. "I suppose we did do that," he said.

"Guilty, as charged." Tweedle Dee's white-blonde hair was combed flat to his head, but it shifted as he eagerly nodded his head.

"How?" I asked.

"You want to know how?" Tweedle Dee asked.

"She wants to know how," Tweedle Dum agreed. They both giggled.

"Yes, how did you open the gates?" I yelled in exasperation. "They were locked!"

"Oh, that," Tweedle Dum arched one eyebrow. He crossed his arms and looked sideways at his brother. "Shall we show her, Dee?"

Tweedle Dee tapped one finger against his chin, thinking. Then he gave his twin a nod. "Show her, Dum."

Tweedle Dum reached into his pocket, slowly drawing something out, which he held up in the air.

A key.

A very old, brass key with a heart molded into the bow.

I reached out to touch it, but Dum snatched it away.

"Is that a key to the gates?" I asked. "But only Alice has a key..." I stared from one Tweedle to the other.

"Only Alice has a key?" Dum asked. He put a hand to his mouth, in mock-shock, and turned to Dee. "I didn't know that."

"I didn't know that either," Dee replied. He tapped a finger against his chin, mock-frowning. "Is that right?"

Dum scratched his chin. "No, that can't be right," Dum answered.

"You've got a key right there," Dee agreed.

The twins grinned at each other.

"So there must be more than one," Dum said, triumphantly. Dum turned back to me. "No, Alice doesn't have the only key."

I clenched my fists, trying to contain my exasperation. "Where did you get it?"

Dum took off his hat and scratched his head, as though he was thinking, but his eyes glittered with mischief. "Can you remember, Dee?"

"Oh yes, I do remember," Dee answered his brother. "Do you?"

Dum grinned, settling his hat back on his head again. "I remember too."

I fought the urge to throttle them both, knowing that interrupting them would only lengthen their explanation. I felt like the pressure of an explosion was building up inside of me, at risk of exploding.

"Yes, as it happens, Her Royal Highness..." Dum

continued.

"Our rightful ruler," Dee added.

"The most rightful ruler as ever there was," Dum agreed.

"And the reddest," Dee added.

"And the heartiest," Dum said, then they both roared with laughter. Then Dee stopped and leaned forward to peer at his brother's coat lapel. Dum stopped to see what his brother was staring at. Suddenly, Dee slapped Dum hard on the chest.

"Hey!" Dum said. Without warning, he slapped his twin across the face.

"Ouch!" Dee answered.

"You hit me first." Dum put his hands on his hips.

Dee held up his hand. A black mark was smeared over his palm. "Bug."

I cleared my throat, putting my hands on my hips. "The Queen of Hearts had a key," I guessed.

The Tweedles turned abruptly. All mirth was gone from their expressions. They both stared at me, sulkily.

"You don't think she would have given up her key to the city when she left, do you?" They said in unison.

I didn't answer, as I turned to rush back down the steps.

◦◦◦

I turned off the engine and pulled up my goggles until they rested on the top of my forehead. Alice's tight grip around my waist loosened slightly, and she jumped off the bike as though it was a wild animal. I'd stopped the bike at the edge of the city center. The Pinnacle rose up in front of us.

I exchanged a look with Alice, but only for a moment

before I stared up at the Pinnacle clock.

In front of my eyes, the Hearts were moving in a rapid and coordinated fashion, forming card towers to hoist each other up the side of the tower. They moved so quickly, I could barely keep up with how they moved, but once the Hearts had finished making a card tower that reached all the way up to the Pinnacle clock, then Hearts started slotting themselves into place in the metal struts that made up the framework of the tower.

"What are they doing?" Alice asked, with both wonder and confusion in her voice.

I shook my head at a loss to explain. "I don't know, but I don't have a good feeling about it."

"Can we stop them?"

I looked over at her, then glanced around. There wasn't another person in the city center. Behind us, the brightly colored shutters on the buildings were shut tight. If there was anyone else around, they'd locked themselves up at the reappearance of the Hearts.

"The two of us?" I shook my head. "I think the Hearts attacked people before because they were in between them and the clock. If we try to stop them..."

Alice nodded. Then she closed her eyes and rubbed her forehead. Her shoulders slumped.

I turned back to the clock, unable to take my eyes off the activity in front of me. It was like a mechanical dance, watching the Hearts climb up the card tower, then slot into the spaces between the tower struts.

Once the cards climbing the card tower had found their place in the tower, the card tower seemed to disappear as the cards that formed it, started slotting themselves into place from the top down.

I stood completely still, holding my breath as I watched the final card scramble up the tower, then slide into place.

When the last card slotted into place, there was a grumble from deep beneath the ground.

Alice called out, reaching out to grab my arm, as though she was losing her balance. I stumbled sideways, falling to my knees. The ground trembled, starting to move underneath me.

I looked back at Alice, who was staring at me with wide eyes. We both looked up. The Pinnacle tower had started to rotate.

"We need to get out of here," I said. We helped each other to our feet. "The bike will be quicker."

Alice was holding out her hands, unsteadily staring around. "Do you think you'll be able to balance that thing while the ground is moving?"

I was standing with my arms out, and my knees bent, absorbing the movement of the ground underneath me. I stumbled over to the bike, taking it by the handles. I was about to swing my leg over the bike when the ground rumbled again as it continued to move. I stumbled again, and the bike fell on top of my leg.

I cried out, but more in surprise than in real pain. Alice helped me to shift the bike to free my leg, then helped me to my feet.

"Actually," I replied. "I think we're going to have to walk."

~

I trudged through the city, moving slower as I walked the steam bike instead of riding it. The shuddering movement of the ground had stopped—at least for the moment—but I was too shaken to get back on the bike in case it started moving again.

The streets were unnaturally quiet. Normally, at this time of the evening, they'd be packed with people—or at least they would have been before the attack of the Hearts. Now, they were empty.

Alice had left me to return to the President's Palace to talk to her advisers about what to do next. I hadn't been able to go home with her. I couldn't bear sitting and waiting—I needed to find out what was happening and why. All of the puzzles still nagged at me, but I *knew* I was on the verge of finding out the truth.

I couldn't sit still. A restless energy pulsed through me like an itch just underneath my skin. I decided to see Raven instead. He might know something more about the Pinnacle clock and the Hearts and how the ground was moving.

I came to a sudden stop as a wailing sound drifted upwards from underneath my feet. I looked down, still shaky though the ground was still, and saw the manhole. A scream wafted up from below.

I leaned the bike on the ground, then rushed to pull the cover off the manhole. I reached inside.

A hand grabbed mine—a small hand that easily fit within my own. I grabbed it and pulled. A child appeared, covered in dust and dirt, coughing and gasping for breath. He collapsed on the ground as soon as he climbed out of the hole. Another hand appeared, grasping for the rim of the manhole. I leaned forward again to help a woman climb out. Then two more people appeared, each of them coughing, crying, and sucking in deep breaths.

Finally, Raven appeared, looking far more disheveled than I'd ever seen him. His coat was torn, he was covered with the same grey dirt that covered the rest of them.

"A tunnel collapsed in the earthquake," Raven

explained. He ran a hand through his hair, that looked grey from the dust, and shook the dirt from his coat.

"That was no earthquake," I replied, reaching out with both hands to grab his hands, then I pulled him towards me and wrapped my hands around his waist.

Raven looked as though he was about to ask a question when there was another rumbling underground and a cracking sound. We scrambled back from the edge of the manhole. Raven grabbed up the child in his arms. The other three scrambled after us, just as the manhole collapsed, causing the ground around it to cave in.

"We need to get these people to the hospital," I said. I stood up my bike, and Raven sat the little boy on the seat as I pushed it. The boy whimpered quietly, and the woman walked alongside him, holding his hand and murmuring comforting noises. Raven followed behind, helping another man who was limping on an injured leg.

It was completely dark by the time we got to the hospital. Even the lamplighters hadn't come out to light the street lamps, and the only light in the city was the light of the swollen moon that hung low in the sky.

Our small group limped into the entry of the hospital, and I blinked as I saw that the waiting room was packed with people who'd suffered injuries with the movement of the ground. The triage nurses were loudly repeating the need to wait patiently to be seen by the next available doctor or nurse.

We left the people in the waiting room, and I took Raven's hand and walked through the hospital hallway to find Gaia.

"What did you mean, it wasn't an earthquake?" Raven asked when we left the crowds of the waiting room, and made our way through the corridor.

"You won't believe me," I said, shaking my head. "I barely believe it myself."

"Try me." He pulled back on my hand until I stopped and turned to face him.

I nodded. "Gaia should be in Genie's room. I'll tell you when we get there."

Raven looked like he was about to protest, but then several nurses rushed by, rolling a trolley occupied by a wailing man clutching a bleeding arm.

I knocked, then pushed open the door to Genie's room to find Gaia perched on the edge of his bed, her phoenix sitting on her shoulder. I was surprised to see Chesh there too. His arm was in a sling, but the color had returned to his face. He stood when he saw me, and a smile lit his face, almost immediately dampened when he saw me holding hands with Raven.

Gaia leapt up from where she sat on the bed and rushed over to take my hands in hers. "Are you alright? We felt the earthquake. It's still rumbling," she said.

As she spoke, the ground rumbled again, and some fine plaster dust floated from the ceiling.

Everyone looked up, warily, as though wondering whether the whole ceiling would fall in.

"It isn't an earthquake," Raven said, then turned to me. "What is it?"

I rubbed at my forehead, closing my eyes briefly as I marshaled my thoughts into some sort of coherent order. "The Hearts got back in. They reached the Pinnacle clock. They seemed to activate the ground movements, as though they were some sort of key."

I stared around at blank, confused faces, then proceeded to tell them the whole story, starting with when I'd climbed the broken scaffolding that morning.

When I finished, the building groaned again, and

more plaster dust fell from the ceiling, as though confirming my words.

"The underground tunnel system has partially collapsed," Raven reported. "Anyone caught down there is probably dead. I managed to save a few, but while the ground is moving, the tunnels won't be safe."

I squeezed his hand, grateful he'd managed to escape. Raven hung his head, no doubt wondering how many he'd left behind.

"Do you think the Tweedles are behind it?" Chesh asked, sounding doubtful.

I shrugged. "Honestly, I think they're working for the Queen."

"I thought the Queen was dead?" Chesh replied. "Alice always said—"

Gaia was shaking her head. "All over the Twelve Kingdoms, those who were presumed dead are returning."

"Why would she be making the ground move?" Raven asked. "For what purpose?"

I sighed, taking out Mr. Pillar's pocket watch that hadn't stopped ticking, no matter that I hadn't wound it in almost a month. I flicked open the face of the watch and stared at the ticking of the second hand mesmerized by the tiny movement. "So many questions," I murmured. The pocket watch had started ticking at the same time that the Pinnacle clock had started working, at the same time the Hearts had reappeared in the city. I now knew why the Hearts had appeared, and why they'd been trying to get to the clock. I still didn't understand why the Queen—if she was behind it all—wanted to make the city move. "So many things that don't make sense."

"Maybe we can't work it out because we're on the

ground," Chesh said, leaning against the wall.

I frowned, looking up at him. "What do you mean?"

"Remember you said there were those machines on the roof that were suddenly working again. You first noticed them when you glimpsed them from the top of the wall, but you'd never noticed them from ground level before. Maybe the movement of the ground and the clock would make more sense from above?"

My mouth dropped open. I'd almost forgotten the machines on the roofs of the city. Another puzzle that hadn't been solved, only overshadowed by so many other things that didn't make sense.

"That's brilliant, Chesh!" I said, beaming at him.

Chesh smiled back, meeting my eyes for a moment, before looking down at his shoes. "You can use my hover if you like."

"You got it working?" I asked, unable to hide the surprise from my voice.

Chesh sighed and shook his head, kicking the floor with his shoe. "Nah, but I'm sure it's almost there. Knowing you, you'll have it working in minutes. I don't know how you do it." He glanced up at me again, with a half-smile on his face. "You and your 'knack.'"

A smile passed over Gaia's face, and she raised an eyebrow at me, but I was already thinking about the plan. I nodded and was turning to leave the room when Raven grabbed my hand.

"It's dark," he pointed out. "You won't see anything. None of the street lamps are lit."

I looked out of the window, and my heart sank. Raven was right. Even if I did get the hover working, I wouldn't be able to see anything until dawn.

At that moment, a nurse bustled into the room, declared the end of visiting hours, and shooed us all out.

As Gaia, Raven, and I stood out in front of the hospital, we looked at each other.

"Shall I walk you home?" Raven asked. He looked up at the sky. "I can't move around underground anymore, so I'll have to make sure I'm home by sunrise. Still, there are a few hours before I need to be safely back inside."

I shook my head. "I'm going to Chesh's workshop. It might take me the rest of the night to get the hover working. Or it might not work at all, but I have to try."

7TH SEPTEMBER

I wiped my hand across my brow, my eyes dry and burning with fatigue. I hadn't allowed myself to close my eyes all night, but now, in the deep lateness of the hour, I felt the effects of lack of sleep.

I put down the screwdriver and looked at the hover again. I put my hands on it, pushing on the accelerator. The engine hummed, lifting the hover off the ground for a moment. Hope buoyed my chest for a moment—maybe, *maybe,* this time, it would work.

Then, the purring of the engine became a wheeze. The machine tilted sideways and started spinning wildly.

I quickly removed my hands from the accelerator and turned off the engine. The machine fell to the ground with a *thunk*, but it didn't land true and, with a clatter, the central spine holding the handlebars upright lurched sideways. I sighed and let my chin fall against my chest. My mind was fuzzy, and I couldn't think properly.

A faint glow lit up the opposite wall as the first rays of daylight peeped through the window. I'd worked all night to make the hover functional but still hadn't managed it.

Perhaps Gaia had been wrong about my magic. Perhaps my "knack" was nothing more than intuition.

I covered my face with my hands, squeezing my eyes shut before I stood abruptly upright and put my hands on my hips. "You *will* work," I demanded aloud. "And you *will* take me up high enough to see what is happening to this city."

I reached out to put my hands on the handlebars, determined to test this "so-called" magic, once and for all. I gripped the handlebars tightly, feeling for the lever of the accelerator with my thumb. I turned on the power again and, without pressing on the accelerator, I felt the power hum underneath the palms of my hands.

I focused on the *hum* as I slowly pressed my thumb against the accelerator. As I concentrated on it, the sound of the engine fell away, but I could still *feel* it humming beneath my skin.

With the pressure on the accelerator, the hover lifted about a foot into the air. I held my breath, waiting for the engine to fail again—but it didn't. I tentatively put one foot on the platform to mount it. The engine hummed, stable and consistent, and I paused a moment before putting all of my weight onto the platform as I removed my foot from the ground.

The hover wobbled, but I gripped the handlebars

416

tightly and focused my attention on *feeling* the inner workings of the engine. I concentrated, focusing all of my thought on it—wordlessly encouraging the machine to continue the smooth running of its parts. The hover continued to *purr*, continuing to hover for longer than I'd ever seen it.

I pressed the accelerator lever with my thumb a little harder, revving the engine, and pushed the hover higher, then higher again. All of my attention was focused on the engine, as I felt all of the parts working together in harmony to make the machine work. The *thrum* of the engine became part of me, as though the hover and I merged somehow. A small smile spread across my face.

Gaia was right—my magic could make it work, as long as I concentrated on feeling it, and not tinkering with it like a puzzle.

I pushed the hover into the next gear and leaned forward, pushing the hover to move in the same direction, toward the door.

I let out a laugh as the hover obeyed my mental commands, moving better than it ever had. I flew out of the door of Chesh's workshop, then pushed the hover to fly higher in the sky.

As I flew through the doorway, the ceiling disappeared, replaced by the dim golden glow of the dawn sky. The engine rumbled as my concentration faded, and I fixed my focus once more on the inner workings of the hover. I turned in the direction of the city's clock and suddenly found myself flying across the street, my hair and skirts streaming behind me as I leaned into the direction I wanted the hover to take me.

Without the friction of wheels on cobblestones, I moved even faster than when I rode the steam bike. The ground became a blur as I sped by.

At the thought, I willed the hover to rise into the air, flying along the line of the rooftops. A shout came from one of the buildings, whose shutters opened, and a woman leaned out to watch my passing with wide eyes.

With a sudden surge of enthusiasm, I let out a whooping sound and took one hand off the handlebars to wave to the woman, whose mouth hung as wide-open as her eyes. The hover wobbled again, and I renewed my focus, gripping the handles tightly with both hands. With the ground still making sudden movements, I had to concentrate on staying between the buildings that rose up on either side of me. To make it easier, I pushed the hover a little higher until I was flying over the rooftops.

I saw the cogs turning on the rooftops, and wished I had the time to examine them—but that would have to wait.

The sun popped over the horizon, bathing the city in a golden glow, as well as casting long shadows. The clock rose up ahead of me, and I felt a renewed sense of urgency to move.

When I approached the spire of the Pinnacle clock, I took the hover in a circle around it, slowing down to a stop in mid-air while I looked over the city.

At first, all I could see was Melfall, its wide avenues leading from the market to the perimeter wall in every direction. The puzzle of narrow streets between the avenues made uneven patterns.

Then suddenly, the ground jerked, and the whole city moved. My mouth dropped open. The twelve avenues that spread out from the center of the city like spokes on a wheel now looked more like the hands on a clock. The Pinnacle clock chimed the hour, and

418

the whole city moved again, so the avenues relocated around in a circle. When the ground stopped moving, Twelfth Avenue was in the place that Eleventh Avenue had just occupied. The ground—the avenues—had moved around like an hour hand, but in the opposite direction—counterclockwise.

I squinted at the ground—I hadn't been looking at Twelfth Avenue at all. The real Twelfth Avenue was pointing towards what would be three on the clock face. Rubbing my forehead, I did a quick count—it was about nine hours since the last Hearts had slid into place into the Pinnacle clock tower, which had set off the movement of the city. There had been regular movements under the city—what felt like earthquakes to anyone who didn't know better—but it hadn't occurred to me that they were happening every hour, on the hour.

So Melfall looked and acted like a clock—but why? And why was it going backward? Unless it was counting down? But to what?

A shiver of fear ran through me. Another puzzle. Now, I didn't have time to figure it out. For once, I knew Raven wouldn't have any more information than I did. But the Tweedles had let the Hearts into Melfall. They must have known what they would do.

It was time to find some real answers.

On Chesh's hover, it didn't take very long until I spotted the ornate rooftop of the Queen's old palace. The residence was whitewashed, with red shutters on its hundreds of windows, rising into four towers, one at each corner of the building, each of which was topped with bright red tiles and decorated with ornate wrought iron hearts at the tips. The palace was surrounded by gardens featuring red roses that had been trimmed into the shape of hearts.

From above, I could see that paths of white gravel ran around the residence and through the neatly mown green grass like ribbons. The edge of the garden was fenced by wrought iron in the same heart shapes as the tips of the towers. Objectively, it was a beautiful building.

From the stories of the reign of the Queen of Hearts, I knew this building had instilled terror in the citizens of The Forge. Not long ago, I'd thought this building had been abandoned.

Now, from above, it looked freshly painted and its gardens neatly tended. It was in even better condition than the last time I'd visited the Tweedles.

I landed the hover on the front lawns, stroking a hand over the handlebars as I switched off the ignition, sending silent thoughts of gratitude—as though the hover would understand—for bringing me all this way without incident. As soon as I lifted my hands from the handles, the machine seemed to lose all sentience.

Heavy footsteps pounded down the gravel, and I turned to see several large Hearts marching towards me.

No, not Hearts—not like the ones that had been stalking the city for weeks. These were double the size and more humanoid than the other Hearts had ever been.

"You do not have permission to enter," the first robot spoke in a mechanical voice. "You are an intruder."

"I wish to speak with the Tweedles," I said, putting my hands on my hips as I determined to stand my ground.

The robots pointed their spears towards me. "Intruders are forbidden."

I swallowed but didn't move. I lifted my chin.

"Forbidden by whom?" I asked, hoping they weren't attuned enough to human behavior to hear the quiver in my voice.

"Forbidden by order of Her Royal Highness, the Queen of Hearts."

My heart did a somersault inside my chest. The first robot reached out and seized my arm.

"Hey!" I startled.

The other robot stepped forward to take my other arm. Together, they lifted me into the air as they turned me towards the gates.

"Intruders are forbidden."

With its other hand, the second robot seized the hover, and, together, the two robots marched me towards the gates.

"Hey, what are you doing?" I struggled, kicking my feet in the air, but it had no effect on the robots at all. "Put me down! And put down that hover, too!"

The robot hurled the hover at the fence, and I gasped as it smashed into the wrought iron fencing, bending the metal column at a right angle as several screws spilled onto the ground.

I froze, wondering if the robots planned to hurl me out of the gates too. I looked over my shoulder and saw someone in a first-story window staring out at us. In that brief glance, I was sure it was Chesh's friend, Oscar Pankhurst, who had gone missing only a week before.

Suddenly, another piece of the puzzle fell into place. The Queen had kidnapped people from the city—those who could build her robots and restore her palace to its former glory and who knew what else. Maybe they'd also been set to work on whatever mechanism was causing the city to move. I clenched my fists. I couldn't let the robots throw me out before I discovered the truth.

"I'm not an intruder," I said in as commanding a voice as I could muster. "I'm here to see the Queen. Take me to her!"

The robots stopped mid-stride.

The Queen of Hearts sat on a throne in the middle of a large room lined with red carpet and large paintings of herself. I had never seen the Queen in person. She'd disappeared before I was born, but I'd seen her pictures in the old newspapers I'd been researching since the Pinnacle clock started unexpectedly working again.

In the flesh, she was more beautiful than the pictures gave her credit. Flawless skin like alabaster, bright red hair pulled into an intricate bun and finished with a gold tiara inlaid with heart-shaped rubies. She wore a fashionably fitted vest and skirts of red velvet. Her lips were heart-shaped and painted red, which made her look as though she was smiling, but her eyes were cold and calculating as she looked down at me without moving her head.

"You are the spawn of the usurper," she said, a statement of fact.

"Exactly right, Your Majesty," one of the Tweedle's said. His voice startled me—I hadn't noticed anyone else in the room except for the Queen. The Tweedles stepped out from behind the enormous throne to come to stand at each side of the Queen.

They both bowed to the Queen, deeply and in unison. She didn't even look at them.

"Of course, I'm right," the Queen said, her voice smooth and rich. "I'm the rightful Queen."

She rapped a finger against the gilded arm of her throne, then raised one eyebrow. "Bow to me, girl. I am your queen, after all."

I lifted my chin, but the robot came behind me and laid a metallic hand on my shoulder, so forcefully that I was pushed to my knees. I glared, but the robot didn't stop, the pressure of its hand forcing me forward until my forehead was pressed against the floor.

"That's better."

The Queen rose from her throne, slowly and gracefully. Her skirts swished as she crossed the floor to come to stand in front of me. The robot held me so that I could only see her embroidered slippers and the bottom of her plush skirts and layered lace petticoats.

"What are you doing here, girl?" the Queen asked. I tried to shrug off the robot's heavy hand on my shoulder, but the robot held me down.

"What are you doing here? You're supposed to be dead," I said, speaking more sharply than I'd intended, the frustration of being held down seeping into my voice.

The Queen rapped me on the head with something sharp.

"Your Majesty," Tweedle Dum spoke up from behind her.

The Queen did not reply.

"He's asking you a question," I said to the Queen.

"He's reminding you of your manners," the Queen replied.

Tweedle Dee walked across the room and slapped me over the back of the head. "You must address our Queen as Your Majesty."

I rolled my eyes.

"Release her," the Queen commanded, and the robot released me from its grip. I looked up at her. She raised one perfectly shaped eyebrow. "Did the usurper say I was dead?" The Queen threw her head back and laughed. "As though she had such power."

"Then where have you been all these years?" I asked. "Why have you come back now?"

The Queen hit me on the head again with her red fan. Her eyes narrowed.

"You have no right to ask questions. You're lucky I do not take your head from your shoulders right here." She waved a hand, as though indicating I wasn't worth such concern. "As it happens, I have been biding my time. Waiting until the right time to reclaim my throne."

"The people won't accept you. The Forge is better off without you."

The Queen's expression darkened as her glare snapped toward me again.

"She lies, Your Majesty," Tweedle Dum kneeled, putting his hand over his heart.

"The Forge cries out for your return, Your Majesty," Tweedle Dee added. "The people seek freedom from the usurper."

"That's not true!" I said. "President Alice has been a much better ruler than you ever were. The people chose her to lead them."

The Tweedles were shaking their heads, their blonde hair bobbing as they did so.

"What the people want is irrelevant." The Queen waved a hand dismissively, then tapped her fan closed, before rapping it against the palm of her hand. "I am their rightful Queen. They are my subjects. Mine. Do not worry, I have a surprise for them."

I frowned. "What kind of surprise?"

The Queen struck me with her fan again.

I rolled my eyes. "Your Majesty," I added.

The Queen reached out and grabbed my chin with her hand. Her fingers were strong and bony, without any tenderness at all. She yanked my chin so that my face was angled upward, and she studied me with her cold, dark eyes. Her lips pursed, pinching at the edges and emphasizing their heart shape.

"Do you think I am so foolish that I would tell you so that you can run back to tell the usurper?"

"You think Alice is powerful enough to thwart your plans?" I said.

Tweedle Dum smacked me over the back of the head, harder this time. I glared at him as I rubbed my head.

"Your Majesty," I added, through gritted teeth.

The Queen laughed. "Of course not, but it would spoil the surprise. I'll tell you a secret, though."

The Tweedles looked at each other, rubbing their hands together, before looking at the Queen in anticipation.

"Tell us, please, Your Majesty," they said in unison.

I rolled my eyes. The Queen didn't take her eyes from me as she narrowed her eyes.

"You are insolent," she said, then she waved a hand as though swatting a fly. "It is of no consequence. No matter what you or the usurper say or do, my friends and I will regain control—not only of The Forge but of each of the Twelve Kingdoms. There is nothing you can do to stop us."

The Queen twirled around and strode back to the dais, where she sat down on her throne, and flicked open her fan to wave some cool air at her face. Her expression was suddenly bored, and she looked out of the window. The Tweedles rushed back to her side, kneeling next to her as though waiting for the next scraps of attention.

"Where are my roses?" The Queen rapped her fingertips on the arm of the throne. "Bring me the gardener."

"Of course, Your Majesty," the Tweedles said in unison, and hurried away.

The Queen's eyes roved around the room then settled on me once again. "Is this one still here? She is polluting my halls with her unbeauty. Take her out of my sight. Throw her onto the street."

The robot behind me grabbed me by the arms again. "Let me go!" I said as I was yanked to my feet. I pulled away from the robot.

"I'm not leaving. I know what you're doing. I know you've kidnapped people from the streets of Melfall. I'm not leaving until you let them go!"

The Queen raised an elegant eyebrow. "Which people?"

"The ones who have gone missing this past month or so. I saw one of them in the window when I was outside. Do you deny it?"

The Queen stared at me. "My subjects are here at my invitation. They are my special guests. They have been given the opportunity to utilize their talents. They are honored to serve me, as they should be."

"They're afraid they'll lose their heads if they refuse," I retorted.

The Queen shrugged. "They are some of the smartest people in this city. They understand the benefits of pleasing their Queen." She motioned to her robots. "She is boring me. Take her away."

The robot lifted me off the floor and swung me over

his shoulder so that my head was hanging down his back. I banged my fists against the metal panels of his back and looked up to see the upside-down figure of the Queen of Hearts as the robot marched out of the hall.

"You won't get away with this," I yelled. "Not you, and not your friends."

The Queen settled herself on her gold throne once again. She curled her fingers around the arms of her chair and watched as the robot marched out of the room. A nasty smile spread across her face, and, for the first time, I saw the glint of her fangs as they pressed against her plump, red lips. Raven was right, she was a vampire, after all.

"You are like the usurper—too curious for your own good," she said. The robot paused, allowing the Queen to finish speaking. "Know this—you will fail." She shrugged one shoulder. "Since you are so curious, if you want to know more, you should go to Urbis. My friends and I will be treating the populace to a party. The party to end all parties, in fact. There will be none like it."

I shook my head, straining to keep my eyes on her as the robot kept a firm grip on my legs. "You won't get away with this. The people won't accept your rule— never again!"

"*My* people will do exactly as I tell them."

"Your Majesty?" A man in dirty overalls, with bits of twig and leaf caught in his hair, came rushing into the throne room and fell to his knees. In his hands, he held a red rose. "You summoned me?"

"Show me my roses," the Queen ordered. She held out a hand.

The gardener shuffled forwards on his knees, keeping

his eyes on the floor. He was shaking as he held out the rose in his hands. "I live to serve you, Your Majesty."

"You may live *if* you serve me," the Queen replied. "I shall be the judge of that."

"Of course, Your Majesty."

The Queen held the rose to her nose and inhaled deeply. "A pleasant scent, and the color is good enough, I suppose. You shall live—for now. See that every rose in my garden is at least as good as this one, and you shall live a little longer."

"Thank you, Your Majesty." The gardener shuffled backward, unwilling to either get up off his knees or to look up.

I struggled on the robot's shoulder again, but its grip was unrelenting. The Queen rose up and walked slowly toward us. She stopped in front of me, then held out the rose until it touched my nose.

"This one is for you, girl," she said. Then she tucked the rose behind my ear. "Next time I see you, I shall add your unbeautiful head to my collection."

The Queen turned her back and waved a hand. "Take her away."

The robot dumped me on the ground and, a moment later, the gate slammed shut, and the key turned in the lock. I rubbed my bruised hip where it had collided with the footpath in front of the Queen's Palace. Metal feet crunched on the gravel, getting softer as the robot moved away.

I sat up, with a quiet groan. The rose was still tucked behind my ear, and I examined it.

A perfect specimen, the rose was a rich, deep red,

like blood, with a lingering scent. It was exactly the same type of rose that Alice had received every day for weeks. Now, I knew where they had come from. Not an admirer, after all. Jack had been right—the roses were from the Queen of Hearts, and they were a message: She intended to take Alice's head.

Our heads, I reminded myself. Both of our lives were in danger.

The sun beat down from overhead, and I squinted upward as I got to my feet.

In the distance, I heard the hourly tolling of the bells, and the ground jerked and shuddered as it moved. I imagined the whole of the city shifting around the Pinnacle clock.

The hover was a crumpled heap next to me. I sighed. Poor Chesh wouldn't see his invention in action. Not only that, I would have to travel back to the hospital by foot. I felt a sudden wave of weariness and leaned against the gate with a sigh.

It was a long walk back.

With the sun beating down on my head, I forced myself to put one foot in front of the other..

8TH SEPTEMBER

Alice closed her eyes as she took a sip of her tea. The cup rattled as she set it back on the saucer. I glanced at the vase of roses, still as red as the day they'd been left on the doorstep. We'd all assumed they were for Alice, but after receiving a rose of my own from the Queen, I wondered whether some, or all, of them might be for me.

"The Queen of Hearts?" Pearl asked, and I turned to find her standing in the doorway. Her hand was over her mouth, and her eyes wide. I knew she'd been standing there long enough to have heard at least some of the story I'd recounted to Alice.

I nodded.

"But...she's dead. You always said so, Mother," she said.

Alice hadn't opened her eyes. She was sitting very still—too still—and her hands were clasped so tightly on her lap that her knuckles were white.

"Mother?" Pearl asked.

I leaned forward to put my hand over Alice's hands clasped in front of her. Alice jerked away, standing abruptly and walking over to the fireplace so that her back was facing us.

"So I thought," Alice replied, her words clipped. "Nobody found her body, but I knew the Queen would not leave The Forge unless she had no choice." Alice rubbed her hands together, as though she was washing them, over and over again. "I was wrong," she whispered.

"Nobody could have foreseen this," I replied, getting up to take a few steps towards Alice. "Don't worry—"

Alice spun around, eyes wide. "Don't worry? You don't know what she'll do to me. You don't know what she'll do to everyone in this city. You don't remember what it was like before—of course, you don't, you weren't even born. People lived in fear. Every word they spoke, every time they left the house, the Queen might execute them on a whim. She took people's heads because she didn't like their hats, or the lace on the trim of their shirt didn't please her eye, or the color of their jacket clashed with her own. You can't know what it's like to live in constant fear for your life."

I watched as her fingers worried at the trim of her shirt, and her eyes filled with tears.

"It has taken many years, but The Forge is changing— finally, changing. Now it may all have been for nothing. The people will be too frightened—too fearful for their lives—to admit the unbeautiful into the city. All these years, I've tried to rule the people of The Forge fairly, so that they could live free from her shadow. Now..."

Alice covered her face with her hands. Young Dinah purred, curling around Alice's legs to rub against her affectionately. Alice sobbed as she bent down to bring her cat into her arms and scratch her between the ears.

Holding Young Dinah in her arms seemed to settle Alice a little, although the moisture in her eyes remained.

I heard footsteps in the hall, and Gaia appeared in the doorway. "Something's happened?" she said, as her eyes found me. I nodded and pulled my sister aside to explain what had happened the previous day.

"So, we go to Urbis," Gaia said.

Alice looked up sharply, starting to shake her head.

"I agree," I said before Alice could voice her misgivings. "The Queen has people helping her. Their next move will be in Urbis. If we're going to stop the Queen from regaining control of The Forge, we need to go there."

"It might be a trick," Pearl murmured. She moved closer to Alice and put an arm around her mother. I noticed how similar they looked. There was no doubt that Pearl was Alice's natural daughter. There were years between them—noticeable by the fine lines around Alice's eyes and the few grey hairs that marked her temple—but otherwise, they were almost identical images of each other.

"We have to take the risk," I replied. "You should stay here with Mother. Gaia and I will go to Urbis."

Alice glanced at us, her eyes shifting from me to Gaia, and back again. "Alone?"

I exchanged a look with Gaia. She hesitated, and I saw a hint of sadness cross her face. Then her features settled into their familiar pattern of determination.

"Genie isn't well enough to come," she said. "He must remain at the hospital—for now, at least."

Alice stared at me. "What about Raven?" she

whispered. "Or Chesh?"

I shook my head. "Chesh is still in the hospital. Raven can only travel at night." I took a deep breath and squeezed Gaia's hand. "I think it must be the two of us."

Alice's face twisted into grief. She clutched Young Dinah until the cat meowed in protest. She reluctantly set the cat on the floor and came over to take my hands in both of her own.

"Take care, my darling girl. The Queen is dangerous— more dangerous than you know. You may have heard stories of her that seem silly—as her shadow retreated, some people talked of her as though she was a comical character. She was not. She was as dangerous as she was unpredictable."

I nodded, but Alice spoke before I had the chance to respond. "You may not be my own blood, but you *are* my daughter. I've always thought of you that way, and I have always loved you. Come back to me."

Tears welled in my own eyes as Alice took my face in her hands. "Promise me."

I nodded, not trusting myself to say anything. Then Pearl was standing next to me, her head on my shoulder and her arm around my waist. "Come back, Ivy. I need my sister beside me. Especially if I'm going to learn how to be a nurse—I'll need you to show me how to study."

I started to giggle. "I'll point out the library before I leave. I'm not sure you've ever set foot in it before."

Pearl laughed, rolling her eyes, but I could tell that she was holding back tears.

"I'm proud of you both," I whispered and put my arms around my mother and my twin sister, clutching them as though it might be the last time.

~

Raven held my face in his hands, his dark eyes studying my face as though committing it to memory.

"I have every intention of coming back," I said, reaching up to pull his hands away. "I promise."

"I wish I could come with you," Raven said. His slouched slightly as he stood in front of me, as though defeated. He'd reluctantly agreed, as I'd known he would, that he could not accompany me to Urbis. Without the tunnels, he was trapped inside during the day. It would be too dangerous and too difficult for us to travel through the countryside by night.

He pressed a light kiss to my forehead, then I lifted onto my tiptoes to meet his lips with mine. I curled my arms around his neck, running my fingers over the feathery softness of his hair. I kissed him, taking note of the feeling of his hands on my hips, the flat lines of his chest as I pressed my body against it, the cool touch of the skin on his neck under my fingertips. I ran my hands over the wide planes of his shoulders, and along the lengths of his arms. I wanted to memorize every line and curve, every bulge and hollow. I wanted our kiss never to end, but in the end, it was I who pulled away so that I could study his face one last time.

"When do you leave?" Raven asked, cupping his hand behind my head so that his fingers tangled in my hair.

"Today. Now," I replied. "When I leave you, I will meet Gaia at the hospital."

"I would feel better if Genie could go with you, at least," Raven murmured.

"He cannot," I replied. "He needs to remain in the

hospital."

Raven sighed. "I would feel better if *someone* could accompany you."

"We'll be—"

"You've never left this city, Ivy," Raven exclaimed, suddenly stepping away from me and turning away. He looked up at the portrait of his mother on the wall of his house. "Now, you're going to travel to Urbis."

"There has to be a first time for everything."

Raven turned around, looking at me with an expression of astonishment. "Are you not at all afraid?"

I laughed, then walked toward him. I reached out to him, hooking my fingers into the edge of his vest and pulling him toward me until we were pressed against each other again. "Of course," I said. "But I will have my sister with me. And it's about time I saw more of the Twelve Kingdoms."

Raven leaned forward and rested his forehead against mine. We were silent for a moment, aware of each other, without moving to disturb the sudden peace between us.

"Be aware of the Queen," Raven cautioned. "She is dangerous. She is ruthless. She might rip out your throat at any time. Do not, under any circumstances, trust her."

I squeezed Raven's fingers. "I don't. I won't."

He gave me a brief smile. "I don't want to say this, but if you don't leave now, you will not have enough daylight to make any distance today."

"It's not goodbye, Raven," I whispered. "I'll see you soon."

I pressed a kiss to his lips, then pulled away and strode out of the door before my reluctance to leave him could betray me.

436

"Are you ready?"

Gaia was waiting for me in the lobby of the hospital. Her eyes were red, as though she'd been crying, but she stood with her head high and determined. I noticed she didn't have her phoenix.

I nodded. "Have you said goodbye?"

Gaia gave me a curt nod. "We'll be back," she said. Then she linked her arm in mine as we made for the door.

"Wait," I said. "I need to ask Chesh something before we leave."

Gaia hesitated, then nodded, and followed me down the whitewashed corridor toward Chesh's room.

I pulled the cover off the steam bike, and Gaia looked at it with a cautious look on her face.

"You're serious," she said.

"It'll be faster than walking," I replied. "I'll drive. You can ride on the back."

"You know how to drive this?"

I chuckled. "Yes, I do. Believe me. I've even taken Alice for a ride on it." I kept to myself that Alice had only gotten onto the steam bike because of the extreme urgency of the situation, and under much sufferance.

I handed Gaia one of the helmets and a set of goggles. She looked horrified.

"Once we start moving, you'll be pleased to be wearing them."

"Ivy, I don't think—"

"Gaia, you can do what you like, but I'm not walking

to Urbis," I insisted.

Gaia sighed, resigned. I put on my helmet and goggles, then helped Gaia to fix her own.

"I look ridiculous," she complained.

I rapped her helmet with my knuckles. "It's a great disguise," I said. "Nobody will know it's us leaving the city."

Gaia rolled her eyes, then pointed at the steam bike like it was some sort of monster that might swallow us in one gulp. "Show me how it's done."

I swung my leg over the bike, arranging my skirts so that they wouldn't fly up when we started moving. Gaia watched for a moment, then settled herself behind me. I positioned her arms so that she was holding me around my waist, then kicked the bike into action.

I revved the engine, laughed at Gaia's shriek, and started rolling out of the shed.

We sped through the city, and I couldn't dampen the elation I felt to be moving—doing something—and finally leaving the city where I'd lived all my life. Even though I knew danger awaited us in Urbis, this felt right. I knew, deep in my bones, that this was exactly what we were supposed to be doing.

Alice and Pearl were waiting for us at the city gates, which stood open. I lifted a hand to acknowledge them as we rolled through the gates without slowing down.

Behind me, Gaia let out a *whoop* of excitement, and I felt the grin on my face. Outside of the city walls, we picked up speed as we followed the road that curled through the fields of green grass like a ribbon, into the unknown.

~

I saw the group of them long before we arrived. They were sitting underneath the shade of a large tree, whose buttress roots raised above the ground, like sprawling feet. Even from a distance, I couldn't take my eyes off them. As the road ran over the crest of a hill, then curved around across the rolling plain, I counted seven of them.

"There," Gaia shouted at me to be heard over the wind. I didn't need to look at her to know she was feeling the same way as me. The road we were on was taking us directly toward them, but even if there had been a turnoff, I would not have taken it.

Every fiber of my being drew me to the small group.

It wasn't until I was slowing the bike to a stop, that they turned to look at us.

I noticed the gold ring around their irises. I gasped, looking back at Gaia, though she didn't seem surprised. My eyes flicked from one to the other, barely noticing anything apart from the gold ring around their irises. These people weren't strangers. They were family.

At their invitation, Gaia and I dismounted and joined them underneath the tree. They shared their small picnic. One-by-one, they shared their stories.

Gaia's was by far the most interesting. She knew more about us than we knew about ourselves. She was the only one who'd seen our mother albeit in some kind of magical flashback. She'd seen her own birth, although she conceded the two babies she saw being born could have been any of us.

"I want to find her," Azia said. The others nodded. It seemed that this had started with our birth and our mother was a big part of what was going on now.

"Where were you heading?" The one called Deon asked..

"Urbis," I said. "The Queen of Hearts said that something was going to happen there."

"I hope you might consider coming with us instead," Deon said. "We were coming to The Forge, but since you're here, we should head to Oz instead. Something is happening in the Twelve Kingdoms."

"We're stronger together," Halia said, smiling at us with a friendly, open face. "Don't you feel it?"

I nodded, noticing it as soon as she'd said the words. "Do you think there are more of us in Oz?"

Deon nodded.

I glanced at Gaia, but I saw the agreement in her eyes before I even asked the question.

"Alright," I said. "I suppose there's no harm in taking a detour. Besides, I've always wanted to see Oz."

JAKON

SON OF DOROTHY

GRAB THE NEXT BOXSET IN THE KINGDOM OF FAIRYTALES SERIES

MEET THE TEAM

The Kingdom of Fairytales Series was a team effort.
Below are the people that made it possible:

EQP Management: Rhi Parkes & J.A. Armitage

Our authors: J.A. Armitage, Audrey Rich, B. Kristin
McMichael, Emma Savant, Jennifer Ellision, Scarlett
Kol, Rose Castro, Margo Ryerkerk, Zara Quentin,
Laura Greenwood and Anne Stryker.

Our Editor
Rose Lipscomb

Our Beta Team
Nadine Peterse-Vrijhof
Diane Major
Kalli Bunch
Stephanie Woodwood

Our Proof Reader
Tina Merritt

And to all the wonderful people who loved the world
we created and reviewed our stories.
Thank you

READING ORDER